# PRAISE FOR

## *Ruthless Gods*

"If you liked *Wicked Saints* and you want more of everything, the sequel *Ruthless Gods* takes the monstrous romance to whole new . . . heights. Get ready."  —*Book Riot*

"*Ruthless Gods* is every bit the sequel that Emily A. Duncan's chilling *Wicked Saints* deserves—even darker, bloodier, and even more complicated. . . . A dark, brutal, and deeply thrilling sequel that will leave you wanting more."  —*Culturess*

"Magic and romance steeped in blood and betrayal. . . . Fans of the first volume will be pleased to have more of the same, with higher stakes and increasingly complicated questions of power and divinity."  —*Kirkus Reviews*

"After the glimmers of divinity and magic in *Wicked Saints*, *Ruthless Gods* opens the door to a world of fallen gods and eldritch horrors and I am absolutely ready to step through it. Gruesome, grotesque, and so, so glorious."
 —Erin A. Craig, *New York Times* bestselling
author of *House of Salt and Sorrows*

"Come for the Gothic horror-fantasy, stay for the eldritch nightmares, cosmic despair, and irreverent, unforgettable characters. *Ruthless Gods* will leave fans demanding the final installment in the trilogy."  —Christine Lynn Herman, author of
*The Devouring Gray*

ALSO BY

EMILY A. DUNCAN

WICKED SAINTS

# ruthless gods

SOMETHING DARK AND HOLY: BOOK 2

# EMILY A. DUNCAN

WEDNESDAY BOOKS
NEW YORK

Published in the United States by Wednesday Books, an imprint of St. Martin's Publishing Group

RUTHLESS GODS. Copyright © 2020 by Emily A. Duncan. All rights reserved. Printed in the United States of America. For information, address St. Martin's Publishing Group, 120 Broadway, New York, NY 10271.

www.wednesdaybooks.com

Interior designed by Anna Gorovoy

Map by Rhys Davies

The Library of Congress has cataloged the hardcover edition as follows:

Names: Duncan, Emily A., author.
Title: Ruthless gods / Emily A. Duncan.
Description: First edition. | New York : Wednesday Books, 2020. | Series
Identifiers: LCCN 2019049591 | ISBN 9781250195692 (hardcover) |
    ISBN 9781250195715 (ebook)
Subjects: CYAC: Fairy tales. | Magic—Fiction. | Princes—Fiction. | Gods—Fiction.
Classification: LCC PZ8.D917 Rut 2020 | DDC [Fic]—dc23
LC record available at https://lccn.loc.gov/2019049591

ISBN 978-1-250-19570-8 (trade paperback)

Our books may be purchased in bulk for promotional, educational, or business use. Please contact your local bookseller or the Macmillan Corporate and Premium Sales Department at 1-800-221-7945, extension 5442, or by email at MacmillanSpecialMarkets@macmillan.com.

First Wednesday Books Trade Paperback Edition: 2021

10  9  8  7  6  5  4  3  2  1

*For the weird ones.*
*And for my brothers, Noah and Ian.*

# prologue

## THE GIRL CAUGHT
## IN-BETWEEN

All was darkness. Vast and cold and alive. She could feel it breathing, shifting, *wanting* from her. There was nothing to stop it from consuming her.

Her arms were bound to a slab of stone—there was no escape from this place she didn't recognize. She couldn't remember when she had stopped fighting. But the real fear—the blistering horror threatening to tear her apart—was that she didn't know *who* she was.

"That will return." A soft voice curled around her, calm, the hand against her hair gentle where all others had been hard and cruel. "You will be allowed one thing, you see. It will be returned when the process is finished. But not until the taste of it becomes a bitter wine that you crave and detest in the same breath. When it is something you would kill for but would kill you if you had it, only then will it be given back."

She yearned to reach for the voice. It was terribly familiar. It was bones and gold and blood, so *much* blood. A boy with a throne and a boy reaching for another and a girl with hair like snow who did not belong.

But none of that mattered here.

The darkness was creeping beneath her skin. Settling inside of her, making its home within her bones and swimming through her veins as it tore her to pieces and re-formed her into something *else*.

If she could scream, she would. If she could fight, she would. But she could do nothing.

She could only suffer her fate.

There was only the dark, stretching on for so long that she wondered if she had imagined it all. There had never been a voice. There was never a gentle hand against her hair. There was nothing, *nothing* but this darkness.

# 1

## SEREFIN

## MELESKI

*A viper, a tomb, a trick of the light, Velyos is always reaching for whatever does not belong to him.*

—The Letters of Włodzimierz

Serefin Meleski inhabited the sliver of night that was ripe for betrayal. It was a time when knives were unsheathed, when plans were created and seen into fruition. It was a time for monsters.

He knew that span of hours intimately, but even knowledge of the inevitable wasn't enough to make it less painful. It wasn't like he spent his nights awake because he was expecting another tragedy.

No, he did it because it was easier to drink himself into oblivion than face the nightmares.

He was awake when Kacper slipped into his chambers. To rouse him, clearly, but he probably wasn't particularly surprised to find Serefin lying on the chaise in

his sitting room, one foot braced on the ground, the other leg kicked up against the back. An empty glass on the floor within reach and a book hanging over the arm where Serefin had put it to mark his place as he considered the same thing he had considered every night for the last four months: dreams of moths and blood and monsters.

Horrors at the edges of his awareness and that *voice*. The thin, reedy voice that needled him from a place past death. It never left. Those strange intonations hummed constantly in his veins.

*"Any trouble is of your own making,"* the voice snipped.

He did his best to ignore it.

"Who is it?" he asked Kacper. The hammered iron crown had long since been placed on his head, his palm cut and bled on an altar as he was named king of Tranavia—his downfall was oncoming. The nobility had never liked him, not when he was the High Prince, and certainly not since his coronation. It was never a matter of *what* or *when*, only *who* would be the first one brave enough to strike.

He had let the tense whispers go on and put off explaining fully how his father had died. He was tempting fate. Tranavian politics were messy. So very, very messy.

"There's a collective meeting happening," Kacper answered, voice soft.

Serefin nodded, not bothering to sit up. He'd anticipated it from the *slavhki* who had been supporters of his father.

"*Ksęszi* Ruminski is involved," Kacper continued.

Serefin winced, finally standing. Nicking his finger, he lit a few candles with the magic sparking from his blood and wiped his hand, movements slow.

Żaneta's family had been demanding answers for months. Serefin was at a loss for what to say. "*Oh, terribly sorry, she com-*

mitted some light treason and the Black Vulture decided she would be better served amongst his kind. Tragically awkward situation, but, there it is! Nothing to be done."

It was a constant, festering point of anxiety that had settled underneath his skin. Yes, Żaneta had betrayed him, and, yes, he had died for it, but did she deserve the terrifying fate Malachiasz had chosen for her?

"You're being unusually calm about this," Kacper noted.

"What will they do, I wonder? Hang me? Toss me in the dungeons and forget about me?"

Kacper deflated some, shoulders slumping. "I hate when you're defeatist," he muttered, shoving past where Serefin stood to make his way into Serefin's bedchambers.

"Where are you going?" Serefin asked. He contemplated the bottles in his cabinet before pulling a miraculously full bottle of vodka from the shelf. "I'm not defeatist," he murmured. "I'm pragmatic. Realistic. This was inevitable."

"A coup is not an inevitability," Kacper snapped from inside the room. Was he packing? "None of this would have happened if you had hanged that damned cleric instead of forcing her into the same odd limbo you've forced on the rest of the country. But you didn't. And here we are with a coup on our hands because we have no one to blame. Do you want to end up like your father?"

Serefin flinched. He took a long drink. Dreams of moths and blood and his father's body at his feet. He had not landed the killing blow but it was his fault all the same.

"No," he whispered, brushing a pale moth away from the flame of the candle.

"No. You don't."

But that is likely inevitable, too, Serefin thought morosely. Kacper would not take well to him saying it out loud.

"Half your clothes have been eaten by moths." Kacper sounded despairing.

The door flew open. Serefin's hand went to his spell book, adrenaline spiking. He shuddered, sighing. It was only Ostyia.

"Oh, you're awake," she said flatly.

"Lock that door."

She did.

"I told him what was going on and he's standing there drinking!" Kacper complained.

Serefin offered Ostyia the vodka bottle.

Kacper poked his head out and groaned as she grabbed it and took a sip.

She winked at Serefin—an exaggerated blink from her one eye.

"Get back in here, Kacper," Serefin said.

Kacper huffed loudly and leaned in the doorway.

"How long have they been meeting?"

"I'm fairly certain this is their first," Kacper replied.

"They won't strike tonight."

"But—"

"They won't strike tonight," Serefin repeated firmly.

He tamped down his rising panic, taking the bottle back from Ostyia. Anxiety had been steadily dogging his steps for months, waiting for him to falter. If he paused and thought too hard about it he would be swallowed alive. He had to pretend this wasn't happening.

Kacper slumped against the doorframe.

"Your desire to see to my safety is, of course, appreciated," Serefin said, ignoring the dry look Kacper shot him. "You're a good spymaster, but a tad hasty."

Kacper slid down to the floor.

"Let's figure out what they want first," he said. He set the bottle down on the table, brushing away another moth.

Ostyia frowned, moving to the chaise and perching on the armrest. She yawned.

"We knew Ruminski would want answers eventually," Serefin said.

"He's been asking for *months,* Serefin. He simply got tired of waiting," Kacper groaned.

Serefin lifted his shoulders in a weary shrug. "Perhaps they can be reasoned with? Surely there is something they want that I can give them."

"Clandestine meetings by your enemies don't suggest a list of demands that can be provided for," Ostyia said.

"The entire court is my enemy," Serefin muttered, throwing himself down into an upholstered chair. "That's the problem."

She nodded thoughtfully.

He had tried to win the court to his favor but nothing was working. There were too many rumors to combat that he couldn't explain. He couldn't reveal who had truly killed his father, and the whispers swirling through the underbelly of the court were starting to drift dangerously close to the truth.

A Kalyazi assassin. The Black Vulture. Treason. Disaster. A missing noble. A dead king. Titles from the common folk that Serefin could not shake: King of Moths, King of Blood. Serefin blessed by something no one could explain. What could the blood that fell from the sky that night be other than a blessing?

Serefin had nothing but questions and resistance from his nobility. The Kalyazi were pressing Tranavia's forces back, and even if Tranavia did not know Kalyazin's only cleric had killed the king, the Kalyazi surely did.

Renewed hope from Kalyazin was the last thing Serefin needed.

He couldn't stop the war. He couldn't answer his nobility's questions unless he wanted Nadya hanged and he found he didn't want that. She had done what he could not, and while she was still from an enemy territory and a force for something Serefin did not trust or believe in, he would not have her executed.

"What do we do?" Ostyia asked.

Serefin raked a hand through his hair. "I don't know."

There was an obvious solution to appease Ruminski, but Serefin was uncertain of how to attempt Żaneta's retrieval. From what he could discern, the Vultures had fractured significantly. He hadn't seen many slinking around the palace, but he wasn't about to go to the cathedral door and knock to see who answered.

He rubbed his eyes, tired. He wanted to sleep through the night, just once. Instead he sought out the cleric, holed up in the library as ever, because, as she put it, where else was she supposed to be?

"So his majesty has deigned to grace the poor *boyar* locked in her tower, wasting away," she said when he found her. She was sitting in a high window alcove, one leg kicked off the edge. Her white-blond hair was loose around her shoulders. Serefin couldn't recall a time when it had not been carefully braided.

He tensed, glancing through the gaps in the stacks to see if anyone was around to hear. But it was too early for any *slavhki* to be awake.

"It's like you want me to be forced to hang you," he muttered.

She snorted softly, dark brown eyes dismissive. She had

dropped the act of the clueless, backwater *slavhka* and the girl who had appeared in Józefina's place was sharp and witty and *completely infuriating*. The handsome Akolan boy she was constantly with, Rashid, had quietly given Serefin new paperwork to explain this girl—pale freckles, pale skin, pale hair but curiously dark eyes and eyebrows—a far cry from red-headed Józefina. The paperwork was forged; the explanation surprisingly solid. Road flooding from the lakes had plagued their journey and they had arrived too late for the *Rawalyk* but couldn't yet return home. It would do. Her given name was functionally Tranavian enough to pass, if spelled differently.

She sighed, shifting to the corner of the alcove, and gestured for him to climb up. He settled in next to her and riffled through the stack of books she had piled up. Tranavian texts on the old religions that were so decrepit and brittle they might fall apart in her hands.

"Where on earth did you find these?" he asked.

"You don't want me to answer that," she said absently as she returned to her book. "But do warn the librarian. Wouldn't want the old blood mage to die of shock when he finds his banned texts collection ransacked."

"I didn't know we had banned texts."

She made a humming sound. "Of course you do. Have to keep all that heresy at the forefront of the kingdom somehow, yes?"

"Nadya—"

"I do have to say," she continued, "I am surprised these weren't burned. You lot seem like the book-burning type."

He wasn't going to take that particular bait.

They were quiet as Nadya read and Serefin paged through another book. He couldn't quite figure out what she was studying.

"Have you seen any Vultures around recently?" Serefin finally asked.

She lowered her book and shot him an incredulous look. "Have I *what*?"

He supposed he hoped the answer would be yes and everything would be simple for him; a mess easily cleaned up.

"I should think the king of Tranavia would have more dealings with that cult than one captive peasant girl," she said primly.

"I hope someone overhears you saying these things and forces my hand," he replied.

That got a short laugh from her. She leaned back, dangling her legs out into the open air. He didn't even know why he was asking her except she had shown up in Grazyk at the same time as Malachiasz and clearly knew him; he didn't know what they'd had between them. He'd never asked. But Nadya had said enough offhand to suggest she and the Black Vulture had been more than strange allies and what he had done was more than a simple betrayal.

Why did he assume she knew more about the Vultures than he did? Her, the cleric from Kalyazin. It was ridiculous; this wasn't getting him anywhere.

He leaned his head back on the wall.

"Why are you asking?" she asked.

"I don't have to give you my reasoning," he reminded her.

"Serefin, every day you make me regret not killing you a little bit more." But there was no heat in her words. They had an uneasy truce, and though Nadya was furious he had kept her more or less trapped in Tranavia, she didn't seem altogether eager to leave, either.

"Żaneta," he said quietly.

Nadya paled.

He nodded curtly.

"What happened to her?" she asked delicately.

"Malachiasz took her."

She tensed at his name and picked at a hangnail, refusing to meet Serefin's gaze.

"She did betray you," she said. It sounded like she was trying to convince herself that what Malachiasz had done was justified.

"And I died."

"And you died."

"Supposedly."

"They're starting to talk, you know," Nadya said. Her hand went to her neck, falling when her fingers met nothing but air. An absent tic he had watched her perform countless times. She had worn a small, silver amulet for a bit, but that too had disappeared. "We weren't the only ones in the cathedral that night. They say, 'Not even death commands this new young king.'"

Serefin shivered.

"My goddess is death," Nadya continued. "No one walks into her realm and returns."

Blood and stars and moths. And that voice, *that voice.*

Serefin shoved it away before it spoke to him.

"And what does she think?"

Nadya shrugged listlessly, gazing blankly out over the library. "She doesn't talk to me anymore."

This was not the conversation Serefin had come here to have. But the desolation in Nadya's voice struck even him.

"What will Tranavia think of a king who was brought back from death?" he said, after a long stretch of silence.

She looked over, one eyebrow raised. He remembered the halo that had shivered around her head, fractured and tainted.

She lifted a hand, one of the pale gray moths that constantly fluttered around Serefin landing on her index finger.

"Serefin Meleski," she said contemplatively. "There has been a mark on you growing darker with each day. I thought . . ." She trailed off, waving her hand at the piles of books. "I don't know what I thought . . . that I could help? That I might want to? It doesn't matter."

"Help me? Or help him?"

"It doesn't matter," she repeated, an edge to her voice.

"If suspicion grows, neither of us will walk away unscathed," he said.

She nodded. It was already treacherous here for her. If his court turned on her, he could do nothing. Though, he still wasn't entirely sure why he wanted to protect her at all.

"I shouldn't *want* to help. You destroyed my home," she said.

Serefin had avoided bringing this up, but had wondered when she would. He closed the book and set it on her stack. Serefin had never had any intention of torching the monastery, and he couldn't speak for what Teodore had done once he'd left. He'd found what he was looking for there: her. And the pressure from his father to capture the cleric to see how her power might augment a blood mage's was gone. Serefin didn't particularly care to discover the answer to that question. He wanted to end a war, and it would be easier with this girl for leverage.

"I did. I would be lying if I said I haven't been waiting for some kind of vengeance."

"I would be lying if I said I didn't want it."

"Look at us, being honest with each other!"

She rolled her eyes. "Do you regret it?"

"It's war," he said. She gave him a pointed look, and he

sighed. "Nadya, if I let myself regret everything I've done, I wouldn't be able to get up in the morning."

She made a thoughtful sound.

"Is this you deciding 'well, revenge it is, then'?"

"Not worth my time. Serefin, having watched your court, I can safely say any chaos that might ensue from your death would hardly be enough to deter anything out at the front."

"Ah, saved by my own deeply dysfunctional court."

Nadya glared at him. "What does all this have to do with Żaneta?"

"Her father is going to stage a coup if I don't bring her forward soon."

"You think that he won't do it regardless of your actions?"

"Ah, ruined by my own deeply dysfunctional court."

She was right. He wasn't going to stop what was spinning into motion. The mysticism growing around him was making everything worse. How could Tranavia be ruled by someone touched by something no one understood?

And that *voice*. It whispered to him constantly, but if he didn't answer, it wasn't real. If he told no one, it wasn't real.

Or maybe he was simply his father's son and losing his mind as well.

They sat in silence. He didn't know what to do, and she couldn't really help—if he was overthrown, she would be hanged.

"We can't get her without a Vulture," Nadya said. Then, softer, "Have you heard anything . . . ?"

He shook his head, cutting her off. Every few weeks she would ask after Malachiasz and he would always give the same answer.

It was a lie. But she wouldn't want to hear the things he had heard. The rumors of deaths and dark magic that could only be caused by his cousin.

"You'll figure something out," she said. "You have to."

Novel, that the *we* had become just *him* fixing things. That was the thing: he had no choice. Nothing would change if he didn't stop this in its tracks.

# 2

## NADEZHDA

## LAPTEVA

*A goddess of winter knows the taste of bitter cold and broken bones, of frozen ground choking out life. A goddess of death knows vengeance and the burning hatred that fuels the wars of men. Marzenya is benevolent—when she wishes—but cruelty sits easier upon her shoulders.*

—Codex of the Divine, 399:30

There were a surprising number of Tranavian holy texts for the last—maybe the last?—hopefully not the last because she had failed so utterly—cleric of Kalyazin to read as she bided her time, captive in the heart of Tranavia.

*Not captive, technically,* Serefin would chide, *you just shouldn't leave.*

*The definition of a captive, then,* she would reply, but she understood. Nadya was in constant danger the longer she remained in Grazyk, but staying in the palace kept her within Serefin's fragile sphere of protection. Granted,

protection he seemed puzzled at extending to her. She had no magic and wouldn't survive the journey through Tranavia to make it home. The well of power she had touched had either dried up or had never been truly hers. And as much as she hated it, she lingered, hoping for the return of the sad, broken boy who had brought her here. She was frustrated with how much hope she felt every time she asked Serefin if he had news and how quickly it crumbled when he told her no.

Why should she hope for the boy who had betrayed her so completely? Her fury had tempered to a numb ache as months of silence passed. She had no more anger left in her to fight Serefin, much less Malachiasz's ghost.

So she skulked around the palace and dragged what religious texts she could find up into the little corner alcove. None of them were particularly helpful. Her gods were her gods, as it was, and there was little a book written centuries ago by a Tranavian priest could inform her that she didn't already know.

But there were occasional glimmers among the pages of what she was missing, hints at why she had failed so fully. Why the gods no longer spoke to her, and how a boy twisted into the form of a monster was able to tear himself into pieces and reassemble in the shape of something potentially divine.

At times the books she found spoke of old religious sects and saints Nadya did not know. How many clerics had been abandoned like Nadya? Her heart would be broken, she thought, if there was anything left of it to break.

After Serefin wandered off, clearly no closer to a decision than before, she left the library—abandoning the pile of obscure, ultimately forbidden texts stacked in the alcove. She hid the ladder in a random part of the room every day. As yet no one had disturbed her ever-growing stacks, but she *was* caught in a silent war with the old librarian who perpetually acted like someone using the library was the worst thing that could possibly happen to him.

"There you are!" Parijahan tugged Nadya away from the direction of the kitchens where she had been planning on smuggling out some bread and cheese, and toward her chambers. "There is a court dinner tonight and you must attend."

Nadya groaned. "Serefin didn't mention that."

"He said if he did you would do such a spectacular disappearing act that even I wouldn't be able to find you. Clearly he was correct."

"I'll kill him," Nadya muttered as she let Parijahan drag her back to the rooms they shared.

"You would have done that by now if you were going to," Parijahan replied evenly.

The Akolan girl was wearing simple, loose trousers and a blouse in complementary shades of dark gold. Her black hair was tightly braided; the golden ring in her nose caught the light every time they passed a window. They had dropped the pretense of Parijahan acting as Nadya's servant, though Parijahan continued to decline Serefin's offers to have her own rooms and be treated as the noble she truly was. Too suspicious, she said, and Nadya had noticed there were a handful of *slavhki* that Parijahan always went out of her way to avoid.

Even with the king of Tranavia finally dead, Parijahan was more on edge than ever, her secrets held with a firm grip from Nadya.

Malachiasz's betrayal was just as brutally unexpected to Parijahan, but questioning her about it got Nadya nothing but cryptic answers that meant little. Asking Rashid was worse. The Akolan boy was far too good at spinning his words, so he said absolutely nothing but took ten minutes to do so.

"Did Serefin tell you anything else?" Nadya asked.

Parijahan shook her head. "Is it me, or does he look like he hasn't been sleeping?"

"Not just you." There had been dark smudges underneath Serefin's pale blue eyes and stubble dusting his pale jaw and cheeks. And he had reeked of alcohol. "Frankly, I don't blame him."

Nadya couldn't say she had been sleeping well, either. The months since that night in the cathedral had been hard, and when she slept she saw things she didn't particularly want to consider. But at least when she was asleep she didn't have to confront the silence in her mind. She wasn't used to being alone with her thoughts and found she hated it.

"Read anything interesting?" Parijahan asked. It was her standard inquiry after Nadya's visits to the library.

Nadya always shrugged noncommittally. She didn't even know what she was searching for. Mostly she was hiding. From herself, from Serefin, from Parijahan.

"There was a Tranavian saint named Maryna Cierzpieta whose head was cut off, but she picked it up and went on her way."

Parijahan cast her a sidelong look. "I can't tell if you're making that up or not."

Nadya pressed a hand over her heart. "This is my *religion*, Parj, would I lie?"

Parijahan snorted.

"I'm serious! She started a cult of personality and everything. It all died out about one hundred and thirty years before Tranavia broke from the gods."

Parijahan made a contemplative noise as they reached their rooms. Nadya flopped onto a chaise in the sitting room.

"You're not locking yourself in that library every day to read stories about saints you already know."

Frustrated, Nadya's fingers went to her prayer beads, the shock hitting her anew when she found her neck bare. It was a daily occurrence and she was still waiting for it to stop hurting. She gathered her hair back and began braiding it instead.

"How did he decide on the path he took?" she finally asked. "How did he get the idea that he should be the one to unseat the gods? He must have read it somewhere. Something started him down that road. I have to find it."

Parijahan moved across the room, sitting next to Nadya. "Or, he's simply an idealistic boy who found something to blame. You're not going to find answers to that problem in old books."

"I don't know what else I'm supposed to do," Nadya said softly.

Parijahan took her chin and angled her face toward hers. "Don't you dare. He hurt *you*. You don't get to fling yourself into trying to save him when he clearly did not want to be saved."

"I know." No one knew the gods did not speak to Nadya anymore. She was nothing but a Kalyazi peasant. Good for little, useful for less. She wasn't trying to save him; she wanted to understand. It was her fatal flaw, her desire to understand. It was what he had used so willingly in the tapestry of lies he had woven around her.

"Besides . . ." Parijahan said, her voice shifting, calculating and sly, "if he got his grand ideas from a book, shouldn't you be looking in the cathedral?"

Nadya shuddered. She had been avoiding that place for months. The thought of going back chilled her to her core . . . and yet . . .

Parijahan noticed her hesitation. "He's not there," she said. "You're safe."

*An impossible position, the hating and the missing all at once.*

"Are you scolding me, or encouraging me? It's very unclear."

Parijahan smiled ruefully. "Maybe a bit of both?"

"How long do we have until the dinner?"

Parijahan noted the sun's position through the window with a shrug. "We have time."

Nadya gazed up at the broken statues lining the entrance of the massive black cathedral, and wondered if she was *more* afraid now that she knew what lurked inside. If the terror settling in her limbs was because, this time, she was walking in unprotected.

Parijahan spared the crumbling face of the cathedral a passing glance, unfazed. Nadya had come to find that indifference a comforting aspect of the Akolan girl. Parijahan wrenched the huge wooden doors open.

It was deathly quiet. Nadya swallowed thickly. She didn't want to remember the last time she was here, fingers tangled with Malachiasz's, trusting him against all reason. And she certainly didn't want to intrude on any Vultures in their home.

*But it wasn't their home once,* she thought. She trailed a hand against the wall, wondering which god this church had belonged to when Tranavia still cared for such things. Panic began to claw at her chest from the silence in her head so she shoved the thoughts away, following after Parijahan, who was—unfortunately—intent on where she wanted to go.

"Oh, Parj, must we?"

"Where else?" Parijahan replied.

She had a point. There hadn't been so much as a whisper as to what had happened to the Black Vulture. Though Nadya asked, the reality was she didn't want to know.

To know would be to acknowledge the blackened scar on her palm each time it heated, a burning itch lasting for hours before it went away. To acknowledge the pull of her heart to something far away, as if linked to someone. She didn't know what had happened the night she carved Velyos' symbol into her palm, then Malachiasz's. Something had happened when she had stolen his power to use with hers. When she had done the impossible.

It remained, still. The sludgy, inky darkness of Malachiasz's magic slumbered somewhere deep within her.

Parijahan tried the door to Malachiasz's chambers, a small smile flickering at the corners of her lips when she found it unlocked.

Nadya hesitated. Nothing had changed since she had been there last. Malachiasz's patched-up military jacket hung off the back of the chair where he'd last tossed it. Paintings were stacked in every spare corner of the room and piles of books surrounded the bookshelves. Piles and piles of books.

Parijahan whistled low. "There you have it." She picked up the jacket, frowning at it before she handed it to Nadya.

She waited until Parijahan turned away before she pulled the jacket on over her dress and tucked her face against the collar. It smelled like him still, iron and earth and *boy* in a way that was comforting and painful, and the pang in her chest was a vicious stab.

It was hard to parse her feelings about Malachiasz's betrayal. With time she had hoped she might untangle her mess of emotions. She knew how she was supposed to feel and how everyone *expected* her to feel. But she couldn't figure out if any of those things were true of her.

Yes, she was furious and hurt, but she also caught herself waiting for him to burst into her rooms, a whirlwind of dark hair and bad jokes and painfully brilliant smiles. She missed him.

But that wasn't who he was anymore. Idealistic, but powerful and cruel, his body twisted and his mind shattered.

Nadya desperately wanted to stop thinking about him altogether. He had lied to her for months, making himself out to be an anxious boy who had made a mistake and needed help fixing it. Instead he had used her to gain a power so terrible it had driven out the last of his humanity.

The silly, condescending Tranavian boy with the sly smile, who chewed on his fingernails when he was nervous, was gone. Maybe forever. And she was so deeply sad that it had swallowed the heat of her anger. He didn't deserve her sadness, but that didn't make a difference to her heart.

"Did he plan this from the beginning, do you think?" Nadya spoke up quietly.

Parijahan looked up from where she was riffling through a stack of paintings. "Are you finally ready to talk about this?"

Nadya shrugged.

"I spent months with him and he never seemed remotely interested in finding you," Parijahan said. "I had to convince him to come with us when we started following rumors about a cleric. In the end, something forced him to flee to Kalyazin, and later return here. He never said what."

"Well, he's a liar."

"He is very good at lying," Parijahan agreed. "If only because he's actually telling the truth while he does it."

The door to his study rested like a black stain in the wall. What did she hope to find here? The thing that set him on his reckless quest to destroy her gods? Something else?

She paged through the books mindlessly. They were eclectic piles: history, novels, magic theory. But she didn't understand blood magic enough to comprehend the latter. She was wasting her time.

Parijahan opened the door to his study. She coughed as she stepped inside the room. Nadya didn't immediately follow, though something tugged her toward the doorway. She heard Parijahan shift around papers on his desk, and she shivered, a chill suddenly pulling down her spine.

Magic.

Something she had not touched in quite some time.

"What do you have?" she called. Her stomach churned. There was something familiar and terrible yanking at her, a call that sent a deep wave of dread crashing over her.

"Some of his spells, I think," Parijahan said, unaware of Nadya's sudden anxiety.

Nadya flinched as she stepped into the study. The palm of her left hand ached, a dull pain steadily and sluggishly working its way up her arm. Sweat broke out on her temples. She was too hot and too cold and she could feel—she could feel—

She snatched the papers out of Parijahan's hand, crumpling them in her tight grip. She was breathing hard and couldn't shake the feeling that something was very wrong. There was something moving, something hungry that *wanted* with such a deep and powerful ache it was going to swallow everything if it wasn't stopped.

"Nadya?"

She slammed a hand down onto the desk. "No," she said flatly. "This isn't how magic works."

She spread the spells out in front of her. Her heart tripped at the sight of Malachiasz's messy, borderline incomprehensible scrawl. She shouldn't be able to feel his power, shouldn't be able to feel *him*. Not now, not after so much time had passed.

She could read Tranavian, but the words blurred. Frantic, she riffled through more of the pages, digging out hastily scrawled notes and diagrams underneath the spells. Endless markings Nadya did not understand.

"I shouldn't be here," she whispered as horror continued to curl around her core. She lifted a page that had clearly been dipped in blood, the bottom stiff and dark. The top she could read, and she wished she couldn't.

Notes on Kalyazi magic, on divine magic, on *her* magic. Notes on how her magic and blood magic might intersect, how they shouldn't but could, how there is *something else* changing very slowly and it might be new or it might be a melding of both.

Serefin had mentioned, once, finding Tranavian spell books with Kalyazi prayers scrawled inside on the battlefield. It was an impossible combination. Why was Malachiasz studying it?

She froze; the something else on the other end of that thread of connection had grown nearly tangible. A gaze from far away turning on her where previously there had been none. It was a power so much greater than her own, infinitely dark. Magic that did not belong to her hummed underneath her veins with a painful tug toward the one who truly owned it.

She never should have stolen his power.

But surely he had known what she intended when she'd dragged that blade across his palm? It had been his idea once—a sly musing she would be stronger if she used his blood. Abhorrent, horrible, and yet, she had done exactly what he wanted in the end. Just another twisting of truth to push her to unwittingly aid his incomprehensible plans.

Nadya had fallen too far, sacrificing everything she believed for a chance to change the world, and she was punished with silence.

She gasped, burning hand curled against her heart. The sludgy power had altered. A tether, a line rapidly pulled taut.

*I should not have come here.*

The monster. *Malachiasz.* She backed away from the power that suddenly was too strong, too much, too *evil.*

Nadya took a few ragged breaths—the muddled sound of Parijahan calling her name glancing off her ears—and let her awareness press out, cautiously brushing her fingertips against the pane of black glass that separated Malachiasz from her, yet bound them together.

*This is my fault.* She had created something when she stole his power and bound it to hers. Of course it lingered, of course there were consequences. Gods, she could *feel* him. He was crumbling, eroding like a cliff face being rocked by an ocean's waves.

Then—as clear as if it were happening right in front of her—she heard the sound of an iron claw scraping against glass. A painful, caustic screech that drove needles into Nadya's ears. Down, down, down. A hand slammed against the glass, slender fingers tipped with dripping iron claws.

Nadya broke away.

She stumbled back from the desk. Nadya willed her last meal not to return. This couldn't be happening. *How* was this happening?

A few agonizing seconds passed without a rekindling of the twisted connection. The brush against the roiling chaos of his madness.

But it had felt like Malachiasz. The monster was still Malachiasz.

Would it be hope, then, that killed her in the end?

Nadya looked up at Parijahan, who stared at her in horror.

"Well," Nadya rasped, "I guess he's not dead."

# interlude i

## THE BLACK

## VULTURE

The hunger would not relent. The gnawing at the edges of his being was too much to bear yet never enough. He could only hunger, *need*, until finally he was released unto perfect oblivion and felt nothing. No hunger, no unceasing, unending emptiness pulling at the core of him, the ever-present threat of fully shattering.

The darkness was a comfort. Torches were few and far between here and easily avoided. It was a welcome escape to remain far from the glimpses of light that reminded him of the *missing*. Of the thing that flickered outside his consciousness, just far enough away that he couldn't grasp it. The relentlessly fluttering wings of a little bird that refused to be choked by darkness.

It was an irritant sweet enough to drive his madness a little further, a little deeper. But ignorance was sweeter. He never moved beyond that initial grasp.

There were glimmers that didn't belong to him, didn't belong to anyone, frustrating in their displacement. A girl with hair like snow, fiercely glaring, pale freckles dusting her skin. A girl arguing, rooted and stubborn and passionate. Beautiful, brilliant, torturously absent. He had no idea who she was and that made everything all the more frustrating.

Eternal and instantaneous, time became extraneous. The glimmers—*the distractions*—faded. Only the hunger, always the hunger, remained. Only the feeling of being taken apart and put back together and ripped to pieces once more.

(Being unmade was, apparently, an ongoing process.)

There was a vague needling that something needed to be done. But nothing was something was everything and couldn't it wait? Everything could wait. Until the darkness was less choking. The hunger less cloying. Until his thoughts were strung in a row on a line, instead of incoherent, scattered bits that jumped and fluttered and—

Fluttered.

*Wings.*

Again.

There.

The little bird.

He reached and missed. His hand slammed into something cold and he pulled his claws down it, slowly, carefully. The sound was calming, clear.

His hands were bleeding. His hands were always bleeding.

There was something there. The wings fluttered away again, too fast, too sharp, too soon, too *real*.

There was

something

   else.

A memory, broken,
                scattered,
     fleeting.
                    Gone.

# 3

SEREFIN

MELESKI

**Svoyatova Elżbieta Pientka:** *a Tranavian who burned in the cleric Evdokiya Solodnikova's place. Where her body was buried, the dead are said to speak with the living.*
—Vasiliev's Book of Saints

Serefin was halfway up the tower stairs to visit the witch before he realized what he was doing. He paused, hand gripping the rail, and wondered if he shouldn't be going alone. But it was too late to turn back. Pelageya knew he was there the moment the door to her tower opened.

He took the steps two at a time. Serefin wasn't wholly pleased he was forced to turn to the witch, but it was strangely inevitable. She had set him on this path, hadn't she? Surely she would have some horribly esoteric advice that he wouldn't understand and would be terrifying in its broad foretelling of future doom.

He reached the top of the tower and found the door ajar, swinging open under the light rap of his knuckles.

*Well, that's less than ideal,* he thought with a frown. A cloud of moths blew into the air. He waved them away.

"Pelageya?" he called, pushing his way in.

Serefin's stomach dropped. The room was gutted.

It was as though the witch had never been there at all. Cobwebs dusted every corner. The fireplace had remnants of ash but was mostly swept clean. A witch's circle stood out in stark relief against the center of the floor. A sigh escaped him—it was only charcoal, not blood.

He moved around the circle, fingers tapping against the spine of his spell book.

This was not what he'd hoped for.

Kneeling down, he nicked the back of his finger on a razor in his sleeve and paged through his spell book. Pelageya wouldn't leave this behind without reason, and while Serefin could not read the sigils scrawled within the circle—knowing sigils was Vulture business—he could charge the spell.

He hesitated. What he was doing was profoundly stupid. If Kacper or Ostyia were here, they would sooner put a blade to his throat than let him deal in uncertain magic.

Except, his voices of reason weren't here. Swiftly he pressed his bloody palm down. His focus pared down to a single point underneath his hand. It caught fire from there, like the powder that lit magic cannons, and slowly filled out the circle, sketching in every sigil until the floor burned with a strange, acrid, green fire.

But that was all.

He straightened away from the spell, faintly disappointed, yet relieved all the same. Just a blank spell the witch left behind to toy with Serefin. He nudged the circle with the toe of his boot, carefully breaking the flow of power, hopeful the spell wouldn't explode in his face. The flames went out.

"I made bets with myself, you know, on which of you would come to me first."

Serefin nearly jumped out of his skin.

"The girl who is a cleric but not a cleric, a witch but not a witch." Pelageya was sitting in the middle of the ruined circle, counting on her bony fingers. "The monster who sits on a throne of gilded bones and reaches for the heavens far past his understanding, or the princeling touched by a power he does not believe in."

Serefin rested his hand against his spell book and waited for his heart to stop rattling his body. "Did you win?"

"Win what?" Pelageya asked, still counting.

"The bet."

"No. Where's the witch?"

"She's not a witch, she's a cleric."

"Can't be a cleric if the gods won't talk to you," Pelageya said, waving a hand. "Can't be a witch with what she is, either. Tainted but holy. A puzzle. She's a lot of things, including not here. Not what I expected. But you *are*. One half of my delightfully bloodthirsty and pathetically delusional blood mage pair."

Serefin's eyes narrowed as he took in the empty room. "What happened here?"

A blink. The room was no longer empty. The witch circle on the floor was now chalk instead of charcoal. The deer skulls hung from their antlers on the ceiling and Serefin found himself sitting in a black upholstered chair, moths fluttering nervously around his face, his head spinning.

"What happened where?" Pelageya asked, suddenly no older than Serefin. Her curls were tied back from her face, black but for a shockingly white lock that disappeared into the mass of hair knotted at the back of her head. "You want something," she chirped, picking up a skull from a side table—human—before sitting in the chair across from Serefin, the skull perched in her lap, facing him.

"I should really be going," Serefin said, moving to stand.

He remained trapped in his chair. A flicker of panic threaded through him.

"Oh," Pelageya said, tapping her chin. "Oh, no. I have the one and the other will come eventually. Meleski and Czechowicz but closer than you know, closer than those who have lied have said. He'll come, soon enough, and then—finally—I can deal with the witch who is a cleric who is not a witch and not a cleric."

"What does Malachiasz have to do with this?"

Pelageya leaned forward over the skull. "*Everything*, dear princeling."

"King," Serefin murmured.

"I'm sorry?"

"I'm the king now," he said, fingers running across the hammered iron crown that rested over his hair. It still felt like a mistake had been made and he had been given something that did not belong to him. He supposed no one truly believed it did. All he wanted was to prove the throne was rightfully his—even if he had to prove it to himself along with his nobility.

Pelageya nodded but he couldn't shake the feeling that she was unconvinced, her gaze drawn to his left eye. He lifted a hand to it self-consciously.

"*She knows.*"

Serefin chewed on the inside of his mouth to keep from reacting to the reedy voice.

"Black and gold and red and gray. Vultures and moths and blood, always blood. A boy born in a gilded hall and a boy born in darkness. Bred in bitterness and bred in lies. Change your place; change your name. Nothing for it, it's a mirror, you see. The blood's the same, the darkness more cloying on one, but a mirror, you look to find yourself and find the one you are terrified of becoming. Two thrones, two kings, two boys to plunge this world into darkness for the sake of saving it."

A shudder wracked Serefin's body. He regretted coming here alone. He wished Kacper's steadying hand was against his shoulder, pulling him away yet again from the incoherent ravings of the witch.

"What are you talking about?" Serefin said, voice low.

"Hide and forget. Hide and remember. You hide from the truth, basking in the lie of a family deceitful from the start. He hides under magic that has burned away remembrance of what he used to be. One day, both will remember, and what will happen then?"

"Remember *what*?" Serefin's nerves were fraying further.

Pelageya stared off into the middle distance, pale fingers stroking the top of the skull.

"Should I tell you a story, dear king of moths, king of blood, king of *horrors*?"

"Yes." The word escaped in a whisper before he could stop it and he flinched. He desperately wanted to flee whatever revelation was about to drop.

"A story about two sisters from the lake country. A story about a girl who married a prince she disliked who became a king she hated. The girl became a woman who bore a son she did not understand but loved anyway. But it wasn't enough. And she would seek oblivion far from the husband she detested. A second son, of the dark, hidden away and born of masked passion and lies."

"No . . ." he murmured, shaking his head. "No." The walls

began to close in around him, everything growing black at the edges.

"Tranavians make it so easy!" Pelageya said, delighted. "Oh no, no, you see, this boy belongs to the sister, not the woman, they said! Hide him in a twisted truth and no one will suspect! Send him away to Tranavia's high order and no one will remember he was anything other than a dispensable *slavhka*! Burn his bones and shatter his body and it won't matter who he came from. Make a weapon; make a king."

*She's lying*, Serefin thought frantically, yet he knew—somehow, deep down in his core, in that place that kept Malachiasz in his thoughts long after he was gone—she wasn't. Maybe that was why it hurt so much when Malachiasz had opened the door to Pelageya's tower and his sharp-toothed smile had no recognition in it.

"Where is your brother, dear king? Where did the Black Vulture go?"

The word *brother* hit Serefin like a punch to the chest. "How do you know?" Serefin asked, voice strained.

Pelageya cackled. "You ask as if you have doubts. But you know, you *know*, the blood is the same."

"Why are you telling me this?" Why now? When all he had was a simmering hatred that burned for the Black Vulture because he had *died* because of him. Because of Malachiasz. His *brother*.

"Who else would tell you?" she asked. "Certainly not your mother."

Serefin shivered. How much did his mother know of Malachiasz's fate? *How is any of this even possible?*

Pelageya's pitch-dark eyes tracked the moths fluttering around Serefin's head. "That," she said, "is an interesting development. Has he spoken to you yet? I'm sure he has. Whispers, though, only whispers because you are Tranavian and thus so very difficult to break. *You are not the one he wanted.*"

Pelageya tilted her head and stood, moving to the heavy curtains that cloaked everything in darkness. She drew them back, flooding the room with blinding light.

"The creeping shadows slither from the dark; retribution falls from the sky," she murmured. "You have time, but fast it slips. And slip away it will. Things are set into motion and you must see if you will stand or fall."

Serefin struggled to his feet, his limbs finally free. This was more than he wanted. He didn't care if there was more to be said. Pelageya turned from the window, giving him a wry smile.

He fled.


Serefin crashed into his mother's rooms, ignoring the protests from her maidservant.

"I'm her *son*," he snapped as she bustled after him, muttering about decorum. He found his mother in her sitting room and slammed the door in the maid's face. A glass vase near the door wobbled precariously.

Klarysa looked up from her book, glancing pointedly at the door, and to the vase.

"When were you going to tell me?" Serefin asked, surprised at his level voice.

"You are going to have to be a great deal more specific, my dear," she said, oblivious to his distress. She held out a hand, beckoning him closer, taking the cloth mask down from her face.

He didn't move. He wanted to take that damned vase and hurl it against the wall. He didn't do that, either.

"You knew what my father was doing," he said carefully, slowly. "You gave me a warning, you knew the whole time."

Her pale blue eyes narrowed and Serefin absently considered that he and Malachiasz had both inherited those eyes.

"And you stopped him," she said placidly, hooking her mask back over her face. "The crown is yours."

"You knew he was acting with the Vultures."

"I did."

"You knew the Vulture whose fault this is."

She frowned slightly. "It was the Black Vulture."

"How do you not know who he is?" Serefin asked, his voice finally cracking. He raked his hands through his hair. For months, he had been steadily tucking away information on Malachiasz as it came to him because eventually he would have to deal with the Black Vulture. He would have to make him stand for his treason.

But now he didn't know what he was supposed to do.

"Serefin, what are you talking about?"

"The witch had to tell me," he said, raw panic tearing at his voice. "You didn't even have the decency to tell me yourself. Did you know, when you sent him to the Vultures, what he would become?"

Klarysa finally tensed. "What?"

"You were never here. Of course you didn't know. Of course you never saw him in passing. But you could have told me. He was here this whole time, so close, and I never knew."

The blood drained from her face.

Serefin collapsed into a chair, dropping his head into his hands.

"Pelageya told you?" Klarysa said bleakly, the thread of tension between them threatening to snap.

He nodded, not lifting his head.

"He was supposed to stay with Sylwia," she whispered. "A bastard has no place at court and there were too many who were suspicious."

"He was never my cousin," Serefin said. "And you let the Vultures have him."

"Don't be sentimental, Serefin, it's a terrible look on you. He was too powerful to go anywhere else."

"Well, now he's the Black Vulture and conspired with my father to kill me, so congratulations, I suppose you're right."

Klarysa looked dizzy, her skin very pale. "You're mistaken."

"I assure you, Mother, I am not. My little brother has committed treason and I can do nothing because he holds the one other high office in Tranavia. We have no official legislature in place for this because no Vulture has ever dared to overreach like this."

Some had ventured close; not every Black Vulture had been content to remain in their cathedral and their mines. But none so far as Malachiasz.

Her hand went to her mouth and Serefin had the fleeting notion that she was going to descend into one of her frequent fits. To be frank he was surprised she had stayed this long in Grazyk; the magic residue in the air did not sit well with her.

"The rumors . . ."

"The rumors are wrong. What happened was worse." Serefin sighed, leaning his head back against the chair. The ceiling of his mother's sitting room was painted with bright flowers and magic symbols for health were scrawled across the plaster. No Vultures in sight. "I thought he was dead for years. I almost wish he was."

*Because his fate rests in my hands.*

"Serefin—"

"I don't want your excuses, Mother, it was all for propriety's sake, after all. How were you to know your bastard son would grow up depraved and soulless? Oh, right, wait, that *is* the fate of every Vulture, isn't it?"

She jerked back as if struck. Serefin wilted.

It wouldn't change anything, this revelation. Malachiasz had to answer for his actions.

"Two thrones and a pair of ruined brothers to sit them," he murmured. "Though, soon, I suppose not." He slid the crown off his head and ran his thumb around the cool iron.

His mother relaxed, relieved to grasp onto a topic of conversation that was not Malachiasz. She had tucked her shaking hands down into her lap in an attempt to still them.

"There is a collective of *slavhki* who wish to see me off the throne," Serefin said. "And I don't know what to do."

Klarysa stood. She clipped her spell book to her waist and moved briskly across the room, placing her hands on Serefin's shoulders.

"You know exactly what to do. You make them regret that their tepid whispers reached your ears." She tilted his chin up. "You are the king. Do you think your father didn't have enemies whispering for his removal from the throne every night?"

"*I* was one of those enemies," he said wearily.

She kissed the top of his head. "You did what you had to."

"Is that how you justify what happened to Malachiasz?"

She sighed. "If I could have kept him close, I would have. You two were the only thing that made this palace bearable."

"Then why did you send him away? Why did you never tell me?"

"The Vultures came for him, there was nothing we could do." She smoothed Serefin's hair as she pulled him to her. "I did not tell you because you would've tried to pull him from the order. You are so stubborn, Serefin, and we are not to concern ourselves with the affairs of Vultures."

He shivered, her nails lightly scratching his scalp.

"Treason is another matter," she continued thoughtfully. "As poetic as my sons wielding the two thrones of Tranavia might be, we can't have treason. But let's see to those *slavhki* first, yes?"

Serefin's panic had cooled to frustration when he found Ostyia in the hallway. He grabbed her arm, ignoring her yelp of surprise as he dragged her into his rooms and slammed the door closed.

"You knew about Malachiasz," he said, tone more accusatory than intended.

"What?"

"You knew. You knew he was the Black Vulture the whole time."

She rolled her eye. "Why does this matter to you *now*? I didn't tell you because I didn't think it mattered."

"I thought he was dead. For years. You let me think it."

"He may as well been!" she said incredulously. "What is this about, Serefin?"

For a brief instant, he considered telling her the truth. Or did she know that, too? What else had she kept from him for his own supposed good?

Ostyia groaned. "It was a few years ago. I saw him without his mask. I know you were close but he was . . ." She trailed off, shaking her head. "Poisonous. I didn't want to break your heart when you had finally moved on."

"It wasn't for you to keep from me," he said.

She shrugged, clearly nonplussed. "Why are you bringing this up?"

Serefin shook his head, waving her off. This was a growing point of contention between them and he was willing to let it fester.

"It doesn't matter," he muttered, hating that everyone hid the truth from him. "Nothing matters. I need to go to dinner."

"Not like that, you're not." She grabbed his wrist and yanked him back. "Clean up first. Don't give them more ammunition against you."

He gritted his teeth, brushing a hand over his jaw. He needed to shave.

If word got out about Malachiasz . . . Serefin was already treading on dangerous ground. He couldn't very well pin his father's death on the Vulture, though ultimately he liked to think it was his fault—the common folk and the *slavhki* idolized the Vultures to a point risking civil war if he threatened their rule.

Malachiasz must have known he would have immunity granted to no one else by sheer lack of precedence. But treason was treason.

Ostyia flagged down a servant, then waited while Serefin did his very best to be halfway presentable.

"We need to find Żaneta," he said, moving to take a razor and getting his hand slapped away by Cyryl, his manservant. He sighed and let Cyryl shove him onto a stool.

Ostyia perched on his desk. She looked thoughtful.

"She's likely in Kyętri . . ."

Serefin shuddered, earning him a scowl from Cyryl. He had to play the game in a way the *slavhki* understood, with power. Żaneta was a piece he held that those who wanted him out of power desired. The problem was his mother wanted him to deal with this issue first, and to leave Malachiasz be until the time came to deal with *him* as well.

To Serefin, it was killing two birds with one stone.

"May I cut your hair, *Kowesz Tawość*?" Cyryl asked. "While we're here . . ."

Serefin waved a noncommittal hand.

"Finally," Ostyia muttered.

She was one to talk, she'd hacked off her bangs herself and they were crooked.

"It would be a risk to leave Grazyk," Ostyia said. "You have to figure out how to do this without leaving the city."

Serefin frowned.

"What if I can't?" he mused quietly.

"They take everything."

Serefin couldn't walk a step without tripping over a new low *slavhka* who had arrived from somewhere in Tranavia, hoping to find favor with the young king.

It was exceedingly tiring.

The dinner was supposed to be a quieter affair than most, yet even this was still too many people for Serefin's liking. If only he were the sort who thrived on social interactions. Instead they made him desperate to escape.

The room was dimly lit with too many dripping candles spread across the table. Torches burned against the wall, casting the lower hall in a flickering, erratic light. The paintings on the ceiling struck Serefin as being vaguely familiar in a different way than usual, as if he had seen them once in a dream, this vast battle between bears and eagles.

The *slavhka* he found sitting to his left was none other than

Patryk Ruminski. Serefin stifled a sigh as he was announced. This was going to be a long evening.

Nadya caught his attention from where she sat farther down, tense and taut before tracking to the nobles seated near him. She shot him a sympathetic look before turning to the person at her right. Masks had not fallen out of fashion, to Serefin's dismay, and Nadya wore the bare minimum with a strip of white lace tied over her eyes.

Serefin recognized the languid way the girl beside the cleric held herself, the pile of black hair and dark blue eyes that kept the room sharply in her attention from behind the iron mask that hid all but a quarter of her face.

*A Vulture.* The second-in-command that hadn't been seen anywhere in months. Serefin scanned the room. No other Vultures in sight.

Nadya lifted her hand slightly, beckoning Serefin over.

Slight *Ksęszi* Ruminski by speaking with a girl who should be far beneath his attention and a Vulture first? Or suffer not knowing what the Vulture was doing here the whole dinner?

Serefin decided to compromise. It was only diplomatic.

He murmured his greetings to Ruminski and the boy seated on his other side, whom he did not recognize at all, before moving to where Nadya was seated, highly aware it should be the other way around. Nadya should be coming to *him*. He was the king. This was breaking all sorts of protocol.

"I'm going to have to suffer the most awkward conversation after this," Serefin said, resting a hand on the back of Nadya's chair and leaning down.

"I thought speaking with those who wanted to depose you was a mundanity," Nadya murmured.

"It *is*, but—" He cut himself off. It was no use talking about these kinds of things with her.

Nadya gestured to the Vulture, but Serefin spoke before she could.

"We've met," he said shortly. "Give my regards to *Jen Eczkanję.*"

The Vulture snorted. "Something tells me he won't want those. My name is Żywia, and you're right, we have met."

Serefin went cold. The Vultures didn't just hand out their names. Nadya was eyeing Żywia with cautious curiosity.

"What's this about?" he asked. He glanced longingly at Nadya's wine glass. He needed a drink. "Did he send you?"

"It took some time, you see, to put everything in order. And I don't know what mess has happened here in our absence."

Serefin's stomach clenched at *our.* But there was no way he was here. Nadya, who had been toying with her dinner knife earlier, now held it in the practiced grip of someone who could make the dull blade kill without difficulty. She appeared calmly dismissive, like it was every day she dealt with the upper echelons of Tranavia's bloodiest cult.

*Well,* Serefin considered, *I suppose she has.*

"Who has decided they lead the Vultures?" Żywia asked. "Not that it matters, let them playact at leadership."

Serefin had met with a handful of Vultures since being crowned. Each one had claimed to be ruling in the Black Vulture's absence, and each one had disappeared, never to be seen again.

"Is that the only reason you're here?"

She shook her head. "We'll speak later, Your Majesty. I am but a messenger."

Serefin nodded, straightening and preparing to return to his seat. He caught a glimpse of Nadya's expression as he moved away.

Her grip on the knife had tightened.

# 4

## NADEZHDA

## LAPTEVA

**Svoyatova Lizavieta Zhilova:** *When the Tranavian blood mage Pyotr Syslo burned her village to the ground when she was a child, Lizavieta—granted vengeance by the goddess Marzenya—hunted him down and fed his eyes to the wolf that haunted her steps.*

—Vasiliev's Book of Saints

"Your story is threadbare," the Vulture said casually as she reached for her glass of wine.

Nadya tensed. She picked up her fork to stab a mushroom scattered with dill and waited until she had finished chewing to answer. "I don't know what you're talking about."

Żywia cast her a wry, sidelong glance before tugging the mask off her face. Nadya heard a few scandalized gasps from down the table.

The Vulture was unexpectedly lovely. Her skin was smooth and her features fine; a series of careful circles were tattooed in a line down her chin, stretching down her throat. "Malachiasz doesn't keep secrets from me, dear."

"That makes one of us," Nadya muttered.

"I was impressed you made it so far initially without the *slavhki* poking holes in your first tale. It was a good story, if a touch macabre."

"Malachiasz came up with it," Nadya said. If the Vulture knew she was Kalyazi, there was no point in lying further. Except that they were at a court dinner and there were dozens of ears listening in.

"That boy never fails to surprise me. But your new story, well . . . and paired with such *convenient* timing . . ."

Nadya's eyes narrowed. "You're not here to give me warnings."

Żywia shrugged. "No. Give Tranavia warnings? Yes. But you? No." She reached up, curling a lock of black hair around her index finger. "You should worry, though. I've only been back a day and the *slavhki* talk. They talk a great deal about the *slavhka* with a suspicious story who is close to the king, yet no one knows who, exactly, her family is."

Nadya swallowed hard.

"I know what happened," she continued.

*Because Malachiasz doesn't keep secrets from her,* Nadya thought bitterly. *But he lied about everything to me.*

"And?"

"And the rumors the *slavhki* are spreading venture dangerously close to a certain shade of truth."

The blood drained from Nadya's face. The only reason she had lasted this long was because the truth was so uncanny that it had been swallowed up in a swirl of even more mundane rumors.

Panic started to press down at her rib cage. She cast a glance down the table at Serefin. He looked miserable, sitting next to the man trying to take his throne away.

Her story had not been made to last this long. There were obvious holes, clear gaps where things did not make sense because she was here on some forged paperwork and a story constructed out of desperation when they were all too devastated to think clearly.

"When his court finally turns on you, do you think you'll have the protection of the king?" Żywia asked.

Nadya needed to get out.

Żywia smiled sweetly. "You've outstayed your purpose, dear, that's all. You did what was required of you and brought our Black Vulture back where he belongs. It's time to take your leave. Consider this me being altruistic."

The air between them had chilled, and malice threaded through the Vulture's voice. Nadya thumbed the bottom of her dinner knife. Żywia's gaze dropped to Nadya's hand and her smile widened.

"By my guess you have only days before the *slavhki* move to have you imprisoned at best, hanged at worst. I'd run, *towy dżimyka*."

"Don't call me that," Nadya snapped, before she shoved her chair back from the table and stalked out of the room.

She yanked the lace from her eyes as she walked, wishing she could tear off the finery as well. Tear it all away and be somewhere else, anywhere else, *home*. But she didn't know where home was anymore. She didn't have the monastery to go back to. And there were no gods to guide her actions.

"It's not fair," she muttered. She reached into her pocket and removed her prayer beads, returned to her after months of reaching for them.

They had been resting on the side table by Malachiasz's bed. Next to his iron mask and a thin book that Nadya had taken but not thought of since. Of course he had her prayer beads the whole time, it made it all the easier to convince her that he could be trusted—that the heretical way she had used magic was necessary.

She settled them around her neck, rubbing her hand over the beads, and continued to her newest hiding spot. Nadya had discovered a few of Tranavia's secrets in her boredom while in Grazyk. Far past the eastern wing, where the floors became less polished and servants stopped appearing with regularity, there was an old door. Its aged, dusty wood was carved all the way down with symbols Nadya could not decipher.

She shoved the door open, overly aware of how the empty hall hollowed out, and her with it. She shivered. The room was dark and she killed the instinct to reach for her prayer beads for a light spell. She had a candle in her pocket from some midnight wanderings Serefin need never know about so she lit that.

Nadya stood in an old, forgotten chapel. She spun slowly, taking in the lines of painted icons on the walls, saints and symbols of gods she knew very well.

And a few she didn't know at all.

She moved past pews covered in dust so thick it was like upholstery. The front of the chapel held an ornate altar, carved with more symbols Nadya didn't recognize.

Nadya had spent a lot of time in this abandoned chapel and still had nothing to show for it, but that never stopped her. She would keep praying. She would try until she heard her goddess once more.

She wove her prayer beads around her hand, thumb working up and down the smooth wood, feeling the rough edges of the carved icons. *I don't know what comes next,* she prayed, like she had a thousand times before. She kept her thumb over the icon of a skull. Marzenya's icon.

Her goddess of ice and winter and magic.

And death. Always death.

Nadya had been chosen to be an instrument of those above all others.

And Nadya had ignored her goddess's calls for death every time Marzenya ordered her to kill Malachiasz. She had strayed from her path and was bound to a monster. And the silence of her gods had followed.

It was the emptiness that scared her the most. The feeling that something which had always been warm and *there* was just gone.

*What I did was wrong. I took the easy path when I should have struggled. I should have . . .* Nadya faltered. She should have ended Malachiasz's life. But even now, she wanted to bring the Tranavian boy *back*, not kill the monster. Heresy.

*I know what I should have done. The mistakes I have made are unforgivable. Please don't let this be the end.*

She didn't expect an answer. Yet the silence pricked at her heart. It wasn't a door closing like before, this was a prayer sent out into the empty air where there was no one to hear it.

Marzenya wasn't listening.

She pulled her prayer beads back over her head, wiping at her eyes. What she *wanted* was something vast enough to swallow her so she could no longer think, no longer feel, no longer spend her time circling around how not only had she failed, that this was it, this was the end. The magic she had known was gone. She was just a peasant girl who had killed a king and would hang for it.

What she did feel was anger.

"I have spent months," she whispered harshly, "reading and

praying that there might be something I can do. I've found nothing. I need your help! I don't understand how I can be Kalyazin's hope in one breath and thrown away like nothing the next."

She had oblique references to a single cleric in history who had petitioned the gods for magic, physically, but that was impossible. And in the back of Nadya's brain, constantly present, were the dreams she had of monsters that were more than just monsters.

She wanted answers and she might never get any.

There was nothing for her here.

There was—

She stopped. Head lifting. The air in the room had grown thick with *his* power.

*None of those words were for you.* She threw it out like a blade, in Tranavian. Her struggle was not one to be shared. Especially not with him.

A roiling, churning madness circled her like a predator, making her breath come too fast and her heart beat so rapidly in her chest she thought it might burst.

The candle flickered where it rested on the pew beside Nadya. The madness shifted. Perched on a pew, watching her intently, but when she turned her head there was nothing there. Only flickers in the corner of her eye.

She didn't want this. It was too soon—it had been an eternity—she could not stand to have him so close. She could feel the monster's mutating incoherence.

What she wanted was to feel horror, anger, disgust, anything, *anything* that would push him far away.

But Nadya was curious, more than anything else.

*Can you speak?* Maybe he was nothing but his madness.

There was an assembly of fragments before a glimmering spark of clarity.

"*Tak*," he replied.

A single word—one quiet *yes*—but his voice was a shard of ice.

"*You are always there, little bird,*" he continued slowly. "*Fluttering outside of everything, but you cannot be caught. I try to cast you out yet you remain, irritating, useless, constantly, constantly fluttering.*"

His voice was low and soft and so very *Malachiasz*, yet threaded with chaos as it slipped quietly through the back of her head.

Of course when she was at her lowest he would be here to remind her of how else she had failed. How she hadn't seen his plan even as he laid it out in front of her—had told her he was not to be trusted.

The cut on her palm itched and her heart squeezed painfully. None of this should be happening.

That flickering in his eyes as he had fled the chapel, the draining dregs of his last shreds of humanity. He didn't know her. She didn't know him.

Four months was a long time to live with oblivion. It had been a long time to live with the shadows of everything she had not seen and could not stop. It was a long time to live with silence.

Nadya sighed. *And what solace would catching me bring? Do you enjoy so much your complete and utter solitude?*

"*The bones of a bird are light, easily broken.*"

*Better, then, to waste away alone in the shadows and crush all that come near. What a fate. Pathetic creature.*

What a fate for the boy who had won her heart with such

ardent loyalty toward his friends. It was one of the few things Nadya did not think was a lie. Parijahan and Rashid had not been pawns in this grand game he was playing. Maybe condemnation to isolating madness was what he deserved, but he had been so lonely that this was a truly cruel twist of fate.

He nudged at the thread between them, searching for a weakness she did not think he would find.

*Surely you can break it. Are you not so very powerful? Are you not a being of dark divinity?*

She was goading him; she wanted to hear his voice, rattled and twisted as it sounded.

*"Who are you?"*

And though she had known this question would come, it hit her like a punch to the gut.

*It doesn't matter,* she managed.

The pieces reassembled, as his focus sharpened to curiosity. As he casually dismissed her as no one at all. She had no magic for him to wonder about; a peasant acolyte from Kalyazin could not hold his interest.

She ignored the twinge of pain at this realization.

*Damned boy. Surely you can ignore one irritating little bird.*

She snapped the connection closed. It was imperfect. He would be back. Maybe he wasn't even gone, but the ominous presence in the air slowly faded, and with it came her ability to breathe again.

And the crack in her heart deepened further.

Fleeing the chapel was like admitting defeat. But who was she kidding? She couldn't help anyone. She rubbed at the scar on her palm as she walked. She wanted it all to end.

# interlude ii

## MALACHIASZ

## CZECHOWICZ

"Fool boy, I won't speak to you like this. Wake up."

Malachiasz gasped, the world jolting into clarity as if he'd been doused in ice water.

"Ah, there you are. That wasn't so difficult."

His mouth tasted of blood as he swallowed, disoriented, his head pounding. He didn't know where he was— wait. The witch's tower. How was he here?

He blinked tears away as Pelageya stood before him, a wry grin on her face.

"You, *Chelvyanik Sterevyani*, were expected first. You lost me a bet and I don't appreciate that."

He tried not to panic as his heart sped too fast in his chest, grasping for something to ground him, but there was nothing.

"I asked you before if this would be worth it," she said

contemplatively. "I'll ask you again. Then you can tell me why you're here."

*Why am I here?*

A flickering fire cast the room in an eerie green light. This place was different than before. It dripped with the skulls of creatures both natural and monstrous. A skull sprouting more antlers than any deer would have hung from the ceiling. He blinked. It had more eye sockets than a deer as well.

"Did you ask me that?" His voice was weaker than he would have liked. Everything was fuzzy, like he was pressing through a fog. He rubbed his temples. Why couldn't he remember?

There were flickers, pieces; he remembered fragments. It was unclear and muddied. He seized onto a whole memory and held tight; Pelageya asking him that very question and Nadya's brow furrowing as she tried to fit the Vatczinki words into her understanding of Tranavian and came up blank.

*Nadya.*

Hells.

The witch's white curls were tied back, throwing the well-worn lines of her face into sharp focus. She wore a necklace of teeth that clacked as she moved through the room. Was this her tower? Or was this somewhere else?

"I did, dear boy, and I must say, you were very confident in your response, but I sensed a faltering. Was it worth it?"

"Yes," he replied steadily.

She stared at him, unblinking. He forced himself to keep still under the weight of her scrutiny.

"You look different," she said shortly.

He didn't want to know what that meant. The iron claws that tipped his fingers were enough. He lifted a hand. There was fresh blood underneath his fingernails.

"And what name do you go by now, *sterevyani bolen*?"

He shook his head, frowning. "My name is—"

"It won't help," she said softly. "You will have it for only a second, fleeting and trivial."

"Malachiasz," he said firmly. "My name is Malachiasz Czechowicz."

Her smile was mournful and that sparked an anger in Malachiasz he didn't quite understand. How dare she pretend like his choices mattered to her?

"Fool boy," she murmured. "Why come to me?"

He closed his eyes, a shiver of horror rippling through him. He should leave. Take what she had given him and run.

"It's not enough," he said. "I thought . . . It doesn't matter. Something is missing. It *almost* worked but it's not enough."

She snorted. "It won't ever be *enough*, will it? They let you taste power too young. That family of yours is a cursed line; you know, you *know*. Somewhere deep in those parts of yourself you've locked away. What will happen when you have nothing left? You're near the edge, but soon you'll fall and there will be no more pieces to give away for scraps of power. What will you do with this magic you hoard?"

He opened his mouth to speak, but she cut him off.

"Oh, no, no, I know, I know, you see. I wait to see if you will succeed where all have failed. Visionary or madman? Such ideals, and such darkness, such cruelty, combined are never good. A clever mind—so very clever—but a hollow heart that pumps blackened blood. But it beats yet, and while it beats it can be broken."

He tensed.

"Unless you break it first . . ." She tilted her head, spinning and staring into the fire. "Who will stop you? Who indeed?"

He wouldn't be stopped. That was the horror; that was the brilliance.

"The girl, the monster, the prince, and the queen," she murmured. She passed her hand over the flames. They licked at her skin without burning her flesh. "Except he's the king and she's not a queen. Not how I foresaw it—you all broke that quite thoroughly—but it does make for a more interesting song. More wily, more clever, more strong-willed than I expected, but they still fit the notes they were given.

"And the darkness, the monsters, the shadows in the deep are waking up and they are *hungry*." She glanced sidelong at him. "The very thing you claim to lord over will tear you apart, because, yes, you are powerful, but you are also blind to what will destroy you in the end. You should take the power you swallowed and accept its limitations."

"A prophecy of doom. How quaint, truly, witch," he said dryly.

"No, you wouldn't listen to that, would you? Arrogant boy, clever, foolish boy. You'll taste regret one day. You'll be claimed by the very thing you hate the most. Wait and see. But you're right. You did not come to me to hear of doom, you came to me for something else. Something I can give that no one else can."

"Or take," he allowed.

She clapped her hands. "Or *take*! Oh, the boy steps further and further away from human and molds into the guise of a monster."

She was suddenly too close, her fingers clutching at his chin as she lifted his face up.

"What will your regret taste like, I wonder? Will it be sweet or a bitter, bitter poison? So confident, so clever, so sure of yourself."

"I have every reason to be all of those things." His voice didn't sound so sure.

"Of course." He didn't notice the shift but the witch looked no older than him. Her black curls spiraled wildly around her pale face; her black eyes unsettlingly sharp. Lines no longer marred her smooth skin, and her lips were full and dark. They pulled into a half smile. "Beautiful and arrogant and powerful."

She trailed her fingers over his mouth. "What will you do, *sterevyani bolen? Chelvyanik Sterevyani? Czarnisz Swotep?* What have you done?"

He froze. He had been awake too long and all that had been broken was returning to the surface. Pale hair, rough hands, freckled features, a nose scrunched in thought.

A Kalyazi girl with blood-drenched hands, reaching for him as he shoved her away. She had given him so much and he had crushed her because it wasn't enough.

He hated the witch for waking him, for making him *remember.*

He leaned forward. The witch pressed her thumb against his lips, parting them until her index finger grazed the tip of his fangs. He tasted her blood, sparking something deep within him.

A hiss of air escaped his chest. The witch's smile grew. She lifted her hand, blood dripping down her fingers. She touched the horns that spiraled back into his hair.

"What a fascinating paradox you are," she murmured. "Again I ask, was it worth it?"

"Yes," he said, his voice little more than a whisper.

She nodded. "Yes. And when you are rent apart, when the boy and the monster can no longer reconcile, when you realize you have gone too far and reached for too much and have slipped into a crevice in the world where only the darkest of horrors dwell, will it be worth it then? What a thing to ponder. But you do not care for prophecies of doom."

She snatched up his wrist, dragging his hand into the light. Had the spiral scar on his palm always been there?

"Oh," the witch whispered.

She touched the center of the spiral before he had a chance to stop her. The line to his heart pulled tight and trembled as though someone was trying to saw straight through it.

The witch traced the spiral, her touch feather light. "Marked ahead of your time. How fascinating. How *unexpected*. How did this happen?"

There had been a *voryen*. Warm breath at his ear. Lips in a fast kiss against his temple. Stealing his power in a way no mage should be able. He shook his head.

"I wonder what this changes," she mused. "Will this claw at you faster or save you? Though," she laughed, "there is no saving you. Damned boy, creature of darkness, what horrors will you unleash on the world under the guise of benevolent protection? What destruction under the lie of salvation? How many will you lead down your terrible path?"

He stood up, anxious tremors wracking his body. He had thought that would stop, was disappointed to find it hadn't. *Damned boy.* But the voice was different and a sigh had followed, wistful. He did not know what he was remembering.

"It would be so easy," Pelageya said, watching him pace. "The door is right there. You could stop all of this. You could go back to the little cleric, be a good monster king, and stop trying to change the stars. She is so very, very close."

He stopped in his tracks, heart in his throat. He let out a long, ragged breath as he stared at the door.

He could stop this. Open the door and beg forgiveness for the thousands of lies. Turn back. She would forgive him. And if she didn't, her dagger in his heart might be even sweeter.

But it wouldn't be enough. He stepped away from the door.

Pelageya gave a small, feral smile. And she asked one last time.

"Was it worth it?"

This time he hesitated. One single heartbeat where he didn't know, he didn't know, *he didn't know*.

*What had he done to Nadya?*

There was so much missing, but what *wasn't* was the Kalyazi cleric, bloodied fists relaxing in shock when he'd taken her hand and brought it to his lips. The girl who rested her blade at his neck over and over and let it fall each time, finding something in him worth saving. The beautiful, infuriating nightmare of a girl he couldn't keep away from even as each twist of her string around his finger drove a dagger deeper into his heart.

He didn't know when his plans for manipulation had turned into real feelings.

He hated the witch for waking him up.

"Yes," he growled.

She grinned. "Then I will take that heavy, mortal burden from you. I will give you what you desire. But, oh, know this, *Chelvyanik Sterevyani*, there is no going back once you walk down this path. I can take and hold this from you, but if you ever want it back the pain will be greater than anything you have yet suffered."

She dropped a handful of bones into his hand.

"This will only be the start. There will be more to come."

She did not give him any more chances to change his mind. She kissed him.

And he shattered.

# 5

## SEREFIN

## MELESKI

**Svoyatovy Aleksandr and Polina Rozovsky:** *Twins born under the double moons of Myesta but not taken by her as clerics. When they were torn apart for sport by Tranavian blood mages, their mirrored souls split the ground in two and swallowed the mages alive.*

—Vasiliev's Book of Saints

*Ksęszi* Ruminski was perfectly civil until Nadya left the hall. His eyes followed her, dark and hooded. Żywia met Serefin's gaze across the table, smiling wryly and standing up to follow Nadya.

"Is that the one?" Ruminski asked, gesturing to the doorway where Nadya had disappeared.

"Sorry?" Serefin waved for a servant to refill his wine glass. He wasn't drunk enough for this.

"The one you chose after that *Rawalyk* went to shit." Ruminski was far past drunk and bordering on belligerent.

"That puts what happened far more delicately than I would," Serefin replied cheerfully. "And, no. Did you want me to say yes? I don't think assassinating her will help me find your daughter any faster."

Ruminski frowned. "Assassination would be too simple, *Kowesz Tawość.*"

Serefin tensed. He turned the glass underneath his finger. He had expected them to go after him, but Nadya? If things turned in that direction he did not know how far he would go to save a Kalyazi girl, even her.

"Oh?"

"Your Majesty, you realize she is not who she says, don't you?"

Serefin lifted an eyebrow. "Are you saying I have an imposter in my court?"

"I'm saying you have something far worse."

Ruminski believed Serefin had no idea. That was good, at least.

"What is that supposed to mean?"

"We are at war, *Kowesz Tawość.*"

Serefin would never get used to being called that. He gritted his teeth. He would also never get used to being reminded of the war as if he hadn't spent most of his short life in the worst of it. As if he hadn't failed to sleep a full night for years because, if the horrors of the battlefield didn't keep him awake, the things he had seen in the aftermath would. He had lost so many people he considered friends to the Kalyazi, had seen the war stripping Tranavia raw as it pulled away its resources year after year.

"We are," he replied, with an edge that clearly took Ruminski by surprise. "Which is why I need my court behind me and my actions. My father ran this country into the ground over

this war; I intend to build us back up. We must return Tranavia to its former glory, wouldn't you agree?"

Ruminski nodded his head graciously. "Of course," he said,
"but it would be unwise of you to get too comfortable. Isn't
that what happened to your father, after all?"

"It wasn't complacency that killed my father, I assure you."

"No, that was you."

Serefin took a long drink of his wine before grinning at
Ruminski. "Are you ready to level that accusation?"

"More ready than you know."

*I doubt that.* Serefin leaned back in his chair, resting his
elbow on the arm. "My father died of an experiment of magic
that he took too far. He is not the first to die in such a way."

"The lies you have been feeding the court are not going to
satisfy much longer."

"Is that a threat, *myj ksęszi?*" Serefin asked blandly.

"Simple truth, *Kowesz Tawość*. I am not the only person who
feels this way."

"What way are you referring to? You forget that when my
father took the throne he did it by killing—quite publicly, I
might add—his father."

"Is that an admission?"

"No, because I didn't do it."

"There are others who agree with me."

"Agree with you on what point? You aren't being very clear.
All I know is you suspect me of killing my father, which is all well
and good—perfectly Tranavian, if you will—but you and I both
know such an accusation would not hold against the crown."

"Then what are you afraid of?"

Serefin swallowed. He was afraid of the truth, because the
truth was much worse and it would absolutely be enough to
tear him down.

"I don't wish to take action, you must understand," Ruminski continued. "But I will do anything to get my daughter back, and to maintain the interests of those who have placed their trust in me. So, if my daughter isn't returned to me, I will do what I must."

Kacper had a list of nobles who had allied themselves with Ruminski. He would need to see it after this; he had a sinking feeling he might know a few of the names already.

Ruminski stood. "Good evening, *Kowesz Tawość,* I do hope my point was made."

"Not really," Serefin replied.

Ruminski leaned down closer, gesturing vaguely to the doorway Nadya had left through. "Her paperwork is forged. She is a fraud. And, *Kowesz Tawość*? You must get some rest, you don't look well."

The man strode away. Serefin hurriedly got up, fleeing the hall before any more *slavhki* could corner him. He was drunk. He was tired. And he still had to deal with the Vulture.

Ruminski thought he had orchestrated his father's death, greedy for the crown. That Serefin had always made it perfectly clear the throne was the last thing he wanted didn't matter. He had a suspicion this was about something else entirely: Serefin wanted to end the war.

His attempts thus far had been fruitless. Kalyazin refused to hear talks of a truce and any envoys Serefin sent returned half out of their minds or never came back at all.

Serefin's left eye blurred—worse than usual—his vision going so fuzzy that he stopped walking, momentarily blinded. His eyesight was never good; he went through life with his surroundings perpetually blurry, but this was different.

*"You could have handled that better."*

A whimper escaped Serefin and he squeezed his eyes shut. When he opened them a hazy vision had superimposed itself in front of Serefin's sight. Like one eye was seeing something different than the other.

There was a forest, dark and deep and primeval. Ominous. A place where the trees were monstrous and large, almost impassable. It was the domain of something ancient, something that had slept for a long time and was waking up.

*"There are a number of things waking up, you'll find."* And that voice, *that voice*. Serefin shook. He was going insane, that was all. These hallucinations were the first sign.

*"Your continued obstinacy is growing wearisome. I wanted the girl, but she is, unfortunately, too deeply wound around the fingers of the others."*

Serefin dragged in an uneasy breath. It had never spoken this coherently before. This was too real.

The forest was growing darker, blood seeping from between the roots of the trees. Panic gripped him and he covered his bad eye, hoping the forest would go away, and was relieved to find it had disappeared into the halls of the palace.

*"It's not so easy as that,"* the voice said. *"Do you think you can live with one eye closed?"*

Serefin finally cracked. *You only have the one. You don't have both.*

*"Yet."*

He did his best to remain calm and continue through the halls like nothing had happened, one hand clamped over his eye. But something had shifted. All the things he had been ignoring and hoping would go away would not be ignored. They were getting louder.

*"Kowesz Tawość?"*

Serefin stopped in his tracks, nearly careening into a *slavhka* who stood before him in the hallway, watching him with some concern.

"Are you all right?"

He held a hand out. The boy was about his age and vaguely familiar. The name came to him a few seconds later: Paweł Moraczewski. A *slavhka* who was most likely aligned with Ruminski and not someone he wanted to know that he was having hallucinations.

"I'm fine," he said shortly.

He swept past the boy, knowing rumors would spread like wildfire in a matter of hours. He staggered into his rooms, lowering his hand and letting his eye open. Then he moved to his liquor cabinet.

When his door slammed open a second later, he nearly flung the bottle in his hand against the wall.

It was only Kacper. "The Vulture wants to speak with you." He shot a rather pointed look at the bottle in Serefin's hand. Serefin wordlessly offered it to him. He sighed heavily. "I'll abstain."

"Well, don't act all high and mighty about it," Serefin replied.

Kacper laughed. "Come on, I left her with Nadya and I'm worried they're going to kill each other before we get there."

Serefin stared at him.

"Blood and bone, you're drunk. Sit down, Serefin."

Serefin frowned, but let Kacper sit him on the chaise. "I saw . . ." He trailed off.

Kacper moved closer. "What?" He crouched in front of Serefin, the warmth of his hand resting where Serefin's shook.

Serefin became very suddenly enamored with the deep, dark brown of Kacper's eyes and the scar that nicked his eyebrow.

But Kacper's attention was on Serefin's bad eye and Serefin had to fight the urge to hide it. He knew it was different. His left eye had turned the dark blue of midnight, pupil gone, only a glimmer of stars remaining. Constellations that swirled and shifted, ever changing.

What had he seen? What was that place? Kacper reached out and gently touched the skin underneath Serefin's left eye. His fingers came away wet with blood.

"That's new," Serefin said, voice cracking. He was strangely warm, the spot Kacper touched almost burning. He must be drunker than he thought.

Kacper nodded slowly. He wiped his hand off and folded a handkerchief into Serefin's palm. "Don't let anyone know." Serefin snorted. If only he knew the half of it.

"They all think I'm losing my mind anyway," Serefin muttered. "They're going to know soon enough." He told Kacper about Paweł.

Kacper looked pained.

Serefin carefully massaged his eye socket. The vision—and the voice—were bad news. Kacper was right, no one could know. Even Kacper and Ostyia. No one.

Maybe if he got out of the palace—away from this place where he had been murdered—it would go away. He had been too frightened to tell his mother, but she might have similar advice. The air in Grazyk was sour—the smog that hung over the city rank and heavy. Maybe he needed to get away. He would be fine.

He wouldn't be running. He was doing what was best for the kingdom. Ruminski was right on one point, Serefin was as unwell as he appeared and it wouldn't do. But it would be a dangerous pivot to make, leaving the throne unguarded.

He didn't think he had much choice.

"Who are the nobles working with Ruminski?"

"Kostek, Bogusławski, Tuszynska, Moraczewska, Maslówski, and Fijalkowski," Kacper rattled off the top of his head.

Serefin sighed. The Maslówski family were spell book binders. The Kosteks were merchants with a trade river that half the country used. They were all nobles with a vested interest in the ongoing war. Ruminski turned a profit because of the war, and while Serefin wished, desperately, that the nobles in his court weren't petty and greedy, he knew without a doubt that they were. It was why he hated court so much.

He stood, wavering slightly on his feet. "Let's hear what the Vulture has to say, then."

Żywia sat with her legs kicked up onto the table, her iron mask by her feet. Nadya was pacing, strangely rattled. Neither of them acknowledged Serefin when he entered the room.

This was going to be a long night.

"Ruminski knows your paperwork is forged," he said to Nadya as he sat down.

She looked like she might faint for a moment, before her expression hardened.

"Told you," Żywia said, singsong.

"Shut up," Nadya snapped.

"He doesn't know for certain you're Kalyazi—I don't think— but he will. He suspects it," Serefin said. "And when you fall it remains to be seen whether I will go next, or whether it will spare me."

The silence in the room was so tense that when the door opened both girls jumped. Ostyia quietly slipped into the chair next to Serefin.

"Of course," Serefin continued, "I could always pin all of this on Malachiasz."

"And risk civil war?" Żywia asked pleasantly.

"That's the issue, isn't it?"

"And you can't afford that, I'm afraid."

He gestured wearily. "I'm not going to like what you have to tell me, am I?"

"Absolutely not."

"Is this coming from Malachiasz?"

Nadya flinched.

Żywia shook her head. "He has other matters to attend to."

"That's what you said last time, and those 'other matters' were planning to murder me," Serefin pointed out. "A fact I have not forgotten and will be dealing with in due time."

Żywia leveled an unsympathetic look at him. "The Kalyazi have discovered a way of using magic that we know very little about," she said. "It's incredibly effective, though its scope seems limited. We are not talking about a resurgence of clerics, but something else. The magic has the same—" She waved a hand, searching for the right word. "—taste as divine magic, but it's slightly different."

Nadya was frowning and rubbing the scar on her palm. It looked strangely, newly infected.

"Troubling," Serefin murmured. "But it explains the rally from Kalyazin."

"The what?" Nadya asked.

He had been keeping a lot from her and he wasn't sure what she had figured out on her own. The fact that Kalyazin was pushing back hard and Tranavia was struggling to hold them off was not something she had sussed out yet, apparently.

He couldn't figure out how Tranavia had gone from nearly finishing this war for good in their favor to struggling to keep the Kalyazi from moving across their borders. None of the reports made sense and some days he was half tempted to return to the front himself.

He ignored Nadya. "When you say the magic is effective . . . ?"

"It hasn't killed a Vulture yet but it's gotten close," Żywia said. She glanced at Nadya. "Should we be discussing this in front of her?"

"What can I do about it?" Nadya asked. She sat and dramatically leaned her chin on her hand.

"You're the enemy."

"I'm *exhausted*."

Żywia cast Nadya another long look before she leaned forward and dropped a handful of bones onto the table. Nadya made a low sound in the back of her throat. Serefin squinted at them, trying to parse their genesis.

"Those are relics," Nadya whispered. Her hand stretched out, reaching for them, eyes oddly glassy before Żywia pinned her arm to the table with a cage of iron claws.

*Oh. Human, then.*

Żywia didn't break eye contact with Serefin, her face difficult to read.

"Keep going," Serefin said.

"The *Voldah Gorovni* have resurfaced," Żywia said, still pinning Nadya to the table. "Whether because of this magic or because the Vultures have been more active, I can't say."

"Active because your king has completely lost control," Serefin pointed out.

Żywia looked like she wanted to argue but nodded.

"How much control does he have?" Nadya asked softly.

"It's limited. His crisis of conscience effectively fractured the order and even with him as he is now—"

A flicker of disgust passed over Nadya's face.

"—it's not been quite enough to reforge the broken bonds."

"There have been *slavhki* who have recruited Vultures onto the battlefield," Serefin said. Those reports had been baffling. There was a reason they did not allow the Vultures at the front. They were unpredictable and the casualties on the Tranavian sides of those battles could have been easily avoided had Vultures not been present.

"And the Kalyazi are, surprisingly, reacting in kind to the threat. We've nearly lost a few to the Vulture hunters."

"Is this all you came for?" Serefin asked. "This is valid information and I thank you for it, but I'm surprised I'm receiving it at all."

Żywia hesitated, finally releasing Nadya and leaning back. Nadya's fingers creeped out toward the relics again before she shook herself and squeezed both hands into fists. Żywia rubbed the line of tattoos along her chin with her thumb.

"Why haven't we seen these before?" he asked Nadya.

"They didn't work," Żywia replied before Nadya could. "Not like this."

"Magic is changing," Nadya murmured.

Serefin frowned.

"Tranavia will not survive with my order divided," Żywia said cautiously.

Tranavia relied on blood magic for everything, and the Vultures were the highest authority on magic. Serefin had been avoiding thinking about the possible repercussions from their lack of leadership.

"What do you want me to do? Intercede? Something tells me Malachiasz considers himself far above my mortal rule."

"No, there's no reasoning with him," she said.

"Then what?"

She gestured to Nadya.

There was a beat of silence before Nadya, still eyeing the relics, said, "Absolutely not."

Serefin frowned.

"He spoke so highly of you," Żywia said, something different in her tone. She was growing desperate.

Nadya leaned over the table. "I. Don't. Care," she said, jaw clenched. "He built that hell for himself, let him rot in it."

"Then why do you remain here? What's the point of hanging around the capital of your enemies?"

"I'm rotting, too," Nadya said flatly.

The Vulture paused for a beat, before smiling slightly. "So you are. Well, it was an attempt. I suppose, then, I came to warn you."

"Of?"

"He's going to move soon."

Nadya tensed, her hand going to a necklace of wooden beads.

"I can't tell you his exact plans—"

"Incredibly helpful," Kacper said dryly.

Żywia smiled, all sharp teeth. "I *literally* can't tell you because he has my allegiance and thus my obedience."

"Why the warning?" Serefin asked. "You lot aren't particularly magnanimous when it comes to the greater welfare of the country."

"He used to care," Żywia said. "Somewhere inside he still does. I didn't—I don't—but you deserve a chance before he strikes."

Nadya paled. Serefin nodded.

"You can't tell us who he's moving on first?"

Żywia opened her mouth and closed it, shaking her head.

"Pity." Serefin was going to have to make a choice, and quickly.

"Isn't telling us *this* a betrayal of your allegiance?" Nadya asked. "Besides, he hasn't acted against us in the last four months, why would he wait so long?"

Żywia lifted an eyebrow, clearly waiting for Serefin to respond.

Nadya's expression wearied as they both hesitated. "Don't tell me what he's done. I don't want to know."

"No. You don't," Żywia said flatly.

"I don't think you have to worry about him striking against you, Serefin," Nadya said softly.

Serefin couldn't pin the stability of his kingdom on her guess that Malachiasz would go after her people—her gods—before he tried to take Serefin's throne a second time. Even if Malachiasz's next move *was* against the Kalyazi, it wouldn't end the war, it would only make things worse.

Kacper suddenly shifted, distant, sensing something. He leaned in close to Serefin. "Someone snapped the spells outside your rooms."

*Shit.*

"How quickly can you pack your things?" he asked Nadya.

Her face went gray. "Why?"

"I would say we have a handful of minutes—at most—before a contingent of guards that, frankly, Ruminski should not have any control over, burst in to arrest you. You will not get a trial; you will be immediately hanged. From there it is likely he will lower accusations upon me for harboring an enemy spy—are you a spy?"

Nadya, eyes wide, shook her head.

"Well, that's good at least. Regardless, this will be used to remove power from me." He brushed at a moth. "He wants Żaneta and he wants this war to continue churning. And you"—he leveled his eyes at Żywia—"have her."

"We do not let our own go without reason," Żywia said.

"Helpful." Serefin stood, gesturing for Nadya to follow. "Thank you, again, for your information and your warning. But if you can't hand over the single thing that will actually help, I suppose our conversation is finished."

He yanked the door open.

"I don't have that power," Żywia said quickly. "You have to petition Mal—the Black Vulture."

Serefin paused. "Is he in Grazyk?"

"No. He does not leave the mines."

Serefin closed his eyes. "And it's from the mines that he'll strike?"

Żywia nodded.

There was something not being said that chilled Serefin. What, exactly, was he up against with his brother?

But there was no longer a choice before him; he was being shoved. "Of course. Well, I suppose I'll be paying him a visit."

This would be for the good of the kingdom. This would be to keep his throne.

# 6

## NADEZHDA

## LAPTEVA

*What of Milyena Shishova? What of the girl touched by the goddess of magic who toiled under her thumb until one day she woke and her goddess was gone? The only thing the gods ever leave behind is heartbreak.*

     —The Books of Innokentiy

Nadya had to run to catch up to Serefin. "You're not serious!" she called.

"Keep your voice down," he hissed, pausing only a handful of seconds to let her catch up. "This is what we're going to do," he said, voice a low hum. "I have to speak to my mother. Return to your rooms and prepare to leave. I'll send Ostyia for you, she'll get you out of the palace."

"Why are you helping me?"

"I don't know," he admitted. "But you're coming with me to the Salt Mines."

"*Serefin—*"

"We don't have time," he snapped. "Go."

She didn't want to find out what might happen if that noble got his hands on her. Being Kalyazi was one thing—if it was discovered she was a cleric, that was a whole different mess. She was glad to be leaving, to be forced out of the place she had let cage her and her guilt, but there was no way in hell she was going to the Salt Mines.

The scar on her palm had hurt since the conversation in the abandoned sanctuary. It had blackened strangely, like veins were bleeding around it into her palm. She tucked her hand out of sight.

"We're leaving," she announced the moment she was in her rooms.

Parijahan was on the chaise in the sitting room, Rashid's head in her lap. She was in the middle of lazily braiding his hair. Her head lifted.

"What?"

"They know my paperwork is forged."

Rashid sat up, swearing loudly.

It took them little time to gather the few possessions they had. There was a knock at the door, far too forceful to be Ostyia, and Nadya froze, exchanging a terrified glance with Parijahan.

Parijahan's spine straightened. "I have an idea," she said. "It'll buy us some time." She untied her braid, letting her dark hair fall in loose waves around her shoulders, and kicked off her shoes. "Behind the chaise," she hissed at Nadya. "Stay quiet and out of sight."

She ran a hand through her hair, and said something loud in her language, yanking the door open. "You better have a *very* good reason for bothering me this late at night. No, no, don't you dare step past this threshold until you tell me who you are and what you want."

"Are these Nadzieja Leszczynska's rooms?" the guard asked.

"Do I look like my name is Leszczynska?" Parijahan spat. "You're inching forward and I told you to stay back. Please, push me further, I would love to spark an international incident with Tranavia."

Nadya inched around the chaise to see what was going on. The guard was pushed out of the way by a well-dressed *slavhka* whom Nadya didn't recognize. He unfolded a piece of paper and shoved it in Parijahan's face.

"Can Tranavia outlast a war with Akola?" Parijahan asked evenly.

The *slavhka* lowered the paper. "I have a warrant for Leszczynska, she is to come with us at once."

"Good for her. You've found the wrong rooms."

The man looked bewildered. "I-I assure you, these were—"

"My name is Parijahan Siroosi, Prasīt of House Siroosi of Akola of the Five Suns, and if you don't step away from my door within the next ten seconds, I will decide the magnanimous relationship that has flourished between our two countries will end this night."

Nadya clasped a hand over her mouth. Rashid was casually, impassively perched on the arm of the chaise, long legs stretched out, with an edge to him that reminded Nadya of how potentially dangerous he could be when he truly wanted.

The *slavhka* stuttered, sounding incredibly flustered, but Parijahan merely shut the door in his face. She waited a bit before she turned, something in her posture diminished.

"We need to leave," she said, voice small.

Nadya climbed over the back of the chaise. "Parj, what—"

Parijahan waved her off. She pulled her shoes back on and picked up her pack from where she'd stuffed it in a bookshelf.

Nadya knew Parijahan was from one of the major noble houses but she'd had no idea just how important the Akolan girl was.

Rashid scratched his jaw. "Your family will know you were here in about three days."

"I know," she replied shortly.

There was a much softer knock at the door and Ostyia entered.

"Princess, huh?" was all she said.

Parijahan's eyes closed. "Can we go?"

"Sure, sure, *Your Highness.*"

Parijahan had the other girl slammed against the wall with a dagger at her throat in an instant.

"Do not," she said through clenched teeth, "call me that. Ever. Again."

Ostyia grinned rakishly at her. "Of course."

Parijahan stepped back, exhausted. Nadya fumbled for her pack as Ostyia slipped back out the door, beckoning for them to follow.

The noble girl took them through the same back passages Nadya had found during her midnight wanderings. She could have escaped a long time ago if she'd wished it, but no, she had waited like a little fool.

Serefin and Kacper met them at the stables at the northern end of the palace.

"What are you going to do about Ruminski?" Nadya asked.

"My mother will hold the throne in my absence," Serefin replied. "Ruminski wouldn't dare stage a coup against her."

Kacper didn't appear as certain. "So long as you return soon," he murmured.

Serefin looked like he was going to say something sharp, but sighed. "So long as I return soon," he repeated.

Swiftly they readied the horses and rode southwest. The city fell away and the outlying villages became nothing but a road that was crowded in on either side with dark, dense forest. Ostyia kept complaining that it had been too easy to get out of the city; Serefin just looked grim. And Nadya was going to fall asleep on her horse and fall right off; she had never been particularly good at riding.

Her hand hurt and she resisted pulling her glove off to study the scar. It was bitingly cold, unseasonably so, as if winter had fallen on the land and fought off both spring and summer.

She was relieved when Serefin finally moved off the road so they could catch a few hours of sleep before setting off again. She thought the breakneck pace they moved at was unnecessary until Rashid pointed out that Serefin had no idea if Ruminski would honor his mother's regency.

"You've effectively left the throne to those vultures," Rashid said.

"The alternative would be to leave it to the actual Vultures," Serefin said. "And I find I am deeply curious if Malachiasz would make a decent king?" He directed the question at Nadya, a thorny barb.

She ignored him, finally pulling her glove off and rubbing her palm. Was Malachiasz's power infecting the scar? Was he what festered beneath the surface?

Nadya had made a terrible mistake in letting him live.

Serefin pulled a silver flask out of his coat pocket and took a swig. "If I deal with this as quickly as possible, there's nothing to worry about," he said, a touch too cavalierly.

Maybe Nadya had made a mistake letting Serefin live as well.

Rashid nodded slowly, also clearly questioning Serefin's intelligence. "Well, then, we better get this finished quickly."

"That's the plan."

"Will they come after us, do you think?" Nadya asked.

"You? Probably. Me? Unlikely."

"No, they'll *hire* assassins to go after you," Kacper muttered, but he looked worried.

Serefin glared at Kacper and jerked the tent out of his hands, moving to the other side of the clearing to set it up.

Nadya went over to Serefin as the others set up the rest of camp. He was working with the practiced ease of someone who had done this a thousand times before. She was surprised, she had known he was a soldier—had witnessed that firsthand— but she had figured the army treated him like a prince all the same and waited on him hand and foot.

After a long silence, he spoke. "I can't exactly let you go on your way."

"Can you, exactly, stop me from leaving?" she asked, sitting near him as he made a pile of the wooden tent poles and began assembling the tent. "Why didn't you hand me over to that *slavhka*?"

He shrugged. "It would be wrong to let you hang for something that was hardly your fault."

"I infiltrated the *Rawalyk* with the sole intent of killing the king," she reminded him. "And I succeeded."

He leaned back on his heels. "You did."

"I was going to kill you, too."

He laughed softly as he rolled his sleeves back. His forearms were dusted with scars, a story of haphazard swipes from an untreated blade in the middle of battle, careless cuts for magic without thought of the damage that might be left behind. Different from the dedicated, careful crosshatch of self-inflicted pain that had been painted against Malachiasz's pale forearms.

"I'm glad you didn't, though my entire court apparently stands to disagree." Serefin finished up the tent and sat next to her. "I don't play their games the way they want me to," he said. He ran a hand through his hair, fingers catching on the hammered iron crown that still rested on his brow. He tugged it off with a sigh. "I had hoped the court—at least the majority— wanted the war to end. I'm ashamed of my *slavhki* to find that is not the case." He rubbed at his jaw, clearly uncomfortable. "And the rumors were not ones easily brushed away."

"And you think bringing Żaneta to her father will appease them?"

"I don't have any other options."

"Why does it feel like you're running away?"

He shot her a half-smile. "Because I think I might be." He sobered. "I have other reasons for leaving Grazyk. The magic residue in the air wasn't good for me. I was having—" He waved a dismissive hand. "—hallucinations."

Nadya froze. "You what?"

He shook off her concern. "Nothing more than old magic. I'm not used to being in Grazyk for so long. The air got to me, that's all. I'll be fine now that we're out of the city. Anyway, I know you don't wish to go to the mines, but I need your help."

"You don't know what you're asking," she said quietly. Her mouth filled with moisture like she was going to throw up. What did he mean, hallucinations? She had felt a little strange when she'd first gotten to Grazyk, but the bad air hadn't bothered her after a while.

"Tell me," he said gently.

She shook her head.

He frowned. "Nadya . . ."

"Come with me," Parijahan said, walking up beside them. "I will tell you what you need to know."

Nadya let Parijahan pull Serefin away. He didn't need to know the depths of Malachiasz's betrayal. Not from her.

The sounds of Parijahan's soft voice explaining what had happened and Ostyia and Kacper arguing over whether they should light a fire drifted through the clearing. Rashid sat down next to Nadya.

She leaned her head against his shoulder. "Is it terrible that I miss him?"

"No," Rashid said. "I miss him, too. We don't have to go with them, you know."

"I have nowhere else to go, Rashid," she said, voice soft.

"Go back to Kalyazin. Find the army. Find Anna."

Her heart twisted. She was no use to the army. And she didn't know what she would say to Anna if she ever found her again.

"I'm just tired. I keep thinking maybe enough time has passed that I can get on with my life, but . . ." She shook her head. She couldn't exactly mention that she could feel Malachiasz's presence *constantly* but the sentiment was the same.

"Why are you and Parijahan still here?" She changed the subject. The thought of them leaving made her so desperate and anxious that she had never dared ask before.

Rashid's dark gaze cut to where Parijahan was talking to Serefin. She was tense, her hand resting near the dagger she kept at her hip.

"I don't think she's done here," he said. "She's not ready to go home, either. So I stay, too."

Nadya followed his eyeline, slightly puzzled. "Are you and she . . ." She trailed off, unsure what she was asking.

He laughed. "No. I don't really go for that. Besides, I'm not

Parj's type. My family was indebted to hers, but I worked off the debt long ago. She's a cold star we all orbit around, but I love her all the same."

Serefin cut a sharp glance toward Nadya and she wondered what Parijahan had told him.

"Did she not get her revenge?"

Rashid shrugged. "I honestly don't know. I would hope so. For this blasted, monstrous country, I sure hope so."

Nadya pulled the first watch, tamping down the fire to embers and sitting with her back to it, the jacket she wore pulled close around her.

She shouldn't have his damn coat. Nadya tucked her face against the collar where it smelled like him and wondered how long before his scent faded. She shouldn't think of him, it would only call him back to her, it would . . . She sighed.

*And here you are.*

*"You're somewhere different."* He sounded curious. It hadn't taken quite so long for coherence this time. She wondered what that meant. What was Malachiasz and what was the monster?

*And you are in exactly the same place. How boring.* An easy guess. Żywia had said he didn't leave the mines; it was heartbreaking. One of the few truths he had shared was his absolute fear of that dark and terrible place.

A shimmer of irritation.

*I wasn't expecting you to return,* she said. *After all, I had been thoroughly weighed, measured, and found wanting. Gods, it must be frustrating. For a being of some divine power to find yourself linked to a mortal with no magic.*

The thing she hated the most about this connection—aside from everything—was the feeling he was so close to her. That he sat nearby, his lean, scrawny frame folded with his long legs stretched out.

But he wasn't. It was only her, alone in the dark with her back to a dying fire.

"*No magic?*" He was puzzled.

*Didn't you say I was of no consequence?*

"*A miscalculation.*"

*Do you make those?*

That little flicker of irritation burst into a flame. She went silent. She shouldn't goad him. But it was so easy. It took this corrupted, nightmarish thing between them and turned it into something almost familiar. Except she shouldn't *want* that. She had to find a line within herself she would not cross.

The clearing they were camping in wasn't far from the road, but suddenly it felt like it was miles away. The trees too tall, spindly branches reaching fingers that would become a cage and trap them inside. The darkness no longer natural, but thick, cloying, and deadly cold.

*Why are you back?* she asked, after the silence between them had grown dangerously comfortable, even as the world around her grew more menacing.

She was aware of him watching her, or whatever it could be called through this scrap of magic tying them together.

"*I don't know,*" he said, and she hated herself for letting her resolve weaken.

There was chaos and darkness in that voice but also the lonely boy who had isolated himself further for a fruitless cause. She wanted to feel the thrill of justice. He had what he wanted and he was miserable for it. But instead she yearned to give him some measure of comfort he did not deserve.

It was too easy to pretend, like this—unable to see him, hearing only his voice—that he hadn't turned into something horrific. She would have to keep searching for the place where she would finally be revolted by what he was.

*Well, we can't exactly keep doing this, can we?* she said. *Surely you have far more important things to attend to.*

Silence. It was as if he was content simply watching. Nadya found it unsettling. She didn't know how much he was seeing, how much of *her* he was seeing.

Suddenly he tensed, a predator poised to strike. *"You're not alone."*

Nadya rolled her eyes. *Of course I'm not—*

*"She's here."*

*She?* Nadya didn't like the hope that lit inside her. He had a tie to the divine that she did not, as twisted and horrific as it was.

*"There are witches, and there is* her. *I will not suffer her again,"* he said.

In a blink, he was gone. Nadya frowned, puzzled, and looked up, right into Pelageya's young, pale face.

She stifled a yelp. Pelageya held a finger to her lips, grinning impishly.

"Hello, child," she said. She held out her hand. "Come with me, there's something I must show you. You're the last, you see, and it's time. It's past time. It's due time."

Nadya glanced to where the others slept. She wasn't about to leave them unprotected, not when the air had gone so wrong around them as they slept. And Parijahan had agreed to take the next watch. She would notice if Nadya didn't come to wake her.

"Oh, no, there's no choice here." Pelageya seized Nadya's wrist.

And they were somewhere *else.*

Nadya staggered to her feet, taking in the dimly lit room. It was the tower in the palace, except the view through the windows was of a dark forest.

The room shook. Nadya pressed a hand to the wall to keep her balance.

"Oh, don't mind that. Gets restless, the house does," Pelageya said.

"I have to go back," Nadya said.

"Why? Go back to pining after the pathetic boy who broke your heart, to a wasteland of your own creation?" Pelageya tapped a finger against her nose. "You haven't felt it, have you? What he's been doing?"

Nadya hadn't felt much of anything recently. She shook her head. Nadya wasn't certain she wanted to know where this conversation would lead.

The witch looked at Nadya with a pity that made her furious.

"Stop it. Take me back. I don't want this."

"Oh, child. I have saved you for last because your road will be hard and long. Fervent and zealous and abandoned in the end. Or maybe not? Or maybe so. It is so hard to say with those divine monsters we call gods. It is so hard to see what it is they are doing to you."

Nadya gripped her prayer beads, tears pricking at her eyes.

"What has he done?" she asked in a hoarse whisper.

It was troubling how much more coherent the witch was than the last time Nadya had seen her. She didn't know where Pelageya's power came from; this force of wind and nature and strange magic. She didn't know if it was a magic she could access herself. She had used power outside her gods' will, but when she reached for it now, there was nothing there.

"Things are waking up. Old things, dark things. The old ones who have slept for so very very long. You set it into motion. You and that Vulture."

Nadya opened her mouth to argue, but Pelageya clapped her hands in front of her face.

"Your intentions do not matter. You and the boy—though something tells me he was not involved so willingly—freed Velyos from his prison. Velyos has found a new mortal to claim. He will wake those who were allied with him in his long fight against your pantheon's leader."

Nadya frowned. Her pantheon didn't have a leader. They didn't have a single god above all others. It was more varied than that, wider than that. And what did she mean about Velyos claiming someone? *Who?*

Pelageya cocked her head. "The little cleric does not know? Yes, a cleric, don't shake your head at me, you may be an odd one—you may bathe in blood and be touched by darkness—but you cannot hide from your fate by denying your reality so easily. Sit, child, we have a lot to talk about."

Nadya sat tentatively.

"Tea? I didn't offer those boys tea. What a strange, brutal pair they are. They wanted information or magic and nothing more. So rude. Their mother clearly never taught them any manners."

*Mother?* She didn't know what to do with that, so she tucked it away.

Pelageya busied herself with a samovar. "Your Tranavians. The Vulture and the princeling, oh, king, I suppose. The boy cast from shadow and the boy cast from gold."

"You've seen him?" she whispered.

Pelageya looked up.

"Nevermind. Don't answer. I don't—"

"You care, little Kalyazi, and that is your weakness. It could be your strength, in another time, another life. But here? In this world of monsters and war? You care too much."

Nadya chewed on her lower lip, trying to will the threatening tears away. She took the warm mug of tea Pelageya handed to her, and sipped it slowly.

"I don't know what I'm supposed to do," she said.

"You have little time, you see," Pelageya said. "So little time before the heavens are ripped asunder and all that fire and damnation comes raining down. Do you think it will only flood Tranavia? Do you think your precious Kalyazin will be spared?"

"It doesn't matter," Nadya said wearily. She drew her legs up onto the chair.

"Broken so easily by divine mischief." Pelageya clucked her tongue at Nadya. "What a shame, what a shame. I had such hope for you, child. Salvation or destruction, capable of either, but giving up will dash all chances."

Nadya's grip on her mug tightened. She wouldn't sit here and be mocked.

Pelageya took Nadya's hand as she passed her chair. Nadya protested, trying to pull her hand away as Pelageya flipped it over.

"You as well," she said, "but yours is different."

"I stole his magic," Nadya said.

"Clever girl. I'm sure the Vulture didn't like that."

Nadya shrugged.

"An impossible thing. But I should have expected impossible things from you, all things considered."

What was that supposed to mean? "Maybe expect fewer of those now."

Pelageya's finger traced the blackened scar on Nadya's palm. She squirmed. "Untapped power that has festered, or something darker that has been waiting to surface?"

Nadya jerked her hand away.

"You didn't get the hellfire you were promised. Now what?"

"I didn't want hellfire . . ."

"Oh, lies. You tell yourself that your opinions were swayed because of a few pretty Tranavians, but I know the truth of your vicious soul."

Nadya shifted uncomfortably.

"I know the truth of the darkness you harbor."

"I don't know what you're talking about," Nadya snapped. Her words meant nothing. The woman was mad.

"That will only get worse," Pelageya said, motioning to her hand. "That, and the silence. Don't give me that look, girl, you think I don't know?"

"Did you bring me here for a reason? Or did you just wish to taunt me?"

Pelageya laughed. "Such a sharp tongue! If you want answers there is one place you can go. You'll have to watch that hand, though."

"Where?"

"You're a smart girl, I'm sure you've heard of Bolagvoy."

The name sounded familiar but she couldn't place it.

"In the Valikhor Mountains?"

Nadya scoffed. *That* she knew.

"Such distrust! You forget we come from the same place. I know my codicies and verses. I know my saints. I know my stories about Valikhor."

Nadya groaned. "I can't *petition* for forgiveness." The seat of the gods was an old legend, and as much as Nadya thought it might have some truth to it, she would never survive the journey. It had come up often during her solitary studies in Grazyk, and she had eventually decided not to pin her hopes on myths.

Pelageya tugged on a black curl. "Can't you?"

"Only the divine are able to reach the mountain. Bolagvoy is locked."

"Well, shame you don't know anyone who has tasted divinity."

Her heart sped. "You can't be serious. He can't be saved."

"Saved? No. Returned? Mmm, well, also no. But do you possess the key to tearing through the armor of madness he has constructed around himself? Possibly."

"And what good would any of it do?" Nadya cried, standing up, sloshing the scalding tea against her hand. "I killed the damn king but I couldn't stop the war. I can't stop whatever Malachiasz is doing. I can't *do anything*. I have nothing. What do you want from me?"

Pelageya laughed, an odd pealing sound. "It's not about what I want, child. What do *you* want? You who have lived at the whim of others your whole life. Is freedom truly so debilitating?"

*Yes.* "I want . . ." Nadya licked her dry lips. She wanted to hear Marzenya's voice. She wanted to see Malachiasz's smile and hear him laugh at his bad jokes. She wanted, so dearly, to do the gods' will. She wanted *too much*.

She scrubbed the heels of her palms against her eyes. Pelageya was spinning a web around her.

"I don't know," she whispered. She had become unmoored and couldn't find her way back. "Would it work? Going to the mountains?" She hated how hopeful she sounded.

Pelageya shrugged. "It could, it could not."

Enigmatic nonanswers weren't going to get her anywhere.

"The forest takes. Sacrifice, always sacrifice, and is it a sacrifice you are willing to give? It burns, it changes, it eats. It's hungry, old things are so hungry. And the hunger, the gnawing, it will destroy and devour and eat you alive."

Nadya closed her eyes.

"It will ravage the divine like it will ravage humanity."

"So even if I can get him to help me . . ."

"It will shred his mind and twist his body even more. Annihilation for a being such as him. Is that worth it, do you think? Is his destruction worth your salvation? What a choice. Can you love someone and ask them to shatter themselves for you?"

"I have to," Nadya whispered.

Pelageya smiled. "Would a boy from Tranavia know the stories? Would he know that the forest always hungers? That it would gaze upon him, divine and mad and broken, and *want*?"

She would have to lie to him. Like he had lied to her.

"Would a boy too much in love with his own country know of Nastasya Usoyeva and her golden heart and silver tongue, who suffered the trials of the forest and looked upon the faces of the gods?" Pelageya went on. "Who was granted the speech of the gods by petition and will alone?"

"No one can survive gazing upon the gods," Nadya said wearily.

"You have."

Nadya stilled. She *hadn't*. She had seen visions of monsters. Horrors, nightmares, nothing more.

"The taste of divinity is a sweet poison, but poison all the same. It infects, it leeches, it destroys, it . . . well, it consumes. Like the forest will consume. Like that hand of yours will consume."

Nadya curled her fingers closed. None of this made any sense.

"Why are you helping me? Why now?" She hadn't heard from the witch since before they killed the king.

"Because something has changed," Pelageya said. She tossed an item to Nadya.

Nadya only barely caught it. A *voryen*, sheathed in black leather, with a pale, white handle. She tugged it out of the sheath. The blade was the same shade of ivory. Her breath caught. The *voryen* was carved of bone.

Her palm ached. She frowned, feeling a strange pulse in the bone dagger as she curled her fingers around it.

"That'll eat you alive if you let it," Pelageya said, nodding to Nadya's hand.

"What is it?"

"What do you think? Power. Monsters have always slept at the edges of your world. Your Vulture created the veil cutting off your gods from the world, what do you think he's done with his power now?"

Nadya's vision tunneled. "What?" she whispered.

Pelageya's head perked up. "Ah, our time runs out. Good luck, *koshto dyzenbeek, koshto belsminik.*"

When Nadya blinked, she was sitting in front of a dead fire, the sun broaching the horizon, with the bone dagger in her lap.

"Well, hells," she swore.

# 7

## SEREFIN

## MELESKI

*The waters sing. Omunitsa howls.*

—Codex of the Divine, 188:20

"I'm concerned."

"You and literally everyone else." Serefin looked up from where he sat. They had traded in their horses for what would be the first of many boats—all the better to evade assassins, he supposed—and his legs were kicked over the edge as they ferried across one of Tranavia's hundreds of lakes. Kacper stood beside him, distress sketched in the hard lines of his body. As if ready to bolt. The others were below deck; it was early yet, the morning light still gray on the water and full of shadows. Only the boat's captain and his skeleton crew were nearby.

Kacper sighed and sat down next to Serefin, almost leaning into him against the cold. Serefin offered him

his flask, surprised when Kacper accepted it. That wasn't a good sign.

"What if this was all a ploy to get you out of Grazyk? What if it has nothing to do with Żaneta? What if—"

"Kacper."

"Your mother is made of steel but her nerves *aren't*. And, what if—"

*"Kacper."*

"You're going to be defeatist again, I just know it," Kacper whined.

"I'm not. All your concerns are valid."

"Then why are we *here*?"

Because Serefin was seeing things that weren't there, and maybe if he was away from all that magic, it would stop. Because Serefin was losing his mind and had no better option before him than to flee and hope he could fetch Żaneta and fix things.

"I'm . . . breaking," he said, very quietly. "And maybe it's nothing, but I think something happened to me when I died."

"Besides all the moths chewing through your clothes," Kacper said, his voice strained.

"Besides that."

"And your eye."

"The eye is definitely part of the problem."

And even as Serefin spoke, everything morphed around him.

*"Something is stirring. Something hungry."*

It was worse this time. His whole body went rigid as it struck—a vision that was not a vision because it was *more*, real and right in front of him. He was not on this boat, not even in Tranavia. He was somewhere else, someplace that did not want him there and would destroy him if it got the chance. Blood dripped down the bark of trees so massive he could not see around them. The sudden snap of twigs was ominous, so full of a promise of oncoming terror that Serefin's heart slammed into his throat.

This place wanted something; his death, his life, he didn't know.

Something slunk through the trees, close to the ground, and Serefin saw only the flash of teeth dripping with blood, too many for the creature's mouth to contain.

*The closer you draw to me, the easier it will become. You cannot fight it, boy, you can only submit or be taken.*

The vision winked out, and Serefin was left, breathing hard, on the deck of the boat. Kacper had dragged him away from the edge, his fingers gripping Serefin's jacket so tightly he thought the fabric might tear.

"You boys all right?" the ship's captain called.

"We're fine," Kacper called, something Serefin couldn't quite place in his voice. It was fear.

"Serefin," Kacper murmured. He raked cool fingers back into Serefin's hair, his palm resting against the side of Serefin's face. "You nearly threw yourself off the side. What *was* that?"

Serefin resisted the urge to lean into Kacper's hand as he pulled away and scrambled to his feet. There was no use in Kacper worrying; there was nothing he could do to help.

"That," he said, voice brittle, "is why I had to leave."

But he was shaken by the notion that the opposite was true. What if the farther away he got from his home, the stronger this voice became?

"You have a plan, right?" Nadya asked, her frustration evident as she sidled up next to him.

Serefin was at the railing of yet another boat—he had lost

track after the scare he had given Kacper, largely thanks to the waking nightmare that was his life—massaging his bad eye after seeing someone impaled on the antlers of a monster he couldn't identify. The visions had been slowly superimposing themselves over his sight more and more, until they grew unnervingly constant. He had come to dread being awake because he never knew when the visions might strike, but he dreaded sleep even more.

"Plans are all I have," he replied. "Whether this one will work remains to be seen."

She tugged the sleeves of her jacket down over her hands. It was a Tranavian military jacket, and much too big for her. Serefin had the faintest idea where she'd gotten it—only one branch of the military had silver epaulets and they technically never saw battle—but it wasn't for him to ask.

Nadya blinked up at the snow falling around them. She held her palm out, watching as the flakes melted against her skin.

An eerie sound pitched up from the water followed by a thud against the side of the boat, a hit so hard that it tilted precariously to one side.

Serefin and Nadya exchanged a wide-eyed glance. They leaned over the railing, ignoring Hanna, the boat's captain, yelling at them to get away from the edge.

The weather changed in a blink, the benign suddenly growing fierce. The water became choppy; the boat rocked so much that Serefin worried he was going to be thrown over.

A strong hand gripped his shoulder and he was yanked away.

"Get back, boy," Hanna said sharply. "You fall in and they'll pull you under and then there's no saving you."

"They?" Nadya asked.

"*Rusałki,*" the woman said. "They're angry today."

The boat rocked, buckets of icy water sloshing onto the deck. Hanna swore. Serefin reached for his spell book, but Nadya grabbed his hand, shaking her head.

"Wrong approach, I think," she said.

Kacper leaned over the railing as another vicious strike sounded. Hanna quickly hauled him away and ordered him below decks with a glare.

Amidst the dark churning water, a flash of pale skin broke through.

"Are we in danger?" Serefin asked.

Hanna looked uncertain. "If there's enough of them down there and they want what's on this ship bad enough, yes, but that shouldn't be an issue. They usually leave us well enough alone."

Serefin couldn't fathom what they could possibly want on the ship. Nadya's face was deathly pale. She winced, rubbing the scar on the palm of her hand before reaching for the necklace around her neck.

A hand slammed against the side of the boat, right above the water. The skin was sickly translucent, and long, blackened claws curled over the fingertips. The claws dug into the hull of the boat, splintering the wood. A piercing, single musical note rang out over the water, turning into a hauntingly strange melody.

Serefin tentatively looked over the railing. A girl's face appeared under the surface. Her eyes were pitch-black and a touch too large to be natural, just enough that something registered as *wrong*, but they were the most beautiful eyes Serefin had ever seen.

Her head broke the surface and her face changed *utterly*. Stringy, black hair plastered to her forehead, her mouth split too far back into her cheeks, and when she smiled Serefin saw rows upon rows of tiny, sharp teeth.

She lunged. He was wrenched back, her teeth snapping inches from his face.

"Stupid boy," Nadya muttered, shoving him away.

Claws dug into the wood again as the *rusałka* began to climb her way up the side. Dozens of pale, gangly arms followed, latching on to all sides of the boat. They were surrounded.

"I've been on the waters my whole life and I've never seen them act like this," Hanna yelled, struggling to keep the boat steady.

Serefin was back at the railing and he didn't know how he'd ended up there. Claws swept inches from his skin. Dimly, he knew he would be pulled under and drowned, but he was unconcerned.

"No!" Nadya yanked him away again, flinging out her bad hand at the *rusałki*.

The *rusałki* froze.

They turned, slowly, in one movement, and stared hard at Nadya. Her face was pale, mouth open. She met Serefin's gaze, panic in her eyes.

What kind of magic did this girl have?

# NADEZHDA

# LAPTEVA

The scar *hurt*, darkness stabbing at its center. Her heart thudded against her chest. This should not be happening. Something was wrong.

Parijahan pulled easily out of a *rusałka's* grasp, its attention locked on Nadya's hand.

Nadya slowly let her hand fall and they all watched it drop. There was a thread of power—one she did not recognize—tying her to the *rusałki* and she didn't understand what it meant, but she felt it when it snapped. The second whatever control she had over the monsters broke, they returned to tearing the boat down into the depths.

She flexed her hand and closed her eyes, an odd stare from Serefin boring into her back. What was this magic? A *rusałka's* claws clasped her forearm, tight and painful. The snow had turned to sleet and it struck her skin in thousands of cold slaps. Nadya's hip slammed into the railing of the boat.

Not witch magic, not blood magic, not divine magic.

There was nothing else. There was *nothing else.*

So what had she just done? And could she do it again?

The thread that tied her to Malachiasz shifted—his attention was on her but it didn't matter, not when these monsters were going to drown them all, and for what? Hanna said they wanted something, but what?

Urgently she pulled at that thread of power, searching past the darkness. A *rusałka* dug her claws farther into Nadya's arms and if she didn't figure out how to use it she was going to die. They all would.

*There.*

The line pulled taut and with it came a thrilling rush of *power.* Power she had missed before; the shape was so very different from the magic she knew.

Nadya threw her will into that power. They would leave. They would not torment this boat. They would not hurt anyone.

*Leave now.*

Everything shuddered around her and Nadya let out a

gasping breath, knees giving out and sending her crashing to the decks.

The silence that followed stretched out for so long she expected them to renew their efforts. Then all the *rusałki* fled.

Serefin pushed away from where he had nearly been pulled over and crouched in front of her, moths bursting into the air around him.

"What was that?" he demanded.

"I'm fine, thanks for asking," she managed through gasps.

He glared, unamused. The only sounds came from the rain pounding against the deck, less violent than before, but all the more freezing.

*Blood and bone.* The Tranavian curse came unbidden. Nadya had just used impossible-to-define magic in front of the boat's captain. She looked up at the woman, who was standing nearby, watching them warily.

"I'm not going to ask questions," Hanna said. She took her hat off and wrung it out—even though it was still raining—before slapping it back on over her dark hair. "I don't want to know. That was too strange for me. The *rusałki* are quiet creatures, they take their fair share of lives, but they've never paid me any mind." She shook her head. "Something awful in the air today."

*Not just today.* Nadya rubbed her thumb over her scar. The darkness reacted to her touch and she shivered. Parijahan slumped down against the railing, her head in her hands.

"Are you all right?" Nadya asked, alarmed.

Parijahan's breath was coming in fast, panicked gasps. "I could have drowned," she said, her voice shaking.

*Like her sister.* She moved next to Parijahan, careful to keep her distance, but Parijahan immediately rested her head on Nadya's shoulder. Serefin watched them quietly.

"Everything is fine," Nadya murmured, but the lie burned her tongue. She couldn't stop rubbing at the scar.

They sat in the rain for a while, already soaked to their skin so there wasn't much point in moving below decks. It took Parijahan a long time to calm down.

"What is that?" she asked after watching Nadya trace the spiral on her palm for the thousandth time.

She still had Velyos' pendant. She dug it out of her pocket and handed it to Parijahan.

"It was the only way to get enough power to do what was necessary," she said slowly. "Using an old god who demands sacrifices of blood. Well, I think Velyos is a god. I don't actually know. That sounds bad. And worse, I stole some of Malachiasz's power with it."

It was still too close, the weight of his wrist, heavy with compliance, the drag of the blade over his palm, carving out a claim on him that he had to be fighting against even now. Why had he let her?

Parijahan cast Nadya a furtive glance. Serefin took the pendant from her, turning it over in his fingers, eyebrows tugging down almost imperceptibly.

Nadya thought about what she'd said, and laughed in a dull, horrified way. "Oh, no," she whispered.

"It's not possible for you to take his magic," Serefin said mildly.

"That's what Pelageya said, too," Nadya whispered. "But I did."

Serefin shook his head. "Magic doesn't work like that. There are rules—"

"Oh, you *sound* like him."

That got him to shut up fast, but not for long.

"Can you feel it?" Serefin asked, his shock turning into

curiosity, also like Malachiasz. She shuddered. Tranavians and their destructive fascination with magic.

"I always feel it," she said softly. "Him," she clarified, voice dropping lower.

Serefin blinked, startled, but Parijahan appeared concerned.

Nadya glanced between them, pressing her thumb against the center of her palm. "It didn't—that didn't feel like his magic. I don't know what that was." *I don't know what's happening to me.*

"I'm a little more concerned that you're constantly aware of the Black Vulture's presence."

Nadya shrugged helplessly. "I did what I had to. These are the consequences."

"Does that mean it works in reverse?"

Nadya chewed on her lower lip. She couldn't bring herself to tell them about the conversations.

"I don't know," she finally said. "I know he's aware of me. Not who I am, just that I'm here."

Parijahan let out a soft breath. Serefin looked ill. He rubbed at his bad eye. Nadya wondered if it was bothering him; this wasn't the first time she had seen him favoring it.

"Well," he said quietly, "this changes things."

"Still hell-bent on breaking Żaneta free from the Salt Mines?" Nadya asked dryly.

"There's nothing else to do," he returned, sounding as helpless as she felt.

"You could start by telling me what happened to you that night. What really happened," Nadya said. She wasn't telling him the full truth, and she didn't expect that courtesy from him, either, but maybe having a better understanding of what happened would help. "I know you died, Serefin. *I can see it on you.*"

"Is this the time for that conversation?"

"When better?"

He sighed. Kacper and Ostyia were below decks, surprisingly apart from their king. Hanna had long since moved to the stern of the boat, muttering about her "good ladies never acting like this." He finally sat, crossing his legs underneath him. He opened his hand and the pendant fell from his fingers, bouncing when the string caught on his knuckles.

He tossed it to her. "I haven't the faintest idea what happened to me." He rubbed at his eye, harder this time.

Nadya smoothed her thumb over the carving. How had Kostya—her mischievous but pious old friend—found it in the first place? Why had it made its way to her?

When she looked up at Serefin, she watched with horror as his hand turned red with blood. She caught his wrist, pulling his arm away. Serefin made a soft sound of protest, but she shushed him.

His eye was deep midnight blue, all trace of the pupil gone, flecked with stars constantly changing their constellations, but the white was crimson, as if every vein had burst. There was blood trickling out the corner of his eye.

His pulse raced under her thumb. She was dimly aware of Parijahan leaving—possibly to fetch the Tranavians, but they couldn't help here. This was not the fault of blood magic; the bad air in Grazyk wasn't making him ill.

"Nadya?" he said. He sounded small and lost, like a little boy suddenly finding himself alone in the woods. It struck absolute fear into her heart. The moths that trailed him created a frenzied cloud of dust around his head.

She made a low, soothing sound, pressing her fingers against the skin underneath his eye. It was darkened as if bruised, blood pooling there as well.

"I can't close it," he said, panic threaded through his voice. "It took this one and I can't control it anymore."

"It?"

Serefin didn't answer. The pupil of his good eye was blasted out, the ring of ice only a mere sliver, awareness flickering in and out. Sweat beaded at his temples, his breath coming fast.

"Serefin, what is it?" Nadya asked. She swallowed back her panic.

A black patch slammed over Serefin's eye. Kacper caught him when he froze and collapsed in a faint. Kacper's face was tense and withdrawn and so worried that Nadya's heart clenched. He tied the patch and smoothed Serefin's hair before wiping at the blood already starting to seep out from underneath. The gentleness in his touch made Nadya feel like an intruder.

"What's happening to him?" he asked, turning to Nadya.

Nadya shook her head. "I don't know."

"Well, you had better find out, and you had better fix it, Kalyazi. Or all his talk of keeping you alive will be worthless because I'll kill you myself."

# SEREFIN

# MELESKI

**Svoyatovi Zakhar Astakhov:** *Astakhov communed with the voices of the forest—some say Vaclav—some say something much older—some say he spoke with nothing more than the leshy who ultimately took his mind and dragged him into the Tachilvnik Forest to feast on his bones.*

—Vasiliev's Book of Saints

He'd recognized the symbol on Nadya's pendant. Was it a Kalyazi god that had control of his eye? Serefin thought the gods abhorred blood magic—that's what this entire bloody war was about, wasn't it?—and his vision had been so much like something that could be reached with blood magic.

Serefin had returned the eye patch to Ostyia—a little worse for wear—after their last boat had docked and they had sought out new horses. Nadya had inspected his eye and declared it fine, given the circumstances, which he understood to mean she had no idea what was going on, either.

It hadn't been the vision that had been terrifying so much as the powerlessness that had gripped him. He couldn't close his eye, couldn't stop what he was seeing. He could barely move.

He was going to lose himself to this *thing* if he didn't do something about it. And now he had the added stress of worrying that Nadya's bizarre connection to Malachiasz was going to compromise everything.

Żywia had come on her own, which meant Malachiasz was actively plotting to usurp Serefin's authority, or worse. And unfortunately Serefin couldn't exactly kill Malachiasz in the Salt Mines—though he wanted to.

He didn't really know *how* to kill a Vulture; they only died under extraordinary circumstances. And he would have to create just that. The *Voldah Gorovni* might have resurfaced, but Serefin couldn't exactly go to a group of Kalyazi Vulture hunters and ask best practices for killing the monsters.

They had long since passed the last village that dared to rest near Kyętri and the dark magic it harbored. The ground was flat here, the trees stunted if alive at all. It was made all the more bleak by the snow falling from the permanently gray sky. Serefin was used to traveling in the cold, but it had been cold without relief for so long that it was growing unbearable.

"He knows I'm close." Nadya's voice startled Serefin as she moved her horse up next to his. She was still wearing that jacket, nearly hidden underneath the second coat she wore. She had a hood up over her hair, the fur collar around her shoulders frosting with ice. Her hands worried the wooden necklace of prayer beads around her neck.

The others had fallen farther back. Serefin glanced over his shoulder. Kacper looked bored; Ostyia was talking to Rashid, as animated as ever.

"Just you?" He turned back to Nadya.

"Yes. He doesn't know who I am."

"Awkward."

Nadya's nose wrinkled. "He's not particularly coherent."

Serefin lifted an eyebrow.

"I forgot you were unconscious for that bit."

"I know what he did."

"Yes, but it's harder to understand if you didn't see it. What's your plan?"

"He has to recognize my authority, regardless . . ." He trailed off at the expression on Nadya's face. He sighed, tugging his hat more firmly over his ears.

"I just told you he's barely coherent. Appealing to protocol isn't going to do you any good."

"Nadya, what I would dearly like is to put a knife through his chest, get Żaneta out, and be done with it."

She flinched.

"Would it fix . . . ?" She pressed her fingers to her eye.

He groaned. "I'm losing my mind."

She was thoughtful. "Possibly, yes."

He frowned. He had been hoping that, what, she would disagree? This girl who spoke to the gods regularly? Stupid.

A flash of dark forest, the scent of old leaves and damp moss, suddenly filled Serefin's nose. He shook his head, trying to dispel the scene before it turned into a full hallucination.

"Do you have a better plan?"

"I go alone."

He narrowed his eyes. "I thought you didn't want to go *at all*?"

She was quiet, gazing out over the barren field scattered with dead trees that would eventually lead to a doorway to hell. There was a vulture sitting in a nearby tree and Serefin couldn't shake the feeling it was watching them, waiting to report back.

"There's no reason for all of us to die down there," she said.

"How noble," Serefin said flatly.

"I am incredibly noble."

"Tell me your motive, Nadya."

"I don't have to."

He tilted his head back, rolling his neck to look over at her. Her eyes widened.

"What?" He straightened in his saddle.

"N-nothing," she said. "I need Malachiasz for something."

"You just told me he was barely coherent and that my going down there would result in disaster."

"I didn't say *that*."

"You implied it. Maybe we should try trusting each other," he said. At her incredulous scoff, he continued. "Just a bit?"

She smiled at that.

"What do we need him for?"

"It's complicated and very religious."

He didn't manage to mask his distaste. She laughed.

"There's no *we*. You only want Żaneta as leverage to get your throne back."

"Oh, don't say it like that."

"You left her with the Vultures for months and are only going to find her now because she's of use to you."

He swallowed. He couldn't really argue with her.

"Tranavians are cruel," she said.

If he took her bait she would never tell him what she was planning. He tamped down his rising frustration.

"What for?" He pressed on mildly, "He committed treason, Nadya, and you're technically the enemy; I need to know what you're planning."

After a few seconds of petulant silence, she sighed.

"There's a place in Kalyazin that myth says is the seat of the gods. I'm going there. Stop looking at me like that; I know what Malachiasz wants to do. It's surrounded by a forest only the divine can walk through."

At Serefin's confused silence, she continued.

"The gods don't talk to me anymore. And you don't care about that, fine, but this?" She waved to the snow dusting the ground. "And the *rusałki* attack, the rumors of other things, horrors, emerging from the deep dark where they slept. There's something coming, Serefin."

*"Something is stirring. Something is hungry."*

He shuddered violently.

"That implies I'm going to let you go," he said.

"Whatever you think about the gods, I don't care. But something is in the air and I intend to find out what it is and how to stop it. You don't have to come with me. I'll get Żaneta for you; you take your throne back, maybe stop this damn war while you are at it. And you *will* let me go. I need to go home. And I need Malachiasz for this."

"So, you think he's divine?"

"I think he's an idiot. But that ritual of your father's was to become—if not a god, then akin to one and I believe Malachiasz has succeeded at something of the sort. He can take me where I need to go."

"Have you told the others?" His voice came out strained.

Nadya shook her head. "I'll probably die down there."

Serefin didn't want her to go down there by herself but the prospect of dealing with his brother—the word was still strange and unfamiliar and uncomfortably *right* to Serefin—was not something Serefin wished to do. He didn't want to admit how much he wanted to let Nadya deal with this problem.

"Tell me you have a plan, at the very least."

"We've been talking, he and I. There's a crack in his armor."

"I'm not hearing a plan."

"Because your plans have been so detailed?" She rolled her eyes. "Whatever he did . . . I don't think it took him as far as he expected."

"You lost me."

She laughed, surprising Serefin, who had never heard her laugh quite that way before. It wasn't derisive, but a gentle, easy sound. "He shattered himself, yes, but if he had the power to dethrone the gods, well, wouldn't we have seen the results by now?"

*Not if the gods don't exist,* Serefin thought petulantly.

*"Oh, wishful thinking,"* the reedy voice chimed.

He held up a hand and a large, dusky gray moth landed on his index finger, its wings fluttering and catching the fading light.

"You think he can be saved?" Serefin asked. He was willing to play the long game. It would make Malachiasz easier to kill.

"Hardly. But perhaps pulled back into a semblance of coherency."

"And if not?"

"If not . . ." Nadya paused. She eyed the vulture that was still watching them. "Then the Vultures will finally accomplish what they were created for and that will be the end of Kalyazin's clerics."

"I thought you wanted him to rot."

"I do," Nadya said fervently. "He deserves whatever nightmare he's in. But he's the only one that can get me where I need to be."

They rode in silence for a while until one by one the horses began to balk, firmly planting their hooves and refusing to go any farther. Serefin couldn't blame them—he certainly didn't want to go any farther—and begrudgingly made the decision to leave them behind.

"Out here?" Rashid protested. They were miles from any sign of life, and the surrounding fields were dry and barren.

"I'm not a monster," Serefin said.

"Debatable."

Serefin ignored him, cutting his forearm on the razor in his sleeve and flipping through his spell book. He ripped out a page, smearing blood inelegantly on it and blowing the ashes that followed toward the horses. He dabbed his fingers in his blood and touched each horse—lightly, there was no need to be messy—on the flank.

"They'll be fine. They'll make it home."

"That's a drain on you," Kacper murmured, disapproving. "Just leave them."

"*You're* the monster!" Rashid exclaimed.

Kacper rolled his eyes.

Serefin turned to Nadya. She was gazing out into the horizon in the direction of the Salt Mines. He wished he didn't have to put so much trust in her—he needed Żaneta, and if she failed he would lose much more in this venture than she would.

A Kalyazi cleric and the king of Tranavia. Sworn enemies turned exhausted allies. There was no good reason for their alliance outside of sheer desperation at this point.

Serefin was going to let her try. It took a lot to kill a Vulture. It would take even more to kill Malachiasz, but Serefin had a feeling that it would be harder now than if Nadya succeeded.

"Don't make me regret this," he warned.

She shot him a wistful smile. "I already regret asking."

# 9

## NADEZHDA

## LAPTEVA

*The taste of blood through broken teeth and a promise, a
reminder that nothing lasts forever. Hunger is eternal.*
—The Volokhtaznikon

When she snuck away from camp, the barren fields were
eerie with the darkness blanketing them. As blithe as she
had been about it to Serefin, she didn't have a plan. She
had a hope and a prayer and that was all. With each step
she walked closer to her death.

It was unsettling, how unassuming the entrance to
the Salt Mines was. Compared to the extravagance of
the cathedral in Grazyk, this was sinister in its quiet.
How easy it would be for the unsuspecting to stumble
upon the plain shack and enter into something horrific.

How easy it was for her to walk into something horrific.

"And so the little bird risks oblivion," he said, suddenly
beside her.

Nadya tried not to flinch at the sound of his voice. She didn't manage such restraint. She kept her eyes locked firmly on the door carved with symbols, the bloody markings painted against the wooden walls.

"I didn't realize you stepped outside your hallowed halls," she said.

*Don't look.*

He snorted softly and stepped past her. She dropped her gaze before it glanced upon him.

"You will follow," he said.

She stepped after him, keeping her eyes dropped low, tracking the bloody feathers of his heavy, black wings as they dragged the ground behind him.

*Don't look.*

She hesitated at the doorway. The darkness past the threshold was suffocating. This was truly stepping into hell. This was following him somewhere she might never escape.

"You came far." Nadya nearly jumped out of her skin at the voice right next to her ear. A hand clasped her arm, nudging her in the right direction as the world plunged black around her.

Żywia.

"Where's the king—wasn't this whole mad business his idea?" There was a pause. Żywia tucked an errant lock of Nadya's hair behind her ear, the gentle scratch of her iron claws grazing her cheek. When Nadya didn't answer, Żywia laughed. "Oh, this is different, is it? This is about *him*."

The Vulture hadn't been like this at the palace. Was it this place that broke them down to their darkest parts, leaving them more monster than human?

"Darling, I'm so glad I got through to you, though this is only going to end in misery. I look forward to your attempt. Come now, and don't trip. It's a long way down."

Żywia twined her fingers in between Nadya's, the motion rough.

"Won't tell him, I won't," she said. "He is so *baffled* by you. So confused, and I won't tell him that you know what you know. You try, *towy Kalyazi*, what is uncertain is whether you will succeed."

The Vulture led Nadya down the steps.

It grew colder the farther down they went and Nadya thought it would never end. She would be trapped on these stairs, in the dark, forever, and that was how she would die. She never would have made it down without Żywia and she hated relying on the Vulture.

It never got any lighter and so she was never able to see. The air tasted of iron, a metallic tinge clung to it. The darkness was unbearable. Things moved in the depths of the dark and she could not tell if the creatures that crouched in the corners of the labyrinthine passages and slunk in the doorways, with their rows and rows of teeth, that *appeared* vaguely human, were real, or if her brain was imagining them.

She had no idea if Malachiasz—*not Malachiasz*, the Black Vulture—was nearby or if he had left her to her fate.

Something screamed in the dark and Nadya froze, gasping for air. It hadn't sounded human, or, it had, but only barely, the last shreds hanging on while nails of iron dragged out everything else.

Żywia stopped walking, waiting for Nadya to move.

"What was that?" Nadya hissed.

"You don't want me to tell you," Żywia said. Nadya could hear the smile in her voice.

She didn't. She didn't want to know.

Her heart was pounding too fast, lodged in her throat, and

no matter how hard she swallowed she couldn't get it to budge. She wasn't getting any air in her lungs. It was as if there wasn't any air down here and she was just going to suffocate as the walls closed in around her. Żywia slowed to prevent Nadya from slamming into the rough stone wall as the passage narrowed, leaving only a sliver of space to pass through. Nadya had never thought herself afraid of small spaces before, but wedging herself through that passageway she couldn't help thinking that she was being led straight into a trap and the walls were going to swallow her alive.

She focused on Żywia's hand in hers—real. The breath in her lungs—real. The nearby screams—not real. Even if they very much *were*.

She started walking again and finally, *finally*, the hall opened up into a vast throne room. Torches cast the room in a sickly pale light. Bloody symbols streaked the walls, bones inlaid on the floor—like that of the cathedral yet without any of the elegance. What this spoke of was far more primal. The throne in this foul place was carved of bone, paneled with gold, inlaid with amethyst. It was a beautiful, terrifying construct—a near twin to the one that sat in the cathedral in Grazyk—that gleamed in the flickering light.

*Don't look, don't look, don't look.*

But her eyes found him anyway.

He lounged sideways on the throne in a way that was achingly familiar, his leg kicked up over the arm. Black veins trailed underneath his pale skin. Spikes of iron dripping blood jutted from his body. Heavy black wings were tucked against the other arm of the throne. He was chewing idly at the pointed end of a claw with razor sharp, glittering iron teeth.

That wasn't the worst of it. That wasn't what made her stomach sour and bile rise in her throat. There was something shivering at his edges that she couldn't quite place. As if everything he had become had twisted even darker as he lurked in the shadows. There were cracks in his skin, but with a shiver, it would all change. Each time her brain tracked him, his monstrous features altered. A shiver. New eyes dripped down his cheeks and jaw, blinking open at intervals. A shiver. Sharp teeth slicing open the skin of his cheek. Her eyes blurred. Eyes on his forehead, bloody and pale instead of onyx black. An ever shifting, chaotic horror.

Despair threatened to drown her. This was so much worse than she had imagined.

His onyx eyes skimmed over her as she desperately avoided meeting them. His inky black hair was long and tangled, threaded with golden beads and pieces of bone. The worst part—the glimmer that shattered the fragile armor she had built around herself—was when the shifting plane of his features rested fleetingly on his utterly human, painfully beautiful face. Transient, quiet, gone in an instant.

Only a monster.

A slow smile stretched across his mouth, revealing iron teeth and hints of fangs as he studied her in a careful, cautious way.

She had to do *something*. She bowed. "*Kowej Eczkanję*, I am here to make your life miserable."

She didn't have time to straighten up from her false deference. He was across the room, hand clutching the back of her head, wrenching it back.

"Easier to kill you now," he said thoughtfully. "Here."

"As opposed to across a magic thread? I suppose so. Easier for me to fight back," she pointed out.

His iron claws scratched against her scalp. It would be so easy. Press a little more and she would be dead. She had to make the idea of her death not quite so compelling.

"But . . ." she said, mocking his thoughtful tone, "that would be a sour end to your curiosity."

He allowed her to straighten, shifting his hand to tip her chin up with one iron claw, forcing her face up to his. She had forgotten how tall he was. "I suppose we'll see, pet."

And in the shifting hellscape that he was, she caught a glimpse of the scared, lonely boy who had been torn into pieces and was searching for something, anything, that might salvage the wreckage.

A crack in the armor.

A weakness for Nadya to exploit.

The Black Vulture let her go. She took a step back. He watched her as a predator might, sharp-eyed, head angled to the side.

"Why have you come here?" he asked.

"There's a *slavhka* that was inducted into your ranks several months ago," Nadya said. "I want her back."

Żywia looked curiously at the Black Vulture, as if she had no idea why Nadya was there. Nadya couldn't trust the girl, but she did wonder why the Vulture hadn't told him who she was. He frowned slightly, returning Żywia's glance. Something sparked in his onyx eyes.

"Oh, the *mistake,* of course. Fetch her, Żywia. Careful, though, it's been a long time since she's seen any light."

Horror settled deep in Nadya's core. She hadn't really known Żaneta, but the *slavhka* had treated her kindly enough when she was pretending to be competition for Serefin's hand in marriage.

Which, Nadya considered, she was glad the *Rawalyk* had ended in disaster. Now that she knew Serefin she couldn't think of a single worse fate than being *married* to him and she had been on the road to winning that whole nightmare.

"What is it you need with my Vulture?" he asked.

"If she's a mistake, it doesn't sound like you have much use for her," Nadya replied.

He was close, lifting her prayer beads with his claw. Time was a circle and Nadya had to relive her past in a new twisted reality. A boy in the snow, too curious for his own good. A monster in the darkness, contemplating a puzzle. His onyx eyes flicked over the symbols on the beads, a slight frown tugging at his mouth.

"Witch magic and divinity," he murmured. "You still haven't told me who you are, *towy dżimyka*."

Hearing the nickname without any of the warmth Malachiasz put into it hurt more than Nadya wanted to admit.

"Neither have you. I suppose we're even," she replied.

A flicker. "Kalyazi, clearly."

"Oh? I thought my Tranavian was rather flawless." It wasn't, Nadya knew, but her grasp of the language had improved greatly since he had first worked with her on it.

"Brave of you, to think you would leave this place unharmed. Or foolish. We're at war, little Kalyazi."

Nadya shrugged. "I thought the Vultures weren't involved in the war. What do you have to fight? There are no more clerics."

"There's one," he said thoughtfully.

"Yes," Nadya said softly, "there is."

He knew what she was. Even in his scattered, barely coherent, soulless state. His mind was shattered but not dulled.

"Will you kill me?"

He frowned at her, thinking. No. Not yet.

*Not yet.* "*Nothing to fear from me, Nadya,*" he'd said, '*not yet*' *lacing his words,* she thought miserably. *And I ignored it.*

Nadya tensed as he stepped behind her. The darkness of his

presence brushed past her, and her fear arced so high she dizzied.

*I should not have come here alone.* Blank horror crept up her spine.

"Will you tell me your name?" he asked.

"Will you tell me yours?"

His laugh was low and grating, a painful sound.

"I have no name." He spoke softly, face close to hers. "I am more than that. More than everything. The darkness to be worshipped, the poison in the hearts of men, heresy, shadow."

"Sounds exhausting."

"Why are you here?" he continued, dragging a claw down her cheek, the graze just light enough that her flesh did not part underneath the razor sharp iron. His breath was hot at her ear. "Why have you come reeking of witch magic and holiness? What purpose do you serve if not for me to ruin? What are your bones worth if not to be crushed?"

"Oh, please, ask the question you actually want the answer to." She was nothing but a little bird and he was the beastly vulture that chewed bones to dust and swallowed the sun. To fear him was natural, it was what he expected, and she didn't want to give him that satisfaction.

He turned her to face him, hands rough against her shoulders. She had to drop her eyes, the shifting horror of his face was too much.

"Is the magic yours?" he asked.

She lifted his right hand from her shoulder, turning his palm face up. She frowned; his scar was clean. Wordlessly, she tugged off her glove and turned her own palm. Her scar was blackened, veins of darkness trailing out over her palm. One vein had started to lace up her ring finger.

Why was his clean, yet hers corrupted like *this*?

He looked puzzled. He closed his fingers around his own scar, his other hand tracing hers with an almost gentle touch.

"The magic is not mine," she said.

His eyes bore down on her. "But you know what it is."

She had assumed it was Velyos' power, but what if it wasn't? What did he know? "I don't know how to break it." She touched a piece of bone that threaded through his dark, wild, tangled locks of hair. It was too far, but he didn't flinch away.

She needed to dig her fingers into the crack in his armor and wrench it open. She had his name—knew how much of himself he had tied to it—but would it be enough? He had to want it to be an anchor. He had to *want* to be Malachiasz Czechowicz.

Somehow, she had to find him. She had to find the boy all while convincing the monster to let her take Żaneta. It was an impossible task.

Tension lay suspended between them. It was an unsettling discovery, to find that she didn't feel a desire to take her *voryen* and put it through his heart.

"Here she is!" Żywia sang, breaking the silence as she shoved a hunched, frail form into the throne room.

Nadya hissed out a breath. The Black Vulture moved away, back to his throne, the moment between them broken.

Żywia skipped up to the dais, settling herself at the foot of the throne. "What do you want with her?" she asked. As if Serefin hadn't told her.

Nadya shot her a glare. Żywia shook her head, ever so slightly.

Was she helping her or not?

Nadya moved closer to the crumpled form that was Żaneta. She was terrified of what she would find under the curtain of limp curls.

"I've been told she committed treason," the Black Vulture said.

"You've been told?" Nadya asked. "You were there."

Żywia shot her a wide-eyed look as the Black Vulture's expression grew distant and confused.

"What?" His voice cracked over the single word, a lost boy, bewildered in the dark until he was pulled back under.

*Stop it.* She shouldn't be separating the two like this. It was all Malachiasz.

Nadya shrugged. He clearly wanted to ask her more, but instead he slouched back on his throne, frowning almost petulantly. Nadya turned away.

"Żaneta?" she whispered, scared to reach for her.

"Her grasp of her name is questionable," the Black Vulture said. He leaned his chin on his hand as he watched. "Her grasp on . . . *reality* is questionable."

"Speak for yourself," Nadya muttered.

She caught the Black Vulture's quirked eyebrow and Żywia's narrowed eyes. She was being too familiar.

Nadya reached her hand out, jumping when gnarled fingers with jagged, broken fingernails snapped over her wrist. The curtain of hair parted.

"Oh, darling, what have they done to you?" she whispered.

# 10

*Part back the flesh, shatter the bone, and see what shapes*
*the beating heart of a being that once was and is not any-*
*more. Velyos is tricks. Velyos is patience.*

—The Letters of Włodzimierz

Serefin had learned very early in life that making Ostyia
mad would only result in his suffering, so he tended to
avoid it at all cost. The more they dealt with Malachiasz,
the more unavoidable it was.

"What do you mean you let her go?" Ostyia said, voice
level.

"We couldn't exactly storm the Salt Mines, could we?"
he returned.

When they had woken and found Nadya gone, Serefin had been more relieved than anything else. He wasn't
ready to face Żaneta, and Nadya had taken the burden
upon her shoulders.

"You let her go to do what? Get Żaneta back?"

Serefin nodded.

Ostyia's eye glared. "And that's all?"

"What she does down there is her business." He moved past her and stoked the fire before digging in his pack for something to eat. The Akolans had wandered off to get a closer look at the entrance to the mines, likely to their detriment. "Stop questioning my decisions."

Her fists clenched. "You can't be serious, Serefin!"

"Do you have a better plan?" he snapped.

"She's going to bring the person who *murdered you* back when we're having a grand old time dealing with things without his meddling, so, yes, I do have a better plan. But it doesn't matter because it's not like you ever listen to me!"

"Why should I listen to someone who has lied to me for years?"

Her jaw dropped. "I never lied," she said coldly. "You weren't exactly asking after him."

Kacper was watching their fight like he was afraid they were going to turn on him next. Serefin couldn't think of a single time he'd fought with Ostyia like this but he couldn't *stand* having every decision he made questioned when everything was falling through his fingers.

No wonder no one in Tranavia took him seriously. He could never get a word out without someone questioning him. "Are you *sure* that's what you want to do, Serefin?" "Isn't there a better way to handle this, Serefin?" "Surely you could stand to have a little more tact, Serefin?"

"You're acting like I've wronged you when you're the one letting the enemy go off to sway back the person who had you killed. I cannot believe I had to say that *twice*."

*"It doesn't matter,"* Serefin said. "It doesn't matter. The decision is made and what's done is done."

"If you make a decision that's stupid and going to end in your death, do you really think I'm not going to try to stop you?"

"It's every bloody decision I make, Ostyia. Not just the stupid ones. It's *everything*. I can't do anything without you questioning me."

She frowned.

"Both of you do," Serefin continued.

Kacper sat up straighter, shooting Serefin a wounded look.

*"How can you rule if your subordinates step all over you?"* the voice said, settling in the back of Serefin's head.

He needed a drink. But the voice wasn't wrong, exactly.

"Blood and bone, that's why the entire court thinks I'm a weak drunkard, easy to plot around, isn't it? Because everywhere I go you two are undermining my decisions."

"Serefin—" Kacper started.

"Or because you *are* a drunk," Ostyia said.

Serefin closed his eyes as anger tore through him.

"Ostyia!" Kacper said sharply, desperately trying to keep this from spiraling out of control.

"We never should have left," she continued. "Your mother isn't going to be able to stand against Ruminski, and no one will believe you left for your health—coincidentally, another thing the *slavhki* love to gossip about. And every single one has decided you're as mad as your father, but at least he knew what he was doing, because you clearly don't. You're right, Serefin, I do tell you when you're reckless, because no one else will. Everyone is happily waiting to see you fall, and—"

"Stop," Serefin said, voice level.

*"Waiting to see the young king fall. Waiting to see him swallowed up by the enemy from the west. An animal, hungry and waiting to snap you up in its jaws so everything can go right back to the way it has been for a century. It will spin on and on and on and you will have let it happen."*

"Why should I?" Ostyia asked. "What's the point? We're not going to have anything to go back to at this rate. And the Black Vulture is going to kill you because you're going to let him."

*"Do you really think you can be free of me, child? Are you really that naive?"*

"Stop." Serefin didn't know if he was talking to the voice or Ostyia, but the word came out strained and snappish and so forceful that she fell silent. "He's my brother," he finally said.

Kacper gave a low gasp. Ostyia's eye was wide with shock.

"No," she whispered. "No, he's your cousin."

Serefin shook his head. "He looks nothing like Sylwia or Lew and you know it. He does, however, look a hell of a lot like Klarysa." Malachiasz was taller than Serefin, slighter, with paler skin and sharper features. But they both had those ice pale eyes.

She was shaking her head slowly. "This changes nothing." But she was rattled.

"Well, yes, in that, at least, you're right." Serefin stood. Ostyia took a step back. "There's no changing what he did. I just get to live with the agony of wondering if I could have done anything to stop it had I known he was alive for the past *eight years.*"

Ostyia winced.

"How long did you know?"

She took a sharp breath and didn't answer.

A thought slithered in and took root. It was horrible and he wasn't sure what led him to voice it, but it didn't feel like *he* was talking anymore.

"You were jealous."

She shook her head vehemently, but there was a shift in her posture, a blow landed.

"You were the only friend I had," she said, voice soft and close to breaking. "After the attack—after—" Her hand lifted, going to her scarred eye socket.

Many noble children had died in that attack. Serefin and Ostyia had lived. No one would ever fault the heir to the throne, but Ostyia had faced the resentment that came with being one of the only ones to walk away.

"I've made my decision. You will not speak to me like that," he said slowly, still unsure who he was talking to. "If you question me again I'll have you sent back to the front on a tour that has no end."

And he didn't know if it was the rod of iron in his voice, the way it had dropped to a toneless, dead hum, or the words themselves, but tears were burning in her one blue eye. She clenched her fist, fraught with anger, and stormed away.

Nervous silence filled the camp before Kacper let out a long breath.

"Whatever you're about to say, don't," Serefin snapped.

Kacper lifted his hands. He was still watching the spot where Ostyia had disappeared.

"Is it safe for her to go off alone?"

"Do you want to go after her? *By all means.*" It came out more venomous than Serefin intended. His skin was too hot, sweat beading at his temples. He dug in his pack for his flask.

Kacper flinched, but his eyes searched Serefin's. "Are you all right, Serefin?"

"Stop asking me that." He scanned the fields. Ostyia was far enough out that his wretched vision couldn't see her. "Are you going to decide what's best for me as well? Because I don't need you, either."

"You know what? I'm going after Ostyia. I'm not about to be your punching bag. Go ahead and drink yourself to death."

Serefin slumped down onto the ground with the flask and watched him go.


The forest was dark. The leaves were thick, heavy, so no moonlight caught between the branches, instead plunging the underbrush into a darkness that was total and complete. A shadow shifted between the trees—too fast to see properly. There was a groaning in the earth, like something ancient and vast was waking up and pressing its way to the surface from underneath. A cold wind blew, icy fangs biting at Serefin's skin as he gasped awake.

He didn't know how he had ended up in this place.

He didn't even know where *here* was.

Serefin turned, searching for a path to follow home, but there was only underbrush and dead leaves.

*"Well, you are unexpectedly talented at being in two places at once."*

Serefin spun around, recognizing the voice. High, melodic, like reed pipes. He didn't see anyone, but he had *heard* someone speak.

"What do you mean?" Serefin spoke out loud. At least, he thought he did. He shivered.

*"I mean what I mean. You are here but you're not. Not much good to me there but you'll come in time."*

Serefin didn't like how confident the voice sounded.

"What do you want with me?"

*"Oh, your power, your status, your clever, clever mind. The realm*

*of the divine is vast and far reaching, but it is mortals who change this world, and mortals will see our whims into reality."*

"You need us?" Serefin asked. He hated having to acknowledge this being. He was Tranavian. The gods were useless. That's what this was, wasn't it? Some god?

"Unfortunately, I have my own problems to deal with and they don't include coming . . . here . . ." Serefin trailed off. Wherever here was.

*"How long do you think you can run, boy? How long do you think you can survive as I take you, piece by piece?"*

The voice's tone chilled him to his core. Serefin touched his bad eye. The fear of losing control of his eye was too close, too real. He had to get out of here.

"As long as it takes," he finally said.

*"It's been so long,"* the voice said. *"So long kept in a prison created by mortal priests. Your world has become a place where my kind watch from the shadows as you build your walls and your veils and destroy a balance that has been in place since the dawn of time. Your arrogance is precious. You think you can control the stars, change the heavens. Little fools. You can't run, little fool, you can't hide from this."*

Serefin covered his eyes. If he stopped seeing the forest, he would stop being in the forest. This wasn't real. He was at the camp outside the Vulture's nest. This was a trick and nothing more.

He would wake up and Ostyia and Kacper would be back and less angry and Ostyia would stop needling him. Everything was fine; everything had to be fine.

Serefin gasped awake.

He was still in the forest.

# 11

## NADEZHDA

## LAPTEVA

*Sofka Greshneva was beautiful, transcendent. She was touched by Marzenya. Until she wasn't. Until there was nothing. Until there was only silence.*
— The Books of Innokentiy

Nadya didn't know what would haunt her the longest: Żaneta's eyes, pitch-black, blasted out, the whites swallowed by darkness, her dark skin uncomfortably sallow, her frantic sobs, or that when she had bared her teeth there had been rows of iron nails and fangs.

Żaneta had scrambled for Nadya's hand when she was being pulled away, desperate and panicked. Her voice garbled and wrong but pleading for Nadya to not let them take her. The noble girl was still there somewhere, just as Malachiasz was within the monster.

Żywia went to lead Nadya out of the room, but the Black Vulture stopped her.

"No," he said softly, "leave her."

Nadya took a steadying breath as something subtly dangerous shifted.

"She's not afraid, isn't it curious?" He slouched back on his
throne. "There's no scent of it on her. Nerves, maybe, but not
fear. Let her stay; let her see." He grinned. "Let her fear."

Żywia let Nadya go, waving her back to a corner; Nadya
gladly fled to it.

"I have better things to do than deal with a Kalyazi witch
anyway," he muttered, shoving himself off the throne. "Tell To-
masz to bring me a new one."

Nadya's hands were shaking. She slowly sunk to the floor,
catching Żywia's eye. The girl nodded as Nadya slid back into
the shadows.

The new one, as it were, was a man dazed out of his mind. His
clothes were ragged and Nadya couldn't tell if he was Tranavian
or Kalyazi but she didn't want to know. Whatever was about to
happen to him wouldn't be less horrible for the knowing.

Żywia crouched next to Nadya.

"What's he doing?" Nadya whispered.

"Always moving forward," Żywia said, watching the Black
Vulture with rapt attention. "Always reaching for the next step,
the next scrap of magic that will make him more, better, and
as far from human as possible."

Nadya's stomach turned. The Black Vulture lifted up the
man's chin with an iron claw. The man stared, unseeing.

"Would be better if he were more lucid," the Black Vulture
murmured. "But I'm not sure he would have survived that
much magic being pushed into him any other way, do you
think, Żywia?"

"That, and he'd struggle when you do the removal."

"Oh, but the fight is half the fun," he said absently.

Nadya covered her mouth, gasping as he slammed his clawed hand into the man's chest, wrenching open his ribs, and yanked out his still-beating heart.

She buried her face against her knees, frozen with terror as it played out again and again behind her eyelids. And the sounds, *the sounds*—was it worse that the man hadn't screamed? That there had been nothing but the creaking and snapping of bone and the sound of *wet* as blood sprayed everywhere.

She could *hear* the blood dripping to the cool stone floor. Hear the thud of the man as his body fell. She lifted her head only slightly, to see the Black Vulture regarding the heart, dispassionately contemplative.

He smiled, slight and cruel. "Ah, there's the fear." He tossed the heart to Żywia, who caught it, close enough that blood splattered over Nadya.

It was still warm.

He licked blood off his slender fingers. "It's not perfect," he said. "But it *is* something."

Żywia, less enthusiastically but just as curiously, tasted the blood coating her hands. She made a soft, affirmative sound.

"Could always . . . take it all, I suppose."

"I just had dinner, too," he said mournfully, and his voice sounded so much like *Malachiasz* that Nadya jolted.

Żywia cast her a sidelong glance before throwing the heart back to him. He brought it to his mouth, biting into it.

Nadya fainted.


Nadya let Żywia drag her through the halls, too dark for Nadya to ever escape. She tried to block out the screaming, but it was *constant*.

"How do you stand it?" she asked.

"It's enough to know that this time, it isn't me who's screaming," Żywia replied bleakly.

Nadya had woken up almost immediately after passing out, but the Black Vulture was gone. Only Żywia remained. Her head pounded and her throat was painfully dry. She felt like throwing up and swallowed hard when her mouth filled with moisture.

"You're not leaving," Żywia had said. "He won't let you. But you can come with me."

"Where?"

"To where we keep our guests, obviously."

"Are you helping me, or trying to sabotage my efforts?"

Żywia laughed. "I'm sure it feels like both."

The Vulture took Nadya to a dimly lit room, sparsely furnished. Not uncomfortable, ascetic in a way that Nadya was used to, in fact. The Vulture lit a torch and set it in a sconce on the wall. She shut the door.

"I thought the king was dealing with this," she said. "I thought Malachiasz was getting what he deserved."

Nadya sighed. She sat down on the bed, suddenly exhausted. Not that she would sleep here. "The situation changed."

Żywia folded her arms across her chest and leaned against the closed door. She wore a crimson tunic, the sleeves long and tattered, over a pair of black breeches.

Nadya's hand grasped for the hilt of the bone dagger at her belt.

Żywia rolled her eyes. "I struggle to believe you've had a sudden change of heart."

This wasn't about Nadya's feelings. This was about being pragmatic. If she was going to figure out what was eating away at her hand—if she was going to fix anything—she needed Malachiasz.

"That is precisely what has happened."

The Vulture regarded her with a frown, rubbing her thumb down the tattoos on her chin.

"It all leads to the same end," Nadya pointed out.

Żywia's gaze grew distant. "What he is now is all we're made to be. But he is so scattered, his brilliance dimmed by the chaos he's caught in. And I selfishly miss my friend."

"A monster can do that?"

"We monsters can do a lot of things."

"But you don't think I'll succeed." Nadya didn't think she would, either, frankly, but she had to try.

"I don't know. He knew what he was doing. I'm glad you're willing. And I'll see what I can do about Żaneta, though I give no promises. It's his call whether she stays or goes."

"Thank you, that is unexpectedly kind."

"It's not kindness," Żywia said. "You're Kalyazi, dear, and this will surely spell disaster for you. But I will go get you some food. *That* will be a kindness."

"Then thank you for that."

She found herself wandering blearily through the darkened halls the next day, aware the choice could very easily end in her death, yet unable to wait until Żywia fetched her.

"Tell me—" He appeared out of the darkness, startling Nadya so badly that she drew her *voryen*. He gave it an amused, dismissive glance, his features settling on Malachiasz's for a split second as he nudged the blade easily to the side.

She slowly sheathed her blade and waited for him to continue. Instead, he started walking down an adjacent hallway.

Nadya let out an exhausted sigh. "Tell you what?" she asked, jogging after him.

"Why would a cleric think herself safe to walk these halls?"

Suddenly her back hit the wall, her hand trembling as it reached for her *voryen*, knowing it would be useless if he struck. Her heart pounded wildly, her breath hostage in her lungs.

He braced a hand beside her head. She could hear the scratch of his iron claws against the stone. His other hand tipped her chin up.

"I'm not safe here," she whispered. "You don't need to remind me."

The heat of his body surrounded her. She would only have to shift slightly for their bodies to touch. She stared at his mouth, at the black veins of poison that settled underneath his skin. In a split second his mood could change and she could be impaled. But there was a curious glint in his eyes as he pinned her to the wall.

"If I kill you," he said contemplatively, "would that be it? Would that be the end?" He trailed one of his claws down her cheek.

"It would be for me, yes," she said, unable to resist the dry quip.

She did not expect the twitch of a smile at his mouth, or the amused puzzlement that played over his face. He touched one of the silver epaulets on her jacket, a frown tugging at the tattoos on his forehead. She had forgotten she was wearing his damn coat. An eye blinked open on his jaw, dripping blood.

After a long silence, he pulled back, immediately turning on his heels and continuing down the hall.

*He is literally just as insufferable as always,* she thought as she took a shaky step forward, giving herself a heartbeat to catch her breath. He was still infuriating and condescending and overly convinced of his own self-importance. He hadn't been consumed yet.

Nadya caught up to him, tried to ignore the little half glance he cast back at her that was, again, too much like Malachiasz. She had to keep her hope in perspective. The pieces of the boy she loved were only that, scattered pieces.

The boy she should not love.

But Nadya could only think of the boy leaning against a boat railing beside her, long hair caught by the breeze, joking how he had never had anyone in his life who cared enough to worry about him. Revealing behind his flippant guise how desperately lonely he was.

Her splintered heart would not let her abandon that boy. Even if she needed him only so that she could ultimately destroy him.

She didn't know where he was leading her, each hallway more horrific than the next, and the thought settled like a jumble of snakes in the pit of her stomach. She considered asking him, as if she were with Malachiasz, who would take all her questions with that gentle, lightly superior way he had but answer them all the same. But she wouldn't give the monster the satisfaction. Finally, he stopped at a nondescript door, looking back at her surreptitiously.

"Where have you taken me?" she asked.

He held one finger to his lips, a smile quirking. "Patience, *towy dżimyka,* patience." A jab of pain stabbed her.

A scream echoed through the hall and Nadya jumped. He opened the door and took a half step back, as if suggesting she enter the room first, but instead he stepped into the dark space, his magic lighting torches near the doorway.

The shadows were slowly chased away as he lit hundreds

of candles throughout the room. Somehow Nadya knew what she was going to see when the darkness finally receded.

"You have got to stop taking me into your poisoned sanctuaries," she muttered under her breath. He was lighting candles at an altar covered in dried blood. It was all too familiar.

She slowly took in the pillars of stone, carved with symbols she didn't understand. A chandelier made of bones was lighting up the vast, vaulted ceiling, but there was an undercurrent of darkness that stirred in the shadows.

A thread of discordant power jolted through her as she stepped farther into the room. Her hand itched.

"Are those . . ." She stopped, forgetting she wasn't with Malachiasz.

He shot her a wicked smile. Too much like Malachiasz. "Yes," he said, his tangled voice sounding utterly pleased with himself.

*Human bones. Lovely.*

As the glow chased the shadows away, it lit upon skull-lined walls, carvings of symbols marring the foreheads. Tears pricked her eyes at how much death she was witnessing in an instant.

The Black Vulture's cathedral had been beautiful. But this . . . this she didn't understand the purpose of.

"Why have you brought me here?" she asked.

He coughed, violently, and pitched over. When he straightened, he was eyeing the blood that covered his hand. An eye opened at his jaw and he pressed at it absently, blood oozing over his fingers.

"I don't know," he finally said. "There's something missing."

*It's an act. He knows how to manipulate, even like this.*

"You're not here for the girl," he continued. He coughed again, spitting out a mouthful of blood.

*This is destroying him.* She watched with mild disgust. "No. Would you let her go?"

He shrugged. "I do not like losing things that are mine."

"But you're one half of Tranavia's political sphere, yes?" She moved around him, carefully, perching on a stone bench.

He made a deeply noncommittal noise.

Something rumbled from underneath their feet, the growl animalistic and monstrous. His head cocked, listening.

"What was that?" Nadya asked, hushed. She shivered, fear trembling through her. There were things in this place that were darker than she knew and older than she could fathom. "Żaneta is a political pawn. I'm hardly here for a noble purpose." She wished she were. She wished she were here to save Żaneta instead of the monster before her that did not wish to be saved.

He tucked a lock of black hair behind his ear. "She is doing no one much good in her current state."

"What happened to her?"

"Why do you wish to know?"

She shrugged. "You called her a mistake."

He watched her silently, clearly puzzling over whether he should bother answering. Who was she to be asking him questions?

"Some don't take to the changes well. She resisted particularly strongly and it resulted in complications."

Nadya felt sick at the impassive way he relayed such horror. "Will you let me take her, then?"

"I have not decided."

She nodded slowly. Another scream, throat searing and piercing, tore through the chapel. She shuddered, wrapping her arms around her body.

"You don't like the songs of my kind?" he asked, his lips pulling into a smile.

"What *is* that?"

"Do you think we're the only monsters that live down here? The Vultures are simply the most capable of appearing palatable."

Her gaze wandered to the door. Would she see more horrors while down here? She was already haunted by the figures creeping in the shadows, hunched like people but with too many teeth, too many eyes.

Movement caught the corner of her eye, and as she watched, blood started to drip from the eye sockets and out the open jaws of the skulls along the wall. She closed her eyes, pressing the heels of her hands against them.

He breathed out a soft laugh. "Most humans who descend don't last nearly as long as you have."

A soft whimper broke from her throat, but that was all. Fear had become her default; this place was so unassumingly malevolent. Things felt wrong, off, and when she went to have a second look the horror would appear.

"Are you not human?" she asked.

A dry glare, but then only fathomless sadness. "No one down here is, anymore."

Her chest ached in the strangest way.

"Why else are you here?" he asked.

*You,* she thought, *because somehow my life has become intertwined with a horror in a way I can't escape. And I need you to find my way back to my gods.*

The gods he wanted to destroy.

Her head hurt.

"Do you remember your name?" she asked softly.

He went so still it was as if he had turned to stone. Nadya's pulse ramped up and she wanted to bolt. The tension in the room had become deadly.

He turned slowly, moving toward her. She slid to the back of the bench until there was nowhere else to go.

"What are you implying, *towy Kalyazi*?"

She reached until her hand hit the next bench, skating back, bridging between the two as he edged closer in a way that terrified her.

"Have you come to be my savior? A benevolent Kalyazi saint come to cleanse the monsters of Tranavia?" His tone was poisonous.

"No," she whispered. "I-I mean, maybe once, but no."

She lifted a hand. He climbed on the bench she had slid off of. He crouched there, forearms resting on his knees, hands tipped with long claws on display.

"I met a Tranavian boy in Kalyazin," she said, voice trembling and words rushing too fast out of her. She had to risk this. "He was strange and thrilling and he stole my heart. He lied to me, I lost him. I am here because I need the help of the king of monsters to bring back something else I lost. I'm afraid this world is going to burn and I need you to help me keep that from happening."

He cocked his head. *That.* That was what she needed to keep drawing up in him. That curiosity. That was the crack in his armor. That was what she needed to wrench apart. He was more coherent here than she had expected; she had to use that.

"Why should I help you?"

Why *should* he help her? What could she possibly say to convince him that, yes, she needed him and, no, he should not kill her here in the dark.

"Because something is missing." She straightened, moving to her knees. He stilled as the inches between them melted away.

She reached out a shaky hand, fingertips brushing against his cheek. She traced her fingers up over the horns that spiraled back into his hair.

He caught her hand, pulling it down to stare at the scar cutting across her palm. She felt a strange pulse of power as his skin touched hers. Was it his magic, or was this ugliness something else entirely?

"What are you?" he murmured.

She shook her head slowly. "I don't know." Her voice cracked.

And with a swift starburst of pain, he slammed her back against the bench, her head cracking against stone, his hand at her throat. "I'll consider your request," he said.

Then he was gone, stalking back across the sanctuary without another word. And every candle winked out, leaving Nadya in darkness.

# 12

## NADEZHDA

## LAPTEVA

*She tore out the throats of those who opposed her, this goddess of magic, this goddess of death.*

— The Letters of Włodzimierz

Nadya was left alone in this hall of horrors. She wandered through the dark passageways, desperately hoping for light and finding very little. But it was the sounds that were starting to grate on her. The screams and odd chanting that hummed underneath it all were *constant* and she couldn't tune them out, forced to listen to the chorus of agony that haunted this place. And anytime she caught a stretch of light she would see the symbols carved into the wall, painted with blood, and immediately wish she was in the dark. There was so much horror here, she understood why there were rumors of those who traveled beneath the earth going mad before they ever made it back to the surface.

The Vultures she passed skirted around her without a glance. She was the Black Vulture's plaything to torment, therefore untouchable. The Vultures that she did see looked like Żywia—or Malachiasz when he was only a boy. Merely people. One would never know they were members of a terrible, monstrous cult. It made her far too bold as she explored.

Żywia would find her before long, she was certain. Nadya entered a dank and uncomfortable space, colder than the rest of the rooms she had been in. She could hear the soft rattling of chains and it nestled down in her bones. A dungeon. She peered through the cage bars and nearly choked on her own breath. There was a crumpled form in the back of a cell that she recognized.

*No. No, I lost him. I lost him, this can't be real.*

"Kostya?" she ventured.

The figure lifted his head, dark eyes clouded, face dirty. "Nadya?" Then he was at the bars, bloody hands wrapped around them.

Nadya crossed to him in an instant, reaching past the bars to grasp at Kostya's shoulders, his arms, his face. He was alive. And he looked . . . if not fine, at least whole. Haggard, but *alive*.

"What are you doing here?" he asked in disbelief. His fingers traced her face almost reverently.

Nadya opened her mouth and closed it. Too much had happened, oh gods, she had changed so much since that day she had fled the monastery. There was no good way to say what she was doing. What she had done.

"That is a very long story," she said softly. She leaned back, scrutinizing the cell door. She was no lockpick—and didn't have the tools for it.

But . . .

She flexed her fingers, casting a glance at Kostya as she tugged away from him and he reluctantly let her go.

"What are you doing?" he whispered, following her along the cell bars as she searched for the lock to the door.

"Getting you out."

*He* would know the second she used this foul magic. Was it worth tempting his anger?

Kostya's strong features were beaten down and covered with fading bruises. The gods had a twisted sense of humor to send him back to her right when she was trying to save an abomination of a boy instead.

Her fingers found the lock and she didn't let herself overthink it. The scar on her palm heated, the magic toxic and dark, but she grasped onto it, willing the mechanism to switch.

The lock fell to the floor with a clatter, ringing out like an alarm.

Pain lanced through Nadya's palm and she hissed through her teeth, watching in horror as the black lines of the scar threaded out farther over her hand like trails of poison, blackening the tips of her fingers.

*All right, never doing that again,* she thought. But the door was open and Kostya was hugging her with such fierce warmth that she almost sobbed with relief.

She had to get him out.

There was an angry shift in the thread binding her to Malachiasz. He would be here soon.

Kostya let her go, but he had the same frightened light in his eyes from the monastery attack, and it filled her with such panic that she spoke before he could say anything.

"I'll show you to the door out," she said. "There's a group with two Akolans to the east. Find the Akolans, tell them who you are."

Confusion passed over his face. "What? But what will you—"

She was wrenched away from him.

"Oh, *towy dżimyka*." The Black Vulture's voice was close, his mouth at the shell of her ear. "Badly done."

Kostya's expression melted into pure terror. The Black Vulture took Nadya's hand, pressing a thumb against the scar on her palm. She whimpered as pain lanced up her arm, her knees weakening. She leaned back against him to try to keep from dropping.

"We finished our discussion far too early, it would seem," he said. "And here you are stealing from me."

"What—" She broke off. She licked her dry, cracked lips. "What will it take to set him free?"

"Nadya, don't," Kostya whispered.

The Black Vulture froze at her name. Nadya looked up at him, afraid to move. A crack shivered in his expression, and he let out a shaky gasp. He trembled against her. His hand shifted to her wrist, clenching it so tightly that he tore open her skin.

He blinked, shaking his head.

"Well, *Nadya*," he said, and her breath hitched. "I suppose we have an arrangement to make. Only one will leave this place. Are you going to save the *slavhka* or the . . ." Disdain threaded his features. "Peasant boy."

Kostya's Tranavian wasn't as good as hers; he'd probably only understood enough to gather that Nadya was going to sacrifice something for his freedom. Noble Kostya wouldn't want that.

"Don't lock him up again," she said quickly. "I'll go with you. I'll make my choice."

The Black Vulture eyed her, and nodded. Immediately another Vulture was there, grabbing Kostya's arms and dragging him away.

"Nadya?" Kostya said in alarm, beseeching.

"It'll be fine," she lied. "I promise."

Żaneta's panicked, hopeful face flashed before her. She couldn't do this. She couldn't make this choice.

Serefin needed her to get Żaneta out. His throne was on the line, and it wasn't something she could ignore in favor of what her heart wanted. Kalyazin would be better served with him on the Tranavian throne.

But she couldn't leave Kostya. Time was running out.

"Come along, pet," the Black Vulture said. "The game has changed."

She followed him to the bone sanctuary, back down into hell, trapping herself into something she would never escape. She could only save one and she wasn't included in that deal, not when he had a piece of her name.

When she caught up, he was lightly spinning a chalice over the bloodstained altar. She didn't want to know what was inside.

"He was taken into these halls ages ago," she said. "Why is he still alive?"

The Black Vulture shrugged. "I don't know."

"Liar."

His eyes glinted, and the air turned dangerous around them.

"The girl or the boy," he said, waving a hand. "Make your choice."

"The stability of *your* country is at stake here," she snapped. "And you're going to turn this into a game."

He grinned and it was the same as punching her in the chest. "Then consider how much you, also, have to lose."

It wasn't a choice. She couldn't leave Kostya to Tranavia's will again. He was her best friend. He was the only family she had left. But saving Żaneta meant Serefin could take his throne back from those who would see this pointless war continue until both countries were nothing but ash. It was twisted and impossible.

"He's not who I came here to save," she said quietly. "But he is the one I will choose." This was the wrong choice and she knew it. She was dooming everyone with this decision. But she couldn't leave Kostya. He was Kalyazi; she had to protect her people first.

But she had another chance here with the Black Vulture. One last attempt. Maybe Żywia—who understood what was at stake—would help her like she had claimed. Maybe Żywia would spirit out Żaneta and save Serefin's tattered kingdom. *Unlikely.*

Nadya had just ruined everything.

"Then it shall be done," he said.

She wondered if there were others from her monastery still here. There was no way for her to save them all, she realized with horror. There was no way for her to do *anything*. She only had scraps of a power that was killing her; she couldn't even convince him to let both Kostya and Żaneta go free. She couldn't even find Malachiasz behind the monster.

Despair chewed at her edges. She shouldn't have come down here.

She stepped closer, moving cautiously. She had nothing left to lose. "You have my name," she said, "or, at least, a part of it. I know yours, *Chelvyanik Sterevyani*, I know you. Do you want it back?"

"No," he said, frowning. The heaving changes in his features were roiling more chaotically than before, as if a storm were raging within him. A cluster of eyes flickered open along his neck, closing again a few seconds later.

She shushed him, pressing her finger over his lips. He went rigid, one hand slipping back against the altar to steady himself as she shifted closer. Her other hand settled on his hip, sliding up to his waist, his bare skin hot to the touch.

His gaze was darkness, but there was an odd, confused look on his face that made it easier for her to continue. To trail her finger over his parted lips, the flash of fangs and iron teeth just visible, a reminder that this was not something she should be doing. This was not how he would be saved.

But maybe he wouldn't be. And she would die here. And thus would kiss him one more time before the inevitable came to pass. He had crashed far past the point of no return and she didn't even know what she would be saving.

His other hand—tipped by the iron claws that could so easily tear her to pieces—glanced against her cheek, her neck. Her hand slid back into his tangled hair.

Then she yanked his face down to hers and kissed him hard.

He made a sound that was a cross between surprise and *want*, taking a shaky step back that knocked him into the altar. He clutched at the back of her head, a hand sliding down her side to pull her closer. She was bleeding from those stupid iron spikes that broke his skin, and his claws were digging into her back, and this was certain heresy.

But what did it matter? The gods had left her anyway.

He kissed her back with a terrifying desperation that made her think maybe—maybe—he could be saved.

His hands slid down her body, drawing a heat that made her gasp against his mouth. He drew back only long enough to sweep her up, turning to deposit her on the altar, knocking over the chalice and spilling blood everywhere. She was level with him, catching his hips between her knees. He diverted his attention to her neck and her breath left her in a rush. She leaned back on her hands, sliding on the blood covering the altar. His sharp teeth grazed against the sensitive skin of her throat and her entire body reacted, jolting against him.

And she let herself fall. Her calculations never quite accounted for the way he always made her feel like there were stars in her blood. Even here.

Her bloody hands clutched at his face as she kissed his forehead, the bridge of his sharp nose, his cheek, trailing back until finally, finally, she wrapped her arms around his neck and whispered, "Malachiasz, please."

He stiffened, hands that had been unusually careful suddenly going taut, claws piercing her sides. She gasped in pain, wrenched her eyes shut as they flooded with tears.

But she held him still; she nudged her nose against his cheek. "Your name is Malachiasz Czechowicz," she said, pain choking her voice as his own hiss of distress plunged ten daggers farther into her body. "You're the stupidest boy I've ever met. You're the Black Vulture, but you're more than that. You're infuriating and gentle and too godsdamned clever for your own good. Please, Malachiasz, please remember."

There was silence. Nothing but the sound of his breath, heavy against her. Nothing but the blood dripping down her sides, her head dizzy as she lost too much too fast.

She cried out as he yanked his hands from her, dislodging his claws from her flesh. He stumbled away.

His eyes were the palest blue and his expression was one of sheer horror.

"Nadya," he whispered.

*Yes, gods, please, let this work.*

His hand caught hers. Bloodstained, pale fingers with perfectly normal fingernails. He caught her face between his hands, eyes tracking over her in disbelief.

"You're here," he whispered, thumb stroking her cheek. He blinked, realizing just where *here* was. He stared at the bloody altar in bewilderment, a rattling breath escaping him in a rush.

"Nadya?" His voice sounded confused, like he didn't know how *he* had ended up here.

She reached up, clasping her hands over his. "*Dozleyena,* Malachiasz."

He shuddered, eyes closing at his name. He mouthed the shape of it to himself. His hands were trembling.

Creeping black decay inched over his cheekbone. An eye flickered open at his temple. Blood leaked out of the corners of his eyes and when he opened them they were onyx black. His head twitched once, a slow, bitter smile pulling at his lips.

"No," he murmured. "Not enough." He pulled away from her sharply, claws growing out swiftly from his nail beds as he regarded her.

"You have something else that does not belong to you, little Kalyazi," he said, cool fingers against her cheek. Then his palm was over her face and it was like her *soul* was being pulled from her body. She choked, scrabbling at his forearm, digging her fingernails into his skin, trying to wrench his hand away, but he was too strong and she had lost too much blood.

Something snapped in her chest. A sob broke from her, a rush of power that was not hers leaving her as he took back the thread of magic she had stolen.

He pulled his hand away, fingertips blackened.

"My curiosity has been sated," he remarked dispassionately. "Your death is your own, *towy dżimyka.*"

He walked away and left her bleeding out on the altar.

# 13

## SEREFIN

## MELESKI

**Svoyatovi Ivan Moroshkin:** *A cleric of Devonya, where Ivan's arrows fell, fire consumed.*

—Vasiliev's Book of Saints

Serefin felt like he had been walking for days without ceasing. Everything ached and he could no longer see out of his left eye. He finally gave up and sat underneath a large tree, closing his eyes.

*What is happening to me?*

He had lived his whole life in perfect normalcy. His own blood magic was the oddest part about it, but that was a perfectly benign thing in Tranavia. Everyone could use blood magic if they really wished to.

But this . . . was more than he could bear. Suddenly the thought of being too much like his father felt uncomfortably close to the truth. Maybe madness was a fate he could never escape.

It took him longer than he liked to admit he was totally alone. If this was real, then where were the others? Where was *he*?

All the frustration and anger he had felt at Ostyia and Kacper were so very small now. He should have left it alone; Ostyia only ever wanted to help, it wasn't her fault that he was such a wreck. And Kacper . . . he . . . Kacper deserved better.

Panic threatened to swallow him. But Serefin had dealt with horrors, and he would deal with this. Yet his fear was that it wasn't true and it would break him.

He closed his bad eye. He was still in the forest.

"Well, shit," Serefin said.

He stood up and tried to figure out which direction was east, giving up after only a few minutes of frustrated gazing into the abyss of forest where everything appeared the same and there were no markers of direction.

*I have not survived this long only to die in a forest,* he thought bitterly.

"Of course not."

He nearly jumped out of his skin at the thin, reedy voice that sounded beside him. The voice he was used to hearing in his head sounding very much *outside*. Slowly he turned, terrified of what he would see.

The figure standing beside him was tall and robed in black but for the jaw bones tied in a string around its neck. If it was human, Serefin couldn't tell; its head was the skull of a deer, moss hanging from broken antlers, blackened pits for eyes and nothing more. A spider crawled from one eye socket to the next before setting at building a web in the great cold expanse. The figure stank of grave rot.

The skull tipped up as if gazing at the canopy of leaves above. "I grew so tired of Tranavian forests," it remarked.

Serefin choked out a gasp. He wasn't in Tranavia anymore? How was that *possible*?

"It won't be too much of a stretch to assume you are at fault for why I am here?" Dimly, Serefin was aware of how casually he spoke to a—a god?

The being had long, spindly fingers tipped with ragged, beaten claws. It pressed a hand over its chest. "Me? Dear boy, you walked here on your own two feet."

"You aren't particularly . . . awe-inspiring for a god," he said, ignoring that impossible revelation. Weren't the gods supposed to burn out mortals' eyes at mere sight? Wasn't it a whole *thing* for the Kalyazi that their gods could never be shown in pictures because their true forms were too beautiful for mortals to handle? Maybe Serefin was making that up.

"Not a god. Once a maybe, now an after, between an essence for change and for chaos and for the dead that wait below the surface."

A chill of fear rippled down Serefin's spine. If this was going to be like talking to Pelageya he wanted nothing to do with it.

"A god would be different, of course, you're right. Ever shifting, ever changing; never staying in the here, the now, but in the future and the past and somewhere else, somewhere different all at once. A sight to kill a mortal like yourself. Well . . ." The being paused and Serefin could feel those gaping black expanses considering him. "Maybe not like yourself. Burn one eye out and keep the other, but no one walks out unscathed. No one walks away clean."

"I don't understand," Serefin said desperately.

"Are you ready to cooperate? Ready to do as I ask for I ask so very very little from you?"

Serefin scowled.

"Ah, so no. Due time, I understand. I can be patient, far more patient than a boy of only a few years stumbling through this world thinking he knows everything. I can outlast you, child. I have outlasted so many others."

"I might be more inclined to consider if I knew what I was being asked to do."

"Presumptuous."

"So they say."

The being crooked a hand at Serefin. "Come." It began to walk deeper into the forest.

Serefin was nearing collapse. How much time had passed? The forest remained dark, dawn no nearer to the horizon.

His one regret, he decided, was that he was probably going to die here and he had left things such a mess with Ostyia and Kacper. He desperately wished they were here. Kacper complaining how this was a terrible idea and Ostyia trying to pull him away. He had been so cruel to them. Too much like his father and he did not want to become that. Anything, *anything* but that.

"Where are we going?" he asked hoarsely, jogging to catch up to the looming figure, gasping from the effort. "And will you ever tell me your name?"

The figure stopped, turning to Serefin, who had stepped too close. The feeling of mad, eldritch loneliness was so choking he had to retreat a few steps as it clawed up his chest and nestled between his ribs, hammering away at his heart. Alien and dark.

"Are you ready to cooperate?" it asked, its reedy voice pleasant.

"No."

The figure turned without another word and kept walking.

"You can't *make* me follow you," Serefin said petulantly.

But the figure was doing exactly that. He let out a panicked laugh, trying to force himself to stillness and finding he was incapable.

"What do you know, Tranavian, about Kalyazin's clerics?"

Serefin stumbled after the god that was not, apparently, a god. He only knew as much as any Tranavian. All but one cleric had been killed by the time he was sent out to the front, the Kalyazi only hanging on by the skin of their teeth.

And while he could say fairly confidently that he *knew* Nadya, he had no idea how her power worked. The skill she had shown during the duel against Felicíja was like no blood magic Serefin had ever seen. And she had used it within Tranavia, where supposedly the gods did not have access. Didn't clerics have to pray for their power? It occurred to him he hadn't seen the girl cast any magic since that night in the Vulture's cathedral. What did that mean? And what about the blackened scar on her palm?

Serefin knew blood magic. He never needed to understand any other path.

In hindsight, he had allowed Nadya a lot of freedom considering what she had potentially done to his country. Except there had been no signs of divine judgment, so he had never acted on any desire to see her punished for tearing down the veil that had supposedly existed.

It didn't really do much for her point that her gods were all-powerful beings. If they really had such power, wouldn't something have happened? Wouldn't Tranavia have been punished for its supposed transgressions?

Nadya couldn't quite argue with him when he brought it up.

The being merely laughed when Serefin brought it up now. Its laugh was a grating, terrible sound. "Your paltry lives are a twitch in their eyes, nothing more. That cleric did many things when she came to Tranavia; you have yet to see the ramifications of any of them. But they will come, in time.

"It's clear you know nothing of Kalyazin's clerics. A pity. Though, what good would that knowledge do you? Except, perhaps, understanding how to deal with the oncoming storm."

Serefin sighed. He was so tired. If he walked any more he was going to collapse. Maybe that was the being's intent, but Serefin wasn't going to bend so willingly. He wasn't going to agree to anything blindly.

"What is it you think you will wrench from me, boy? A story? An explanation? I owe you no answers. I owe you nothing. You owe me everything. Your father would still be alive if not for me. *You* would still be dead if not for me."

Serefin froze, coming to a standstill.

The being turned back to him.

They appeared to be standing underneath the exact same tree as before. Huge and vast, unreal in its size, with shriveled brown leaves still clinging to the branches as the bitterly cold wind whipped around them. Serefin's stomach dropped.

"Ah, didn't you know? Of course not. *Tranavian*, I forget. Do you think most people would survive what your father did to you? Do you think most people live with a scar like that?"

Scar? He had no scar except the one that cut across his eye.

The being snapped its fingers. "Right, right, right. So little your kind sees. So little they know. Like children, staggering through the world, playing with forces they do not understand. You are stubborn, but you will break. You are already breaking."

Serefin closed his eyes. His shaking hand trailed up over his chest, fingers catching against raised, smooth skin across his throat, the aftermath of a knife parting his flesh. He didn't remember what had happened after Żaneta had shoved him down into the darkness. That was probably for the best; he didn't want to remember how he died. But he hadn't realized, he hadn't *noticed*.

How had he not noticed this?

Had everyone around him been politely ignoring it?

"Your kind created the Vultures, fascinating constructs, but that's not what you are. You, dear boy, are something else entirely, and I have made it so. I will tell you what I want, in no simple terms, for you will break and I will have to put you back together again and truly that is so very exhausting. I hardly want to be picking up after a child who can't keep himself together.

"Oh, oh, wait, that's the other one. So hard to keep track of you all, you all look the same. He will be for another, but you, *you* are *mine*. And I have dragged this game out long enough."

Serefin slumped down the side of the tree.

"Have you not put the pieces together yet? Have you not figured it out? You are very clever and yet not clever enough by far."

The god—not a god—tilted his head and Serefin could've sworn that hellish skull face was grinning.

"I want revenge."

# interlude iii

## THE BLACK

## VULTURE

If being unmade was violence, being remade was horror. The screams of the Salt Mines, inconsequential before, dug underneath his bones, raking their claws through him and leaving him half-formed and so very broken.

This was . . . worse, somehow, than before. He didn't want this. He had worked so hard for oblivion, for this raw, dark power, and he could feel it slipping away.

And as much as he did not want it to go, as much as he welcomed the silence, he could feel her hands in his hair, her mouth on his skin. She had wrenched open the door and yanked him back into a semblance of something he did not think he could be anymore. She was maddening and powerful—too powerful. He had been caught in her fire before and there was nothing left to keep him from burning up completely this time.

There were flickers, pieces of him waking up, and he

tried to shove them back down, but *he didn't know how to stop this.*

His fingers scrabbled against bones in the wall as his legs gave out, his body revolting. The quiet chanting that always crept along the depths of the mines became agonizing. He dragged himself back up, shoving his shoulder into the doorway to the bone chapel.

She was lying in a pool of blood—too much blood. He could smell it, sharp and metallic and *hers*.

His hands were shaking.

His hands were bleeding.

He needed to move closer, but he couldn't confront the possibility that he had done the impossible. Not when he was on the precipice of coherency. Not when he nearly had it; it was in his grasp.

His name was . . .

His name . . .

It was there, just out of reach, and he couldn't fight toward it. He didn't want it. But he did *he did*. How could it be possible to want something and to hate it so much?

He was close enough to see the shallow lift of her lungs, to feel the pulse fluttering at her throat like a drumbeat against his skin, pounding but weak, light, fading. Blood stained her pale hair, streaked over her face.

His was not a power that could save. He was made for nothing but destruction, chaos, disaster, pain, pain, *pain*.

But she was dying and he had her name. He *remembered*. There was snow on the ground and the fur of her hat was crusted with ice. The cold reddened her cheeks, covering the pale freckles that dusted her skin. She had rested her hands on the hilts of her *voryens*, watched him with a wary kind of curiosity that never simmered into the hatred he'd expected, that he'd wanted, because if she had hated him all of this would have been easy.

Everything would have been perfect.

She had not given it up easily. Held it close, kept it safe, but gave it to him nonetheless. (How was he here; what had he done?)

Her voice, whispering his name. The only anchor he had. The only thing that had not been taken from him, that he had not cast aside himself.

Until the monster had.

He didn't know how to reconcile the wanting and the revulsion. Knowing it was too late and yet yearning to look back. It was within his grasp. It hurt, it was too much, too far. He shied away from the pain.

Her heartbeat was fading.

He thought nothing would be more painful than the act of being unmade. But this was worse.

The drumbeat growing quieter was all too loud. And while he was a fractured, shattered being, he could not let that pulse stop.

She had whispered his name in his ear. An anchor to something human.

Malachiasz woke up.

"Hells," he groaned, spitting out blood. His head pounded, a blinding pain behind his eyes. He took the last tremulous step toward the altar, chest seizing at the damage he'd wrought but didn't remember.

*Less than ideal.*

He could still hear the flicker of Nadya's fading pulse and there was nothing he could *do*. She couldn't die here of all places, he wouldn't allow that.

*Well, there's one thing, I suppose.* "She's going to kill me," he whispered. The sanctuary was empty but he recognized the bones strewn everywhere. Blood and bone, what was he doing here?

His vision shattered—a kaleidoscope of fractured light—and he crashed down, gasping. It took a heartbeat to realign, he watched as an eye opened on the back of his hand, his vision splintered again, it closed, he saw clearly.

"That's . . . also less than ideal," he said, pulling his aching body back up and spitting out another mouthful of blood.

Blood magic couldn't heal. He was effectively useless and she was *dying*. But it could do one thing.

He used his thumbnail to slice down his forearm, noting absently the gashes not made by him that ran down his arms. The degradation at his skin ate down to his wrist like a corpse months into the grave and disappeared moments later, leaving his arm whole and him more rattled than before.

"I would apologize for this, but you *did* steal my magic first," he said. Talking was the only thing keeping him from panicking his way into uselessness. If he thought about how close he was to losing her he was going to fall apart.

He touched his blackened fingertips to her lips, letting magic seep into her. Hearing her heartbeat strengthen as power darker than blood magic coursed through her.

He squeezed his eyes shut as his vision splintered.

"*Taszni nem, Malachiasz Czechowicz,*" he whispered, gritting his teeth as he started to slip. He was unmoored, unbalanced, and less human than ever.

He couldn't stay here. He didn't want her to see him like this. Though, if she was here . . . she had seen worse.

Malachiasz moved a lock of bloodstained hair away from her face and gently kissed her forehead.

He left her on the altar and hoped he wouldn't come to regret it.

Żywia caught him in the hallway, and yanked him down a different passageway, ignoring his protests.

"Shut up, shut up!" she snapped, gripping his arm. "Did you kill her?"

"What? *No.*" He massaged his temples. His head *hurt.* Every time his body shifted pain seared through him. His knees started to give out again, decay rippling down his arm, eyes blinking open. He clapped a hand over a *mouth* that opened on his neck, whimpering softly.

Żywia's hand was all that kept him steady.

"I didn't feel this before," he said through clenched teeth. The haze of power had been enough that the changes didn't register. This was agony.

"You need to kill the girl. Malachiasz, *there's something wrong about her.*"

Everything was fuzzy and he frowned at Żywia. "She's a cleric," he said, confused.

"It's not that. It's something else."

He made a dismissive noise and started to tug away.

"I threw bones, read entrails, did all the things I'm supposed to, and I swear to you, Malachiasz, you will regret the path she will lead you down. There's a darkness in her waiting to come out."

"Żyw—"

"Listen to me for once in your *damned life,* Malachiasz," Żywia said. "The king has a tenuous hold on Tranavia and Kalyazin has—"

"Relics," Malachiasz murmured, unsure how he knew.

"This is our chance to keep Tranavia on the brink of chaos

while you fix the order from the inside. That's what's most important. Not some fantastical notion about the Kalyazi gods, but the Vultures. Your kind. *Your* order."

Żywia let him go and turned to leave. He grabbed her, wrenching her back around, his hand on her jaw.

"Take her up to the surface. And don't you dare harm her." He invoked the magic that bound the Vultures to him and Żywia flinched.

"You're making a mistake," she muttered.

"Then I'll deal with the consequences."

# 14

## NADEZHDA

## LAPTEVA

*Not every story is sweet. There was a cleric of Zlatek, An-astasiya Shelepova, who was discovered dabbling in blood magic. She was burned as a heretic after Zlatek stripped her of her magic and her voice, her miracles discounted and all references of her burned out of the texts because of her ultimate transgressions.*

—The Letters of Włodzimierz

Nadya had no recollection of leaving the Salt Mines. She must have put one foot in front of the other; she must have staggered up hundreds of stairs. She *must* have, because she stumbled back into the campsite, freezing and incoherent from blood loss.

Parijahan jumped to her feet to steady Nadya, and gave her a cold once-over before asking, "How long should I wait before I say, 'I told you so'?"

"At least a week," Nadya said.

Parijahan sighed. Her face paled as she took in Nadya's bloody dress. "This is your blood."

"My blood? Yes. Mostly. Some of it's his. A lot of it, frankly, I have no idea where it came from because there is *so much blood* down there. It's—it's everywhere, and I—"

"Nadya, you're in shock."

She nodded thoughtfully. "Yes, that *does* keep happening to me." And she collapsed.

In the rare moments Nadya was conscious afterward, everything was a blurry haze, and each time she descended into unconsciousness she thought maybe this was finally the end. She didn't really know what was worth coming back *for*. Dying would have meant not having to reconcile her failure. No more Tranavians, no more anything.

When she finally awoke, Nadya was in a warm room in what appeared to be a farmhouse. An oven burned in the corner, and dried flowers and herbs hung from the rafters. Her sides were tightly wrapped with bandages and she was wearing a clean shift.

And curled up asleep in a wooden chair, in a way that had to be terrifically uncomfortable, was Kostya.

Nadya's heart clenched. The fleeting thought that she had saved the wrong boy slithered through the back of her head and, though she could not take it back, she regretted it. That wasn't fair to Kostya. It wasn't fair to the best friend she thought she had lost forever.

But maybe that was why she was having trouble comprehending that Kostya was *back*. She had mourned him and moved on, she had become a person she wasn't totally sure he would recognize, and she wasn't ready for how that might affect their friendship.

He woke when she shifted, blinking blearily in a way that

suggested he was unsure of his surroundings, before his eyes cleared and he was at Nadya's side in an instant.

They stared at each other in weighty silence.

"Hello, Kostya," Nadya finally said.

He grinned. He looked like he was about to hug her, so she rested her hand against his chest.

"That would almost definitely hurt," she said.

He laughed a little. "Of course." A shadow passed over his face. "I'll kill him," he said, deadly serious. "For what he's done to our people, to you."

*Oh, we're getting right to it, are we?* This wasn't a conversation she could have. She had been so close. For a glimmering fraction of a second, she'd had Malachiasz—and lost him. She wasn't particularly good at saving the people she cared about, she considered. But she had saved Kostya, hadn't she?

Except she had saved him at the expense of Serefin, someone who could help stop the war that was killing so many. And she didn't know how she was going to deal with that guilt on top of everything else.

She shushed Kostya and let him take her hand even though she remembered the look he gave her before the monastery attack, and she knew better, now, what that meant.

"A different battle for another day," she said.

He nodded, clearly dissatisfied. Surely he wasn't already seeing whoever it was Nadya had become? The girl who was so tired of war that she couldn't build up the righteous indignation to hate Tranavians simply based on who they were. Simply because it was *expected*.

The old Nadya would have agreed with him vehemently. The old Nadya would have ignored how her sides were only held together with some thread and bandages and raced back to kill the Black Vulture herself.

But the old Nadya had the gods and power and fell for a monster anyway. And was left with nothing.

She reached up, smoothing his dark hair back from his forehead. "I've never seen you with your hair this long." He always kept it short, with Veceslav's holy symbol shaved into the side.

"There wasn't much space for hygiene in the Salt Mines," he said ruefully.

His dark eyes were haunted, his time in the mines written across his haggard face. Her hand skimmed over her prayer beads, and she remembered the pendant. She still had it somewhere. The necklace that had trapped Velyos, and—from what Pelageya implied—set this madness into motion.

"Nadya, what's happened?"

She shook her head wordlessly. She didn't know where to start. She couldn't tell him about Malachiasz. Or Serefin. She made an attempt to relay the events of the months since the monastery was destroyed. Dancing around the obvious hole her story created when Malachiasz was missing. She couldn't explain how she'd become so fluent in Tranavian; she couldn't explain how she had accessed the Salt Mines, why she had been so relaxed around the one person who was Kalyazin's enemy among others.

*The enemy of my people is a ridiculous eighteen-year-old boy,* she thought, not for the first time.

It was obvious Kostya could sense her side steps. Nadya wasn't doing a very good job masking her hesitation.

"But the king is dead?" he asked, after she told him a watered down and, frankly, blatantly untrue version of that night in the cathedral.

She nodded.

"And the prince?"

"Serefin?" she asked without thinking.

His eyes narrowed.

If Kostya was here with her, but hadn't met Serefin . . . where was he?

"Serefin lives," she said quietly.

"But . . ."

"I know, Kostya," she said, her voice cracking. "I *know*." Serefin was the reason everyone she had ever known was dead. Gods, she had made so many terrible mistakes.

Luckily she was saved by Parijahan coming into the room. "Blessed mother," she murmured, relieved. "I wasn't certain you were going to survive that. How did you get out?"

Nadya shook her head slowly. "He didn't . . ." She glanced at Kostya.

Parijahan cast him a pointed look. Clearly he had been less than friendly with them.

Nadya frowned, thinking hard. Those last seconds came back in hazy flashes. Someone's hand, gentle against her face. A touch of magic filling her body.

Though she vividly remembered him taking it back—she could feel Malachiasz's magic still.

Nadya flipped her hand over, where the blackened veins had spread out over her palm. Kostya moved, as if to take her hand, and she pulled it away.

"I failed," she said to Parijahan. "But I had him, for a moment."

Parijahan's eyebrows tugged down. She nodded.

"We lost the other one."

"*What?*"

"Woke up one morning and he was just . . . gone."

"What about Kacper? Ostyia?" Nadya was highly aware of Kostya's body language as he recognized the names as Tranavian. His broad shoulders grew rigid with tension.

"They had already left. Those three had some falling out. There was a lot of yelling. Truly, I don't think Serefin is well."

Kostya was growing impatient beside her.

"What do you mean, they're gone?"

"Nadya," Kostya said urgently.

She ignored him, looking beseechingly at Parijahan.

"I wish I had answers. Things deteriorated with Serefin very quickly and I didn't think to have someone watching *him*. I thought *his* people would do that."

Nadya leaned back. A gift or a curse?

"So what do we do?"

"Unfortunately, as insufferable as those Tranavians were, they were incredibly useful. So, I'm not sure. For now, you should rest." She threw Kostya a glare that he met in kind. "Come on, Kalyazi, get out."

Kostya didn't respond. Nadya nudged his hand. "I'll explain later, I promise. Just . . ." She bit back the urge to sigh. "You aren't going to like it, so prepare yourself."

Confused and more than a little upset, he nodded and left the room without another word. Parijahan shot Nadya a knowing look.

"Don't give me that."

"And I thought *you* were a little zealot—"

"I'm going back to sleep, Parj."

Parijahan laughed and sat at the edge of the bed before considering further and shifting so she was next to Nadya.

Nadya rested her head on her shoulder.

"I'm sorry it didn't work."

"I was so close," Nadya said, blinking back tears. "He's *there* but he's so thoroughly *gone*."

Parijahan was quiet before finally saying, "We'll have to stay here a little longer. Rashid has no idea how you survived that, you lost a lot of blood. You need to heal."

"Where are we?"

"A village a few days west of Kyętri. A farmer has very graciously let us stay in this empty house for the reasonable price of ten *łowtek* a night."

"Good grief."

Parijahan shrugged. "I can pay it, but I'm nearing the end of my funds. He said his son owns the house but he's at the front and trade has all but stopped out here."

"Nothing changed," Nadya said softly. "If anything, everything has gotten worse."

"Maybe," Parijahan said. "Or maybe it was only a first step and there are merely more steps to come."

"I'm not sure how much more I can withstand." She was bewildered and exhausted and couldn't stop thinking about the stricken expression on Malachiasz's face before it had all been wiped away.

Parijahan pulled Nadya's corrupted hand to her lap. "This feels like it should be a priority," she observed.

Nadya flexed her fingers. "I'm not sure what to do about this, either."

"Rest," Parijahan said. "That's all you can do."

Nadya was no longer in the farmhouse.

"How do you keep doing this?"

Pelageya looked up from a string of chicken feet in her hands. "Doing what?"

Nadya gestured around her. They were in the sitting room where she had met Pelageya before, middling light flickering in through dusty windows. Bundles of dried flowers now hung from the ceiling alongside skulls strung up through their eye sockets. Nadya was tucked in a chair, her hands wrapped around a warm mug of tea. Her sides hurt, but it wasn't unbearable.

Pelageya ignored her. "Failed your noble quest, did you?"

"All right, send me back," Nadya said, struggling to get out of the chair.

"So sensitive," Pelageya said, clicking her tongue at Nadya. "You'll stay where you are if you know what's good for you."

"It's been established that I do not know that, actually."

Pelageya barked out a laugh.

Nadya winced as she settled back in the chair, worrying she had pulled a stitch. Pelageya eyed her.

"You should be dead."

"Many times over, I'm sure," Nadya said dryly. It was easier to be snappish with Pelageya when she appeared no older than herself.

"The Vulture's claws are poisoned. And I'm sure your boy's are worse than any other of his kind."

Nadya frowned. Her hand strayed to her side. How *had* she survived?

"But you live and you persist. I can't give you answers, only advice."

"I never asked for advice," Nadya said, ignoring the implication that Pelageya had answers for Nadya that she was withholding.

"What are you going to do? You don't have your pet monster to pull on a leash into the country of his enemies—"

"And I have no magic," Nadya muttered.

"Haven't you ever thought about why it is you exist?" Pelageya asked.

*That sounds deeply unpleasant,* Nadya thought. She stuck her face back down into the warm steam coming off the tea.

"A cleric who communes with the entire pantheon—unheard of—arriving during a time of strife when no other clerics were to be found. What makes you so special?"

Nadya ignored her. It wasn't for her to question.

"I thought you were like any other cleric—with a talent for magic of your own that the gods exploit and inflate to make it appear as though you could do nothing without them, but I was wrong."

"Wrong because I have no magic to speak of anymore?"

"Wrong because you draw your power from somewhere else entirely," Pelageya said. She stood, setting the chicken feet onto a table before taking Nadya's hand. The black tendrils had snaked up her ring and index finger. "What do we think this is, hm?"

"I used Velyos to steal Malachiasz's power," Nadya said.

"And so that makes you some kind of magic *kashyvhes*? No, child, this is something long ignored that you woke up and which now seeks what it has been owed."

A shiver of fear rippled down Nadya's spine.

"I'm not used to being wrong," Pelageya mused, "but I was wrong about you."

Why couldn't she just be a foolish cleric who had made bad choices? That was simple. She didn't want to know what was different about her, because then she *wasn't* just a cleric, and that was all she wanted to be. Except she was the cleric destined to stop the war, and she had *failed*.

"I don't know what I'm supposed to do," she whispered.

Pelageya perched on the arm of the chair across from Nadya.

"I thought . . ." Nadya trailed off. "I thought tearing down the veil would change things, even if killing the king didn't—but I did both and nothing changed."

"Are you not seeing your divine retribution?"

"Clearly not."

"You don't think abstractly enough, child. You thought the gods' wrath would come in hellfire and destruction? The gods don't work like that. You are seeing your retribution, it's merely falling on Kalyazin as well."

The blood drained from her face. *The winter.* The unceasing winter. It was going to freeze them all; starve them. And it would be retribution for Tranavia, certainly, but what was it worth if the Tranavians didn't realize who caused it?

"You think that's it? Some pesky weather? Nadezhda, you are far cleverer than this."

Was she? She hadn't been clever enough to see through Malachiasz's lies. Or to bring him back. She wasn't feeling particularly clever at all.

Pelageya sighed. "You think that the new young king is struggling to keep his throne because of incompetence? He is as ruthless and bloodthirsty as a Tranavian king is expected to be—more so, even."

"Oh," Nadya breathed. "Bozidarka?"

"Or Veceslav. Any number of your gods could be twisting the king's plans around him until he truly falls."

Nadya gazed up at the dark wood of the ceiling. It made a sick kind of sense. She had been expecting an apocalypse but she had received exactly what she had wanted for Tranavia: chaos.

"You really want Tranavia to crumble?" Pelageya asked. "They are on the precipice and it would only take the lightest push to tip them over the edge."

"How?" Nadya asked. It was the only way to stop the war, the only way to redeem herself.

A small smile pulled at the witch's mouth. "Soon," she murmured. "Very soon."

It took a few more days before Nadya was well enough to get out of bed. Every movement was minor agony—breathing *hurt*—but if she stayed in bed any longer she was going to mope herself through the floor.

Kostya continued to hover around her edges, but tension was building, waiting to explode with each day she let pass without telling him the truth.

Honestly, she had been hoping to get away with it. She didn't want to see his disappointment.

He sat down at the table, pushing a mug of tea her way. The bruises on his face were healing, more yellow than black.

"Nadya, you need to talk to me," he said quietly.

*Not technically true,* she thought sullenly. Rain pounded against the dirty windows and she dug her toe into the packed earth floor.

"I only want to know what happened, *all* of it. Why were you traveling with the prince?"

"Wait," she said, holding up a hand. "Wait. There are things you need to tell me as well."

He paused, puzzled.

"This isn't going to be an interrogation, it's going to be an exchange of information."

"I thought it was a conversation," he said.

"It would be if you weren't so dead set on hating everything I'm about to tell you."

"I'm not—"

"It's worse than you know, Kostya. It's worse than probably the absolute most terrible thing you can imagine. And I'm not going to be interrogated, but I will tell you if you want to listen."

"I want to listen," he said without hesitating.

"Then you have to answer my questions, too."

He nodded, uncertain what that meant. His expression didn't sour too much when she explained why she had been with Serefin, even as she glossed over the *other* reason for being in the Salt Mines. But before she could ask about the pendant, about Velyos, a knock, tentative and soft, sounded at the door. She exchanged a confused glance with Kostya as Parijahan cautiously went to open it.

Nadya heard a surprised gasp and the sound of something hitting the ground. She got up to investigate, taking her mug of tea with her, and froze when she recognized the voice speaking in rapid Tranavian.

# 15

## SEREFIN

## MELESKI

*No one knows what Lev Milekhin's slight against the
gods was; no one knows what happened when he made
the pilgrimage to Bolagvoy except that he returned touched
by a different god than the one who abandoned him, and
never spoke again.*

— The Books of Innokentiy

Serefin woke up from a horrifying nightmare only to discover it hadn't been a nightmare at all. He was still in the
damn forest.

At least the eternal night was passing. It was dark, but
the occasional flicker of light through the thick canopy
of leaves and the sound of birds flitting through the trees
was more of a relief than words could say.

He was tired, and hungry, and certainly had no desire to stay in this bloody clearing, so he got up and
started walking. The creeping dread was gone. The forest

was . . . normal. It would be pleasant if he wasn't so terrified he would never make it back to his friends.

He had a vague feeling the voice had not been lying when it claimed he was no longer in Tranavia, and he didn't understand how that was possible, even as he began to stumble toward the outskirts of a Kalyazi village.

*How far did that creature take me?* he thought, horrified. Quickly, he shrugged out of his military jacket, shoving it deep into his pack. He went to pull his signet ring off but paused, the metal cool underneath his fingers. Removing it felt wrong, though it might very well get him killed. And if that didn't, his accent would. The wiser choice would be to bypass the village entirely, but he was dizzy with exhaustion and hunger.

The winter had been hard on this village; it was suffering. The fields should have been sprouting green with growth and the farmers doing their best to make up for the winter's bite. The buildings he passed were worn down, the thatched roofs thin and patchy. It was similar to the poverty in Tranavia, and he tried to not let that get to him.

This war was destroying everyone.

He wanted to cry with relief when he found an inn because it meant the villagers weren't looking *too* closely at him—though he'd garnered some odd glances. This place saw travelers, and even if they didn't like them, they were used to them. He'd pulled his hat farther down in an attempt to shadow the scar on his face, though he knew it was fruitless. His hat was Tranavian in style, another mistake.

He ducked into the building, grateful to get away from the villagers outside even if it meant facing the ones within. It was warm, a fire burning in the center of the hall. Serefin was immediately struck by the sharp earthy scent of the dried herbs hanging against the wall. This whole thing was terrifically foolish of him, but he didn't care. He was tired, he was in the country of his enemies, and at worst he would be recognized as Tranavian and then . . . what? Hanged? Thrown to the military? That'd probably be doing him a favor.

He wished Kacper was here. For a hundred thousand reasons, he wished Kacper was there, but also because Kacper was very good at these sorts of things. They had never really been in this kind of position before, but Kacper liked to *know* things, especially if those things had to do with how people worked and what made them tick. Kacper could pass himself off as an incredibly convincing Kalyazi.

*I'm not trained for this,* Serefin thought wildly. He was a soldier, not a spy. He couldn't pretend in that way.

He had to risk it.

Serefin lightly thumbed the lining of his pockets and pulled out a thin pouch containing a handful of Kalyazi *kopecks*. It wasn't much but it would be enough for a hot meal and a warm place to sleep. Also a drink. Maybe two. Hopefully two.

The crowd sitting around a long, nearby table didn't spare Serefin a passing glance, caught up in a fierce discussion that was moving too fast for him to keep up with. He caught bits and pieces; it was some kind of political debate, and an old man with a long, graying beard was scolding a younger man and telling him that they were in a *korchmy* and the *neznichi krovitz* had no power there.

Serefin frowned slightly. Were they near a low prince's stronghold? Surely not. And why would a low prince have no jurisdiction in an inn?

He spoke as little as possible to the innkeeper, the man merely waving him to one of the two long tables that stretched across the room. Serefin avoided the large group. He just needed to survive this and find his friends—and ignore the pull farther west, to *where* he couldn't yet say. The voice wanted revenge, but on whom? Serefin wanted revenge, too, though he would rather call it justice to better sleep at night. Killing a father and a brother might be enough to finally make him snap; he was so close to crumbling as it was.

"Your hat's ugly."

Serefin glanced up from his broth—it tasted terrible but was warm. At least the black bread was good and the alcohol already working its charms, small mercies. A woman slightly down the table from him—wearing an embroidered scarf over her hair and a look that said she knew *exactly* where a hat like his had come from—was watching him.

"Ugly hat from an ugly soldier," he said gruffly. "Can't be choosy in this weather."

He had said about seven more words than he'd wanted, but the woman nodded and her attention shifted away from him. He'd let out a sigh of relief when the door to the inn slammed open, frigid air sweeping into the room. Serefin reacted without thought, slicing open the back of his hand.

Someone screamed and the table across the room overturned as the group scrambled to move away from the Vulture entering the room. Serefin's eyes flickered closed for a second; he was in no state to fight off one of those.

And it was definitely here for him.

So much for getting out in one piece.

He ducked as a blade fashioned with magic came flying at him. His head was spinning. Why did they *always* wait until he had been drinking?

He supposed it was his fault for wanting to get drunk while being fully aware that assassins from Ruminski were inevitable. But what were the alternatives? *Not* getting drunk? Unlikely. And why a Vulture?

Maybe it was from Malachiasz, not Ruminski.

He shouldn't use magic. Using it would paint him immediately as the heretic he was because everyone knew there was only one cleric and she was far from here. But the Vulture was moving closer and there was power shivering underneath his skin and moths fluttering around his head and in his hair and it took no effort at all to dip into that chaotic place and pull stars out of the air and send them right into that jagged iron mask. There was a terrible, gut-wrenching scream as the light burned through the mask and into the Vulture's skin, the flesh bubbling underneath. Serefin looked away but he couldn't escape the throat-tearing cries of pain.

*Interesting,* he thought.

He hoped this wasn't going to come back to bite him in the ass. It wasn't wise to be using a power he didn't understand.

The Vulture caught under his guard, tearing his side with its claws. He was only wearing a simple shirt and no protection. He hissed through his teeth, blood running down his side. But with all that blood came an unintentional surge of power he had to tamp down, because if he survived this he was going to be in trouble.

He swiftly sidestepped the Vulture's next attempt, pressing a hand to his bleeding side. Suddenly his vision shifted, going oddly sharp and focused in a way that was so massively disorienting he almost tripped over his own feet. For a beautiful, shimmering second he could *see.*

But as fast as it came, it went, and everything he saw was horrifying. Those fleeing the inn were corpses, their flesh blackened and rotting. Appendages worn to bone, extremities broken off, black blood pouring from their eyes. And Serefin stood in a forest that was dark and oppressive and going to swallow him whole and spit him out half a person, only a creature, nothing but a boy whose mind had been cut in two after being thrown about by gods and cast aside.

Then the forest was gone and Serefin's mind cleared.

Magic pooled in Serefin's hand and he slammed it into the Vulture's face so hard the monster dropped like a stone. His knuckles split.

Serefin let out a long, shaky breath and rubbed his eyes. That was nothing. That had to be nothing. He couldn't stomach the alternative.

He crouched next to the Vulture, dazed but alive.

"*Czijow*," he said amiably. There was no use *not* using Tranavian anymore; he doubted he would get out of this village alive. "I assume you're from Ruminski." He paused, and tore the Vulture's mask off.

He was about Serefin's age. Pale blond curls fell over his forehead. His face was bleeding where Serefin's magic had cut through his mask, his dark blue eyes venomous.

"Yes? No? The Black Vulture, then?"

The Vulture spat, narrowly missing Serefin's face.

"Ah, you're one of the ones that hate him, we have that in common. So, Ruminski. Excellent. Did he say I was a weak drunkard and an easy kill? He's having some trouble, isn't he, taking over my throne? Are there a handful of *slavhki* that keep him from claiming it without due cause and without proof of my death?"

The Vulture did not speak. His hand scrabbled for something at his belt but Serefin caught his wrist, taking a vial from him and swirling the liquid inside.

"Going to kill yourself instead of talking to me? Seems extreme." He tossed the bottle over one shoulder, heard it shatter. "You're going to run along back to Tranavia and tell Ruminski that I hope he spends his nights sweating. That his plans are never going to work. If he thinks I let him have the throne by leaving the city then he is as great a fool as he appears. You tell him"—Serefin leaned in close—"that his daughter is well and truly among the Vultures and no amount of negotiations or threats to my throne will get him what he wants. He can treat with the Black Vulture. But you knew that! You just never told him, did you? He should enjoy the time he has! I have some things to deal with first, then I'm going to tear him limb from limb and enjoy every second."

Serefin plucked a moth from the air and shoved it down between the Vulture's lips. He fought but ultimately choked it down, eyes going wide.

"Ah, yes, thought so," Serefin said, with a sly smile. "You go straight back and deliver my message. And, please, if you'd like to make it more gruesome, go right ahead." He let the Vulture struggle to his feet and walk into the night as if in a trance.

*I have no bloody idea what I just did,* Serefin thought mildly.

Surely someone had gone to the nearest military outpost. Maybe he could get out of the village before the Kalyazi army arrived.

He got up as if in a daze of his own. He took a step forward and his leg gave out.

He made it back to his feet, moving to the door.

And straight into the tip of a blade.

*Shit,* he thought, lifting his hands, gaze traveling down the length of the sword, up the blue Kalyazi coat with high-order medals emblazoned on the jacket. A black braid draped over a slim shoulder. And right into the sharp green eyes of someone he recognized and wished he didn't.

"Shit," he said out loud.

Yekaterina Vodyanova, the *tsarevna* of Kalyazin, grinned brightly. "Well," she said, delighted. "The king of Tranavia is a long way from home, isn't he?"

# 16

## NADEZHDA

## LAPTEVA

*The storms did not always come by Peloyin's hand; that
usurper, that fraud. There was another once, one and one
and one. Smoke and shadow and a voice like thunder,
a corpse of a tree struck by lightning. He who held every
movement of the air before his abrupt defilement.*

—The Books of Innokentiy

Nadya gaped, burning tea spilling onto her shaking fingers. She quickly set the mug down.

Malachiasz looked dreadful. He was soaked to his skin and covered with mud; dried blood caked the side of his face, as if he had been struck on the jaw. His black hair dripped and he was shivering, his lips blue from the cold. She could see the tracks of his veins underneath his pale skin. No claws. No iron teeth. No spikes of metal jutting from his flesh. Just a teenage boy, arms wrapped around his body emphasizing how rail-thin he was. He

wore a frayed gray tunic over a pair of mud-stained breeches, a battered pack slung over his shoulder.

Nadya was relieved. And then all the anger she hadn't been feeling struck her at once. She was furious enough to kill him.

His pale eyes met hers, wary. Nadya's fist clenched.

Rashid grabbed her arm. "Absolutely not. You'll rip out your stitches."

"There's nothing I want more right now than to punch his stupid face, do not take this from me, Rashid," Nadya replied, but her side twinged.

"Stitches?" Malachiasz questioned gently, and all the air in the room was sucked out. He was picking at his cuticles and his right fingers were already bleeding. He coughed violently.

This was the boy who had convinced her so earnestly that he *cared*, only to throw it all in her face. How dare he come back and act like they could slide back into the comfortably strange friendship they had before, when it was all a lie.

"That's what happens when you impale a person with all ten of your godsdamned finger blades," she snapped, livid.

*Finger blades,* he mouthed, puzzled, before his hands slowly curled into fists—not combative, protective. A flicker of panic crossed his face. He looked to Parijahan beseechingly but she took a step closer to Nadya. The subtle shift in allegiances made his panic grow more pronounced.

"What did I do?" he asked slowly.

Nadya scoffed, resisting the urge to roll her eyes. Rashid was frowning. Malachiasz had gone from leaning against the door to appearing as though his legs were about to give out.

"But this is what you wanted," Rashid said to Nadya.

"I said I needed him back, I didn't say he was going to be forgiven," she replied.

Malachiasz flinched as if she'd struck him. She watched

as he tried to shutter away the anxious boy and . . . failed. He lifted a hand and started gnawing on a hangnail. She didn't trust this—couldn't possibly—but there was something strange about the way he was acting.

"Malachiasz . . ."

He startled at his name, eyes flickering closed briefly.

"What's the last thing you remember?"

He frowned. Shook his head slowly. Kostya had come up behind her to lean in the opposite doorway, the hatred radiating off him in cool waves.

"I woke up in the mines," Malachiasz said. "But it was Grazyk, the cathedral. I—there are other things, flashes, but . . ."

"The cathedral was nearly six months ago," she said.

He shook his head again and raked a hand through his hair; his fingers caught on a piece of bone threaded amongst the gold beads caught in the strands, and it only rattled him further.

"All right," he said softly. "That was not a calculated result."

Parijahan snorted. "You idiot."

He smiled weakly. His gaze returned to Nadya, fell on her necklace, and his face paled. "I didn't . . ."

"That grand plan of yours? No," she said, voice sharp. "Or maybe? Who knows. We need to talk."

"Yes." He sounded like he would rather do anything else.

"You should get cleaned up first," Parijahan said.

He let Parijahan pull him into the room. He stood there listlessly, lost and bewildered before she nudged him in the right direction.

Rashid left to heat the bathhouse and Malachiasz followed as quickly as he could, clearly wishing to be away from Nadya. And as angry as she was, it hurt. Because she had missed him and he was right in front of her—*so close to her*—but she couldn't have him because he had lied and was trying to destroy her gods for the sake of some extreme ideal. Because she didn't know what he was and she couldn't see past that monster in the dark.

She shivered hard, wrapping her arms around herself. The monster she had kissed. But he didn't remember. That sheer blasphemy was for her to bear, alone. For her to forget, alone. It had been a kiss goodbye.

Parijahan glanced over Nadya's shoulder at Kostya. "Leave him be," she warned.

"Nadya—" Kostya tugged her around to face him. The anger and confusion and bewilderment in his face was a barrage.

"He was my friend," she said, voice hoarse. "But something happened and he's not anymore but I need him for something. I need to do something big, something that might fix everything, but I can't do it without him."

Kostya furrowed his brow. "I don't understand."

"I don't know if I can help you understand," she whispered.

A painful silence stretched between them until, with a disgusted grunt, he stepped past Nadya and Parijahan, out the door and into the rain.

Nadya bit her lip, willing back tears. "I didn't expect this to be so hard."

"Do you want me to talk to Konstantin?" Parijahan asked.

"It's kind of you to offer, but no, I'll do it. He'll cool off," Nadya said, though she wasn't sure that was true.

"And?"

"Oh, I'm definitely talking to the other one, too," Nadya said. "How dare he act like that? Like nothing happened at all. Like he doesn't remember."

"Maybe he doesn't," Parijahan said.

"Even if he doesn't, he sure as hell remembers that everything he ever told me was a lie," Nadya said. It did bring up a problem, though. How was she ever going to figure out what exactly he had been up to if he didn't remember? She couldn't dismiss that lost time, optimistically shoving it away with the explanation that he had been too incoherent to do any real damage. It wasn't true.

Parijahan frowned. "He did lie," she said, but her gray eyes were, as always, too discerning. "Is this how you're going to punish him, then?"

"He's deserving of whatever I decide." And it was true, but she knew that wasn't what Parijahan was trying to say.

She couldn't help it. She was angry at everyone. She was angry at Malachiasz for lying. She was angry at Marzenya for turning her back when Nadya needed her most. And she would see this through—use him the way he used her. If she was the one who was supposed to stop this war, then she was damned well going to do just that, regardless of what it took.

# PARIJAHAN

## SIROOSI

There were only so many dry Tranavian military reports Parijahan could stand before she wanted to burn down the whole country herself. She left Rashid, who was still puzzling over a report that Parijahan was fairly certain meant nothing and Serefin hadn't intended to bring with him. She wandered into the tiny kitchen to find a significantly cleaner Malachiasz intently boiling water for tea. She watched him—

the way he tensed at her footsteps and relaxed again without looking.

"Parj."

"Are you trying to bribe your way to forgiveness?"

"I," Malachiasz said, voice prim, "am trying to bribe my way out of getting my throat slit or nose broken. Forgiveness is hardly a factor and does require remorse."

Parijahan laughed and hopped up onto the table. "You look wretched."

"Thank you," he replied. "That is exactly what I want to hear right now, you do know all the ways to make me feel better, Parj."

He had found raspberries and withered apples somewhere, and was steeping them in the tea, but Parijahan supposed he would know exactly where to find ingredients for a very Tranavian drink in this little Tranavian farmhouse.

Parijahan's personal vendetta against his country was nothing like Nadya's and she didn't particularly care about the monsters and the heresy—whatever that meant. If Malachiasz were some rich *slavhka*, her feelings might be different.

"I missed you," she said. "I wish you had told me the truth about what you were planning."

"I have not had the capacity for missing anyone," he said, falsely cheerful.

She was quiet. His cavalier tone wasn't masking everything like usual. The cracks were showing. She knew how lonely he was, but she hadn't realized how scared he was, too. And she wished, so badly, that things hadn't ended up this way because, despite everything he was, she wanted to help him and now she wasn't sure if she could. Her circumstances were rapidly shifting and she didn't know how much time she had left here. Soon she would have to leave him behind.

"No remorse, then," she finally said.

He drummed his fingers against the table. "I didn't know if you would trust me or tell her," he said, his voice nearly inaudible.

Parijahan opened her mouth to protest but he held up a hand.

"You can't fault me for it when I am very aware that you would like to see my entire country in flames," he pointed out. She sighed.

A cluster of eyes, in unsettling colors and dripping blood, opened up on his cheek. He pushed away from the table before he could get blood on anything. A few seconds passed before they disappeared and he could clean off. She grimaced. It was sickening.

It had been obvious there would be nightmarish ramifications from what he had done, but she hadn't expected this. She thought of the night where his control had slipped and he'd admitted to her just what he was; the way his voice had trembled, how she'd thought he was going to cry when she'd taken the revelation with a shrug and told him it was his turn to make dinner. She hadn't expected he would *want* to be worse than he already was. A lapse in judgment.

"We need to talk."

"Do we?" He was immediately wary.

She almost laughed. "Not about any of this." She didn't know why Malachiasz was the person whose help she wanted in making the decision that was before her—he had *lied,* and how was she to know if he was going to use what she had to tell him against her? It was politically tenuous, and he was ambitious, to say the least.

A quizzical head tilt from him. He poured the tea into two ugly, misshapen mugs and offered her one.

"You know I'm picky about tea."

"If you hate it, I will make it my new life's mission to get you tea from Akola."

She wrinkled her nose. "You *do* need a new life mission."

"You're not allowed to hate it on that principle."

She didn't hate it. It was much sweeter than she usually liked, but the sweetness wasn't cloying, it was pleasant.

"I suppose you get to keep your fool's quest."

He grinned. She eyed him over the rim. He was barefoot, his hair haphazardly tied back, hardly the incoherent monster Nadya consistently implied.

"What did you want to talk about?"

She shook her head. "Not here, somewhere the others can't hear, later." She didn't want to talk about Akola with Rashid within earshot, wrong as it felt to hide something from him.

He waited for her to continue.

"I'm in trouble."

"And you need *my* help?"

"I need advice." Parijahan took another sip. "You should take Nadya her tea. She probably won't hit you."

He frowned at her, debating whether to press further or wait. But he knew her; he understood she would tell him eventually.

Because, though he had proven he didn't feel the same, she trusted him. Terrible as it was, the betrayal he had enacted was one she understood, even if she wished he had gone about it in some other way. She knew how much he wanted to change things, how willing to go to extremes he was. He could have told her, even just a piece of it. Then there wouldn't be this awkwardness between them where before there had only been ease. They had crashed into each other—quite literally—but he had fit in so well with the odd band of Kalyazi that Parijahan had gathered around her since fleeing Akola. She missed them, the ones who had left, and she had always been very aware that he was the one who had *stayed*; the Tranavian, the Black Vulture, the boy who wanted too much and knew too much and was too much. She didn't want to lose him like she had lost the twins and dear, sweet Lyuba. But she also didn't want to lose, well, everything because of him and his rash actions and his lies.

So she would grant to him what he refused to grant her, even if it might end in disaster. Frankly, she wasn't sure how things could get much worse than they already were.

He gave a quick nod. And, looking like he was staring down the executioner's block, he took the mug of tea to the other room. Parijahan didn't immediately hear any yelling, so she supposed Nadya had decided to spare him. This time.

# NADEZHDA

# LAPTEVA

Kostya still hadn't come back in from the rain, and Nadya sat at the table with a map open before her, trying to figure out how they could get to Bolagvoy without it taking half a year. The prospects weren't good.

She would be eighteen by the time they made it that far into Kalyazin, she considered with no small amount of distress. The country was massive, and the Valikhor Mountains were on practically the opposite side, right up along the border to the Aecii Empire with its flatlands and horse lords.

A fresh mug of tea slid over the table to her. Malachiasz sat down across from her, his movements slow and careful, as if he was in significant pain.

A cluster of eyes opened up on his cheek. He flinched, a shaking hand immediately flying up to cover his face. Nadya watched in silence as he let out a long, tremulous breath before slowly lowering his hand. The eyes were gone.

"Well," she said.

He pressed his fingers against his cheek, searching. There was no hiding what he was. The shield of the anxious teenage boy was too easily fractured by the monster out of his control.

Gods, she wanted to rage, because he looked so *sad* and she didn't know if that was him playing at human to get the response he wanted.

She took a small sip of the tea, finding raspberry seeds floating at the top. It was sweet and *good*. She didn't want to think about how Malachiasz was the only person in the farmhouse who would prepare tea like this.

He had cleaned up, his long black hair drying tangled and wild around his sharp features. Exhaustion painted shadows under his pale eyes and hollows under his cheekbones. The features of his face didn't shift as wildly as before, but decay crept over his cheek as she watched.

He was quiet, scratching at the table with a chewed up fingernail, but Nadya had missed his thoughtful silences and that frustrated her, too.

"Nadya, I—"

"Did you—"

They spoke at the same time.

Nadya glared and continued. "Did you ever regret what you were doing? Did you ever feel bad for all the lies?"

He cleared his throat but didn't speak. He nodded slowly.

"Not enough to ever tell me the truth."

"I had to do what was best for Tranavia," he said, voice hoarse.

"Of course."

"I—thank you. For—"

"Stop. Just stop, Malachiasz. If this is all a game to you, I don't want any part of it."

"Yes," he said sharply. "Because I'm nothing but a monster. It's what I will always be. No matter how hard you pray, no matter how many times you throttle me into the semblance of something human. I am barely that. I was barely holding it together before and I am barely holding it together now."

Her jaw clenched.

"But apparently, you need me," he continued.

So she did.

He sighed. "I never wanted to hurt you."

"It doesn't matter. It doesn't matter what you wanted or didn't want. You sat on your throne and watched while the king nearly slaughtered, not only me, but Serefin—you executed a plan to destroy my gods. You did all of those things. They happened." She paused, knuckling the bridge of her nose. "I went into those mines for *you* and it wasn't only because I need you, but I can't . . . I can't do this. Not right now."

He lifted an eyebrow, distant.

"You're right, though, I need you for what you've turned yourself into."

He winced.

"Not what you expected?"

"No."

"Did you truly think it was going to be sentiment?"

He shot her a dark glare, his eyes flashing black to pale blue again so swiftly she almost missed it. A shiver of ice trailed down her spine. How quickly he had gone from a boy shivering in the rain to something vicious.

"One of your gods can't help you?"

She looked down. Away from his pale eyes that were too capable of seeing a part of her she didn't think anyone else saw. The girl that simply didn't know what to do. Maybe he was the reason that girl was even there, his words drawing up an ocean of doubt within her. And because he was *Malachiasz Czechowicz* he didn't need her to explain. His eyes widened, his expression fracturing sadly.

"Oh," he said, gentle in a way that she didn't want because she didn't want anything from him that might make her forgive him.

"*Stop,*" she said, because she was being drawn to this awkward, terrible boy beyond all reason. And she had to fight it off. She wouldn't *dare* let him lie to her again.

He gave a slight feral smile. He folded his tattooed hands on the table and leaned over to inspect the map.

"Where are we going?"

"I haven't told you what the plan is."

"You will. I'm sure it's something particularly ill-advised that will go against my tender sensibilities—"

"You have those?"

He took a moment of thoughtful contemplation before he shook his head wistfully.

A laugh escaped her. And her heart faltered at the way his smile shifted to a genuine grin, quieter than before, his former brilliance dimmed. His teeth a little sharper, darkness all the more present at his edges. Every little facet of him that was slightly off before had become utterly monstrous.

She sighed heavily and pointed at a spot on the map. He stared at it before getting up and coming to the other side of the table. He leaned over her chair. She couldn't tell if his face had paled or if his complexion was just that sickly in the dim light of the farmhouse.

"That's on the other side of Kalyazin," he said. A crack in his voice confirmed that, yes, he was definitely paler.

"Yes."

He rubbed his jaw, perplexed, and asked distractedly, "Who's the boy?"

She cast him a long look, not sure if he was being serious. He lifted his eyebrows.

"His name is Konstantin. We grew up at the monastery together."

"Ah," Malachiasz said.

"He's been in the Salt Mines."

"*Ah.*"

He tugged on a piece of bone that was threaded through his hair, anxiously searching for something to do with his hands.

Nadya couldn't figure out if the small piece of spine was from an animal or something . . . larger. She decided to not think about it. She shifted away from him and he returned to his seat across from her. Tension threaded back through the room as the temporary ease between them passed.

"Have you taken into consideration that I may refuse to cross your entire frigid country for no other reason than you asked?"

"You could, certainly," she replied. "And that would be the end of this." *And the end of whatever we had.* But maybe that would be better. They part here, now, and she would no longer have to lead him to his own destruction. He would survive a little longer; so would she. She wouldn't have to lie like this.

He scowled.

"I'm hardly trapping you here, Malachiasz."

Each time she said his name there was a second where his eyes flickered closed and his body shuddered, where he pulled a little closer to *the semblance of something human* and she would have him for a little longer before he took a step back to the monster.

He coughed like his chest was caving in. There was blood at his lips that he hastily wiped away.

"At the risk of sounding suspiciously earnest," he said carefully, his voice scratchy, "I would like to help."

"You might change your mind when I tell you what I need you for," she muttered down at the map. "And you're right, it is suspicious."

When she looked up, he was watching her. No, studying her, as if he wanted to get back the lost months they had spent apart. The feeling was ridiculous. They had barely known each other for a year—less, truly. He had lied about *everything*. Anything more from him was another game to get back into her good graces.

Except . . . what would be the point? She had already done all he had wanted her to.

What if he was being honest with her?

Nadya met his icy pale eyes. This was going to be harder than she thought.

# 17

## SEREFIN
## MELESKI

**Svoyatovi Arkadiy Karandashov:** *Tsarevich of Kalyazin,*
*he united the east and the west. Many miracles have been*
*performed over his grave.*

—Vasiliev's Book of Saints

He was surrounded. Even as the *tsarevna* lifted her sword
and rested the flat against her shoulder, looking Serefin
up and down with a wry grin, he couldn't see any way
to run. Blood magic could only do so much when swords
were held inches away from major arteries.

"It's funny," she said, "when someone burst into the
outpost, saying there was a Tranavian in the nearby village, I expected some half-dead soldier, not, well, the *most
important* of Tranavians." Her sharp, dark eyebrows turned
down in mock confusion. "Who knew the king of Tranavia
was so reckless?"

Serefin sighed. He went to pull a hand through his hair and found the point of a blade inches away from his neck.

"Easy," he said. "I just fought off an assassin from my own people, I don't want another fight."

"No," she said soothingly. "Of course not."

He unclipped his spell book and let it fall to the ground. "You've rendered me powerless, congratulations."

She motioned to one of her soldiers who quickly picked it up. Serefin couldn't help the light twinge of panic at losing it, but there were worse things that could be lost here.

Yekaterina eyed Serefin. "And cut off the sleeves of his coat."

"And leave me defenseless against your Kalyazi winter? How cruel."

"You shouldn't be in Kalyazin to begin with," she replied. "And I do hope you have a good explanation for this. I didn't think this was the way you lot did things. Covertly and what-ever." She waved a hand vaguely. "Or get your hands dirty—well, outside all the blood, I suppose."

"It's complicated."

"A shame." She hefted her sword and rested the tip against Serefin's sternum. "I suppose killing you won't do me much good, will it? We've heard things aren't going so well in Tranavia."

"Oh? Your spies are that good?"

She sneered. She had fine features and pale skin. The Kaly-azi royal family wasn't much better off than the Tranavian, because as far as Serefin knew, Yekaterina only had one invalid of a younger sister. So like Serefin's father, the *tsar* had sent Yekaterina off to the front when she was only a young girl. Unlike his father, her father had not had her murdered for a blood magic ritual. What a lucky royal that made her.

Yekaterina considered him. She sighed. "I'll have to actually talk to you, won't I? Ugh. Misery."

"Truly, I am terribly sorry this isn't the time for senseless slaughter. My heart weeps."

"Gods, you're worse than I imagined."

"Infinitely flattered."

She rolled her eyes. Serefin noticed a necklace of teeth strung around her neck and his stomach dropped. His message would never reach Ruminski, because the Vulture was never going to make it out of Kalyazin. He hadn't known the *tsarevna* was *Voldah Gorovni,* and yet it made a sick sort of sense.

And gave Serefin a terrible idea.

"Did you add him to your collection, then?" he asked, nodding to the teeth.

Yekaterina frowned, her hand lifting to touch the necklace.

"I was hoping he would send a message for me, but it is what it is. He did try to kill me," Serefin continued. "Are you very good at hunting Vultures?"

"Fix this place back up," she ordered, her soldiers rushing to obey her commands. "I'm starving. Put him somewhere while I find some food."

Serefin was pushed onto a bench, his wrists tied behind his back.

Yekaterina sat down across from him, a plate of herring and rye bread already in her hands. She was wearing the military outfit of a Kalyazi officer, though Serefin couldn't figure out her rank, which suggested she didn't have an actual military ranking and the army only deferred to her because of her blood.

Awkward.

"Kind of you to not kill me on the spot," Serefin said.

"The rumors say you killed your father to become king," she replied.

He tilted his head. "Actually, your cleric killed my father."

Yekaterina went dead still. "What?"

"Nadezhda Lapteva? Nadya? An absolutely infuriating girl. Someone so small should not be able to be so opinionated."

"The cleric was in Tranavia?"

"I thought your spies were *good*?"

She flushed.

"Don't worry. She's fine. Well, she might not be fine. The last time I saw her she was going into the Salt Mines to treat with the Black Vulture." Yekaterina's expression waned further. "A boring story really, and frankly, I would love to do away with my current Black Vulture. She probably made it out alive, though, the two of them had a stunningly bizarre relationship, but truly who can say?"

She sat in stunned silence. Serefin smiled.

"Ah, I see I have something you want."

"You know where she is?" Yekaterina asked, voice hushed.

Serefin had no bloody clue where Nadya was, but he had to hope Kacper and Ostyia were still with her. He had to hope they were all right because he wouldn't be able to survive the alternative. He missed them desperately. He missed *Kacper*, he realized with a shock. He had grown too used to Kacper's calm and constant presence and the days without him had a very specific kind of loneliness to them that Serefin wasn't ready to parse.

Yekaterina leaned back in her chair. He heard her swear softly in Kalyazi.

"You have me in an awkward situation, you know that?" Yekaterina said.

"Oddly, I'm not feeling a great deal of pity for you."

"What's wrong with your eye?"

"You are incredibly charming, do you know that? Do people tell you that?"

"There are rumors about you . . ." She leaned forward again, resting her chin in her hand. "But they were so ridiculous I wrote them off."

"The war has changed and we all know it but no one knows how to stop it," Serefin said. "What are we even fighting for?"

"You are heretics."

"And you lot are deluded," Serefin replied. "What are the rumors?"

"You died the night before your father. You were brought back in a tide of blood."

"Yes."

She stiffened, but recovered remarkably well. "But there have been no whispers of the cleric's involvement."

"The whole affair was rather messy. I tried to keep her out of it for obvious reasons."

"Why would you protect her?"

"Because I didn't need Kalyazin storming my capital to get her back. I'm a strategist, dear, and knowing where your cleric was would only bring your people more hope."

Yekaterina considered that. "You're more trouble alive than dead," she said.

"You don't have to flatter me." He shivered, nonetheless. The *tsarevna* would either lock him up or have him executed; there was no in-between here.

She finished her meal and stood, moving around the table. She ran a hand through Serefin's hair, then wrenched his head back.

"You're very pretty for a Tranavian," she murmured.

"Thank . . . you?" He had to get out of here.

"Shame. My father says a beautiful king will always hide a cruel agenda." She leaned her face close, mouth at his ear. "Better if you had been ugly." She traced the scar down his face. "Better if this had done its job."

A chill settled in the pit of his stomach. Yekaterina reared back.

"What do you think, hanging or beheading? Should I cut your throat? Looks like that's already been done to you once; let's just finish the job. What kind of execution does the king of Tranavia deserve?" She grinned. "Actually . . . I have a better idea."

Serefin closed his eyes. There was going to be no talking his way out of this one.


Serefin had been taken to a stone church outside the village. Not so much a building as a carelessly carved out boulder that had slid down from the mountains thousands of years ago with onion domes slapped on top.

The *tsarevna* had wrapped a black headscarf around her hair, iron temple rings swinging at the sides of her face. She shouldered open the door, nodding a greeting to the priestess in the entranceway. She kissed her fingers and touched an icon near the door to the sanctuary.

There was a fragile silence in the church, thin ice near breaking, and underneath it something horrific. Serefin had been in plenty of Kalyazi churches during his time at the front. But never one that felt . . . *alive*.

Serefin's vision split. He hissed through his teeth as the icons changed—faces clawed out and defaced—the candles melted down to pools of wax, the patterns carved into the walls turning to bones inlaid into the stone. He froze, a shudder rippling through him, and the Kalyazi soldier had to shove him forward.

But his bad eye wasn't finished yet. He wished he could cover it and make this stop.

*You cannot live with one eye closed.*

He could try. But like on the boat, his left eye refused to close and he was forced to watch as terrifying shadows with too many teeth and too many eyes slunk about in the dark corners of the church.

He had stepped into the domain of something large and ancient and its gaze had turned upon him.

Sweat beaded at his temples. His vision snapped back *back back* until there was no church, no boulder to carve it from, only a clearing and an ancient stone slab, blood dripping down its sides. A blade stained crimson lying in the dust. The eye of the gods on a sacred place.

There was movement around the altar, or the memory of it. Of people long turned to nothing more than dust and ashes, and an action, committed so many times that the bones of the earth remembered it. A life taken on that altar again and again and again, a circle returning to its origin point.

Everything Serefin knew about the Kalyazi was turning out to be fantastically deluded. He had thought them pious, backward people, afraid of magic that wasn't sanctioned by their gods. But he also thought their gods only sanctioned a specific kind of magic—that of clerics. He was no longer certain that was true.

It answered why Kalyazin had spent a century fighting a war against a country that used a great deal of magic when they had very little. But what magic were they using and how had it gone unnoticed by Tranavia for this long?

He had a terrible feeling he was about to find out.

"Take him downstairs," Yekaterina said, sounding bored. "I want more answers before I deal with him."

His arm was gripped by a middle-aged man. He was unassuming in appearance; blond hair, dark eyes, half his face in shadow from his lopsided hood, not particularly memorable, unlike the cult members in Tranavia.

Until he pushed his hood back and Serefin got a look at the scars ravaging half his face. Made by claws—claws with the right distance between them to be fingers. He wore a necklace of teeth like the one around Yekaterina's neck.

"You're back early," the man said, eyeing Serefin.

"Yes, well, my plans were changed by this one," she said. "I'll be with you both shortly."

The man yanked Serefin down the hall, opening a door that led to a set of stairs, descending into darkness. The man took a torch from the wall and went first. The hallway stretched on and on—it seemed like they would never reach the end—but finally the man stopped. He did not open the door, instead turning to Serefin after placing his torch in a sconce.

"None have passed through these halls not of the order in a very long time. Especially not the enemy," the man said.

"No? How shocking."

The man watched him a bit longer. Serefin let out a sigh of relief. He had no idea who Serefin was. Likely the *tsarevna* only knew what he looked like—as he knew what *she* looked like—on the off chance they met in battle.

This was exactly the kind of mess he *would* get into without Kacper around to keep him from doing something senseless. The man shoved Serefin into the room, a dimly lit study. He indicated for Serefin to sit, and waited by the door.

The man was clearly *Voldah Gorovni,* same as Yekaterina.

Though Żywia had mentioned that the Vulture hunters had had a resurgence, Serefin hadn't expected to find them. This was the luck that he needed, strangely enough. This was the answer to his Malachiasz problem.

Maybe he could talk his way out of this, after all.

Yekaterina appeared a few minutes later. "What do you know about what happened at Kartevka?"

Serefin stared up at her blankly. What? He considered the mountain of military reports Ostyia had shoved in his face back in Grazyk. He had read maybe half of them before falling asleep at his desk. Kacper had woken him, gently dragging him back to his chambers, talking the whole way about how he should have let Serefin stay there so maybe the ache in his back the next day would be enough to get him to take care of himself.

"I understand this is something of an interrogation, but can I ask questions?" he asked hopefully.

Yekaterina's lips twitched. He thought she was going to refuse, but she nodded, gesturing for him to continue.

"Do you actually kill Vultures, or are the teeth for show?"

Yekaterina quirked an eyebrow.

"Because," Serefin continued, "I haven't really heard of any Vulture killers until recently, which suggests you aren't very *good* at your job. But, that aside: Would you like to kill the Black Vulture?"

She froze. "Surely you don't share the rule of your entire country with a monster."

"My confidence in your abilities is severely waning as your information appears to once again be incorrect."

She scowled, reached into her jacket pocket, and tossed something at Serefin. He leaned forward—they hadn't tied his hands, an oversight on their part, he could still cast magic so long as he could draw blood—and caught a string of iron teeth.

"How disgusting," he said, examining the trophy. "But I'm listening."

"Monsters are monsters," she said. "They can all be killed."

"How?"

"You think I'll reveal our secrets to you?"

"Ah, you're right, the weird eye just isn't enough, is it?"

Serefin had her at that. She knew what his eye meant, even if he wanted to deny it to himself.

"I *would* like the Black Vulture's teeth for my collection," she said thoughtfully.

"He has lovely teeth, I promise you."

And even though this was working out in Serefin's favor, even though this was something that had to be done, hearing those words rattled him. All he could think about was the scrawny boy with wild black hair and a vibrant grin that he'd dragged around the palace as a child. The boy who had carried a pile of books into his room to read to him when Serefin was recovering from his eye injury and couldn't see a damn thing. Who had probably kept him from going mad with boredom.

Thinking about that clever boy sent another pang of regret through Serefin. Malachiasz had the potential to be a powerful ally. Instead he had made himself the enemy.

His brother had to die and Serefin had to do it before whatever had claim of him led him into the forest and tore him to pieces.

# 18

## NADEZHDA

## LAPTEVA

**Svoyatova Aleksasha Ushakova:** *Stricken by Devonya, she was stripped of all power. Her bones are cursed and rest in the vault underneath the Baikkle Monastery, ruining all who touch them.*

—Vasiliev's Book of Saints

Someone latched onto Nadya's forearm, dragging her into a derelict barn on the farm property. She yanked out a *voryen*, the stitches in her side pulling dangerously and warmth blooming at her waist.

She was face-to-face with Kostya. He ignored the dagger trained at his side, studying her with a strangely dispassionate expression.

She relaxed. "There you are, I've been looking for you."

"I've been trying to discern what happened to the Nadya I know," he said.

She flinched. The coldness in his dark gaze was that of a stranger.

"Because," he continued, voice distant, "the Nadya *I* know would never treat with the enemy. The Nadya I know is so dedicated to the gods that she would *never* leave an abomination against the gods alive."

Nadya closed her eyes.

"The Nadya I know wouldn't do this," he said, looking at her intently. "Do you know what he's done?"

She nodded without opening her eyes. Was she a coward for being so wholly unable to face him? Maybe so.

"I don't think you do," he said carefully.

"Kostya," she said, voice breaking. He wanted to think the best of her and that was only making this worse. She reached out but he stepped away. "I know."

She clutched her hands close to her chest, painfully aware of sticky wetness seeping through her tunic.

"Do you know what happened at the monastery after you left?"

"No," she whispered. Nadya had not mourned for the home she had lost. Not truly. There had been no time. She was terrified that she had moved past it, had become so bitter, so fallen, that it wouldn't matter what Kostya said, she would remain numb and cold.

He took in a sharp breath. "You're bleeding," he murmured, reaching for her against his better judgment.

"I'm fine," she said. "You're not going to stop being mad at me because I pulled some stitches."

He wavered. "I'm not . . ." He stopped. "No, you're right, I am. Nadya, I don't understand."

"I can't make you understand," she said slowly. "Most of the time, I don't, either."

"They killed Anton," he said softly.

Nadya's heart wrenched. Kostya and his younger brother had arrived at the monastery together, Anton only a baby at the time. The boy was always running after Kostya and Nadya, getting underfoot, a generally obnoxious and lovable younger sibling to them both.

"Kostenka . . ." she murmured, pulling his name into a closer diminutive.

It was dim in the old barn, but she could see the bright film of tears shining in Kostya's eyes.

"He died while we were still at the monastery," Kostya said. "The prince used him as bait while he tortured me."

Nadya squeezed her eyes shut, the emotions she had shoved aside threatening to crash down on her all at once.

"Father Alexei died in the Salt Mines," Kostya continued. "They had no use for him, too old, so the Vultures did away with him. No one really knew what that meant. Day by day they would take more of us away, until there were so few left. Until there was only me."

No amount of trying to fight it would keep the tears away. No pretending deep down inside that everyone had gotten away unscathed. Everyone she had loved. The only family she had: gone.

"This is what Tranavians do, Nadya. All they know is destruction and chaos. This is how it has always been and always will be."

She pressed the heels of her hands to her eyes to try to force the tears back. She couldn't break here, not now, not yet. There was still so much farther to go.

"You can't make excuses. Not for him," Kostya said, but his voice was gentler.

She felt his hand on her arm as he tugged her closer. She let him, burying her face against his shoulder.

"I'm sorry," she whispered.

And even after so much time in the Salt Mines, even in his decimated, broken state, he still smelled like incense. He smelled like home and she missed it. The world was cold and cruel and she wanted to be home.

She needed Kostya to understand that she had done what she had to, that the failings of her heart were her own and she was trying to be better. But she had failed her people; it was as simple as that.

"I couldn't think about it," she said, hollow. "I had to move forward and the only way to do that was to just . . . move past it."

"What's going on, Nadya?"

She leaned back and tugged out the pendant Kostya had tucked into her hands before the monastery had burned. "Where did you get this?"

All the blood drained from his face. "You kept it," he said softly.

She flipped the pendant around on its cord so it landed on her palm. "Do you know what it is?"

He nodded.

Things were potentially far worse than she had guessed. "Why did you give it to me?"

"To keep it safe," he said. "The Church— I mean— I was supposed to—"

"Who gave this to *you*, Kostya?" His words made her cold. She wasn't supposed to *use* the pendant. But of course she wasn't. It had taken blood to free Velyos from the prison, and wasn't she the great holy cleric who would never sully herself in such a way?

*What have I done?*

"A woman came to the monastery several years ago. She

asked to speak to me. Father Alexei said she wanted the person who was closest to you, to keep an eye on you."

"Keep an eye on me," Nadya repeated. What was that supposed to mean? What did the Church think she was going to do?

Kostya frowned. "She gave me the pendant but she wasn't very clear on what I was supposed to do with it, only that it was imperative it stayed safe and near the cleric because you'd keep the terrible inevitable from happening. Those were the words she used," he said. "The terrible inevitable."

Nadya had allowed that to happen. Worse still, she had practically urged it on.

"She said it was just as dangerous to have near you as it was necessary, but I never figured out what she meant."

*I was never supposed to use Velyos' power,* Nadya thought, with sick realization. She started shaking. *I was never supposed to set him free.*

"You never told me why the Black Vulture is here," Kostya continued, voice cold once more.

"I need to use his power. I need to go west."

Kostya was shaking his head. "There is nothing you need to do that would include such a monster."

"Kos—" she started, exasperated, but he pushed on.

"No. You're making excuses," he replied. "We need to go. You're well enough to travel. If we leave tonight it will only take a week or so to get to the monastery in Privbelinka. Come with me, Nadya, we'll go back to Kalyazin together, find the army, everything will be like it was meant to be."

*Like it was meant to be.* But meant to be for whom? For the old Nadya, who knew nothing outside the monastery walls and was supposed to be shuffled around the country as a figurehead and a weapon? She couldn't return to that.

She didn't respond, but Kostya wasn't deterred. He took her hands, his demeanor changing instantly.

*He thinks I'm going with him,* Nadya thought, heart sinking. How she wished it would be that easy.

"Kostya," she said slowly, beseechingly. "I can't."

Bewilderment passed over his features. "What? Of course you can. We'll fix this, Nadya, together. Everything will be fine." He kissed her forehead before she could stop him and got up, starting back toward the farmhouse.

"Hells," she whispered. She stood there for a long time, letting the cold burrow into her bones, before she finally followed.

Malachiasz glanced up when she wandered into the house and gingerly took a seat at the table. A strange, wary look came into his eyes when he saw the blood on her tunic.

"He went in there," he said, pointing to the other room. "What happened to you?"

"You, technically," she replied dryly as Parijahan made a disapproving sound and went to fetch Rashid.

"Right," he said quietly.

"You know, in the grand scheme of things, literally impaling me is not your worst offense."

Malachiasz rolled his eyes. She sighed. So that was how it was going to be. Fine. She didn't need to be friends with him. She just needed to suffer him a little longer until she had fixed things, then this could end.

Rashid came in, saw the blood on Nadya's tunic and groaned, gesturing at Malachiasz.

"I didn't punch him," Nadya said. "I still might, though."

Rashid slid down onto the bench beside Nadya. "May I?"

"Only if he looks away," she said. Malachiasz rolled his eyes again and dropped his head onto the table.

Rashid chuckled and tugged her tunic up to peel the bandage away from her side and clean the sluggishly bleeding stab wound.

"Ease up or these will never heal," he said gently.

She made a noncommittal noise. His hands were warm as he dressed her wounds with fresh bandages. "I don't want to sit around any longer. We should figure out where Serefin went."

Malachiasz lifted his head.

"No!" Nadya said.

He dropped his head back down against the table with a soft thunk. "Why do you need *him*?"

"You haven't caught him up?" she asked Rashid.

"He's directly responsible for a portion of it. I assumed he knew."

"I don't remember anything," Malachiasz muttered dejectedly. He lifted his head cautiously. Rashid had finished so she decided to spare him. A cluster of painfully bloodshot eyes blinked open on his cheek, and he jolted—his actual vision must break every time—his expression fracturing, and she wondered if it was a lie.

"You do see why I have a hard time believing you, right?"

Malachiasz nodded petulantly.

"It's just terribly convenient."

He rested his chin in his hands, frowning. But she remembered the look in his eyes before he fled the sanctuary and his lack of memory wasn't exactly far-fetched.

She leaned her head against Rashid's shoulder. Parijahan came in and slapped a map on the table. Kostya trailed in behind her, slid a mug of tea Nadya's way, and, finding the only available seat was near Malachiasz, leaned against the doorway.

"What are we doing?" Parijahan asked.

Nadya took a sip of the tea. The way Malachiasz had prepared it had been better. She closed her eyes briefly, scolding herself inwardly before leaning forward. She tapped the Valik-hor Mountains. "I need to be here."

"That's on the other side of Kalyazin," Parijahan said warily. "And what is it you need him for?" She nodded to Malachiasz.

"I thought we needed him for his glowing personality," Rashid said. "And because we missed him."

"Flattery will get you everywhere, Rashid," Malachiasz replied.

"Only for you, Malachiasz."

"There's a temple at the base of the mountains. There are rumors it is a direct line to the gods."

"I thought that was something you had inherently," Mala-chiasz said.

For some reason the bite in his words was far better than sympathy she knew would be false. She was very aware of Kostya's gaze burning into the side of her face.

"It is very far away," Parijahan said thoughtfully. "Far enough that no one would be able to find me."

Malachiasz shot Parijahan a curious look. She didn't clarify, but what passed between them spoke of an understanding.

Nadya frowned. She placed her hand on the table, face up. The spiral scar had blackened nearly her entire palm, twisting up to stain her fingertips. Kostya took in a horrified gasp, but his reaction was to be expected. There was something infi-nitely more terrifying about the way Malachiasz paled.

"Regardless of the fact that my interactions with your power should, frankly, be impossible, right now I have nothing. Well, I have this, but I think it might be killing me."

He leaned over the table, shooting a tentative glance her way, and took her hand in his. The scar on his palm was pale and healed.

His thumbnail was an iron claw and he touched the back

against her palm. She hissed at the cold and the sudden feeling of something *else*. A magic she hadn't felt in months. He frowned, concentrating, then a smile quirked at his mouth. He let the map roll up and climbed *onto* the table, folding up his lanky frame and sitting on the table cross-legged. He pulled her hand closer to his face.

"It's like it's just being held there," he said thoughtfully. "I did . . ." He hesitated. "You should have died from those wounds in the Salt Mines."

"Blood magic can't heal," Parijahan commented.

"No—I didn't. What I did was give you a touch of my power to keep you alive." He looked up at her from under his cloud of tangled black hair. "But it shouldn't have stayed like this."

"It was there before," Nadya said. "It's been there since I stole it in the cathedral."

"Have I mentioned how annoying that was?" he asked idly as he returned to inspecting her hand. The warmth of his hands against hers was distracting. He isolated her index finger, skimming the pad of his over her fingernail. He made a contemplative sound and showed her his finger.

It was bleeding.

A shiver of foreboding settled in the pit of her stomach.

"Interesting," Malachiasz murmured. "May I open it?"

"Open it?"

He poised an iron claw over her palm and raised both eyebrows expectantly.

"I'd rather you didn't," she said.

"I wouldn't take another step if I were you, Kalyazi," Malachiasz said pleasantly. "This really isn't your concern."

Nadya glanced at Kostya and shook her head. His expression was stormy as he returned to the doorway, folding his arms over his chest.

Malachiasz sliced the edge of her palm. She bit her lip. It didn't really hurt, but a weird feeling of dread horror rushed through her. She shuddered, and Malachiasz lifted his eyes to her face. Her fingers tried to curl closed and he gently pried them back open.

"It's not my magic," he said, puzzled.

She frowned. She could feel power that wasn't her divine magic and had assumed it was his. What was it? And was this why she couldn't talk to the gods? What if they weren't ignoring her at all?

Malachiasz pulled a handkerchief out of his pocket and wiped the blood off her palm.

"I have no idea what this is," he said.

"I love hearing you say that."

He laughed. Her heart flipped painfully in her chest and she wanted to kick herself. She wasn't supposed to be doing *this*. Not with him, not again. This was exactly what she needed to avoid.

She didn't pull her hand away from his.

"There is no priest to go to for answers," Nadya said, her voice low. "If I don't get answers . . ." She shook her head. "Maybe nothing. Maybe I'm inflating my own importance and I've done all I was meant to. But nothing has changed for the better. Kalyazin and Tranavia are still at war. Serefin might lose his throne to a group of warmongering nobles. You—" She paused, waiting for Malachiasz to acknowledge her words. His clear reluctance was telling. "—have shattered something in this world and it's only a matter of time before we see how it manifests. I need to get to that temple. But it is surrounded by a forest only the divine can pass through."

Malachiasz screwed up his face, wrinkling his nose.

"You're the closest thing we've got. But it will be difficult." More like impossible. It would require something of him that she wasn't sure he would be truly willing to give up.

Her hand was cradled in his, resting in his lap. He was lightly, absently, toying with her fingers in a way that was softly intimate.

He had betrayed her. Why couldn't she hate him for that? Why wasn't the anger that simmered constantly under the surface spilling into anything more?

Why did she want him to weave his fingers between hers and press his thumb against her palm?

"Truce," he said, his voice barely above a whisper.

She closed her eyes, swallowing hard, and pulled her hand away. "That's not enough."

When she opened her eyes, he had shuttered everything away. They stared at each other for a long time and, oh, she was *very* aware of the disgust pouring off Kostya, but she was caught again in this boy's colorless gaze.

"It's. Not. Enough," she said through clenched teeth.

Something yanked in her chest as he tilted his head, the bones in his black pile of hair falling into her field of vision. A smile pulled at his lips, feral and cruel, and he leaned closer to her. He took her chin in his hand and roughly pulled her face to his.

"No, of course not," he murmured, breath feathering her face. "But nothing ever will be, will it? A little peasant girl from a monastery would want nothing more than to see the monster self-flagellate at her feet. I won't do it, Nadya. I'm not going to play that game."

He lifted his other hand. "Don't you dare," he spat out at Kostya, who had taken a step forward.

"You'll play," Nadya said, ignoring Kostya, ignoring everything. She couldn't drive him off before he got her through the forest. "You would have stayed in your hellish mines if you were not going to play. Did you expect to return and find everything exactly like it was before you burned it to the ground? There are only ever ashes after a fire, Malachiasz, and I'll have you at my feet yet."

His eyes narrowed, the faint smile never quite dropping from his lips even as the air around him turned dangerous. He tucked a lock of her hair behind her ear.

"We'll see, pet."

# 19

## SEREFIN

## MELESKI

**Svoyatova Kseniya Pushnaya:** *Named Svoyatova of Thorns, Kseniya lived in the deep forests and granted gifts of power to those who sought her out and survived the trials that her god, Vaclav, set before them.*

—Vasiliev's Book of Saints

It was difficult to hear about the conquests of the Tranavian forces and not feel openly delighted. What Serefin hadn't realized was just how dire the situation was for the Kalyazi, how close to the end they truly were. Yet the Kalyazi were turning things around, and Serefin had to stop them before it got any worse.

The *tsarevna* wanted information about something that had happened at some military outpost, and Serefin had nothing to give her.

"So you weren't at Kartevka."

"I only have the vaguest notion of where that is."

Yekaterina was flipping through Serefin's spell book and landed on a spell halfway through. Serefin couldn't remember what it could possibly be, but it made her pause and consider him further. The magic he kept in his spell book was mostly offensive with a tidy collection of persuasive spells.

"It was a massacre," she said. "I'm shocked you Tranavians aren't heralding it as a miracle, what with the monster that was there."

Serefin shifted uncomfortably in his seat. He knew where this was going. "When did this happen?"

"Three months ago or so," she said. "But this came after. The front has been consistently attacked by a creature who only comes under the cover of darkness. We've fought this damn war as fairly as you heretics deserve, but—"

"War isn't fair," Serefin replied evenly. "It never has been. And it's not our fault you have no magic to speak of."

Yekaterina inclined her head. "So little you know, Tranavian."

"Listen," Serefin said quickly, before she could continue. "I'm not asking for trust. But it sounds like our goals align. How many Vultures have been seen at the front? Since when?"

"A lot of questions."

"You've not yet killed me nor taken me as a prisoner of war, so clearly you think I'll be useful."

"Useful might be an overstatement."

"But I want the Vultures taken down, if not for good—I am Tranavian, after all—at least a peg. I want the Black Vulture dead. If he lives, it won't matter who wins this endless war."

Malachiasz wanted both thrones. Serefin couldn't let him take his. And his plot to kill Kalyazin's gods wouldn't end anything.

"Kartevka happened without warning. One moment, it was

as peaceful a night as any can be on the front, the next, the skies split open and magic poured forth; a creature coming with it that ravaged the entire camp to ash."

"What about the location made it special?"

Yekaterina frowned. "What do you mean?"

"If it was the Black Vulture who did this—did anyone survive? Any witnesses? No? Well, he's smart—it wasn't without reason. He's not one for mass destruction because he *feels* like it."

"Shocking," she said dryly.

"He's exceedingly clever," Serefin said absently as he considered. "Was there something there he might want?"

"*Vashnya Delich'niy . . .*" the man at the door said, a warning.

But the *tsarevna* only looked thoughtful. "Gods, what does it matter, you probably already know. We kept our most powerful relics and icons at Kartevka."

*The relics again . . .*

"All this for some bones?" Serefin remarked.

She smiled slightly. "Pray you never see those bones at work."

"Oh, I think something was lost in translation. I'm a heretic. I don't pray."

Serefin thought about those spell books he'd found in a Kalyazi camp. They had to be related.

"But regardless, those are now in the Black Vulture's hands?" Serefin asked.

"They weren't retrieved from the wreckage, so the assumption is, yes."

*Interesting.* What could the Vultures possibly need with a handful of old bones?

"You could get those back if you help me kill the Black Vulture," he said.

Yekaterina shook her head in disbelief. "I don't understand

the game you're playing," she said. She shoved her chair back and stood, picking up the string of iron teeth and draping it over her neck. "Bring him," she said to the man, before sweeping out of the room.

Serefin was led deeper underneath the church, into a wide room with wax candles dripping down sconces and strange stained-glass pieces embedded in the walls, lights flickering behind them scattering rainbows onto the polished stone floor. There were statues of strange creatures in each corner that at a glance unnerved him.

"This is holy ground, take off your shoes," Yekaterina said, sliding out of her boots.

He frowned. "Holy ground for *whom*?" he muttered. She continued to stare at him. He sighed, untying his boots and stepping out of them and onto the cold floor.

"I can't imagine a Tranavian could hope to understand matters of divinity."

"You'd be surprised," he replied, rubbing at his eye. His hand came away wet with blood. *Hells, not now.*

Something scratched just underneath his skin, a foreboding that he couldn't quite identify until Yekaterina crossed the room and opened a door. Serefin caught only the barest glimpse of the stone altar within before panic drowned him. The *tsarevna* gestured and the man clubbed him in the back of the head, dropping him like a stone.

A stone altar worn down by the threads of thousands of years. He had seen it before and he saw it now.

Well, *felt* it, rather.

His hands were bound to the altar. He tugged at the chains

to see if there was any give. Nothing. The air was thick with the scent of incense, pungent and cloudy in the dim light of the flickering candles.

"The gods have been quiet since your father died," Yekaterina said from somewhere outside Serefin's limited field of vision. Her voice was quietly contemplative.

His left eye was showing him strange patterns in the hazy incense smoke above him. He started to chew at the inside of his mouth. He wouldn't need a lot of blood, only a little, just a taste to catch his magic.

"The old ways haven't been practiced in a long time. Ever since the clerics started to disappear. Kalyazin forgot our magic is as fueled by blood as that of the heretics, only we spill it for divine purpose. We spill it in subjugation to our gods, and thus, it is deemed sanctified."

Serefin rested his head back. "And how is ritual sacrifice any different from what our Vultures do in their caverns below ground?"

Yekaterina made a thoughtful noise. "I just told you."

He heard the click of her fingernails against the stone slab right beside his ear, felt a sharp pain across his chest as she dragged the point of a dagger horizontally just under his collarbone.

A cloud of moths burst into the air. She reared back, making an odd sign with her fingers over her chest.

*Superstitious Kalyazi,* Serefin thought.

"What are you?" she hissed.

He tasted blood from his shredded mouth, and shivered with power. Yekaterina frowned and cut another line into his chest, carving a symbol in flesh, sending more moths fluttering into the air.

The *tsarevna* muttered in Kalyazi, words flying too fast for Serefin to keep up, but the drone of her voice lodged panic deep in Serefin's core.

He was going to die here. He struggled against the chains, but they held fast.

There was a tension of power from the carving in his skin but it wasn't his magic; it wasn't power he could access, though it had been his blood that was spilled.

His chest tightened; he was struggling for air. Yekaterina watched dispassionately.

"What will this give you?" he rasped, face contorting at the sudden waves of fiery pain that licked at his skin. "Power?"

"I want a message," she said, wiping the blade clean and straightening from the altar. "I want the ear of my goddess turned toward me. I want to send a sign to Tranavia that we will not be cowed by your heretical magic and we will suffer this war no longer." She smiled slightly. "I want to kill the king of Tranavia. And you're right, the Black Vulture, too. This will help."

She lifted the dagger to plunge it into his heart.


The walls of the palace always made Serefin feel like he was walking in the home of giants. Everything was so tall and loud and he much preferred the seasons when his mother declared that the air in Grazyk was killing her and swept Serefin off to stay in their home by the lakes near her sister's estate.

"What are you doing?"

He had been lying on the floor in one of the great halls, staring at the paintings on the ceiling. There were painters working on the far side of the hall who had only recently finished the portion Serefin was eyeing. More than once a servant had stepped over him instead of going around.

His cousin leaned over him, before looking up to the ceiling. He sighed in his resigned way—as if the younger boy constantly had better things to be doing, which Serefin always found amusing, because Malachiasz had also been absent from their lessons that morning and no one had been able to find him. He did that, just disappeared, sometimes. *Ćawtka* Sylwia was never particularly concerned, though it drove Serefin's mother senseless.

He had dust on his clothes and in his mess of dark hair that Serefin knew Wiktoria, Sylwia's maidservant, had valiantly spent half the morning trying to tame. There was dried blood on his hands, hardly an oddity, though neither boy was supposed to practice their magic without supervision, especially Malachiasz.

Serefin had a knack for blood magic; Malachiasz had something entirely different and altogether *more*.

Malachiasz finally unceremoniously flopped onto the floor next to Serefin.

A servant huffed out an irritated breath and stepped over them, carrying a tray of silvers.

"Nothing," Serefin replied because he had, in fact, been doing absolutely nothing. "What's going on in that corner?" He pointed to where the painters were working.

Malachiasz was quiet, fighting with his desire to remain perfectly indifferent and his love of art. Malachiasz liked to trail behind the royal family's portrait artist while Serefin carted around old Tranavian history books.

"Vultures," he said thoughtfully.

The ceiling above them was covered with vultures, the birds painted as hulking and dark. Serefin shivered. He barely noticed the powerful blood mages that lurked in the palace halls and took their order name after the carrion birds. Malachiasz was both terrified and fascinated by them.

"Where were you this morning?" Serefin asked.

Malachiasz ignored him, pointing up at the ceiling. "It's a battle."

"What?"

"They're painting a battle."

Serefin frowned, tilting his head to try and see what Malachiasz saw. It looked like a lot of animals to him, but there was something vicious to it.

"The bears are Kalyazi. The white eagles and the vultures are Tranavian."

The bears were definitely losing this particular battle. Serefin could see it now.

"Is it a specific one, do you think?" Malachiasz asked.

Serefin *did* know entirely too much about the military history of Tranavia and the war they had been fighting against their neighbor for nearly a century. He squinted, trying to make out any defining features that might denote important Tranavian generals.

"Kwiatosław Rzepka," he finally said.

The focal point of the piece was a white eagle with only one wing and golden talons, tearing out the heart of a bear with a flaming sword at its feet.

Rzepka wasn't some bygone Tranavian general; he was a figure out of Tranavia's oldest myths. Even before the war with Kalyazin, Tranavia had never gotten along with its bigger neighbor to the west, and there were plenty of children's tales about Rzepka and his magic. It wasn't blood magic, this was before Tranavia, it was old magic, one that had long since been lost to Tranavia after Kalyazin did its very best to wipe it out entirely.

"Why would your father have him painted on the ceiling?"

Serefin wasn't sure. His father far preferred cold military

facts to the fanciful stories of an old mage missing a hand who had cut a mountain in half and killed dragons in the lowland hills. He shrugged. Malachiasz almost definitely knew more about Rzepka than Serefin. Malachiasz liked anything related to magic.

His cousin tilted his head farther back, curious.

"They're not the best," he said skeptically.

"This is one of the little halls," Serefin replied.

"I guess that explains everything."

Serefin wished they weren't lying down and he could throw something at Malachiasz. His cousin sat up and grinned at him.

"I'm hungry," he announced and got up. "Come on. You're not doing anything better."

"If you hadn't missed breakfast *and* lunch this wouldn't be a problem," Serefin said, but got to his feet and followed after Malachiasz. "Where were you, anyway?"

"Around," Malachiasz said.

"My mother is going to kill you."

He was unconcerned on his quest to the palace kitchens. He wouldn't get in trouble, he never did. It was frustrating. Everything Serefin did earned him a disapproving glare from his father, and a scolding from his mother.

But he was a prince and Malachiasz was not.

They darted around the legs of servants and *slavhki* until Malachiasz knocked into a tall figure wearing an iron mask. He stopped dead still as the figure slowly turned, the plain iron mask revealing nothing but the Vulture's green eyes.

"Careful," she said, her voice laced with something that made Serefin immediately want to flee.

Malachiasz took a step back, running into Serefin. He *was* going to run, but froze once more as the Vulture dropped into a crouch in front of him, her movements loose, and took his hand.

"Practicing?" she asked. "You're Czechowicz's boy, yes?"

Malachiasz nodded.

"Show me what you can do."

His expression was terrified as he confirmed Serefin was still behind him. "I don't have a spell book," he said.

"I do," she said, unclipping a thick book bound in black leather from her hip.

Malachiasz shook his head. "I'm not supposed to use magic." A beseeching entreaty to Serefin, pleading for him to step in.

But Malachiasz was very good at magic, and Serefin didn't want to tell a Vulture no. He nodded encouragingly as the Vulture tore a page out of her spell book.

"I don't—"

There were iron claws suddenly tipping her fingers and she slashed one down Malachiasz's forearm. He jumped, eyes filling with tears, but his expression quickly went glassy and he reached for the spell book page.

For a terrible second it was like time stopped. The air went white and hazy and Serefin was slammed back into the wall. The Vulture straightened, inscrutable behind her iron mask.

"Interesting," she said, voice soft, and without another word, she swept away.

Malachiasz stood there, blood dripping from his fingers and tears running down his cheeks, before he noticed Serefin wasn't beside him any longer.

He whimpered, flinching back when Serefin stumbled to his feet.

"I'm fine," Serefin said, trying to be reassuring until blood dripped down his face. His head *did* hurt.

"Don't tell," Malachiasz whispered.

It wouldn't matter if he told or not if someone saw. Serefin grabbed Malachiasz's arm and dragged him into a servants' hall.

"You just overpowered a Vulture's spell," he said.

Malachiasz nodded, eyes wide.

"Where am I bleeding?"

"It's only a cut on your forehead. I'm sorry, Serefin. I could have killed you." He was panicking.

They needed to let Andrzej know what Malachiasz had done. The mage would know what to do about a boy who had blown so far past the spell a *Vulture* had given him that it had backfired. Usually the Vultures trained the royal children in magic, but they weren't old enough yet. They were still learning from a mortal mage, and after *that* Serefin didn't particularly ever want to train with a Vulture.

But Malachiasz was trembling and trying bravely to rub away the tears streaking down his cheeks. Serefin sighed.

"Let's get cleaned up," he said. "Then we'll get something to eat."

"You won't tell?"

"No one has to know."

# 20

## NADEZHDA
## LAPTEVA

*Marzenya and Velyos have a bitter rivalry, one a goddess of*
*death, the other a god of the dead.*
—The Letters of Włodzimierz

Nadya sat cross-legged with her prayer beads in her lap, Parijahan asleep in the bed beside her. Prayer used to bring her comfort, but there had been a return on her prayers before. It was foolish of her to ever think of the gods as anything resembling her *friends,* but when Nadya was at her lowest they had always been there, her one constant.

She pressed her thumb over Marzenya's bead, flexing her corrupted hand. What if this was the root of all her problems? What if Marzenya could take this away and things could go back to the way they were supposed to be?

A naive and foolish thought. There was no going back.

And what if the answer was killing Malachiasz? Serefin? Destroying two strangely vibrant boys whom she found fascinating because they were so very *very* different from everything she had ever known? As much as she hated in her core the horrors that Tranavia had wrought, it didn't feel right.

She wished she had a Codex. She needed something to ground herself with. Kostya wasn't enough, not with Malachiasz here. Not when all Kostya wanted to do was speak of tragedy.

He would come for her that night and all she would do was disappoint him. She couldn't run. She had to fix herself first, find her way again. The temple, the mountains, they were the only thing that felt like maybe *maybe* they would put her back where she belonged. Not the girl from the monastery but a cleric of Kalyazin—of the gods—who knew what she believed and was capable of. Someone who could shift this godsforsaken never-ending war for the better.

It hadn't worked before. But maybe she could have a second chance.

Kostya slipped into the room, appearing puzzled that she was merely sitting on the bed. She held a finger to her lips, glancing at Parijahan, before slipping her prayer beads over her head and getting up. She pulled him into the main room.

"What are you doing? Let's go." There was a threat in his tone that frightened her.

"You've not been listening," she said. "I'm not going, Kostya."

His whole demeanor darkened. "Who *are* you?"

She stared at him sadly. She just wanted him to see what she was trying to accomplish, even with the compromises she had been forced to make, and she was afraid he would never look past her dealings with Tranavians.

"I was going to ignore what I saw earlier, but . . . . you've been bewitched somehow. I—" He broke off when she lifted her corrupted hand.

"Creature he may be, he knows a lot about magic. And whatever this is? It is magic."

Kostya took her hand, horror etched onto his features. He dropped it, disgusted.

"It's *you*," he said quietly.

"Kostya . . ."

"They got to you. I was warned, gods, they told me you'd be susceptible. They *told* me you would falter." He began to pace.

"Who did?" The woman who had given him the pendant?

He shook his head. "I shouldn't have let you go. I've ruined everything."

"*You?*"

"You were supposed to go west! You were supposed to listen to the gods! Not some monster who has done this . . ." He waved to her hand in revulsion. "To you."

"Supposed to," Nadya said flatly. "There was never a definitive plan. I was *supposed to* go to the nearest military base, but when the monastery burned I was stranded in a forest with Tranavians swarming the mountains. I did what I had to to survive."

"It would have been better if you hadn't," Kostya muttered.

She recoiled. Something in her heart split off. He couldn't see *her* anymore. She was only the sum of her mistakes.

"You don't mean that."

He didn't speak.

"Kostya, who told you I would falter?"

"Does it matter?"

*More than you know,* she thought. The idea that there was some other greater plan that she did not know about terrified her.

She closed her eyes. Let out a breath. "If I tell you the truth, promise you will listen to me."

"What *else* could you possibly have to tell me?" he cried.

"The gods don't talk to me anymore," she whispered. She didn't open her eyes. She didn't want to see his face.

"Nadya." She heard the horror in his voice. The anger. The betrayal.

"I am trying to make this better," she said. "I am trying to fix what I've done wrong. If I go with you I can't do that."

She opened her eyes. Kostya stared at her, his face blank, eyes hard. He reached out and very carefully took her string of prayer beads in his hand.

"I thought . . ." he said quietly. "I thought you were supposed to be elevated above all others. *Perfect.* I thought the whispers about you were wrong, but . . ." His grip tightened. "Then there's no hope."

Nadya didn't have a chance to ask him what *that* was supposed to mean. He pulled hard against the necklace, yanking her forward and snapping the cord. The sound of her wooden prayer beads against the floor was loud against her ears.

And something snapped inside of her.

Tears filled her eyes. The only thing she had left of the gods was broken. "What have you *done*?" she cried, shoving him away and scrambling to pick up a bead, trying to rethread it onto the broken cord. She couldn't get the bead to slide over the frayed edge and suddenly everything she had pushed aside came rushing to the surface. She choked back a sob, pressing the back of her hand to her mouth.

Kostya made a sound of disgust and slammed out of the house.

After another bead slid through her fingers and rolled away

she collapsed on the floor, shoving her hands against her eyes as she tried to bite back sobs.

He hadn't let her explain. He hadn't *listened*.

She had thought . . . what? That Kostya would forgive her? That he would ignore how she had forced him into the same quarters as the monster who had kept him prisoner?

A soft hand stroked her hair in passing. Malachiasz padded barefoot across the room, stooping to pick up a handful of beads. He returned and sat down in front of her.

He was quiet. He was the absolute *last* person she wanted right now. She couldn't see the frayed cord through her tears but that didn't stop her from attempting to rethread one of her beads. Would she even be able to remember their order?

"These are literally burning my hand," Malachiasz finally said. "Please take them?"

That startled a laugh out of her. She held out her hands and he gently placed the beads into her palms, closing her fingers over them.

He settled back, pulling his leg up and resting his chin on his knee, watching her.

"Sorry," she said, sniffling. "I woke all of you up."

"Nothing to apologize for, I wasn't asleep anyway. Rashid, however, might kill you come morning."

That somehow cracked another laugh out of her. She pooled her beads in her lap, counting them. She was still missing a few.

"I thought I could make him understand." She swiped at her eyes. "If I just explained . . ." But there was so much she couldn't explain. "He wants me to be the girl from the monastery and I lost her long ago."

Malachiasz inclined his head. "Is this something you want to talk about with me?"

"No, I . . . I want you to leave, Malachiasz."

Sadness cracked across his face before he shuttered it away. "That's fair," he whispered. He started to get up.

"I thought . . ." Nadya trailed off. Malachiasz paused before slowly sitting back down. "I don't know. I'm stupid. I shouldn't have expected him to trust me." She stuck the cord in her mouth, trying to smooth the strands so she could get the beads on. "He was my best friend and I thought he knew me but I guess . . ." She stopped, unable to voice what she feared. That Kostya had only ever been friends with the *cleric* and not *Nadya*. She didn't want to believe the worst in him. He had a right to be furious. He had a right to want Malachiasz dead. What she was doing didn't make sense and it was impossible to ask him to understand.

She only wished he had listened.

"You're not stupid or naive," Parijahan said, sitting down next to her.

"Well, a *little* naive," Malachiasz interjected.

Parijahan kicked him.

Nadya laughed but it quickly morphed into a sob. Something flickered across Malachiasz's face that she couldn't bring herself to think about. She was going to lose the only family she had left because of *him* and she couldn't stand it. She wished she didn't need him for a greater cause.

She wished she didn't *want* the boy who had ruined so much.

Parijahan gently took the cord away from her. "You give me the beads in order and I'll string them."

Nadya nodded. She handed her the bead she thought was next but worried she was wrong.

"Do you think he'll come back?" Malachiasz asked. He coughed into the crook of his arm, a harsh, painful noise.

Nadya shrugged. They were still in Tranavia and Kostya

barely spoke the language. He wouldn't last long out there. But she didn't know if he could stand to look at her anymore.

"What if I can never go back?" she said softly.

Malachiasz sighed. She rubbed at her eyes before she met his gaze. Understanding filled his pale eyes, and that frightened her. Feelings of solidarity between her and a monster were not things she ever thought she would have to battle with.

Parijahan gathered up the rest of the beads in Nadya's lap and even though they were holy objects, Nadya let her. Parijahan stood and put the cord and beads on the table.

"Come on," she said, returning to Nadya and holding out her hands. "Bed. Things won't seem as bleak in the morning. Morning is wiser than evening."

"Still pretty bleak," Malachiasz said.

Nadya kicked him this time. "That's a Kalyazi saying," she said to Parijahan, frowning.

"It is."

She let Parijahan tug her to her feet. Everything was strange and wrong. She couldn't stop seeing Kostya's face. The disappointment on it was chewing her up inside.

She followed Parijahan back to their room. Parj was right. Sleep would help.

Morning was wiser than evening. Things would be better then.

She would make things right.

# 21

## SEREFIN

## MELESKI

*A slow corrosion, a deep hunger. Tens upon hundreds upon*
*thousands locked in a tomb, alive, whole, screaming, waiting.*
*Waiting. Waiting.*

—The Volokhtaznikon

Serefin woke up in that damn forest again.

His right eye was completely blind. He started to panic—heartbeat fluttering wildly in his chest, because his right eye was the one that *worked*—but a distant part of him knew this wasn't real.

He could feel blood dried on his cheek, but his left eye wasn't bleeding. It was crystal clear, jarring; he was used to compensating for his bad eye and his sense of equilibrium was off.

*Not real not real not real,* he thought, spinning around.

This was . . . not like the last forest. This wasn't *real* like the last forest.

The tree to his right was pale and scarred, the branches stretching up into the sky, splintering into shards of bone. There was something dark and slow dripping down a hollow in the trunk. *Blood.*

A scream tore through the forest, wrenching and agonized. A sharp crack like a tree branch being snapped in two nearby. Serefin whirled. He forgot to breathe. Where the deer skull had appeared like a mask the last time, now it was a grotesque reality. Ivy grew around the neck and into cracks in the skull. The jaw bone was decayed, the teeth sharp like nails.

"I'm surprised to see you so soon," it said. "I thought you were *resisting.*"

"I didn't come here because I wanted to," Serefin said sullenly.

The creature—monster, *god*—leaned a spindly hand against the tree of bone. The skull tilted to one side. The bottomless darkness of its eyes was unsettling. Serefin had to look away but everywhere he turned were more things to fear.

Had the damned *tsarevna* killed him? Was that how he had ended up here? Could he wake up from this?

"Are you finally ready to talk?" the creature asked.

"Anytime we talk you give me enigmatic responses to my questions and tell me you want revenge. That's not particularly helpful," Serefin said. But he *was* ready to talk. He was ready to put a name to this horror so he could figure out how to escape it. He wasn't going to be able to fight off its pull much longer.

But did he give in? Let this creature take his eye and his mind and do whatever it wanted with Serefin? There had to be another way.

He tried to step away from the creature and nearly tripped, unused to his center of gravity being flipped.

"I suppose it's easy to infer the particulars of your goal," Serefin said. "You're a Kalyazi god, clearly, but which *one*."

"I have told you: I am not a god. Velyos is my name. You have not earned it, but you may keep it if it will cease your struggling."

He hadn't taken that as truth before. Surely gods thought of themselves as . . . something else?

"Then what, pray tell, are you?"

"What happens to a god who becomes not a god?"

A monster, then. "So, you were banished?"

"Banished, condemned, imprisoned, there are many words for what happened to me," Velyos replied.

"And you want revenge on the pantheon that kicked you out," Serefin said flatly.

How on earth could he do *anything* about that?

"We all want things," Velyos said. "The goddess of death wants that little cleric of hers to burn your paltry country to ashes, and she will go to drastic measures to see it through. She is a goddess of vengeance. I am a creature of a more particular sort."

Dread threaded through him. He knew he couldn't trust Nadya, but he rather wanted to be able to; it was disappointing to be reminded he couldn't. It was only a matter of time until she stabbed him in the back.

But maybe *this* was his way out. A mortal deal, a cosmic deal, surely one would lead him to the goal he sought. Nadya was granted power by her gods. Maybe . . .

"If I want to kill a Vulture . . ." he started.

The claws on the bone tree shifted, scraping down and leaving blood and scratch marks in its wake.

"If you want to kill a monster, you come to the one whose domain houses the greatest of monsters," he said. "And, thus, have come to the right place."

Serefin feared he had made a grave mistake, given something to Velyos that he shouldn't have. But it was too late to turn back. Serefin was dealing with something greater than himself.

He feared the creature would see his threats through and take Serefin's eye. And even though it hardly worked, Serefin wanted to keep it in his head where it belonged.

What hid underneath that skull?

Serefin didn't care to find out.

The forest of bone cleared to a massive stone temple. Dark pillars were carved in front of a doorway that stretched out of sight. Serefin paused, taking it in. He could *feel* power emanating from that place, but he couldn't identify it. It was just sheer, raw power. An ache in his chest, in his bones. Something older than the earth that hungered, deeply. Waiting, always waiting, to split apart and devour everything.

"What is this?" he asked.

"You want to kill monsters," Velyos said simply. "I have brought you to the being who can accomplish that."

Serefin's whole body went cold. "Not you, then?" He thought he was only going to have to be caught up in the affairs of *one* of Kalyazin's horrors.

"Not me, no. This one is stronger. *This one* knows monsters. He sleeps, though, you see."

Well, that didn't make him feel any better.

"The problem with claiming—" Velyos started. Serefin hated that word. "—a Tranavian is that you don't *know* anything," Velyos complained.

"Alas," Serefin said dryly. "I suppose you should pick someone better suited."

"Dear boy, I'm afraid she made herself unavailable and now there is no one better suited than you."

Serefin swallowed hard.

"I don't have time to give you a lesson in my kind," Velyos said wearily. "Find someone else to help you with that. My domain was once the forest . . . and the dead."

"And what about this other one? The one who sleeps?"

"The darkness and the hunger therein," Velyos said simply. "Entropy. And monsters of the dark were kept by his hand. They are waking up, you see. That boy, the other one—"

"Malachiasz," Serefin whispered.

"Yes. Another Tranavian. Funny, that. He has awoken a darkness these lands have not known in many an age. In everything, in himself, in someone whom darkness never should have touched."

"Can it be stopped?"

"Is that not what you're doing here?" Velyos asked.

He supposed it was. Would stopping Malachiasz stop whatever was waking up?

"Time is limited, of course. The rest of the pantheon will eventually rain their destruction on your paltry country. Perhaps they've already begun? It is so slight, the way the divine touch the world. Such discord that only a few peoples have sown over so few years. Such wrath from the gods."

Serefin felt sick. He looked up at the massive doorway. "What has stopped them?"

"The gods cannot *directly* touch the mortal realm. That is what clerics are for."

"But Nadya—"

"You think the little cleric has lost her power? The girl held in the grasp of not only vengeful Marzenya, but the entire pantheon? *No.* That girl is so much more than she knows."

Serefin frowned.

"Don't mistake a moral lesson to be a revoking of power.

Don't underestimate how easily the girl can get in the way. How quickly everything can spiral into disaster if she wakes up. Let her sleep forever, let her never know the truth."

Serefin didn't know what to make of that. Or if it was any of his concern, all things considered.

"I just want to kill the Black Vulture," he said. "I want my throne and to end this ceaseless war. I want *our* business to be at an end."

"Mostly all things that can be seen to reality."

*Mostly.*

"I go no farther here," Velyos said, stopping. "It is not my place, though it borders on my domain."

"You're fine with me getting power from someone else?"

"You see things so simply." Velyos sounded amused.

"I hardly see at all, actually," Serefin said.

Velyos waved a hand.

Serefin didn't particularly want to go inside the temple before him. The last time he had been shoved toward a great unknown, he had died. If he thought hard about it, searched the dark corners of his mind, he could almost remember what it felt like. The flash of pain; the darkness.

But his father could barely cast a spell, and that left only one other person who could have killed him. Serefin could call it protecting his people from a horror. He could call it punishment for treason. Or he could call it what it was: revenge.

With a final glance toward the creature at his side, Serefin began to climb the steps up to the doors.

Around the pillars were strange, unnerving carvings. Skulls—open mouthed—facial features displaced from their faces. Jagged teeth and wide, terrified eyes. Chaotic and obscene. Serefin hurried past and up to the doors, which weren't much better. He paused.

Whatever waited for him inside couldn't possibly be good.

But Serefin was the king of Tranavia. He was the king of a country of monsters. He wasn't afraid.

He was lying to himself.

But he wasn't awake and he wasn't asleep. He was . . . dead? Again? Truly, what could happen to him here?

*Terrible things. Well, at least Ruminski won't have to waste coin on assassins.*

"I told you he sleeps and yet still you linger," Velyos said, clearly irritated.

"If he sleeps how can he help?"

"Simpleminded fool," Velyos muttered.

Serefin rolled his eyes. But the creature had a point. The longer he lingered, the more time passed in reality. If that mattered.

How long had Serefin been tied to that altar?

Serefin placed his palm flat against the door. Something gave. Something caught—pulled directly over his heart.

The door began to move.

"Wonderful," Velyos said, oddly delighted.

Serefin glanced over his shoulder.

"All the others became nothing but a pile of bones when they touched the door. I knew I liked you, Tranavian."

Serefin gritted his teeth. He brushed a moth off the door. Then shoved it open.

The thing about looking at something unknowable was that the human brain did its absolute best to make it utterly *knowable*. Coherent, at the very least.

Serefin padded barefoot through snow, but didn't feel cold. He didn't feel . . . anything, in fact. It would have been incredibly disturbing if Serefin hadn't already willfully disconnected from reality.

"The last time something like this happened to me, I was dead," he said aloud and gratefully discovered that, yes, he could still speak. He couldn't really see, though. His vision had moved in the opposite direction from before and was dulled and blurry to the point of uselessness. It should have panicked him more than it did.

He had no choice but to continue.

But he didn't know where he was supposed to go. There was nothing around him. And that was quite possibly the most terrifying thing about this.

Being unable to see made things exceedingly more complicated. He knew he was in a wide open space, covered with snow. What he didn't know was how he was supposed to petition a sleeping being. Simpleminded fool he may be, but it still didn't make sense.

And the inside of this place—this temple—didn't make sense. The ceiling was too high, and an impossible to miss, massive doorway suddenly stood before him.

*That* he knew not to enter. It instilled a dread horror within him that he couldn't quite shake. As if he knew, utterly, totally, that behind this door lay madness.

The door parted. Serefin took a step back.

*Oh good,* he thought.

The voice that came from the dark depths was deep, guttural, horrible. It was as if burning coals were being held against his ears while something unforgiving raked its claws over his bones, splintering them into shards.

His left eye was bleeding. A distant realization. The warmth dripping down his cheek.

There had to be a better way than this.

But Serefin knew there wasn't. Not after what Malachiasz had done.

"Treated with kings before, I have. Dead kings whose bones have petrified at the forest's edge. Old, insignificant bags of rotting flesh that call themselves *humanity*. And you dare stand before me, in my hold, at the edges of my domain, *barely* a king, no more than a boy. I know. I *see*. There is nothing you can hide from me, Serefin Meleski, son of Izak, son of Bogumił, son of Florentyn. You wear the touch of death upon you. How long, then, until it is your bones I toss to the edges of my forests?"

Serefin froze. Power shredded his edges the longer he stood before it.

All his ease of disbelief when dealing with Velyos didn't serve him here. Whatever this was . . . this was different. Vast and ancient and uncomfortably, terrifyingly real.

"Don't disturb my solitude with your irritating mortal words," the voice continued. "We can make a deal, you and I. You need power to kill the meddler. I want the meddler dead."

"How fortuitous," Serefin croaked.

A hand, massive and taloned, and so much greater than anything Serefin could fathom, slammed out. And another, and another, until dozens of clawing, bleeding hands were desperately trying to escape. Pulling, tearing, rending at the doorway, struggling to get out while the massive, incomprehensible power emanating from within only heightened. A vastness that Serefin was so very, very small before.

"How fortuitous, indeed."

One of the hands grabbed Serefin and yanked him into the dark.

# 22

## NADEZHDA

## LAPTEVA

*Cautious and careful is Zvonimira, for her light can be a balm but it can also be destruction, and there are those who would take her light from her.*

—Codex of the Divine, 35:187

Nadya was abruptly shaken awake by Parijahan.

"Get your things, we need to go," she said. Her dark hair was a mess, as though she had barely slept.

Nadya was out of bed in an instant, ready to flee. Her sides hurt and she moved carefully, afraid of pulling her stitches again. "What is it?"

Distant voices shouted in Kalyazi, and she knew deep in her core the voices meant battle. But they were still in Tranavia. How could that be?

"Feeling better?" Malachiasz asked, suspiciously cheerful, when Nadya entered the main room.

"Did Kostya come back?" she returned.

A flicker of annoyance crossed his face. "He did."

Relief flooded her. Nadya hadn't expected him to return. She moved to the window. She couldn't see anything, but she knew all too well what she was hearing.

"Your friend tried to kill me last night."

Nadya glanced sidelong at him. "Oh. Did he succeed?"

Malachiasz frowned. "No?"

"You don't sound sure about that."

"Well, I was until you asked."

"A shame, really, that he failed," she said, with more bite than she intended.

He nodded, not appearing offended. She sighed and dropped the curtain.

"We're all about to die, anyway, so I suppose it's moot," he said.

"Has Kalyazin pushed the front into Tranavia?" she asked uncertainly. She knew the war had been shifting; Kalyazin had rallied. But the war had never moved into Tranavia before. What had given the Kalyazi the means to accomplish this?

She had been in Tranavia for too long.

Malachiasz shrugged. "Kalyazin and Tranavia have both suffered equally significant defeats recently."

He had returned to gazing out the window, unaware of her watching him. He was a little less destroyed than he had been appearing, like he had slept for an hour or so despite the dramatics. His black hair was tied back, throwing the lines of his face into sharp relief. He was wearing his old military jacket and there was a pang in her chest at the loss. But it couldn't really comfort her anymore.

"Some Vultures have been on the battlefields," he continued, oblivious.

Nadya stared at him. He caught her incredulous expression.

"I have the control of only half my order," he said. "This is not by my hand."

"I don't believe you."

He didn't respond.

"How do you know of the defeats?"

He opened his mouth and closed it.

"You're lying." Of course he was. *Of course.* "You can't know everything and yet also remember nothing since the cathedral," she said, voice low. There was movement at the doorway. Kostya.

Malachiasz lifted an eyebrow. "Waiting to catch me in a lie?"

"It's all you do."

A rueful smile pulled at his mouth. "Serefin left a whole stack of military reports behind. Rashid has them."

The tension leaked out of her.

The smile went cold. "Comforting to know how thoroughly you distrust me."

"You don't deserve it," she said. "Not when every word you've ever said to me was a lie."

He lifted a single curl of hair from the nape of her neck. She shivered, wishing she hadn't missed that piece when braiding. "Not every word," he murmured. His expression grew distant. "They're getting closer. Time to go."

Nadya turned, made eye contact with Kostya, and immediately pushed past him, shouldering her pack. She heard his voice as she was leaving the house, heard Malachiasz's soft reply, but wasn't able to make out the words.

She couldn't imagine anything those two had to say to each other could possibly be good.

She stuffed her hand in her pocket, running her thumb over her string of prayer beads. It couldn't act as a necklace until she found a new cord and she couldn't shake the feeling that a bead was missing even though every time she counted she ended up with the correct number.

It was still dark outside and it sounded like the nearby battle was happening to the southwest.

"Keep us from being noticed?" Parijahan asked.

Malachiasz pushed his sleeve back, a cut already bleeding sluggishly down his forearm as he tore a page out of his spell book.

Nadya found it oddly relieving to watch him use blood magic the normal way. Utterly heretical and perfectly banal. He could probably cast magic without his spell book entirely. It was upsetting to think on.

His head tilted back and his whole body seemed to relax into itself, his magic growing thick in the air around them. It was worse than before, darker. But she had been living with it underneath her skin for so long, she had been desensitized to it.

When his eyes opened they were pitch-black. Nadya frowned, glancing at the others. Her hand wrapped around the hilt of the bone *voryen*. She grabbed a fistful of his hair, yanking him down to her level, pressing the point of her blade against his throat.

He froze. The air was strange and wrong, suffocating.

"This will be the last time I hesitate, Malachiasz," she murmured. Her *voryen* pricked his skin, drawing a thin trickle of blood. His flesh parted, a mouth with razor teeth opening against the cut she made. He jolted, gasping, eyes blinking clear. She let him go and he brought a hand to his throat, bewildered.

She grabbed his wrist and lifted his other hand. His nails were long iron claws. He frowned, flipping her grip over so the bone knife was visible.

"We don't need the Vulture. The blood mage will do," she said.

He ignored her. "Where did you get that?" he asked, voice low.

Parijahan shoved between them and startled him. "We're going north," she said shortly. "Stop wasting time."

Rashid loped after her. Kostya followed without looking at Nadya.

"Did that hurt?" she asked, trailing the blade over his forearm. A muscle in his jaw fluttered. She carefully slid the tip of the blade down against his inner arm, parting the smallest sliver of flesh. Blackened decay bloomed up his arm from the point of contact.

He hissed through his teeth, yanking away. His hand moved over the cut. "What is that?"

Nadya ran her thumb down the flat of the blade. She hadn't really considered it since Pelageya had given it to her, but now that it was in her hands, Malachiasz's blood dripping lazily down the edge, she could feel how *alive* it was. How it had tasted his blood and wanted more.

"A relic, I think," she said thoughtfully.

There was a decided wariness to the way he kept his hand over his arm, a frown tugging at the tattoos on his forehead.

"How does one kill a Vulture?" she mused.

Genuine hurt flickered over his face before it shuttered away. "Ready to finally kill me now that you have something that might do the deed?"

"Did you think my other threats were false?"

"Nadya, it's hard to be truly frightened of your threats when your Kalyazi *voryens* are merely an inconvenience."

She regarded the bone knife in her hands. "But this might . . ." she murmured.

"You would kill me so easily," he said, a tremor in his voice that Nadya wasn't expecting. He failed in hiding how truly wounded he was by her thrill at finding a weapon that could harm him.

"It wouldn't be easy," she whispered. "Even though it should be."

He shook his head and started after the others. She was slow to follow. She hated this.

"If you're going to complain the whole time, monk," she heard Malachiasz say in his thickly accented Kalyazi when she finally caught up, "the army is right there. Go cry to them."

Kostya snapped. He lunged for Malachiasz, who merely sidestepped, grabbed his arm, and wrenched it behind his back.

"Let's put the past behind us, shall we?" Malachiasz said amiably. "I am, of course, rather put off by how you've been treating our dear cleric here, but I don't want to involve myself in your petty religious squabbles."

Kostya looked murderous. His gaze caught Nadya's and before he dropped it she saw something she was too hopeful to believe was regret.

"I will kill you," Kostya practically growled.

"You tried that and ruined a perfectly good shirt," Malachiasz replied dryly. He winked at Nadya. The tension between them dissipated now that he had a new target. "Cut it right through the chest."

"You tried to stab him?" she asked incredulously.

"I *did* stab him!" Kostya said. "He's unnatural, Nadya."

"What a bleeding revelation!" Malachiasz said. He dropped Kostya's arm and kicked him, knocking him to the ground. He stepped on Kostya's back. "And a vast understatement. We don't have to get along, you and I, and I'd prefer if we didn't, but if you try anything like last night again, I will kill you and then Nadya will be cross with me."

"*That's* an understatement," Nadya said.

"See? And then no one will be happy. If you wish to go, *go*. If you're going to stay then work out your fanatical zealotry soon, please, so the rest of us can get back to trying to stop this blasted war."

Nadya knelt down and smoothed a hand over Kostya's hair. "Kostenka, for the sake of the friendship we had—*have*—I can't continue with this," she gestured a hand between them, "whatever this is."

Malachiasz took his foot off Kostya's back. Parijahan huffed, irritated, and started walking. Nadya waved the others away. They would catch up. Malachiasz stared at her before loping off after the Akolans.

Nadya sat down next to Kostya. She rested her cheek on her fist and sighed.

"I know, all right? I know it doesn't make sense that Malachiasz is here. I am sorry for what you suffered at his hand. But, Kostya, we're not in the monastery anymore. Things aren't as simple as us versus them."

Kostya lifted himself to his knees and spat out a mouthful of dirt.

"But things are as simple as good and evil."

"Are they?" Nadya thought about the voice, about her dreams filled with monsters. She wasn't so sure anymore.

The desperate way Kostya looked at her was a stab to the heart.

"I'm sorry," she said. "I'm sorry I'm not who you thought I was. I can't fathom what you've been through and you can't do the same for me. But Malachiasz was right. You can leave. I won't hold you to me. I got you out of the Salt Mines but there's no debt to be repaid. I missed you, Kostya. Every day since the monastery fell I thought of you. I never imagined that I would have you back alive. But . . . ." Her hand lifted to her neck and fell when there were no prayer beads to hold on to. Kostya winced. "If our paths have led us apart, I won't force you to remain around him."

"But—" Kostya's voice wavered. "You're choosing him?"

Nadya stared at him, uncertain what to say and knowing she had to do it fast. The voices in the distance were growing closer.

"When you are a half-divine, half-mad creature who can get me through the Dozvlatovya Forest to the Bolagvoy temple, then we'll talk," she said, bumping her shoulder against his.

"That's not what I'm talking about," he muttered.

"I know," she said quietly. "But right now, that's all there is. I need to set my path to rights and I need him to do that."

"That doesn't make any sense."

She shrugged. "I needed him to get to Tranavia to kill the king and I need him now. It doesn't make sense, but that's the way it is."

He let out an agonized sigh.

"I'm done sitting here, trying to convince you when there's a skirmish at our backs." She stood up. "If you choose to leave, I understand. If you want to come . . ." She shrugged ruefully. "I would like that, Kostenka. I don't expect you and Malachiasz to get along. Hells, I don't get along with him. But I do think it's worth listening to the Tranavians sometimes."

Kostya scoffed.

"The whole reason this war hasn't ended is because no one will listen to each other," she finally said. She turned to catch up with the others. "Though Malachiasz really isn't worth listening to on a good day. Such a heretic."

The journey was strange. Nadya couldn't shake the constant feeling that they were being watched. Like her, Malachiasz was perpetually on edge, jumping at every shadow. At least Nadya hoped that was why. She didn't know how she would pull him back a second time.

It was for him to pull himself away from becoming the monster, and she wasn't certain he wanted to.

She avoided him as they traveled, sticking by Kostya, who was making an effort to remain civil, thankfully. It was exhausting enough to be around Malachiasz, who mostly spent his time with his head buried in his spell book. Nadya was curious to know what he was trying to figure out, but sensed she wouldn't like the answer. Things settled into a fragile kind of peace. This journey would be a long one, and they all seemed to recognize that constantly biting at one another was only going to make it insufferable. It was almost comfortable, almost like the journey from Kalyazin to Grazyk, a lifetime ago. Nadya and Malachiasz's arguments never spiraled past trivialities. Kostya had cooled and seemed to enjoy Rashid's company.

Nadya knew it would never last, and that the only reason things weren't growing worse was because they were pushing their pace so hard that they were all too tired to fight.

But passing into Kalyazin from Tranavia was like breathing fresh air for the first time in months. The moment Nadya was back on Kalyazin soil something inside her settled and came to rest. She relaxed.

She didn't want to call it hope, but it was good to be home. Even if the world was falling apart.

But it was so *cold*. It should be summer already. How would anyone survive? The monastery had always relied on what little they could grow in the perpetual chill of the mountains, and what Rudnya donated to them, but for the rest of the country things must be growing desperate. This would be a killing blow for Kalyazin, never mind the war.

There was a monastery in Takni'viyesh, nestled within the woods. From there, a long stretch of forest cut through the heart of Kalyazin, leading up to the northwesternmost point they were trying to reach. It would be unwise to make the journey all the way through the forest—especially with the eyes of once sleeping monsters upon them.

Nadya had only seen flickers out of the corner of her eye. The antlers of a *leshy*. The cut of black cloth and singular, gleaming eye of a *likho*. And other, darker creatures long shunted away into myth and fable that Nadya knew with growing certainty weren't so false.

But the monastery was a bastion of calm in the midst of the dangers of the forest. High wooden walls surrounded the complex, and yet, as they advanced, Nadya grew inexplicably terrified.

Would this monastery feel like home? Or would it feel alien and strange to the person Nadya had become? This was a very bad idea, she suddenly decided.

Someone leaned out over the top of the wall as they drew closer. Kostya squinted up, an odd look on his face.

"Is that—"

He didn't have the chance to finish as the figure disappeared. The gates opened shortly after. Nadya glanced at Kostya, confused.

A giant of a man with a long graying beard, sharp, dark eyes, and brown skin strode out past the gates. He wore a sword openly at his belt.

"Oh," Kostya murmured. "Ivan Novichkov."

Nadya blinked, bewildered, as the man approached them. She knew the name, but it was a vague recollection coming from far away, from before.

"I was going to ask your business but now I see two faces

I have not seen in many years," the man said, his voice unexpectedly warm.

Kostya clearly wasn't as confused as she was. Had she met this man before? Why couldn't she remember him?

He inclined his head to the monk. "You know us?"

"From Baikkle, yes?" The man's gaze trailed back to the others, sharpening slightly on Malachiasz before he returned to Nadya and Kostya, who nodded. "Impossible to forget the only Kalyazi who lives what I've spent my life studying."

Nadya blinked. Ivan bowed slightly to her. "Nadezhda."

"Have we met?" she asked.

"My wanderings took me to the Baikkle Monastery many times," he said. "But you were very young. You did not grow much taller."

Kostya laughed. Nadya's heart clenched at the sound. Here was the boy she grew up with, found once more at the walls of another monastery.

"And what companions do you travel with?"

"Oh, a strange group," she said, formality kicking away some of her nerves. "We seek the monastery's aid and shelter."

Ivan nodded as if she needn't even ask, calling over a sister and instructing her to heat the bathhouse for the travelers.

"Brother Ivan," she said, moving forward, voice low. She hesitated. She had to warn them of Malachiasz, but she didn't know how this monk would react. "One is Tranavian."

His countenance did not waver. Though Kostya's face darkened and he rolled his eyes.

Ivan gave Nadya a wry smile. "So I see. And how did little Nadezhda come to be the traveling companion of a Tranavian? Are we not at war, child?"

"We are. It's a long story."

"I should like to hear you tell it."

Nadya nodded encouragingly to the others as members of the monastery came to take them to eat and rest. Malachiasz immediately shot to Nadya's side.

"I don't think—" he started in Tranavian before he broke off, glance flicking from Ivan to the monastery. "I don't think I can go inside."

Nadya grabbed Malachiasz's arm, pulling him away.

"It's hallowed ground, Nadya, I can't—"

"You'd have to believe in the gods to believe hallowed ground is a real thing," she said.

The desperate look he gave her said that he didn't think now was the appropriate time to be making jokes or picking a fight about theology.

"What do you think is going to happen?" she asked.

He shook his head. "I don't know—I just—"

"So, you're saying that grand plan of yours worked and you're some god?" she said, voice low enough that no one would hear her.

"No, blood and bone, clearly that I'm *here* means it didn't work, haven't you picked up on that yet?"

He blinked rapidly, anxious, fingers picking at his cuticles, the skin around his thumbnail welling with blood. When a cluster of eyes opened up at his cheek, her stomach dropped. They were rimmed with . . . teeth.

*He's getting worse.*

"I'm sure the gods are waiting for a better time to strike you down," she continued.

He glared.

"Can you hide that?" Against her better judgment, she reached up and touched his cheek near the eyes.

He flinched. She dropped her hand.

"Doubtful, but I'll try," he said, covering the spot. He

snapped his hand back down, yelping. His fingers were wet with blood.

He looked horrified.

"Did your own face just bite you?"

He made an odd, strangled sound, nodding slowly.

"Go," she said, before she did something regrettable and made this worse.

The trembling energy around Malachiasz quieted as he cooled to jagged pieces of ice. "There is no reason I have to follow you there."

She reached out, taking his hand. He tensed. "You'll be fine," she said softly, pressing her thumb against the base of his palm. The same way she had when they had first arrived in Grazyk and he had seen the Vulture's cathedral. But that had been a lie. Was this a lie, too? "We'll talk when we're inside. I promise."

She had been avoiding him. And it had been the wrong move. Push him hard enough and he would be gone and she would have no way to get to the mountains. He had been a perfectly good teacher in how to manipulate and she wasn't above using his own methods against him.

He so clearly did not want to go inside but she nudged him toward a sister waiting to show him into the monastery and he went. She returned to Ivan, who was watching Malachiasz.

"Darkness clings to him like a shroud," the monk said quietly.

"Ah, yes, that's the Tranavian, and he's a strange one," Nadya agreed, totally ignoring how she had just been given something very near to an omen.

She also ignored the look the monk gave her. At least she wasn't being blithely ignorant. She was well aware of what Malachiasz was. Kostya was watching him, as if waiting to see if Malachiasz died on the spot once he stepped past the threshold.

"I would like to hear what has brought you to this corner of Kalyazin," Ivan said.

Could she talk to this man, trust him? He was blindly trusting in her because she was the cleric, but she couldn't remember him. She had barely admitted to Kostya what had happened to her, could she truly tell another Kalyazi the truth and expect them to listen without judgment?

"I don't have a particularly happy story to tell you," she said, voice soft.

Ivan wasn't deterred. "We do not live in particularly happy times, Nadezhda, but I should like to hear it. Go with Sister Vasilisa, we will talk later."

Nadya waited until Kostya left, not wanting him to be the one to tell Ivan who Malachiasz was. Kostya clearly knew what she was doing because she was on the receiving end of yet another of his dark looks as he entered the monastery.

"Not a happy story at all," Nadya muttered, before she went off with Vasilisa.

# interlude iv

## TSAREVNA

## YEKATERINA

## VODYANOVA

Katya wiped the Tranavian's blood off her hands with some measure of disgust. She almost felt bad about the whole affair, especially knowing there was a pair of Tranavians waiting at the inn who almost certainly knew the king and she would have to deal with them. But it had to be done and she did like the dramatics of it all.

"You're just going to leave him down there?" the priestess of the small church, Pavlina, asked.

Fyodor's scarred face was as impassive as ever.

"If he doesn't come up in a few hours, he's dead. Do with him what you will," Katya said, drying off her hands. "He's probably fine, though, and should stagger out of here in about an hour."

Pavlina pursed her lips, disapproving.

"I'm not going to tell anyone that your church still has an altar to the old gods underneath it, and you're not going to tell anyone that I tested a theory and carved open the king of Tranavia's chest in your basement," Katya said.

"*Vashnya Delich'niy . . .*"

"It's *fine*."

"If you make this war go on longer because you had a theory, the gods will never forgive you."

"The gods," Katya said, shrugging on her coat, "have let this war go on for too long as it is, so I honestly can't say I'm too concerned about their forgiveness."

That earned her another disapproving glare; she would probably have to make an awkward confession later. Not here, perhaps with a different priestess. She had terrorized this one quite enough. She'd wait till she was home. *Told off a priestess in the middle of nowhere! Carved open the king of Tranavia! Had a grand time, ultimately.* Dionisiy, her priest back home in Komyazalov, would not find it as amusing as she did.

She left before she could say anything else to make the priestess pray harder for the *tsarevna*'s obviously damned soul. She had to face those two damn Tranavians anyway. She had received the report of her soldiers dragging them in from the woods right as she'd entered the church and she was simply not in the mood for more Tranavians. Katya had read enough military reports to know what the pair who shadowed the king looked like; it wasn't a far leap to assume these two were here with him.

Katya thought she'd had her heart's fill of dramatics for the day, but when she returned to the inn and went to the room where they were keeping the Tranavians, she slammed in, shouting, "The king is dead, long live the queen!"

She enjoyed the horrified silence that followed maybe a little too much. But then the boy's shoulders slumped in a truly ag-onized way and *there* was a pang of regret.

"Only kidding! He should be fine, if a little banged up. You're with him, right?" She kicked the door closed, ignoring her guard Milomir's protests. They had taken the Tranavians' spell books; she wasn't really in danger here.

The boy exchanged a glance with the girl. "We were search-ing for him, yes. What did you do to him?" There was an un-dercurrent of anger in his tone, but mostly he just sounded worried. He was pretty. Dark skin, long eyelashes, an edge to him that made her think, if the king was truly in danger, he would be the one she should worry about.

"Oh, no, I'm still asking the questions here," she said, tak-ing a chair and sitting down, immediately kicking it back onto two legs so she could rest her legs against the side table.

The Tranavian girl was perched on the bed. She was *also* pretty. Pale, with one gorgeous eye focused in on her. If Katya wasn't trying to make a point she might be flustered.

"Letting your king wander off by himself while in the middle of enemy territory isn't particularly wise," she noted.

They both appeared as though they hadn't slept in a very long time. As if they had been riding very hard over a very far dis-tance. Katya frowned. Had they *lost* him? She was intrigued—by Serefin, but mostly by the god that had him in its clutches. How did *that* happen?

"Has he been acting strange lately?"

"Sorry, who are you?" the girl asked.

"Oh, was the—" Katya pointed at the door. "—introduction not enough? My name is Yekaterina, Katya to friends—"

"Are we friends?" the girl asked.

"*Are* we?"

"Ostyia," the boy said, his voice edging on disapproving.

"*Tsarevna* of this frigid horror show at your service." Katya affected something close to a bow without getting up or dropping her feet from where they were propped on the table.

The Tranavians exchanged a glance.

"Anyway! Serefin! Acting weird with that strange eye? Yes?"

"Yes," the girl, Ostyia, said. She wasn't wearing an eye patch over her scarred eye socket and her black hair looked like she'd hacked it off herself with a dull blade.

The boy—Kacper, if her reports were correct—frowned, then crossed his arms over his chest and leaned back against the wall next to the window.

"Interesting. Since he was killed by his father, yes?" Katya asked.

Kacper flinched.

Katya waved a hand. "We have good spies and you *slavhki* are rumor mills."

"Why are you asking?" Ostyia asked.

"I'm not a *slavhka*," Kacper muttered.

Katya tucked that little tidbit away. "He's the one who blundered into *me* with all that strangeness swirling around him. I'm just trying to figure out if it can be useful."

"Useful for what?" Kacper snapped.

Well, he was certainly the more hostile of the two.

"I would like this war to end as much as anyone else. But," she allowed, "I don't have that power."

"But your father—"

"My father will not accept a truce. He will accept surrender and nothing more," Katya said. "We are risking invasion from the Aecii in the north with each year this war continues, but," she waved a hand, "victory or death." She paused. "Gods, I didn't just tell you that."

"Where is Serefin?" Kacper asked.

"By the time our conversation is over, he'll be here. He's not dead—well, he's probably not dead. If I'm right about any of this, he's not dead."

Kacper stiffened.

When Katya had first set eyes on the king of Tranavia, what was most apparent was that there was something wrong. She had heard the rumors that the Meleski heir was a drunkard—and he had certainly been drunk or was trying to be when she arrived—but there was more to it than that. His eye held the touch of the gods. She wanted proof, and proof was what she got. And maybe if she killed him here it could end the war, but Tranavia had their Vultures and those were becoming a growing problem with each passing day. The Black Vulture *had* to die to stop that order and if the Tranavian king wanted him dead, Katya thought maybe they could come to an understanding.

The king arrived not much later. Milomir practically shoved him inside. His shredded shirt was hanging open, showing the—rather excellent, if she did say so herself—job Katya had done on his chest, blood and dirt streaked against his face.

He let out a whimper at the sight of his friends, stumbling and nearly collapsing. Kacper was across the room in a heartbeat, clutching Serefin's arm and keeping him steady. Serefin paused, pressed a hand blearily against the side of Kacper's face, and stepped back to turn on Katya. He had a knife in his hands.

"Oh, silly me, I left that behind, didn't I?"

"What. Did. You. Do?" he ground out through gritted teeth, the blade at her throat.

She studied his face. The thing was, none of the rumors their spies had brought them from Grazyk made any *sense*. She was hoping the ritual would shed some light on what had happened but she still wasn't sure.

And he knew the cleric somehow! Katya had been searching for her with little success for *months*.

She looked at him intently. His eyes had gone that strange midnight blue with shattered stars instead of pupils.

"Velyos, huh?" she said. "You've been caught by a fallen god."

Serefin blinked.

"Most don't even know who he is," she continued.

"But you do," he said flatly.

"I do."

Serefin grimaced. He considered her, his hand absently resting over the carving on his chest. "This hurt, you know that?"

Katya shrugged. "I'm sure you've had worse."

"He's had worse," Kacper said.

Serefin shot him a wounded look before slowly tucking the blade in his belt.

"What do you want?" he asked.

"End of the war, riches and fortune without having to work for it, the admiration of as many pretty people as possible?"

He moved to gingerly sit at the edge of the bed next to Ostyia.

"I think the war is the least of our problems," she finally said, growing serious. "If I could sit here with you and end this damned war right now, I would. But neither you nor I have the power to do that."

"I mean, *technically*, I have that power. Blood and bone, don't ask me for a truce," he said with a groan. "I'd been trying for months to get you people to listen to me without success. This isn't on me."

She shook her head. Katya had no power and the mere fact Serefin was in Kalyazin meant he didn't have nearly as much power as he should. It would be pointless for them to kill each other here even though the idea of killing the king of Tranavia was still so *very* nice to think about. Katya liked dramatics, but she didn't really like murder. If the latter led to the former, that was acceptable, but killing the rightful king of Tranavia in a tiny Kalyazi village tucked at the edge of the Dozvlatovya reach wasn't particularly dramatic.

"Why are you out here?" she asked.

He leaned back on one hand, very plainly not wanting to answer. She could wait him out too if she needed.

"Velyos?"

He nodded slowly. "And you?"

That was a harder question to answer. Officially, Katya had been sent to the front. In reality, she had been sent to a military encampment that saw no action. It was *boring*. And with the rise of the Vultures, the order she had joined at thirteen as a curiosity was suddenly useful and not boring at all.

"I follow whatever promises to be the most dramatic," she said, winking at him.

Disgust crossed his face. A hard one to win over, this Tranavian.

"Kalyazin can't survive this winter," she said, sighing. "Something tells me Tranavia can't, either."

Serefin glanced at Kacper who slowly shook his head.

"I didn't think so," Katya said softly. "I was hoping to figure out why this was happening, and I have a feeling you might have an inkling."

"Not really," Serefin said. "I'm sure you don't want to hear my theories that it's your gods causing this."

Katya frowned. That didn't make sense. It did, however, sound like a deeply Tranavian theory.

"Something happened with the Black Vulture on the day my

father died," Serefin said delicately. "It was all his plan, ultimately, and what we suffer now is his doing."

"I don't understand."

Serefin grinned, but the smile didn't really reach his eyes.
"What happens when a monster tries to become a god?"

Ice coursed through Katya's veins. "Did he succeed?"

"Well, that's the thing. How are we to know?"

"And you want to kill him?"

"I think we have to."

Katya's hand went to the necklace at her throat. She had
fought a number of Vultures, but most were in the past few
*months*. Once, the Vultures were nothing more than tales *ba-
bas* told to keep children frightened and in their beds. Go to
sleep or the Vultures will take your blood and unlike the blood-
drinking *kashyvhes* they'll take it all and leave you dry.

"Is he in Kalyazin?" she asked, almost afraid to know. She
had faced these monsters countless times but there had always
been whispers about the Black Vulture. And they had grown all
the more terrifying when this new one had taken the throne.
This one hungered in a way the last had not. This one had committed atrocities on a scale that they had never seen before.

"Not only that, but it's altogether likely he's with your cleric."
He rubbed at his scarred eye. "Can you tell me about Velyos?
What he wants? I can get nothing out of him except a cryptic
pull to the west I'm struggling against."

Katya was intrigued. This had just become far more interesting. She might even say there was potential for it to be exceedingly dramatic.

"Wait, do you know what he's planning?"

"Who, Malachiasz?" Serefin shrugged. "He wants to kill a
god."

Her heart skipped a beat. "What does he think that will accomplish?"

"Feels fairly obvious to me. The gods won't meddle with Tranavia if they're dead."

Katya swallowed hard, her mouth suddenly dry. "That will destroy your foolhardy little country if he succeeds."

He paled. "What?"

"The gods work outside of time. A slow death, meticulous. Retribution is not swift, it's little fatalities all in a row. If he were to incite that kind of war—topple that kind of empire—the retribution would not be quiet, it would be complete destruction." Katya closed her eyes. It would bleed into Kalyazin. The whole world would crumble under the wrath of the gods.

"If we're going to do this, I need some wine," she murmured.

"Oh, blood and bone, me, too," Serefin muttered.

Katya grinned, kicking her chair farther back and opening the door. Milomir was going to kill her. "Be a dear?" she asked sweetly.

He sighed deeply.

When he had returned with an all-suffering expression and a carafe of wine and cups for them, Katya was sufficiently prepared to begin.

"The world forgot, you see, they all forgot. Velyos was cast out a long, long time ago. The Codex was stripped of all reference to him and the others."

"Others?" Serefin asked.

Katya had forgotten she was speaking to a Tranavian. "There were more, many more. The twenty we have now were not always the twenty that have been with us. Velyos, Cvjetko, Zlatana, Ljubica, and Zvezdan." She paused, then allowed,

"Chyrnog." But she didn't want to talk about an elder one. The fallen gods were enough.

Serefin frowned and leaned back on one hand. Katya was overly aware of how intently the Tranavian girl was watching her. She took a sip of wine to hide her blush.

"What happens to gods who have been cast out?" Ostyia asked.

Katya shrugged. "They're known as the fallen. It's said they were trapped by the clerics of the gods who remained." But that was the wrong question to ask. "*Why* were they cast out, eh?"

Serefin rubbed his eye again, confused. The way he fiddled with his eye was starting to make her twitchy.

"What happens when gods decide to directly interact with the mortal realm? What happens when they fight amongst themselves to the point that it spills over into our world?"

"Disaster?"

Katya nodded. "Even so. The war would be the least of our concerns, because they would no longer be bound to treat carefully with mortals. They would burn us to pieces to get what they wanted."

She studied the sheer disbelief on his face. If he was truly dealing with Velyos, how could he still be holding on to that?

"You don't believe me."

"It sounds ridiculous, you have to understand that."

"Your eyes are the most inhuman things I have ever seen and there are moths in your hair. Do you know what moths symbolize to the Kalyazi?"

He shrugged.

"Twofold. They are of the gods and they are of death."

He cringed.

"Also *kashyvhes*? Which is a little odd, and probably less relevant here. Threefold, then, I suppose."

Serefin took a deep drink of his wine.

"The what?" Kacper asked.

"*Striczki*," Serefin said flatly. Blood drinkers.

"Was that a joke?" Ostyia asked him quietly.

"I don't know," he muttered, shifting forward to rest his elbows on his knees. Serefin looked ready to collapse. "He told me he wanted revenge, but he refused to say more than that."

Katya's breath caught in her throat. "There are two gods that Velyos would want revenge on, and it does explain why he did not attempt to claim our cleric. One is Marzenya, the other Peloyin."

Serefin's eyes narrowed.

"The five who were condemned were constantly trying to usurp Peloyin's power," Katya continued. She had grown up on stories of petty battles between the gods, but mentions of Velyos' tricks were few and far between until eventually he disappeared altogether. It took her a long time to put the pieces together. Really she had only done it out of sheer boredom and a desire to be as willfully difficult for her priest as possible.

She had never thought this esoteric knowledge would be *useful*. Especially not with regard to the king of Tranavia.

Especially not in . . . helping the king of Tranavia? Was that what she was doing? As much as her brain revolted against the idea, she wondered if this was what she was supposed to be doing. Something had led her to this specific spot in Kalyazin; *something* had kept her here waiting, as if some part of her had known the king would eventually show up.

She didn't particularly want to think about the potentiality of the gods guiding her actions, though, because then she would have to confront all the many things she had done that would damn her in their eyes.

"Of the fallen, Velyos was the most vindictive. It was called an eternal war, that which raged between Velyos and Peloyin. Marzenya was the one who finally cast him out; she had him bound into a pendant of iron that was locked in a vault beneath the earth."

"So, it's not only revenge he wants," he said slowly.

"Unlikely. He wants it to start again. War eternal. And not this holy atrocity we're trapped in, but one between the gods. I'd wager he wants you to wake the others."

Serefin blanched.

Katya didn't like where her thoughts were leading her. If Velyos wanted this boy to wake the others, well, most were potentially survivable.

But no one would survive the return of any of the elders.

# 23

## NADEZHDA

## LAPTEVA

**Svoyatova Nedelya Ojdanic:** *As a young girl, Svoyatova Nedelya heard the voice of Vaclav and entered the dark woods near her village. She never returned, but when her village was attacked by Tranavian forces, a leshy moved the woods and consumed them. This is thought to be at her influence.*

—Vasiliev's Book of Saints

The bathhouse was glorious for Nadya's tired bones. After, she dressed in clean, plain clothes. She shoved her handful of prayer beads in her pocket, braided her hair and coiled it behind her head, and felt, for a moment, like everything was going to be perfectly fine. She was *herself* again.

The feeling ended as soon as she found Brother Ivan in the monastery's nave. She slid onto the bench beside

him and looked up at the iconostasis. Her heart wrenched, loss threatening to swallow her.

This was to be an act of confession, but still she hesitated. She didn't know if she could trust Brother Ivan. She admonished herself at the thought; she shouldn't be protecting a Tranavian at the expense of her own people.

But what about protecting herself?

"I don't know where to start," she finally said.

"The beginning is usually the best place," Ivan replied amiably. "Nadezhda," he sighed, "you were but a child when I saw you last. I know you do not remember me, I don't expect you to. It's all right. I would simply like to help you, if I can."

Nadya let out a rush of breath. "I have made so many mistakes."

Nadya was living with so many lies and half truths and she could not maintain them all or she was going to crumble under their weight.

If only she could hide away and never let it slip that she had failed; that she had committed heresy; that there was a hole in the world because of her and it was only going to get worse. So much was her fault and she didn't know if she could stop any of it. Marzenya demanded complete and utter dedication and she had failed her, she had failed everyone.

But he was right, she could start at the beginning. Her words grew halting as the story drew into the capital of Tranavia. As she charmed a prince she should have killed and fell for a boy who made terrible jokes and, in hindsight, was a little too willing to help.

Ivan listened in comfortable silence, asking no questions, letting Nadya pause and consider when the story got to places that were dark and hard to remember.

But she was careful; she did not say what Malachiasz truly was.

"What matters is this," Nadya said, edging away from the heresy of falling for a monster—even if she had been burned for it—and toward a very different kind of heresy. "While I was in Tranavia, there was a veil over the kingdom that almost totally cut off my access to the gods. It was blood magic. A spell that had been on the country for decades, refined by the Black Vulture to be even stronger."

She explained working past the magic. Explained the *Rawalyk*. Being kidnapped by the Vultures and siphoned for blood because the king of Tranavia was going to turn himself into a god.

This was where she got a reaction from Ivan. A pursing of his lips. Alarm.

"When I was in Tranavia, I saw . . . things . . ." Nadya didn't know how to explain that part. The monsters Velyos had shown her and told her were truth. The nightmares that still plagued her every night that she ignored and tried to forget. The knowledge that something had broken, but she didn't know what.

"I committed heresy and now the gods are silent. I do not know if they hear my prayers. The only magic I have is what I am able to draw from within and using it feels like poison. I thought I could stop the war. But . . ." She shook her head.

"And there's this," she said, clutching her hand. "I don't know what I've done and I'm scared."

And now the monsters of Kalyazin were stirring. Monsters that had slept far longer than those in Tranavia. Monsters kept at bay by faith alone. It meant a cataclysm.

Ivan contemplated her hand. Silence grew and stretched between them, and Nadya sunk further and further into despair. This was truly the end. This was the thing she would burn for.

EMILY A. DUNCAN

He finally broke the silence. "There has been a disturbance in the heavens," he said slowly, "that the priests have not been able to discern. You have given us part of the answer."

"Will I be excommunicated?" Nadya whispered.

Ivan's cool fingers were underneath her chin, tilting her face up. The monk was unreadable and Nadya shivered with fear.

"You were always a curious child, Nadezhda. Full of questions. Full of trouble. But you are the only cleric walking Kalyazin today," he said. "We do not know why the gods have not touched any others. We do not know why you have been touched the way you have. Perhaps this means a change is coming, one we are not prepared for. I do not wish to make you relive past hurts, and I do not see any sins worth dying for in your past."

Nadya blinked, releasing a startled laugh even though she wanted to cry. "The gods might differ with you, and I feel like their opinions are more important." His absolution gave her little comfort. And she didn't understand how this old monk could know her so well. "Did you come to Baikkle often?"

"Often enough, but that was a long time ago. When poor Alexei—"

A pang in Nadya's chest. Alexei was gone now.

"—had a godstouched child dropped on his doorstep and knew nothing of magic, he asked for my help."

"But you knew—know?" Nadya straightened.

"I know as best as one can who does not experience it fully."

She flexed her fingers. "I don't think I understand magic," she said quietly. And the only person she had to teach her was a wildly condescending Tranavian boy who saw it all as something to be controlled.

"Is it for us to understand divinity?" Ivan asked. He paused, peering at her face. "But you're right, I see you have not grown any less curious."

"Is the nature of divinity so fixed?" she asked.

"Seeing a man try to become a god and fail would draw up those questions, I would wager."

"He didn't fail."

Ivan went very still.

"The king failed, yes, but someone else did the ritual and succeeded."

"And?"

She shook her head, gazing at the iconostasis. It was ornamented with gold leaf and the impassive expressions of saints. "Maybe, if the gods spoke to me, I would have answers, but I don't. And they don't like talking about the nature of divinity anyway."

"Magic and divinity are two very different things, intertwined into reality. Can you have divinity with no magic, as magic is bound in divinity?"

"But you can have magic without any touch of the gods," Nadya said. "Are the Tranavians not proof of that?"

Ivan inclined his head. "And it is heresy. They are doomed for it."

*They most certainly are.* But not, Nadya thought, in the way that the Kalyazi were expecting.

But what of Pelageya and her words that Nadya's power wasn't being drawn from within at all but from *something else*? Curiosity about Tranavian magic was one thing; she couldn't very well ask this monk if he knew about witch magic.

"So, you think this is still some working of the gods?" she asked, flexing her fingers.

Something flickered on Ivan's face. "What else could it be?" he asked kindly.

What else, indeed? It would be so easy to take his answer as truth and turn away from this, ignoring what was happening to her, even if it was to her own detriment. She didn't *want* to uncover some dread magic, she wanted this to be simply another avenue of the gods' punishment. That would be easily understood.

She wasn't satisfied, but her weary heart didn't want to fight.

"What of the Tranavian?" Ivan abruptly changed the subject.

Nadya sighed. "Malachiasz," she whispered.

Ivan nodded. "It took convincing to get him inside. Are Tranavians so afraid of the truth?"

"I-I want to trust you the way Father Alexei did. The way I know I should. But if I am to tell you, I need you to swear to me that Malachiasz will not be harmed. I defied my goddess's orders to keep him alive and I live with those consequences. But he must not be harmed. I need him. If I'm to fix anything, I need him."

Ivan's bushy eyebrows drew together.

"Please, Brother Ivan, please swear."

Slowly Ivan nodded. "So long as he is under your protection, he shall not be harmed, I swear."

She did not comment on the loophole he had included in his phrasing.

"Who is he, Nadezhda?"

She hesitated. She didn't want to disappoint anyone else.

"Tranavia's Black Vulture."

Ivan's face remained perfectly blank.

A war battled within Nadya as she fought with separate pulls. To find Malachiasz and run from this place, or to let Ivan kill him and end her problems right there. She almost bolted when Ivan stood up without a word and walked out the door.

Nadya rose to her feet so fast she nearly sent the bench flying. "You swore, Brother Ivan!"

Ivan flagged down one of the sisters. "Where's the boy? The sickly looking one?"

She dogged Ivan's heels as they followed the nun to one of the cells. Malachiasz was pacing the room when the door went flying open. He froze, eyes wide at the sight of the giant monk in the doorway. He saw Nadya and relaxed a fraction.

He had cleaned up. His hair was already drying in a thorny tangle. If the sisters had offered him clothes, he had refused them, instead wearing a black tunic embroidered with red blocking on the cuffs and leggings.

He stared at Ivan for a beat, and Nadya watched as his entire demeanor shifted. The anxious boy was closed away and the Black Vulture returned in his place. The cold and calculating and utterly cruel parts of Malachiasz that were the cult leader.

"That didn't take long," he said. The look he shot Nadya wasn't betrayed, but it was fairly close.

She winced.

"What do you hope to gain by coming here?" Ivan asked. "What destruction do you plan to wreak?"

"Do you think I care for a monastery in the middle of nowhere in Kalyazin?" Malachiasz caged his heart with long, pale fingers. "I am here because she is here, nothing more, nothing less."

"Come," Ivan said gruffly to Malachiasz.

Malachiasz glanced at Nadya, gaze hooded. He had counseled kings. He could handle whatever Brother Ivan wanted. She touched the back of his hand as he passed. He jerked in surprise before catching her fingers as they slipped by.

Nadya watched him go, terrified of the way her heart started to mend at the hope in his eyes at that careful touch. This was a mess. And Brother Ivan hadn't given her what she wanted. She wanted *answers*. When they disappeared from sight, she went back to the nave.

It was quiet as she knelt before the altar.

She nudged the dark thread of magic within her, white flame lighting at her fingertips. It was really all she could do. She lit a bowl of incense. The smell of sandalwood swept over her and she breathed in deeply, sighing. She carefully took her prayer beads out of her pocket and laid the ones that were on a string in front of her. She lined up the rest.

She chewed at her lip and eyed the iconostasis, searching until she found Marzenya's icon.

*I'm not sure why it feels right to try again here. Something about being out of that godsforsaken country? I don't know. Wait. This isn't how I wanted to start this.* Her prayers sputtered to a stop. She scrubbed her hands over her face. Something that was once so natural to her now felt awkward.

*I'm sorry. I know that's not enough, but I don't know what to do.* She rubbed at the scar on her palm. *Was Velyos telling me the truth?*

"Oh, child . . ."

Nadya sucked in a sharp breath. Her fingers scrambled for Marzenya's bead but she didn't know where it was in the mess of beads in front of her. She bit back a sob.

*I don't understand what's happening,* she prayed. *I thought I was doing what I was meant to. I didn't see his plans.*

"Didn't see them, or didn't want to?" Marzenya's voice was severe.

*Both,* Nadya admitted.

"And how badly, truly, do you want to make this right?"

*I'll do anything.*

There was a long silence and Nadya started to panic.

*"The boy is inconsequential. A creature to be eradicated, but no more."*

*But—*

*"There is another. Rising from the dark, given power on your mortal realm. You spoke with him. He is waking one by one those we cast aside for the sake of this realm's safety and the worst begins to stir. You released him."*

*Velyos.*

*"Cast aside, but he is not alone, darkness never works alone."*

*But what about—*

*"The ritual?"* Marzenya's voice was biting. *"A maggot trying to become a dragon. Pathetic. He has caused a shiver, a crack, yes, he toys with powers no mortal should possess and you allowed it."*

*I didn't know how to stop him.*

*"Lying to me is unwise."*

Nadya rolled the bead around in her fingers, thinking.

*"You have failed and must be punished."*

Nadya's hands began to shake. She lowered her head.

*"But there is much left to accomplish,"* Marzenya continued. *"So much left to be done and you are still my vessel on this world."*

Nadya swallowed hard. She pressed her thumb against the scar on her palm. The black veins had grown, swirling about her wrist. She wondered what would happen to her if they continued all the way to her heart.

*I was traveling to Bolagvoy. I wanted answers . . . Why did you stop talking to me?*

*"Continue on that path. We will speak again."*

Marzenya was gone. Nadya tasted copper. She spat out a mouthful of blood onto her hand.

# 24

## SEREFIN

## MELESKI

*Ground underneath the heels of their betters and cast down
from the heavens, confined in tombs, under mountains,
in waters. They are the silenced. They are the dead. They
know the chosen is coming to free them one by one by one.*

—The Volokhtaznikon

Being spat out of the jaws of a monster was, unsurprisingly, not a pleasant experience. Serefin had woken up, feeling like every part of his body was bruised down to his bones, and immediately choked on a mouthful of blood.

He'd blinked quickly several times, willing his vision to sharpen, but even blinking hurt. Like daggers had been driven through his eyes, too. He'd felt strange, *different,* jittery and wrong. He didn't know what had happened once he had been dragged through those doors. His memory cut off disarmingly in a way that terrified him.

He didn't know what he had given up and was afraid of what would happen when he inevitably found out.

And now he was back in the Kalyazi inn and *Kacper* was here and he had missed Kacper and Ostyia so much. Katya had taken her leave to figure out with the scar-faced man what she would need to kill the Black Vulture.

Serefin tipped backward on the bed until he was lying down. He closed his eyes, knuckling the bridge of his nose. He ached and his head was pounding. He should be moving west, and he was so tired of fighting.

"Serefin, you look positively disgusting," Ostyia said, flopping back onto the bed beside him.

"Fitting, because I feel positively disgusting," he replied. "That girl did not give me enough wine."

Kacper still hadn't spoken outside of that initial greeting and Serefin was trying to not worry about it.

Ostyia made a small distressed sound. Her hand, fingers cool, gently touched his neck. He had forgotten about the scar.

"Has that always been there?" she asked, voice small.

He grunted, noncommittal. He sensed that, yes, but there had been some magic keeping it from notice until Velyos had shattered it.

"Your throat was cut."

"Yes, well, I *did* die."

She was quiet. He didn't open his eyes.

"You didn't ask but I will get you more wine because I am magnanimous and I missed you," she said after a long stretch of silence, her voice raw and full of an emotion Serefin wasn't currently equipped to handle.

Serefin opened his eyes and grabbed Ostyia's wrist as she was sliding off the bed.

"I'm sorry for what I said."

She paused. "You haven't been yourself," she said. "It's no excuse—at all—if you talk to me like that again, *I'll* cut out one of your eyes. I thought about it, though, and you're right, I push too hard sometimes."

"I do deserve it."

"You absolutely do, but I've forgotten that your role has changed and mine has, too, and I can't exactly rib you in public and expect that nightmare of a court to still respect you after it."

"It will be so boring without you ribbing me in public."

"Somehow, I think you'll survive."

Kacper was still looking out the window. Serefin wasn't so certain Kacper agreed with her easy forgiveness. She patted his hand before she left the room.

Serefin sat up with a groan, raking a hand through his hair. He needed a bath. He needed clothes that weren't these to wear. He needed to feel like he wasn't about to crumble into dust but unfortunately he didn't think he would make it to that point.

"Kacper?"

Kacper turned slightly to glance at Serefin, one eyebrow raised. Well, kind of. He wasn't very good at that.

"I lost my pack and have been in these clothes for far too long," Serefin said. "Can I borrow some from you?"

The tension at Kacper's shoulders lowered a notch. Weariness sketched across his face and he nodded.

Serefin stood up as Kacper began digging through his pack. This wasn't normal—this strain between them. He had been just as cruel to Kacper as he had been to Ostyia and maybe Kacper wasn't as forgiving. Kacper had a lot of siblings; he liked to hold grudges.

"Kacper."

No response. Kacper pulled a shirt and breeches from the pack and set them on the bed. "Kacper, I'm sorry—"

"Blood and bone, Serefin," Kacper said, straightening and sounding exasperated. "You're hopeless."

And then Serefin was knocked back against the closed door and Kacper had his face between his hands and was kissing him.

Oh.

*Oh.*

Serefin's hands worked without his brain—that was still thirty seconds behind and static with shock—grabbing the lapels of Kacper's jacket and tugging him closer. A single, piercing instant and everything made *sense.* Every time Kacper had stayed behind to pick drunk and incoherent Serefin back up and drag him back into camp without anyone knowing the High Prince wasn't dealing well with the war. Every time Kacper had sat in his tent and listened to him panic ceaselessly about his father and never once been anything but attentive.

He'd thought Kacper was just a distressingly kind person who had no business being around someone as delightfully wretched as Serefin.

But Kacper kissed him with a kind of reckless, passionate abandon borne of desperation.

*Maybe I missed a vast number of signals.*

Kacper broke away. His expression was soft and he was close enough for Serefin to see the scar that nicked his eyebrow. He pushed back a lock of Serefin's hair from where it had flopped over his forehead. "You are so bleeding dense, Serefin."

He had definitely missed some signals. "I am?" Serefin asked breathlessly. "Do that again."

Kacper grinned and shifted closer, hips pressing against Serefin's in a way that made an odd sound leave Serefin's throat. He kissed him again, gentler, softer. His hands tangling in Serefin's hair, his mouth moving to kiss a line down his jaw.

"You are," he said when he'd pulled away and left Serefin feeling unbalanced against the door. "Also you are very filthy and your eyes are ghastly."

"I'm afraid to ask," Serefin said. He tilted his head back and leaned it against the door. "So, er, how long, then?"

"How long, what?" Kacper asked.

"Please."

Kacper grinned sheepishly and it took everything in Serefin to not yank him back and kiss him again. His heart was rattling in his chest in a most distressing way as he contemplated all of the lost time that could have been spent doing *this*.

"I'm going to get a bath drawn for you," Kacper said, sounding flustered. He went to move Serefin away from where he was in front of the door, but Serefin held his ground.

"Kacper, how long?" he repeated, voice low.

"Blood and *bone*," Kacper murmured, lifting his eyes to the ceiling. "A long time, Serefin."

"Then why . . . now?"

Kacper sighed. "Because you were gone. Because Ostyia and I couldn't find you and none of our tracking spells would work and it was like you had just *disappeared*. And then you were in *Kalyazin* and it was so far away and I was going to lose you and you would never know how I felt." He smiled wryly. "Because I kept having girls shoved at me when we got to Grazyk and I want it to stop."

"That wasn't nice?" Serefin asked innocently.

"I don't like girls, Serefin," Kacper said, exasperated, but that was rather his default tone with Serefin. "You know that."

"I do?" Serefin didn't, in fact, know that.

Kacper frowned. "I thought you did. You know Ostyia doesn't like boys."

"Ostyia makes sure everyone knows she doesn't like boys,"

Serefin said. He peered at Kacper, who was making every effort to avoid eye contact. "Ostyia," he continued carefully, "flirts with any girl that crosses her path. It's hard not to notice. She is almost definitely down there flirting with Katya. It's not like I've ever seen you flirting with any particularly pretty boys."

"Because I spend all my time trying to get the attention of one particular boy," Kacper said. He winced. "Please don't panic about this."

"I'm panicking a little, but in a good way, I think," Serefin said. "Maybe? I don't know."

Kacper groaned. "I just thought—with you and Żaneta—I thought—I never said anything because I never saw you with *anyone* and because of Żaneta I didn't think it was possible."

*Kacper is the one panicking,* Serefin thought idly.

"I liked Żaneta before the whole treason business," Serefin said with a shrug. "I've never cared one way or the other about anything like that."

Kacper's dark complexion was strangely sickly. "I shouldn't have done that. You're not supposed to kiss the king."

"If I take the signet ring off, will that help?"

"I'm going to hit you."

"You're not supposed to hit the king! I still have my ring on!" Serefin lifted his hand.

"Take the ring off and just be Serefin," Kacper said.

Serefin did and tucked the ring in a pocket of his jacket. "I'm always just Serefin," he said. "I think that's the whole problem."

"It's never a problem," Kacper replied.

"We're in the middle of nowhere Kalyazin and the *tsarevna* is downstairs and I think we just became allies with her? I cannot see how my being *me* and taking the throne hasn't been a massive problem."

"You were going to have problems with Ruminski and the

rest no matter when or how you took the throne. How many *slavhki* did your father have to execute when he took the throne?"

Serefin leaned back against the door. "Half the court," he said softly.

"Keep going," Kacper urged.

"My grandfather was lenient but only because he sent most of the court to the lake country. Before that at least a quarter of the court was executed."

"How many *slavhki* did you reprimand or execute when you took the throne?"

*None.* Serefin was quiet.

"I wanted to be better," he said. All he wanted was to be a better king than his father, but what if that was impossible?

"Ser, you're not a particularly nice person. I know you don't want to make these hard and messy decisions, but you *can.*"

No one had called Serefin by that nickname in a very long time and his heart gave a jolty kick at hearing it.

"You're so much less nervous when advising me about murder," Serefin noted.

Kacper laughed. "I'm fairly good at advising about murder."

"You're fairly good at the other thing, too."

Kacper smoothed a hand over his tight black curls, supremely flustered. Serefin grinned at him.

"Does this mean . . . What does this mean? I never expected to get this far. Everything always gets murky from here on out because I've always assumed you would rebuff me."

"*Kacper.*" Serefin groaned. He thought about how Kacper had been in the midst of the *Rawalyk*, how Serefin was always putting himself as close to Kacper as possible as if a part of him knew, even if the rest of him didn't.

He took Kacper's face between his hands. Kacper was tense,

as though he thought Serefin *was* going to outright reject him after all this.

"I have an ancient Kalyazi god rattling in my head and you have chosen the absolute worst time to do this," Serefin said. "And blood and bone, I'm glad you did."

Kacper nearly collapsed with a helpless wheeze of a laugh. Serefin kissed the side of his head. "We've never been good with timing," he said, thinking how when they'd met, Kacper had just had his arm broken by Ostyia.

"I'm going to go see about that bath," Kacper said, reluctantly tugging away.

"You're not my servant. You've never been."

"See, I knew this would happen. You're mistaking someone who is forced to do things for you to earn a wage for what Ostyia and I do, which is thankless work because we care about you."

Serefin frowned. "I'm not that bad, am I?"

"I haven't made a habit of merely telling you what you want to hear—contrary to what you might think in light of the accusations leveled against me—"

Serefin scowled. Kacper smiled.

"I'm not about to start now. You're an absolute menace, Serefin."

"Ah."

"Wouldn't have you any other way," Kacper continued as he finally got past Serefin and opened the door.

"Well, a bath does sound nice."

"You should probably . . ." He frowned, brushing his thumb across Serefin's cheek. "Your eyes."

Serefin cringed and moved to the mirror as Kacper slipped out of the room. His right eye now matched the left, a deep midnight blue with no pupil. Instead, points of light like stars swirled in the impossible depths.

It was unsettling. Ghastly was definitely a word for it. Serefin sighed. This was just one of many terrible things to look forward to from his devil's deal.

# 25

## NADEZHDA

## LAPTEVA

*Peloyin is a god of great benevolence, of great anger, of great storms. He can send the waters of life or the fires of destruction.*

—Codex of the Divine 355:23

Nadya slid onto a bench in the refectory beside Malachiasz. He studiously ignored her, tension coiled across his thin shoulders. She stole a piece of warm black bread off his plate and chewed on it while inspecting her hand in the bright, natural light streaming in through the windows.

He slid his plate over. She wasted no time in drawing her *voryen* and carving out a hunk of *tvorog* and slicing a withered radish into bite-sized slivers. It had been so long since she had eaten anything that wasn't stale bread and thin cabbage soup and admittedly had gotten a little spoiled with Grazyk's finer fare before they left. But she had missed the simple food of the monastery all the same.

He leaned his cheek in his palm and watched her. "You didn't have to say anything to the monk," he finally said.

"He deserved to know what he was allowing inside the walls," she replied evenly. She poured herself a cup of *kvass*. After a thoughtful pause, she poured one for Malachiasz.

"Fair enough," he said. She heard a calculation in his tone.

"Upset your act at the gates didn't work?"

"You think so little of me," he said.

"That is entirely your fault."

"Blood and *bone*, Nadya, just tell me to leave. You don't want me here, fine, I understand. Let me go if you want me to go."

Nadya picked at the table with a fingernail on her corrupted hand. It was sharper than before.

"I finally spoke with Marzenya," she said, and felt his little jolt of surprise beside her. Because *gods* even though she was supposed to be keeping her distance they were still sitting close enough for their shoulders to brush. "She was so dismissive of you." She reached past him to pick up a withered apple and cut into it. "*A maggot trying to become a dragon,* she said."

Malachiasz frowned.

"You don't understand how relentless her orders were. How frequently I was told the very many ways I could—and should— kill you. Everything I ignored, because for some reason, I wanted you alive."

"For some reason," he repeated, voice flat.

He wasn't looking at her anymore and she flipped her *vo-ryen* around and used the hilt to turn his face toward hers.

"I don't want you to go. But *you* betrayed *me*," she reminded him. "You are the leader of a cult that has been tormenting my people for generations and I cannot be so foolish as to overlook that a second time."

He studied her face, then pushed her knife away and turned

on the bench, putting his foot up on it as a barrier between them.

"If I had killed a god don't you think you would *know* by now?" he snapped, voice low. "If I had done anything that would save my country from your peoples' fanatic torches, don't you think it would have happened?"

"No," she said simply.

He shot her an incredulous look.

"You played a long game that led me on a string for months."

"To arrive at an end that would help Tranavia survive this blasted war, except Kalyazin has pushed all the way into my country. I played a longer game than even you know and it *failed*. Nadya, I failed."

And even though the evidence of his failure was before her, that he was here at all implied he hadn't reached the state he thought he would, she could not believe him.

But what was divinity? What was this power he was trying to reach and was it possible? It wasn't for her to know the genesis of the gods and yet *and yet and yet.*

"What have you done to yourself?" she asked quietly.

"I haven't slept in months," he said, sounding wretched. "I remember some things from when I was . . ." He trailed off. "Like that. But only pieces. You're right about other things, too. I am the monster you spoke to in the Salt Mines. There is no *me* and *it*. It's only me. I am the horror you kissed on an altar made of bone. It's all just me."

Nadya flushed horribly, grateful he had said the last part in a whisper so quiet even she had barely heard it.

"You thought letting your gods into Tranavia would destroy it, I know that. You were willing to do it, no matter how much I tried to show you it wasn't the way." His voice was lowering and fear flooded through Nadya.

"Nadezhda Lapteva, I know so many things." His hands were tipped with iron claws and he stroked the back of one down her cheek. "The end of the king and the veil wasn't the end of anything. It was only the beginning. And now your goddess will use you to create a reckoning that will swallow everything."

Nadya shook her head slowly. Marzenya was a vengeful goddess, but Nadya had her own will and she didn't want Tranavia destroyed. Quieted, but not destroyed. Not anymore.

She shifted slightly, her blade resting a hair from his ribs. His lips quirked to one side in a slight smile.

"I will not let Tranavia fall," he said softly. "Not even if I have to go through you to save it." He studied her face. "You will need magic of your own, magic you are *willing to claim,* if you hope to continue toying with powers beyond your comprehension."

"Why are you still here, Malachiasz?"

"I am curious. You've asked me to help."

He was too willing to help, *again*. But . . . what if he was making amends? She hated this impossible cycle she had been caught in. He eyed her for another minute before getting up and leaving the room. Nadya set her *voryen* down onto the table and rested her head in her hands.

There was no one she could go to for help. She couldn't trust Malachiasz, but she already knew that. She was uncertain of Marzenya, whose silence had only left her confused about what she had seen in Grazyk.

She feared what was happening to her. She feared what Malachiasz was planning.

Claiming the dark well of power terrified her beyond belief. And she was afraid how, despite everything—despite her anger, the frustration—she couldn't stay away from him; she couldn't tell him to go. The thought of losing him was devastating. It shouldn't be. She shouldn't care.

But she did.

Maybe it was worth the risk of another betrayal—maybe it was worth the risk of knowing *she* was inevitably going to betray him.

Or maybe she should be forgetting all of this.

She tried to place the pieces of what she knew together and they didn't paint a coherent picture. She was still sitting in the refectory when Kostya entered, looking better than she had seen him in days.

He hesitated when he saw her, but slid onto the bench across from her. He was clean, the bruises on his face from the Salt Mines had finally healed, and his hair had been cut short, Veceslav's symbol shorn into the side. To see it cheered her. She missed Veceslav.

"*Dozleyena*," she said.

He gave her a wry glance. But it was so very much like the old Kostya that relief spread through her.

"How are you holding up?"

She shrugged. He sighed and after a pause placed both of his hands on the table. She hesitated, then slotted her fingers in his.

"It's hard," he said, "to realize that I couldn't be there when you needed me and thus you had to make choices no one should ever have to make."

"Don't blame yourself for what I've done. I knew what I was throwing myself into."

He shook his head slightly. "I was supposed to help you. I *wanted* to help you. Instead I was locked up in that hellhole with those monsters. I felt useless, *weak*, and I took my frustration out on you. I apologize."

"You have every right to be upset with me. I don't expect you to understand my decisions."

"I hate that Tranavian with everything in me," Kostya said bluntly. "I hate that you care for him."

She looked down at their hands, his tightened on hers.

"But you're my best friend. I'm not letting him ruin that."

Nadya wasn't certain she deserved this grace from Kostya. She smiled weakly. He rubbed his thumb over hers.

"Do you want to go to Mass?" he asked.

"I really do."

Kostya paused. He studied her closer, then stood up and waited for her to follow, and when she did he pulled her into an embrace.

Struck once more by the way he smelled like home and how near to tears that brought her, she clutched at him for a tremulous moment.

"I want us to be friends again," she whispered against his shoulder. "And I'm scared that it's impossible."

He leaned back and cupped the side of her face in his hand. "We never stopped, Nadya." He gently kissed her forehead. "Come."

Kostya would never understand what had changed within her. But he had also changed. He was quieter, no more constant talking and teasing. Solemn and far more pious. She couldn't begin to fathom what he had suffered in the Salt Mines. And she didn't begrudge him for trying to kill Malachiasz, the gods knew she'd had the urge often enough. She couldn't really begrudge him of any of the things he had done. She was in the wrong here. She just didn't know how to claw her way out of the mess she had made for herself. She couldn't make her heart stop with its traitorous pull to a monster.

"It's nice, isn't it?" she said, following him out into the courtyard. "Being back in a monastery. I missed it." She wanted nightly prayer, to mold into the day-to-day schedule of the monastery, a pattern her body longed to return to, as familiar as breathing.

"It is nice," Kostya agreed. "You could stay, you know," he said after the briefest hesitation.

"You know I can't," she said, hooking her arm through his.

"I don't, Nadya. It sounds to me like you've done everything expected of you."

She screwed up her face. Why didn't it feel like enough, then?

He cast her a sidelong glance. "You always were one for glory."

"I don't know what you're talking about," she said primly.

"My *divine calling*," he said in an uncanny mimic of her voice.

She shoved him, laughing, knocking him off pace. "It's true, though!"

"But it doesn't have to be true forever," he said, his grin fading to seriousness.

Nadya wasn't naive—well, as naive as she used to be. She knew what Kostya was trying to say. But it wasn't just a matter of saying, *Yes, when all this divine nonsense is finished, I'll find a nice monastery and live quietly ever after.* Making that kind of promise was only tempting fate. She had tasted something *different* outside the monastery walls and she wasn't ready to give it up yet. She wasn't ready to leave Parijahan and Rashid. She wasn't ready to leave her country and that of her enemies to a never-ending war.

She wasn't going to make him a promise she couldn't keep. So she shrugged.

His expression twisted before he smoothed it out and nodded.

A fracture of Nadya's soul began to heal during the service.

She wasn't home, but it *felt* like she was. No matter what happened, the routine liturgy of the Divine Codex would always be the same. Some things would never change, even if she did.

She wasn't expecting her goddess to pipe up in the middle of the service.

"*I did not abandon you, child,*" Marzenya said.

Nadya stiffened, heart lifting. Kostya shifted next to her and she ignored him.

*Then what happened?*

"*Tainted magic, poison. I have been trying to return to you, but the others cannot, not yet.*"

Nadya frowned. Did she mean Malachiasz's magic? It would make sense if Marzenya's absence was his fault, but it didn't quite explain everything else.

"*You thought the Tranavians were finished with their atrocities? They have only begun.*"

Malachiasz had said this was only the beginning. Nadya shivered. She received another nudge of concern from Kostya.

*What do I do? Continue west?*

"*Continue west,*" Marzenya confirmed. "*This is no longer a matter of Tranavia's heresy. Something must be done to stop them totally.*"

Nadya pursed her lips, wary. *I don't want them destroyed. I won't aid in their annihilation.*

"*Destroyed? I said nothing of destruction. No,*" Marzenya said, a gentle croon in the back of Nadya's head. "*Our tactic must change. We'll make them see Kalyazi might. We'll show them why they should lay down their arms.*"

This, Nadya liked the sound of. This could bring an end to the war without the total destruction of a country Nadya had come to appreciate, even as she abhorred their practices.

*What do I need to the west?* Nadya asked.

*"A way to reach the others. You cannot do this on your own, my blessed child. You must come to the west, taste of divinity, and show the heretics their time has ended."*

Nadya's resolve hardened. The plan wouldn't have to change. For all Malachiasz would know, she still needed to get to the temple in the west. He would never have to know what she was doing.

Marzenya was right, what she had accomplished was not enough. Tranavia would keep reaching, keep searching, until they had what Malachiasz wanted—complete and total dominion apart from the gods.

*"We will end this once and for all."*

Nadya smiled ever so slightly. Once and for all.

# 26

## SEREFIN

## MELESKI

**Svoyatovi Nikolay Ostaltsev:** *Spoken of only in whispers, fragments of broken text that speak of a boy blessed by Veceslav and ruined by the monstrous Vultures of Tranavia.*
— Vasiliev's Book of Saints

Serefin didn't really sleep anymore. At night, everything he had tucked away for the sake of his own tenuous sanity returned. The stone temple and its massive doors. The many, many hands reaching for him.

It was easier to stay awake.

It made it easier to fight the losing battle of the pull to the west.

One day he was going to wake up and find himself miles away like before. He couldn't stay here; he had to leave.

He must have fallen asleep, though, because he woke up halfway down the hall of the inn, to Kacper pulling him back to their rooms, clearly worried.

"Not again," Kacper said, and took his hand as he pulled him along.

Serefin rubbed his free hand over his face. Again? Right. He gently tugged away from Kacper, not wanting it to seem purposeful. There was a strange feeling at the back of his neck, like he was being watched, like whatever it was that was holding on to him was merely waiting to take him.

*"I thought you had stopped fighting. Struck a deal, you and I. Don't force my hand, I can make things worse for you."*

Serefin ignored Velyos.

*"It would be a shame, wouldn't it? Mortals are so fragile. All it would take is one Kalyazi deciding there are too many Tranavians here. And my assurance the Kalyazi blade finds that boy's heart."*

No. Serefin had stopped walking and Kacper was looking at him with tired puzzlement. Sleep softened his edges, his shirt hung open, and Serefin wanted to bury his face against Kacper's neck and hide from all that his cursed eyes were showing him. Serefin covered his left eye instead. Everything was fine. The corners of the world were no longer bleeding. He still had one. But he had lost the other, completely.

*"Do you think you can so easily be rid of me?"*

Serefin couldn't keep fighting.

*If I do what you ask, will this end?*

*"I certainly won't have any more use for you."*

Serefin swallowed. He very carefully lowered his hand, readying for the shift in his terrible vision. It was becoming hard to know what was real.

He took Kacper's hand and squeezed before letting go. "I'm fine," he said, a little too forced.

Kacper's eyes searched his. But he simply sighed and returned to his pile of blankets on the floor.

*"They are no longer scattered, you see,"* Velyos hissed. *"Once*

*they were bound into objects, tucked into tombs. But there were those still faithful. They took the pieces to Tachilvnik. There they wait the touch of someone whose magic can set them free. There they wait for a reckoning."*

*If all you need is a blood mage,* Serefin said dryly, *you really didn't have to choose me.*

"I wanted the girl," Velyos snapped. *"Having the girl would have righted so many wrongs. I waited for so long until I was finally in her hands but your infantile father cast that spell and sent out a call I could not ignore. You'll do. You're desperate enough, you see. And we're not alone anymore, you and I."*

Serefin couldn't breathe. He needed to get outside. He leaned over the edge of the bed, checking that Kacper had fallen back asleep.

His heart squeezed painfully. He wanted to smooth the dark curls away from Kacper's forehead. He *wanted* to crawl down beside Kacper and tuck his face against Kacper's shoulder, to feel *something.*

He slid back out of bed, careful to be silent. Kacper slept light.

He shivered. What else would he do while he slept?

He made his way down to the inn's common room. Two of Katya's soldiers sat at the doorway, playing a game using a wide array of differently shaped tiles. One looked up when Serefin approached.

Serefin lifted his hands. "I'm unarmed and I only want to go outside. I don't know what orders your *tsarevna* gave you—"

"You can leave," the one said with a shrug. "Can't guarantee a villager won't put a blade in your back, though, once you're out there."

He let out a long exhale. Everyone knew, then. Katya's general lack of interest in taking advantage of having the king of Tranavia held captive would not extend to other Kalyazi. The soldiers looked like *they'd* like to put a blade in his heart as well.

Serefin couldn't even blithely pretend the Tranavian noble they should be mad at was his father. He had done terrible things to their people during this war. He would do them again. He wasn't here to play nice with Kalyazin. It was the Kalyazi's fault he had their gods rattling around in his head.

This was the *entire reason* for this bloody war. Anger coiled deep in Serefin's core and he pushed through the door to the inn and into the darkness.

It was the damn Kalyazi and their damn gods and he had been *fine* before all of this. He had been *fine* when all that was required of him was victory on the battlefield and slaughtering these backward people. And Tranavia had been so close to victory. They had been so close and then the missive had come from Izak Meleski that ordered Serefin to the Baikkle Mountains because of rumors a cleric was hiding there.

He should have ignored the missive. Burned it. It wouldn't have been the first time one of his father's messages was "lost." Serefin had turned battles to Tranavia's favor by ignoring his father's orders; this war would be over if he had done it that day.

But he had wanted to see the cleric for himself. He had wanted to know if this girl the Kalyazi clung to as their hope and savior was real.

And then . . . disaster.

This god had wanted *her*. Could he be convinced to leave Serefin and go torment her instead?

*"It doesn't work like that, boy. You are always so quick to run from your demons."*

*Oh, is that what you are?*

"*That would be too easy.*"

Serefin was careful as he moved away from the inn, the soldier's warning hitting a little too close. There had to be a way of breaking this connection without destroying himself. He didn't want to turn to the *tsarevna*, but if anyone could help it would be the princess with the knowledge of the esoteric.

The carving on his chest suddenly ached with a pointed fierceness, and he covered his left eye as the world's distortion grew even darker.

"*No more fighting, child.*" Serefin nearly passed out. It was the new presence. The lingering darkness. The one who prowled the edges of a forest scattered with bones. The one Serefin had been desperately hoping would not deign to speak to him.

"*There are powers at play that you cannot stop,*" the voice continued. It was deep and grating, bones splintering, a landslide consuming everything in its path. "*If you do nothing. If you don't act. What will the gods of your enemies do?*"

Serefin leaned back against a tree. He shouldn't have let Velyos lead him into the forest, but he only had a shred of control left and it was taking all he had to keep his hand over his eye; to keep the horrors locked there. His hand trembled.

*You are my enemies' gods,* he said. It was petulant, but he couldn't help it.

"*You are so simple. One day you might find your home crumbling because everything it has used to build itself up has disappeared. Those gods you hate so much, beings you turn to.*"

The taste of copper filled Serefin's mouth. The thought was abhorrent. He had fought too long for his cause; he *believed* in it.

*Never.*

"*You misunderstand. You would not have a choice. All it would*" take is one simple action, by someone with enough power to take away a single choice and change this world forever."

Serefin frowned. He almost lifted his hand away from his eye.

"The girl. You tracked her down once and she escaped. Now you must go under the guise of friendship."

I thought you wanted the Black Vulture dead.

"You do not need to understand how the pieces in this game are being moved. You cannot see. You cannot understand how vast this is, just how insignificant you are. I want many things, boy, and you have given yourself to me so I might take them. Stop the girl, kill the boy, or you will lose more than you can imagine."

Serefin closed his eyes. This was going to destroy him.

# 27

## NADEZHDA

## LAPTEVA

**Svoyatova Maruska Obukhova:** *Only a young girl, Maruska prophesied the death of Tsaritsa Milyena and was burned at the stake for it. Tsaritsa Milyena died of a snake bite a mere hour after Maruska.*

—Vasiliev's Book of Saints

Nadya slipped out of the cell she had been given and onto the monastery grounds. She was restless to move on, and a dull, unceasing ache in her hand wouldn't allow her to think about anything else, much less sleep.

The night air was the painful kind of cold she knew well, the kind that settled deep in her bones, with a permanence to it she had almost missed while in Tranavia.

She walked up to the wall's ramparts, settling her elbows between the gaps in the wooden spikes that lined the wall.

Hushed voices pierced the dark. Across the ramparts,

Nadya could make out Parijahan's tall form leaning over the wall. Malachiasz's lanky sprawl was recognizable sitting at her feet, his back against the wood.

She hated the twang of distrust that pulled in her chest. They had been friends before Nadya crashed into them, and while she knew for certain she couldn't trust Malachiasz, she also wasn't entirely certain about Parijahan, who had her own moral code that didn't align with Nadya's pragmatism nor Malachiasz's sheer disregard.

Nadya didn't know what game Parijahan was playing and it worried her.

"Oh, so no one is sleeping."

Nadya jumped as Rashid leaned against the wall beside her. He watched Parijahan and Malachiasz before turning to Nadya.

"What are they up to?" Nadya asked.

Rashid shrugged. "Parijahan is worried that someone from her Travash will track her down."

"The Travash are like royal families, right?"

"A simplistic way to put it, but yes. Her house has held power in Akola for the last three generations, which, for Akola, is a very long time."

"Are you from a different house?"

"That is also more complicated."

"Enlighten me," she said, shifting slightly closer to Rashid's warmth. He moved, wrapping an amiable arm around her shoulders.

"You mean you *don't* know Akola's long and delightfully convoluted history?" He pretended to be shocked.

"My education was rather specialized."

He smirked. "It used to be five countries. Tehra, Rashnit, Tahbni, Yanzin Zadar, and Paalmidesh. All very different cultures, very different languages. I'm from what was once Yanzin Zadar, Parijahan is from former Paalmidesh. Her people are closer to . . . well, Lidnado, if we're thinking in borders. Mine are closer to the middle of Kalyazin."

"Those are opposite ends of the country," Nadya said.

"Indeed. The Travasha were an attempt at unification that—" He paused, searching. "—mostly failed. The three richer countries have worn down the others as the families wrest power from each other any chance they get."

Nadya considered that. "So, what we call the Akolan language?"

"Is mostly you foreigners being rather dense."

She snorted.

"It's Paalmideshi. I truly don't expect any of you to know this. You're rather busy up here in the north. Our squabbles aren't really of the world-ending variety."

"Understatement of the century, Rashid."

He chuckled.

"So, how did you and Parijahan meet? You never said."

His face fractured and smoothed. "There was a debt my family needed to repay. I worked in her household."

Nadya could hear the things he wasn't saying. A whole world of stories the scribe wasn't yet ready to tell. She wouldn't press him. She knew part of Parijahan's story and part of Rashid's. That was enough for her.

"I'm still not quite sure how Parj and I found our way into this mess," he said softly. "But I'm glad we stumbled our way to you."

"Flattery will get you everywhere, Rashid," Nadya said dryly, but he winked at her, his usual irreverence laced with sincerity. "Do you ever miss it?"

"Akola? Yes. Though, I don't really have much left there. My sister is happily married and my parents died of an illness that nearly took half of Irdistini with it. I was in Paalmidesh when that happened."

Nadya leaned her head against his shoulder. "Well, I'm glad you're here."

"I could do without the near-death dramatics myself."

Parijahan eventually made her way over to them, leaving Malachiasz sitting on the ramparts, his head tilted back as he gazed up at the sky.

"Is he all right?" Nadya asked as Parijahan ducked under Rashid's other arm.

"No," Parijahan replied.

Nadya sighed. She worked her way out from under Rashid's arm and crossed the ramparts. Malachiasz didn't move when she leaned against the wall next to where he sat.

"*Dozleyena, sterevyani bolen,*" she said quietly.

"*Czijow, towy dżimyka.*" His eyes were closed and his lips tugged into a small half smile.

She dropped her hand into his hair. A strange tug of power momentarily canceled out the ever-present ache in her palm—before Malachiasz reached up and twined his fingers between hers.

*Odd.*

But she didn't pull her hand away. Their argument in the refectory had made her realize she was tired of pretending she didn't want him near. If she was going to betray him in the end, would it make it worse if she let him in—just a little—or better? Had he wrestled with these same feelings when plotting to betray her?

"Ow." She shifted her palm away from his, the ache becoming a sharp pain.

Malachiasz frowned in concern.

"There's nothing to be done, don't look at me like that."

"Sit," he said, a gentle plea.

She hesitated, but sat down, back against the wall. "You're not going to be able to fix it."

"Does it hurt now?" He was still holding her hand but his palm was cradling the back of hers, fingers twined together.

She nodded, biting her lower lip. He rolled her sleeve back and she shivered as the cold hit her skin.

He smiled, thumb tracing the line of her arm, and dipped his head, kissing the inside of her elbow. Her breath caught, eyes closing as he trailed his lips down the sensitive flesh of her inner forearm. He kissed her wrist and she was fairly certain her insides flipped completely upside down. Then, very carefully, he pressed his mouth to her palm.

Everything inside her lit up. Her hand moved to his cheek so she could yank him to her. She kissed him hard, gratified by the startled noise he made, how his hand wrapped around her side and pulled her closer.

"It's yours," he said when they broke apart, warm breath mingling in the frigid night air. His pale skin flushed, pupils blasted out. He was painfully human. He kissed her again, tugging at her lower lip with his teeth in a way that *burned* through her.

She had to force herself back. To pass through the haze and focus on what he said. His mouth looked bruised in the moonlight and it only made her want him more.

"What is?"

"The magic pooling in your hand. It's your power."

She shook her head, confused, lifting her hand between them.

"Then why is it doing *this*?" *Why does it hurt?*

His eyebrows tugged down, pulling at the tattoos on his forehead. "I don't have it all figured out yet, but I think it might be because you're rejecting it?" His voice dipped up hopefully.

Pelageya had said Nadya was drawing power from somewhere else, but even she hadn't known what that meant. Now Nadya said as much to Malachiasz, and he frowned. He tucked her against his side where it was warm, and continued to inspect her hand. Their breath steaming out before them in the bitter cold. His slender hands were red, and she was starting to miss her glove.

"What changed?" he asked, after the quiet had grown comfortable between them.

"Nothing," she said, wrapping and unwrapping a lock of his hair around her finger. *Marzenya wants me to topple Tranavia and I can't bear to keep shoving you away because I'm going to lose you for good,* she thought. *Because I haven't told anyone the stories about the forest and crossing the border is going to destroy you.*

He shot her a dry look.

"I don't—I don't know, Malachiasz. I don't know how to fight this." That was the truth; she could give him that, at least.

He made a thoughtful sound. He was only half listening.

"It feels like your power but *different*. Darker. Like it's you but also something else."

"How can you tell?"

"I've always been able to sense magic. Everyone's magic feels unique to them."

She had been avoiding her hand, but as she leaned her head against his shoulder, she studied it. The black from the scar twined around her fingers in inky vines, pouring down over her wrist to taper off like veins on her inner arm. Her fingernails very nearly like claws. She waited for the sick feeling to overtake her but there was only curiosity. She wasn't the same girl horrified by every monstrous thing.

"What does my power feel like?" she asked.

"When it's you, or when it's one of your gods?"

"Is there a difference?"

He nodded. "It feels distorted, when it's their power. Yours feels . . ." He trailed off, considering. "Warm, bright, but not necessarily with light because there's always been a thread of darkness. Like a fire in the center of a blizzard."

*Darkness?*

"This feels like *you,* not like you're channeling something. What if you used it? Stopped fighting it?"

"You can't explain this part," she said, wiggling her fingers at him. "Until I know it's not going to kill me, I'll pass."

"What's life without a little experimentation?" he asked lightly. His grip on her hand shifted so he was holding it again.

The way he looked at her made her want to flee. But mostly she wanted to press into his warmth and kiss him. And she hated that she was trapped in this place of wanting him far away and close all at once.

He coughed, burying his face in the crook of his arm, an uncomfortable sounding rattle in his chest. There was blood on his sleeve when he lowered his arm.

She rested her fingers against his chest. "Are you all right?" she whispered.

He leaned away from her and spat out a mouthful of blood, his face contorted. He let out a ragged breath.

"You know not to worry about me."

"Not to interrupt." Rashid's voice drifted over from the other side of the ramparts. "But we have company."

Nadya blushed and buried her face in her hands. Malachiasz

grinned wickedly at her, kissing the side of her head before jumping to his feet and leaning over the wall.

*So much for distance.*

"This is a nightmare," she muttered. It took her a few seconds to collect herself before she stood.

"I *am*," Malachiasz said as Nadya leaned over the wall next to him.

"Please don't make me want to toss you over the edge more than I already do."

He glanced down dubiously. "Oh, I'd survive that."

"Pity."

"Why is your heart's desire defenestrating me?"

"There hasn't been a single window involved in this."

"Semantics."

"Gods," Rashid said to Parijahan. "You owe me so much money."

Parijahan sighed.

There were spots of light dancing within the dark forest that could only be torches. "Oh no," Nadya whispered.

"Place your bets," Rashid said. "Tranavian or Kalyazi?"

Neither option was good. Malachiasz shivered. Whatever spell he had used to mask the shifting plane of his face slid away.

"Tranavian," he said, voice bleak.

"How can you tell?"

"There's a Vulture with them." His voice tangled around sharp iron teeth, eyes darkening.

Nadya's *voryen* was in her hand, the blade flat against his cheek as she turned his face down to hers.

"If you let yourself fall, can you bring yourself back?"

He gritted his teeth before nodding once. She hoped he was telling the truth. She was fairly certain he was lying.

"The Vultures still want you, Nadya," he said. "They want the potential that can be unlocked with your power."

"So why didn't they take me in the Salt Mines?"

He shot her a blank look and pointed at himself.

"You think you're very important," she said primly.

"I am *incredibly* important," he replied, vaulting over the wall and disappearing.

"He's also incredibly stupid," Rashid said dryly, peering over the wall.

"This monastery is fortified," Nadya said with a sigh. Large structures made of sharpened logs lined the wall, traps that would be sprung only by blood magic. "He's not impaled himself down there, has he?"

"No," Rashid said. "He's fine."

"I hate him."

Rashid dashed off to alert the monastery. Nadya watched the lights in the distance, a nervous calm settling over her.

"Should we run?" Parijahan asked.

Nadya shook her head. "I ran last time. I won't run again."

This monastery was far more prepared for an attack than Nadya's home. There was no need for tolling bells; those would have alerted the enemy. The Kalyazi knew they were there.

A woman joined the girls on the ramparts, her gaze dismissive until she recognized Nadya as the cleric.

Nadya wished she could tell her to expect no miracles from her.

"How's your aim?" the woman asked Parijahan.

"Good."

She tossed her a crossbow and a pouch of bolts. Malachiasz returned, black feathery wings vanishing into twin splashes of blood against his torn coat back as he landed on the ramparts. He slammed a hand over one of the sharp points of the wall, blood coating the wood under his palm. Nadya watched him carefully; it was taking too long for his eyes to clear. A cluster of eyes flickered open and closed down his cheek before they shivered away. He removed his hand, grimacing.

Nadya supposed that was as effective a method as any for him to drag himself back to clarity.

The Kalyazi woman's face had gone white as a sheet, her trembling hand pulling out her *venyiornik*. Malachiasz casually wiped the blood off his palm and wrapped his hand before tying his hair back.

"And?" Nadya prompted him.

"Three Vultures. One full company."

The woman looked at Nadya, eyes wide. *Oh, they'll expect me to kill the Vultures, then.*

Malachiasz rubbed his jaw, covering an odd swirling decay that chewed at his skin. "Are you in charge here?" he asked the woman.

She nodded, fear turning into bewilderment. "Anya."

"Malach—actually, no, that doesn't matter. That monk didn't tell anyone I was here, did he?"

Anya shook her head.

"Excellent." He scaled the wall, balancing on the sharp points in an uncomfortably graceful and vaguely inhuman way.

"He's with me," Nadya said wearily, the lights growing ever closer. She had assumed Ivan would have told everyone. "Just— warn your men about him."

Anya's shock had not yet melted to anger. Hopefully she would remain pragmatic. Nadya moved to where Malachiasz crouched, his lanky body hunched and rigid, the monster settled right under the surface.

He wordlessly held out his hand and Nadya placed her wasted hand in his.

"Stop fighting it," he said softly. "If your goddess won't give you the power you need, you must use your own."

"I'm not fighting it," she hissed.

His eyes were murky, but his touch was soft. He lifted a lock of hair that had fallen from her coiled braid and tucked it behind her ear. She could still feel the pressure of his mouth against her lips.

Suddenly he slashed an iron claw across her palm. She yelped, more in surprise than pain, and he shushed her.

But as blood welled readily from the wound, power raced up her arm and flooded her body. A torrent, once held back and far away. She grabbed the wall, her other hand clutching on Malachiasz's as her knees weakened. He wasn't even unbalanced as his grip tightened on her hand, holding her up, blood smearing between their palms.

"Blasphemy on holy ground," he murmured appraisingly. "Look how far you've come, Nadezhda Lapteva."

"Blasphemy requires intent," she snapped. Nadya wiped at the blood dripping from her nose and reached into her pocket to anxiously roll Marzenya's bead through her fingers.

She was granted calm disdain in return.

Malachiasz was eyeing something just past her head. "*Towy szanka,*" he said softly. The same thing he had said to her in the cathedral before he left. *Little saint.*

"Does it bother you to fight your countrymen?" she asked. She was dizzy, jittery, like when Marzenya gave her a particularly powerful spell. And this magic was just . . . hers? Inherently? She was terrified of the prospect of burning herself up from the inside out. She didn't know how witch magic worked, didn't know how *this* magic would work.

"I hate it." He paused, then allowed, "Deal with the Vultures however you can."

"I don't think—"

"Don't sell yourself short, *towy dżimyka*."

"You've been doing plenty of that yourself," she said flatly.

He smiled wryly and lifted her hand, kissing her bloody fingers. He let it fall right as Kostya stepped up to the wall beside her.

"Don't get hit by crossbow bolts this time," she said, bumping his shoulder.

"Are they here for her?" he asked Malachiasz.

Kostya recoiled when Malachiasz turned his murky gaze on him. Malachiasz grew thoughtful, a hand moving to tug on one of the bones tied in his black locks before he shrugged.

"I can't tell. It could be a random movement of war. That there are Vultures here says otherwise."

"Could they be here for you?" Nadya asked.

"That would be suicide. I'm not particularly forgiving toward traitors."

"How many of the company are blood mages?" Kostya asked.

"Hypothetically, all of them could be," Malachiasz said, a thread of condescension in his tone that Nadya knew all too well. "That's how blood magic *works*."

Kostya's jaw clenched. "Anya," he called over his shoulder. "Do you have any relics?"

Anya stopped from where she was barking out orders. A slow smile spread on her face.

"Aye, we do."

"Relics?" Nadya asked. "What relics?"

Malachiasz had gone very still beside her.

"What relics?" she asked him.

He shot her a *very* dry look. She thought of the bone *voryen* and how easily it had hurt him when nothing else could. What could she do with that coupled with something *else* divine?

Was that the easy way out? To use divinity through an object imbued with it instead of going to Marzenya? She didn't trust Marzenya now to give her the magic she needed, and she had this *thing*, this darkness, this power, but using it would be turning her back on her divine calling. It was a step she would never return from. She closed her wasted hand into a fist and tugged her bone *voryen* from her belt.

"Get them," she said. "I'll use them."

"Wasting your precious few resources on a haggard group of Tranavians far from home?" Malachiasz said, voice jagged, mouth full of iron nails.

"We'll leave one alive to tell the rest of the country that we're done with them razing our villages and churches to the ground," Kostya snapped.

Malachiasz held Kostya's stare, his eyes shifting darker and darker.

Nadya sensed his decision before he moved. She reached out to stop him, fingers slipping off his elbow as he leapt from the wall, his black, feathery wings bursting forth as he disappeared into the darkness.

"*Shit*," she swore.

"Where is he going?" Kostya asked.

"To warn the Vultures."

# 28

## NADEZHDA

## LAPTEVA

**Svoyatova Inessa Besfamilny:** *A cleric with no record of which god or goddess had touched her. Inessa's life was one of anguish. Her lover, Marya Telkinova, was corrupted by a* kashyvhes, *forcing Inessa to kill her and the entire village Marya had corrupted upon turning. It is said the Govanitsy River was created by Svoyatova Inessa's tears.*

—Vasiliev's Book of Saints

Nadya took the reliquary with shaking hands, opening the box. Inside was a cloth, stained with blood. Power emanated from the cloth, and her scarred hand pulsed as if there were a heartbeat in her palm. The power being hers didn't explain why it hurt or why it was reacting this way. Maybe Malachiasz was lying. Except somehow she knew he wasn't. There was something wrong with *her.* She just didn't know what.

She carefully took the shroud out of the reliquary, eyes

closing as a rush of divine power spread through her. She shivered.

Anya's breath caught. She was looking at a point just past Nadya's head.

"Can anyone use these?" Nadya asked her.

Anya shook her head. "Only some can feel the power left behind. Fewer can use it."

So, these were no replacement for Kalyazin's clerics. A shame. Nadya wrapped the shroud around her hand, hissing through her teeth at the influx of power. But she knew how to handle a massive amount of power. It was the lack of it that was a struggle.

The shroud belonged to Svoyatova Vlada Votyakova. The second it met her skin she saw the girl—her age, maybe a few years older—hair cut bluntly to her chin, tears streaking down dark cheeks as she pressed the cloth uselessly over a wound bleeding from her stomach.

Nadya considered further and instead carefully wrapped the shroud over her hair, freeing her hand. Anya fetched a headband from a nearby sister, the temple rings made of dark iron. The temple rings of a high priestess.

Nadya swallowed hard and fitted the band over the shroud. She didn't deserve to wear this.

"We lost our entire advantage because that *monster*—"

Nadya didn't let Kostya finish, snapping her hand out to clutch at his jaw and wrench his face level with hers.

"You don't need to tell me what Malachiasz has done, I am well aware. Shut up and keep yourself alive."

His dark eyes flashed. He looked at a point just past her head. Why was everyone *doing that*? "I'm supposed to protect you."

"You *were*. I don't need protecting. Not anymore."

He flinched under her hand. She paused, tugging him down so she could press her forehead to his.

"Keep yourself safe," she said. "I can't lose you again."

She started toward the stairs, yanking her *voryen* from its sheath. Rashid caught her arm as she passed.

"What are you planning?"

"To say hello to the Tranavians," Nadya said.

Rashid scowled. "That's not what I was asking."'

She rolled her eyes. "He's made it perfectly clear. Tranavia over"—she waved a hand—"whatever this is. So be it."

"Don't kill him," Rashid called as she took to the stairs.

"No promises!" she called back.

She ordered the gates opened and no one questioned her. No one questioned why a girl, small and wearing high priestess's temple rings, was going out to meet a Tranavian company alone.

Power, Nadya considered, had a tendency to make her a tad reckless.

She tugged her other *voryen* out, flipping the one and catching it by its hilt.

Votyakova had been a cleric of the god Krsnik. Nadya delighted in finally having access to fire without having to plead with Krsnik for it. But she didn't know how long this power would last; how much magic was imbued in a relic after a cleric had passed?

Cold flames licked at her blades and she worked quickly, dragging her blade along the ground, crossing the entrance of the monastery. Flames shot up from the ground where her blade touched, creating a wall of fire the Tranavians would be forced to traverse. She backed up to the gates so she wouldn't be facing an entire company on her own.

Reckless didn't have to mean foolish.

She tensed at movement amidst the trees, going still at

the sight of Malachiasz's thin frame. He shot her a grin—
half-crazed—eyes onyx black; he was completely covered in
blood, and from what she could tell, half of it was his own.
Her grip tightened on her *voryen,* unsure if she was about to
fight *him* or—

A snarling shape slammed into him.

The Tranavians were upon them.

It was different, accessing one very powerful kind of magic
instead of all of it, and this made her clumsy. A ball of flame
sent off the tip of her blade not quite hitting her mark, her
movements slow enough that a blood mage's spell caught
against her shoulder, knocking her backward.

This was the way clerics before her had fought, but she could
feel something underneath the heat that licked at her skin but
did not burn; it was something older and far more dangerous
that she reached for, a singular thread underneath a tapestry
that spelt out a defined type of magic. The remnants of a god,
unfiltered, pure. The kind of power that a god would tem-
per before they granted it to a mortal, here left to fester into
something vast and uncontrollable.

*Ah, this is what she meant,* Nadya thought, as she ducked under
a spray of power and shoved a Kalyazi monk out of the way.

The fire had allowed them more preparation; a way to earn
back the advantage they had lost. But it became clear very
quickly the Tranavians were there for a single reason: Nadya.

She yanked on the thread of power from the relic just as a
Vulture stepped through the flames.

Old magic, untamed and rotted from decades of solitude,
quaked within Nadya. She tasted copper and spat out a mouthful of blood. The Vulture's mask was strange, nothing more
than jawbones with teeth still attached tied with strings crossing her face. Her eyes were pools of black.

"Can't kill me with what you have," the Vulture taunted.

Nadya could feel the fire behind the Vulture, an extension of her will. She grinned back, and pulled hard at it, engulfing the Vulture, whose screeches ripped through the chaotic air.

There was someone at her side and she whirled, but it was only Kostya. He eyed the flames, which were keeping the Tranavians back and giving the Kalyazi a chance to pick them off with crossbows. He grinned at her.

The chaos had not truly hit, and Nadya wondered what was stopping them. Surely they had a mage who could counteract her magic. Surely one of the Vultures could. A blast of power shot through the flames, and Nadya only barely stepped out of its way. The Vulture she had burned slammed into her, throwing her to the ground.

Her flames went out.

It was the sound of battle that truly jarred Nadya. A loud cacophony of shouts and screams and of blades hitting flesh, the scent of burning magic. Iron and heat.

She got her legs underneath the Vulture, kicking her off and slamming her back into the monastery wall. If the Vultures attacked the monks, none would survive. Nadya had to keep the monsters trained on her and her alone, but she didn't know where the other two were. She hoped Malachiasz was dealing with them instead of warning them that Nadya had a relic that could do them true harm.

True harm if she figured out how to harness it. The power was fluid and unlike what she was used to. It didn't want to bend to her will; rather it moved chaotically through her. She took a step and the ground underneath her blasted out, a chunk of stone hitting the Vulture, another one slamming into a monk.

There was no time for apology. The Vulture's claws grazed

inches from Nadya's chest. Blood dripped from her eyes, staining the jawbones red as it caught between the teeth.

Nadya had a bad feeling about where those jawbones came from. She kicked out, her boot slamming into the Vulture's head and snapping her neck. But physical blows were useless. She had seen Malachiasz run a Vulture through with his claws and have her step away like nothing had happened.

Magic, however. Magic could stop one of the beasts. She hoped.

She had never been told how Malachiasz killed the last Black Vulture and ascended his throne. He would never give her such a secret, he would never tell how his kind were rendered mortal even as they could withstand such horrors done to their bodies. But her relic bone knife had hurt Malachiasz and surely this magic could, too. The relic's power of fire surged, desperate to be used, and she whirled away from the Vulture, casting out a hand and throwing a spray of white flames that caught on approaching Tranavian soldiers. Divine power quieted, she yanked on the old thread again and grasped the chaos.

Everything went white. Her vision blanked out. She was vaguely aware of magic at the Vulture's bloodied hands. A clawed hand reaching for her throat. The Vulture's blond hair shining against the flames still burning in patches on the ground.

The gods were ancient and unfathomable. There were older, deeper things, but how much farther back could a mortal's brain comprehend than beings of forever? Nadya had so much more to learn about the gods who had touched her and led her down this dark and terrible path.

The relic retained the power of the cleric that had died with it; but it also held something more, and it was that something more Nadya grasped as time went sludgy around her.

Nadya grazed against the will of a god.

Everything stopped.

She dropped back, breathing hard. But nothing moved. She reached up and touched the shroud wrapped around her head. This was not like her divine magic. That was condensed. That was power granted from divinity to be palatable to a mortal. Just enough for her fragile body to contain. This was far more than that, far more than any mortal should ever touch. And here it was, held within the piece of a dead saint.

How many relics held power this way? What could she do with power of this magnitude?

It was building within her, light edging out underneath her skin like veins, and it would destroy her. It would rip clean through her and there would be no putting her back together. Heat and flame and an anger so profound and so deep that it became the very core of her.

How was she surviving this?

Nadya pushed it out of her body.

The magic shot out around Nadya in a wave of fireball. It struck the Vulture and she burned. Not like last time, not a heat so easily shaken. All that was left was a pile of charred bones at Nadya's feet.

Bile rushed into Nadya's mouth, tinged with copper, and she retched. She turned, wiping at her mouth with the back of her hand. She could hear the battle but it sounded calmer, less chaotic, like the Tranavians had been fought off.

There were still more than a handful of Tranavians, perhaps seven or eight. But Nadya's power blast had hit more than the Vulture and charred bones were scattered in the clearing like discarded garbage. She clapped her hand to her mouth, horror rippling through her. There was no way she had only struck

Tranavians with that blow. Kalyazi must have been caught in the chaos.

She had just killed so many people.

She staggered back a step. The remaining Tranavians were tossing down their spell books. A pair of monks were cutting off the sleeves of their coats and she could feel the horror of her people at her back.

This had not been what she intended. She hadn't meant to take in that much power.

*"This is what happens when a mortal plays at the power of gods."* Marzenya's voice was calm and calculating and deeply pointed.

Nadya threw up again.

Something hard hit Nadya, sending her to the ground. Her head cracked back against a stone, vision going black and white and fractured as pain crashed through her.

*He said if he fell he could bring himself back,* she thought frantically, but he had been lying and she knew, deep down, he would kill her for destroying one of his Vultures.

She rolled to her feet, head spinning, reaching for her *voryen*. His boot slammed down onto her hand and a choked cry of pain escaped her. Her other *voryen* was out of easy reach and the power blast had left her dizzy and weak. She could pull at the thread of power from the relic but she had already done more than she could stand. What she had survived was impossible.

Fear spiked adrenaline through her as he dropped into a crouch, his weight shifting on her hand. She had to bite her lip to keep from whimpering.

"What have I told you about taking things that are mine, *towy dżimyka?*" he asked, brittle and chaotic. Black hair shadowed roiling, monstrous features. Blood dripped from his onyx eyes.

"You said to do what I had to," she spat. Her other hand scrambled for the bone *voryen* at her belt but iron claws caged her wrist.

"Did you think I truly meant that?"

He cocked his head and moved suddenly, Kostya's blade cutting through the air where he had been.

Nadya struggled to her feet. Malachiasz would kill Kostya. She moved faster than she thought she was able, stumbling to put herself between them. Both boys froze. Kostya's eyes flicked away from Malachiasz to meet hers.

There was reassurance there. It had always been Kostya and Nadya, two little orphans wreaking havoc in the monastery to hide from her fate. He smiled slightly.

Clawed hands dug into Kostya, horror crossing his face as one of the remaining Vultures pulled him away. Malachiasz lunged to strike at her.

Panic thudded in Nadya's chest. She reached past the relic's magic for Marzenya—fire would do her no good here and she was terrified of touching the deeper magic again.

Marzenya granted her a line of power, careful and controlled. A definitive message—Nadya was pushing too far and needed to hold back. Nadya would take it. She grasped onto the power and slipped away from Malachiasz's claws, lashing out and cracking him on the jaw with her foot. She heard the sound of bone crunching underneath her boot.

"Sorry," she said as he hissed in pain, blood dripping from his chin.

She didn't know how to stop him like this. Kostya staggered into her and her irritation morphed into horror. The blood covering him was his own.

"Kostya?"

Everything moved too fast. A crossbow bolt thudded into

Malachiasz's shoulder, then another, knocking him back into a tree. His head slammed into the hard wood and he dropped like a stone.

Parijahan loaded another bolt into her crossbow and shot the remaining Vulture, who simply laughed as he watched. Nadya, desperate, yanked harder on the careful piece of magic Marzenya had given her and threw her *voryen*. The blade lodged itself in the Vulture's eye and he dropped, too.

Not dead, that was too much to hope for, but hopefully down for long enough to be dealt with.

She was knocked off balance as Kostya fell. This couldn't be happening. Kostya would be fine, he had to be fine.

But his chest had been flayed to ribbons. A sob caught in Nadya's throat. She reached for more power, for anything, but it slipped through her fingers.

*"You will be no more, child,"* Marzenya said gently.

*I don't care,* Nadya snapped. *Give me more. Give me enough to save him, or I'll use my own.* She reached for the ache in her palm, the power nestled underneath her skin. But that resisted her call as well. No one was meant to hold this much magic.

If another scrap were channeled through her, she would be nothing more than a charred pile of bones. But she couldn't bring herself to care. Kostya was going to die. She had grieved his death once, but it was different to watch it happening right in front of her, to see the life slowly leave him.

She wondered too long why everything was blurry, finally realizing she was sobbing and that was why air was only rattling through her lungs and she couldn't see through her tears. She couldn't lose Kostya *again*.

"You're here this time," he said weakly. "I don't want to die alone."

"No, don't do this," she said. "You're going to be fine."

But he wasn't going to be fine and they both knew it. Everyone had always treated her like a relic, like something to be tiptoed around and whispered about, but Kostya had accepted her for who she really was: a girl who messed up sometimes and was painfully human and had a destiny that was too big for her.

Their paths had gotten muddled along the way, but he had never done anything but love her.

She bit back a sob and cradled his head in her lap, tracing Veceslav's symbol against the side of his head.

"I'm sorry I failed," he whispered.

"No, Kostenka, no, never."

He took in a shaky breath. "There are older gods, worse ones, ones they feared to tell you of because . . ." He coughed, struggling past the blood dripping from the corners of his mouth. "Nadya, you're dangerous. They're frightened of you."

She didn't understand why he was telling her this *now*. But she nodded through her tears, stroking a hand over his head.

"Kostya, I don't understand, I—"

But a final, dreadful sigh passed his lips and he was gone. Something deep cracked within Nadya. She thought there was nothing left of her to break, she thought believing him to be dead before was enough to destroy her, but this was so much worse.

She curled up against him and let herself shatter.

# 29

## SEREFIN
## MELESKI

*Trickery, vengeance, a snake in the grass as Velyos watched
and waited and moved to strike a blow against Marzenya
and Peloyin that would topple the heavens. He failed and
was cast into the ether.*

—The Books of Innokentiy

"You can't do what Velyos wants, that's imperative," Katya
told Serefin as they left the small Kalyazi village behind.

Serefin had to keep his eye closed permanently. He had
borrowed a patch from Ostyia and that had helped, but
sometimes his vision still blurred, the world taking on a
cast of horror.

"What direction are we going? Vaguely west?" he asked.
She nodded with a slight frown.

"Well, he wants me to go west, so we are failing at that
part of the solution."

Katya groaned.

"Surely there's a way to break this off," Serefin said.

Katya waved a moth away from her face. It returned to Serefin's orbit. He lifted a hand and it landed on his palm, large and black and white.

"I have an idea, but it would mean going even farther west," Katya said. Her decision to go off with the king of Tranavia had not been met with support from her soldiers. She had allowed one to come with her, Milomir, a dour looking boy, but no one else. She had sent the rest east, which Serefin had thoughts about—mostly that he was letting a group of well-trained soldiers refresh some inevitable war zone against Tranavia. This had all become far messier than he could have fathomed.

It was too early and painfully cold. Serefin's breath clouded out before his face. Snow had fallen in the night and they crunched through it toward a forest, dark and looming at the horizon. Katya tugged her fur hat down over her ears.

"Everything I know is from apocryphal texts," she said. "It's a bad sign that Velyos was woken; it will be even worse if the rest are, too."

*Oh good, the ones that are all waiting for me to come make a racket,* Serefin thought grimly.

Ostyia frowned. She was always hovering wherever the *tsarevna* was. Serefin wondered if he should discourage the healthy crush Ostyia obviously had on the Kalyazi girl. But no, let Ostyia have her fun, it wouldn't harm anything.

"There are stories," Katya continued. "It's hard to know what is true, especially about the fallen ones. Like I said, Velyos always wants chaos and to tear down Peloyin." She waved a hand. "That in itself isn't particularly apocalyptic. We're always caught in the middle of any wars between the gods."

"Speak for yourself."

"Ah, you Tranavians are not immune," Katya said.

"We were, until your cleric came along and ruined that," Serefin said. The veil separating Tranavia from the gods had been doing a whole lot more than providing simple protection. As soon as it had fallen, the winter had swept upon Tranavia, vicious and unforgiving. He wondered if he could get it put back up.

Katya rolled her eyes. "Regardless. You've found yourself in the middle of an ageless battle between gods. You can't even deny it."

"I can deny my feelings on the word *god* being ascribed to them."

"I'm not here to argue theology with you, Tranavian."

Serefin shrugged. "It's not a topic I'm particularly well-read in anyway."

"Yet here you are."

"Here I am."

It was disquieting, though. He wanted it to stop. Even with the eye patch, his good eye swam with darkness. He was constantly jumping at things that weren't there. He kept hearing whispers in the back of his head that did not sound like Velyos *or* the other voice. He only wanted silence and if he did not get it soon he was going to go insane.

"What's odd is that all this chaos is happening but Velyos *isn't* a chaos god. We don't have any of those; we did, but they died," Katya mused.

"They *died*?"

"Chaos is so volatile. Those gods are usually killed by one of the others."

"I'm sorry, you have dead gods? Your gods are just constantly murdering each other?"

"Are you willfully dense or is this a trait only I have to deal with?"

"I *am* your problem now."

She snorted.

"What's your idea, then?" he asked.

"There's an old ruin up in the Valikhor Mountains. It's where Praskovya Kapylyushna was stripped of her power. There's precedent for the gods turning away from chosen mortals, forced away, even."

"And you think I can break myself free from Velyos if I go there?" Serefin asked skeptically. He didn't like it. Each step west was one step closer to where Velyos wanted him to be.

"It might be your only option," she replied. "If you're working with something ancient and forgotten, you have to go somewhere ancient and forgotten to deal with it. But first, we find the cleric because to get to that temple, I think we'll need her."

Serefin glanced at Kacper, who lifted his eyebrows and shrugged. Too much divine nonsense for a former farm boy from Tranavia.

It was connected, somehow, Velyos and Malachiasz, but Serefin wasn't quite sure how. Malachiasz had wanted the power to kill the Kalyazi gods. No Kalyazi gods were dead by his hand—as far as Serefin was aware—but Malachiasz had been stealing relics from the Kalyazi, for what purpose?

Would one thing lead into the next? Did he have to prepare for it all to just . . . implode? The other voice—other god, Serefin supposed—wanted Malachiasz dead as well. The meddler, he had said, but that was almost suspicious. It was what Serefin had wanted to hear. He didn't tell Katya about the other one. Something about the way the carving in his chest ached whenever that terrible voice spoke and how it had crushed through Serefin's defenses so quickly terrified him. So he kept that one to himself, let them think this was only the problem of Velyos, not this greater being who had no name.

He had no idea where Velyos specifically needed him to go so going west was an unbelievable risk. But he had to do *something*.

"Where, exactly, are we?" he asked Katya.

"Just past Rosni-Ovorisk."

The name was familiar. That was where the war had supposedly turned back in Kalyazin's favor. It was inexplicable, the renewed vigor from the enemy. His father had planned to tear them down with his wild plan but obviously that hadn't happened. And when Serefin had taken the throne, the front had returned to its stagnant back and forth. But it was shifting out of its stagnation, and Tranavia might be losing.

Serefin couldn't tell, even from the whispers he heard passing through inns as they traveled. Katya never bothered to make herself appear any different when they passed through Kalyazi villages. The country was too big, she would say, no one had any idea who she was.

"It's certainly not my face on the money," she would joke. Though there had been an evening where she'd suddenly disappeared underneath a table in an inn because a low prince had come through the door. Ostyia had wordlessly slipped her food down to her. She'd remained under the table for the rest of their meal, then climbed back up after the low prince left and went to bed like nothing had happened.

They had passed out of the reach of the armies and now the villages they passed through were not ravaged by battle, but by the poverty that came from decades of war.

But it was worse, somehow, as they passed out of civilization's reach. The air was different and Serefin didn't like it. The nights were cold and the feeling of being observed was constant, but he could never find anything watching, no matter how much magic he poured into the area. Katya had clearly noticed, and Serefin didn't think she had any true magic to speak of. But maybe he was being paranoid.

As strange as it was, Serefin and the *tsarevna* got along well. They both had the shared life experiences of growing up in courts that cared very little for their young heirs, shipping them off to the war as soon as they were old enough. However, there the stories diverged. Serefin was a high-ranking officer; Katya had joined a cultic sect of monster hunters.

They passed the carcass of a village. The houses were only skeletons of wooden boards, mostly burned away.

"What happened here?" Kacper asked.

"*Zhir'oten*," Katya said. "We're nearing the forest of monsters. Villages here don't survive long. This one fell a few years ago."

*Wolf changers.* Serefin shuddered. Did they have those to look forward to?

Trailing the cleric's steps was turning out to be an arduous process. Serefin couldn't figure out how far behind they were and one day his tracking spell simply cut off. He had no idea where she would even be going.

They camped in the decimated village, despite how eerie it was.

"We might not be able to find her," Serefin said, as he and Katya sat with a map before them.

Milomir was arguing with Ostyia about their supplies and how much they could afford to use for dinner if they were going to reach the forest soon. Katya eventually stopped the argument by wearily ordering Milomir to backtrack and hunt for small game before it grew too dark. He left grumbling.

"He's a fabulous tracker," Katya said, rolling her eyes. "We'll be fine." She returned to the map.

"I lost her around here," Serefin said, indicating a spot on the map that was relatively close, but she could have since moved on.

"Valikhor is up here," Katya said, pointing.

Kacper, leaning over Serefin's shoulder, made a tiny, distressed sound.

It was very far away and it cut through a huge swath of forest that bisected Kalyazin in two.

"There's no easier way to this place?" Serefin asked, trying not to think about how very close Kacper was.

Katya shrugged. "If you want to take the merchant roads it will take you about half a year to get there."

Kacper grimaced. Serefin had been away from Tranavia for too long already. For all he knew, his mother had been deposed by Ruminski and exiled to the lake country. He might not even have a throne to go back to. He needed this to be successful, not only for his own sake, but for Tranavia.

"How much time will we save by taking the forest road?" Kacper reluctantly asked, shifting a little so his chin was tucked against Serefin's shoulder.

"A few months. It will still take time but the route is direct." She paused, thoughtful. "And incredibly dangerous. Very few people survive the forest roads."

"Well," Serefin said grimly, "we don't have much choice."

"Not if we can't track the cleric anymore, no." She sounded disappointed. It would have been easier had they found her; divine nonsense was her wheelhouse, surely she could help. Serefin should have talked to her about it in the first place.

"Don't you lot have a way to track Vultures?" he asked.

Katya shrugged. "If you have something of importance of his, I could do it."

Serefin's stomach turned. "What if—what if you used blood?"

"I don't treat in heresy," she snapped.

"But what if that's what you had to use?"

She leaned back on her hands, chewing on her lower lip. "Do you just happen to have a vial of the Black Vulture's blood on you?"

Serefin shook his head. "He's my brother."

Her dark green eyes went wide, jaw falling open.

"A bastard, technically. It's complicated. But, it would be a way to do it, I suppose, if however you use magic is anything like ours. I thought only clerics could cast magic?"

"It's complicated," Katya said, voice hoarse. "The saints can bestow power. It's significantly weaker than the gods and the training to hear the saints at all is incredibly rigorous. We can do very little, comparatively."

"But you could do it?"

She blinked rapidly. "I think I could."

"Well," Serefin said, tugging a blade from his belt and ignoring the way Kacper tensed. He offered Katya the blade. "Let's find my brother."

# 30

## NADEZHDA

## LAPTEVA

*Ljubica's tears filled all the lakes of Kalyazin and still her agony has not run its course.*

—The Letters of Włodzimierz

Nadya stood in the monastery's quiet cemetery and broke under the weight of her grief. She had done nothing but fail over and over and now Kostya was really truly gone and she had killed ten of her brothers and sisters because she had been reckless and couldn't control her power. Her magic had obliterated them. And that magic had felt *good*, which made it all the more abhorrent.

The aftermath was like living through a nightmare. She scrubbed at her tears but they fell unceasing. She had been allowed to help prepare Kostya's body for burial, inscribing the headband and belt the dead were buried with in prayers to Veceslav. It was usually Marzenya who took the burial prayers, but Kostya would have wanted

Veceslav. It was the least she could do. The dead were buried in unadorned white, no embroidery, to ease them across the mortal bounds.

Nadya didn't want to think about how she would fail to see to the proper days of mourning. The third, the ninth, and the fortieth days were to be set aside for remembrance and she couldn't linger here that long.

What was the point of her if she couldn't keep people she cared about safe? All she ever did was make things worse. Her monastery never would have been attacked had she not been there—everyone would be alive. Kostya would be alive. So many people would still live if she had never existed.

She touched the grave marker, running her fingers over Veceslav's symbol carved into the stone, over the dips where Kostya's name was set. *Konstantin Ruslanovich.* He was so far from where his brother died. So far from everything he had ever known.

Nadya had spent so much time frustrated and scared that he wanted her to be something she wasn't, that she had wasted the short time they'd had together since finding him.

She was sitting out in the cold when Ivan found her. The old monk sat down on the frozen ground next to her.

"Peace, sister," he murmured when she tensed, prepared to flee.

Her fingers glanced against the stone. "I'm sorry," she whispered, but she didn't know if she was speaking to Ivan or Kostya.

Ivan sighed heavily. "Child, you have only ever done what was asked."

He looked so much older than when they had arrived, his dark eyes weary.

"People died," she said. "If I was better at this, if I had better control, no one would be dead. Kostya wouldn't be dead."

"If the Vultures did not exist, Konstantin would not be dead," Ivan said. "You cannot blame yourself for every tragedy that befalls those around you."

Oh, she very well could.

"If Malachiasz wasn't here, Kostya would be alive," she whispered.

She hadn't spoken to him since the attack. Parijahan had told her that no one would see to his wounds, so Rashid had done his best with what was on hand. Nadya wasn't really concerned—he was a Vulture and they could survive graver injuries than a broken jaw and crossbow wounds. The whole night was confusing and unreal in hindsight, like it had been a dream.

But it wasn't a dream, it was a nightmare, and the gravestone under her hand was very real and she could not wake up.

Kostya's last words were a torment that never left her. Who were the old gods they were too afraid to tell Nadya about? Who was *they*? And why?

"Brother Ivan, do you know about gods older than the ones we worship?" she asked, casually rolling one of her prayer beads through her fingers.

She saw him stiffen out of the corner of her eye.

"What do you mean?"

"I was given this by someone at my home monastery," she said, lifting Velyos' pendant from under her collar. "Kostya said the symbol was for a god older than ours. That there were more as well."

"I don't know where he would have heard something so preposterous," Ivan scoffed. "There are the High Twenty. No more, no less."

"Having a *High* Twenty implies that there are lesser beings as well," Nadya pointed out.

"Is this what you do now, child? Question your betters?" Ivan tried to sound friendly but his sharpness cut at Nadya.

"What if there were others?" she mused, ignoring him.

"You stray dangerously close to heresy, Nadezhda."

Why wasn't he telling her the truth? Why did the Church think it would be dangerous for her to know of the other gods? How long had they been lying to her, and what other lies had they told?

"We cannot see the threads the gods have used to weave this world together," Ivan said. "Not even you, Nadezhda. Could that battle have gone differently? How many Vultures have you killed, child?"

He was changing the subject to avoid her questions. Why was he lying? Could she trust *anyone*?

"We have always been fighting a war against a people who have gone so far against the gods that they have reached for power we do not have," Ivan said. "And those abominations are proof. I trust when the time comes you will do what is best for Kalyazin."

Nadya closed her eyes. It was so much worse to hear from someone else than when she told herself what she needed to do.

"However," Ivan continued, "no battles are easy. And this is war. Lives are lost during war. You, Nadezhda, you are the one who will stop this war."

"But what if I can't?" she asked, despairing.

Ivan shrugged. "It continues. And more good souls like Kostya will die." She heard what he did not say aloud. *And more evil souls like Malachiasz will live.*

"Marzenya wants me to go west. To the seat of the gods."

"And from there?"

"Touch divinity and make the Tranavians finally *see*," Nadya said.

Ivan was quiet.

"I don't know if I will survive this," Nadya said softly.

"If you don't, you doom Kalyazin," Ivan said.

*Comforting.*

He left her sitting alone in the cemetery, feeling all the more lost and confused. It had long puzzled the priests that she was able to commune with the entire pantheon. But now she realized the Church did not trust her.

Why were they *afraid* of her?

A sick feeling settled in the pit of her stomach. There was only one person she could talk to about magic who wouldn't hold back the truth. He might lie about literally everything else, but he wouldn't lie about magic. She needed to talk to Malachiasz.

Nadya stopped Malachiasz in the hallway, shoving him back against the wall harder than she meant to, hearing his hiss of pain and hardly believing it. She braced an arm across his chest—easy enough to slam her forearm back against his throat—and leveled her bone *voryen* at him.

"He would be alive if not for *you*."

Malachiasz, tired and wrecked, flinched.

"Can you speak?" She didn't know how badly she had broken his jaw.

He nodded almost imperceptibly.

"Good. We need to talk. But first, give me the name of the Vulture who killed him." She needed to have some other point of vengeance to rest herself upon.

Malachiasz's pale gaze darkened. His posture shifted underneath her arm as he slid away from the boy and into the monster. He said nothing.

"I see." She adjusted her grip on the blade, letting it nick his throat. Black veins spread out from the point of contact, and she watched the thin trickle of blood against his pale skin. "You've made what you care about profoundly clear, Malachiasz." She said his name with as much venom as she could muster. "Tranavia. The Vultures. But not me. I guess this was inevitable."

He tilted his head back against the wall, closing his eyes. An ugly bruise bloomed against his jaw, made only more sickening as decay crept along it. It would be so easy to finish him. He would not stop her like he had in the forest a lifetime ago.

"Why did you warn them?" she asked. Tears burned at her eyes but she refused to cry.

He didn't answer.

"You don't care," she said flatly. "I don't know why I made the effort, going back for you, it's clear you don't deserve it. You don't *want* it."

He trembled underneath her forearm, brow furrowed, but silent. She wanted to grab his jaw and yank him down to her level, make him *see* how much pain he had caused her. Cause him equal pain.

There was a moment of disconnect, and then she heard his sharp whimper, his jaw shifting under her tightening fingers.

"You told me you didn't want to cause me pain," she said slowly, trying valiantly to keep her voice from shaking. "But you're the only thing that hurts me, again and again. How am I to ever know if your pain is more than an act to keep me near enough to hurt?"

His knees gave out and he fell. Nadya didn't bother loosening her hold or dropping the blade from his neck.

He knelt before her, forced supplication, breath rattling his chest. The sun through the window lined his edges, jagged and corrupt, but in the light, becoming something beautiful.

There were no warring pieces with this boy. He had made a choice to sink into the darkness and there would be no pulling him from it. She couldn't *save him,* and continually trying was only going to end in more misery.

"I would have a god on his knees before me," she whispered, her dispassionate tone strange in her ears. "I told you I would have you like this."

A tear glistened on his cheek. He was shaking. She pulled her hands away, horrified with her own cruelty. He wasn't a god—as much as he wanted to be. He was a monster, a horror, a nightmare. He was only a boy.

He dropped his head, hand going to his jaw, shudders wracking his thin shoulders.

"I—" She took a step back.

His hand snapped out and caught the edge of her skirt, his fist curling into the fabric. A shiver of fear trailed through her. He slowly straightened, one hand cradling his jaw, pain sketched across his face. He pulled her closer, and carefully worked his way to his feet.

But he only rested his forehead against hers. A heartbeat passed, the crack in Nadya's armor grew wider, and the tears she had been holding back fell.

"So you did," he rasped. "You wear cruelty well, *towy dżimyka.*"

She took a step back, looking up at him. It was as much his fault Kostya was dead as it was hers and it only added to the aching rift between them. Another reminder she *could not* give in to her heart's demands.

Yet she was finding it harder and harder to fight.

She took his hand. It was cold where usually he was warm.

She twined their fingers together. "Come with me," she said quietly, rattled. "I want to talk."

The sanctuary was blessedly empty. Nadya pulled him inside, ignoring his reluctance. She sat down on the first bench, lifting her feet and sitting to the side so she could face him. He studied the vast iconostasis before them, gilded and shining in the fading light of the high windows. His hair was loose and tangled around his shoulders and he hadn't bothered with a spell to cover up the shifting chaos of his features.

A cluster of eyes opened on his cheek. They were a sickly white and oozed blood. His hand immediately went to the spot.

"Everyone is lying to me—"

"Ksawery Opalki," he said at the same time. He glanced at her before lowering his pale eyes. "The Vulture's name. Nadya, I am so sorry."

Her armor shattered. She closed her eyes, tried to cobble it back together. She needed a barrier between her heart and him.

"Did you know the whole time that Kostya was in the mines?"

"I'm not omniscient. I have a thread of control over the Vultures. Well, I had that. No, I didn't know."

"You were the reason he was still alive, though, weren't you?"

He laughed softly. "You know I'm not so noble as that. His was a senseless death and you deserve to take your revenge."

It left a lot unsaid between them. He had chosen his country and his order over her, and she would choose her country over him, and what would happen when the time came for that choice to be the final one? What they had was not made to last.

"Why did you warn them?"

"I didn't. I tried to give an order to spare the monastery. It didn't go over well."

Nadya masked her surprise carefully. "I'm not sure I believe that," she said.

He nodded.

"I'm sorry I broke your jaw," she said.

"Are we just going to trade apologies, because we'll be here literally all night," he said, picking up her badly bruised hand.

"How *did* I break it?"

"If we're prepared for the blow, we can work around it."

"So, if you're caught off guard . . ."

"It would not kill me," he replied cheerily. "It's much more difficult than that, Nadya."

"But you're not unbreakable." Though he could talk, so he healed remarkably fast, but she already knew that.

"I am not. Are you planning on breaking me?" he asked, voice rough.

She shivered at his tone.

"I should've chained you up in the monastery's cellars."

He considered that. "That would have certainly been effective."

"Next time, maybe," she said seriously.

Malachiasz made a thoughtful sound.

Nadya sighed; this was getting her nowhere. She tugged at her core and tiny points of white flame lit along her fingertips. But that was all. Magic ached in her palm but she didn't know how to get to it. Magic borne of desperation wasn't so easy to recall.

Malachiasz lifted an eyebrow, a small smile pulling at his mouth as he recognized what she wanted. He unhooked his spell book from his hip and dumped it unceremoniously in her lap.

"I do not want this," she said dubiously.

He ignored her. He tugged his dagger free from its sheath

and offered that to her as well after a wry glance toward the iconostasis.

"I don't need that."

"No?"

She shook her head. She chewed on her lower lip, contemplating the spell book. He hadn't pulled off the icons she had put on the cover when she had borrowed it in Grazyk. She trailed her fingertips over Marzenya's icon.

"Malachiasz . . ." Why had he kept these?

He misinterpreted her intent, eyes widening a fraction. "You don't *have* to," he said quickly.

She laughed and he relaxed. "I'm not going to." She started to pick at one of the icons and startled when his hand landed over hers.

"You don't have to do that, either," he said, voice unbearably gentle.

She jerked, surprised, studying his face. He carefully avoided touching the icons as he drew his hand back. He offered nothing more by way of explanation and as much as Nadya wanted to know why, she didn't ask.

"The Church is keeping something from me," she said. "And I think it has something to do with how I use magic."

He idly chewed on a thumbnail, looking up at the iconostasis again. Nadya could name every symbol and painting of every saint. Her faith was the only thing she knew without question, yet here she was with a boy who had profaned everything her faith stood for. The knowledge useless when confronted with so much so unlike everything she had been taught.

"You've used my spell book before, if unintentionally, and forged a bizarrely inexplicable magic link through stolen power," Malachiasz finally said. There was an underlying thread in his voice she could not decipher but it made the back of her neck grow warm.

"And?"

He flipped the book open. "Magic is magic," he said slowly, as if expecting her to argue.

She turned the pages of his spell book, passing over dozens of meticulously constructed spells, his messy scrawl edge to edge. She paused, landing on a page covered with charcoal sketches, smudged and imperfect.

They were sketches of *her*. There were canvases stacked in every corner of his chambers in the cathedral. She had thought he simply collected beautiful things when the whole time he had been the one creating them. Her face heated, the gentleness with which he had captured her all too visible.

"How about a different approach," he said, the words rushed.

He shut the book with a snap and set it aside. He was blushing and slightly mortified.

*Oh, hells. I'm in danger,* she thought hopelessly.

"You're very good," she said.

His hand moved to hover over the book. He adamantly did not look at her. "Thank you," he said quietly.

*Such absolute and irreversible danger.*

"Kostya said the Church is afraid of me discovering old gods outside the pantheon. That they were afraid of my corruption." She lifted her hand wryly.

Malachiasz took her hand, curling it into his. "Because they're afraid you might commune with those beings?"

It was certainly plausible. "I wasn't supposed to free Velyos, and I did. I can't help but feel like it's connected."

He hesitated. "If—if we figure out how to reach *your* power, will you even need to continue west?"

"Yes," she said. Yes, because she needed to put an end to

Tranavia's terrors. Yes, because this was doomed between them. Yes, because she was going to destroy him and it was much too late to stop it. The pieces were already in place. There was no turning back.

He nodded. "Well, you've talked it up so much that I'm curious anyway!" He pushed back her sleeve so the dark stain was visible to her elbow. "I don't think you're going to like the answer we find for this," he said, meeting her eyes from underneath his long, dark eyelashes.

He shifted, drawing his legs up so he was rather precariously perched, cross-legged, on the bench. "So, we know about Velyos," he said, "and he's not a part of your pantheon, yes?" He waited for confirmation.

She nodded.

"All right. A fallen god, then, whatever that means. Your power is your own, regardless of where it was initially drawn from. You used Velyos' power in the cathedral, did that feel similar?"

"No. Just like any of the gods' might."

He tilted his head, eyeing a stained glass window behind her. She smiled as she watched the curious, inquisitive boy who loved a puzzle.

"We can rule out that this is a fallen god's power, then, because it would feel like *that*."

"That doesn't really leave anything else, though. I'm not a witch, like Pelageya. She said I was drawing from somewhere else." But was it someone else? Or some*thing* else? Or if it truly was her magic alone, what was it that made it feel so dark and out of reach? Why couldn't she get to it herself? "Pelageya said that witch magic and cleric magic is no different, so why can't I do anything with this? And why is it changing me?"

The tattooed lines on his forehead wrinkled as he frowned.

"Divinity tastes like copper and ashes," he murmured. He held her corrupted hand gently, looking down at it for a long time before his gaze lifted past Nadya's, as if just over her shoulder.

Nadya stilled. She slid her other hand over his.

"And a fractured halo . . ." He slashed open her palm.

She flinched, biting her lip. "Couldn't you *ask* before you do that?"

He didn't answer, dipping an index finger in her blood. He stuck his finger in his mouth.

"Gods, Malachiasz, what are you doing?"

She reared back as he waved vague, bloody fingers in front of her face, shushing her absently. "I have a theory."

"Is it that you're disgusting?"

"No, there's enough evidence of that to conclude it's true," he said distantly, staring right past her. He paused, and with an odd note in his voice, whispered, "Divinity," his eyes unfocused.

Nadya went cold, watching him in horror as he turned whatever pieces he was putting together in his mind. She couldn't tell what it was he had figured out and was not telling her.

"Not of your gods, not of those fallen, something further, something older. Ancient, hungry, *mad*."

"Malachiasz?"

He twitched, blinking back to himself and down at the blood pooling in her palm, paling. "Sorry," he said, pulling a cloth from his jacket pocket and carefully wrapping her hand.

She waited, dread coiling inside her. He took her face between his hands, something in his eyes she had never seen before; it frightened her.

"It won't harm you if you claim it," he said, hushed and almost reverent in a way that didn't make sense from this heretic boy. "You'll merely become magnificent."

"What—"

He kissed her. He was a storm and she was going to drown. He broke away too soon, leaving her feeling unmoored and shaky. Malachiasz very softly kissed the backs of the fingers on her corrupted hand.

"Everything will be fine, I promise," he said. "But you have to take the next step yourself. It's you, Nadya, it's all you." He got up to leave, pressing a hand lightly against her hair before he slipped out of the room.

"What?" she whispered, pressing a hand to her mouth.

As long as they walked on opposite sides of this conflict, they would be cruel to each other even if they wanted to be tender. And when they were tender, her heart would beat too full. There was no escaping it.

The moment he was gone Marzenya's presence swept over her.

*What does it mean? What does he mean? What do you mean for me to do?*

The goddess did not answer right away. Nadya got up from her seat and almost fell over before she made it to the altar and lit another stick of incense. *And will the other gods ever speak to me again?*

*"They cannot,"* Marzenya said simply, not deigning to answer her other questions.

Nadya's heart faltered. Oh. *But the veil?*

*"Another veil, a different magic,"* Marzenya said. *"Different in creation, a similar end. More focused, more defined. Stronger. The Tranavians have crafted something that will crack Kalyazin in half if they are given the opportunity. That is why you must change their minds."*

*Change their minds?* Nadya questioned. The war had gone on for nearly a century. Tranavians like Malachiasz and Serefin wanted the war to end. But Tranavia itself? Kalyazin? Did they want the war to end? Serefin had mentioned how lucrative it was for the Tranavian nobles and Nadya wondered if it was the same for Kalyazin.

It made her so tired.

*"We will change their minds,"* Marzenya repeated. *"Permanently. There is a well from which you must drink. We will fix this. We will bring balance back. We will bring Tranavia back into our graces."*

Nadya swallowed. This was a very different song than Marzenya usually sang for her.

*Do you know why the Church has lied to me? About old gods, the ones that have fallen away? About what this power of mine is?*

There was a long pause. *"It is not the time for questions. It is the time for action. Go."*

Nadya should be grateful all-consuming destruction was no longer on the table. She should be grateful to end this without destroying the country that the boy she cared for loved so much even if she had to tear him apart to do it.

Malachiasz's strange behavior still bewildering and present, she buried her doubts, lit another stick of incense, and left the sanctuary.

# interlude v

## PARIJAHAN

## SIROOSI

The letter was folded into a tiny square and pushed as far into the bottom of her pack as she could get it. She didn't know how the messenger had even found her. Her family's reach clearly went farther than she thought.

> *His Most High Majesty, King of Kings, Ruler of the Travash of House Siroosi, In Whose Hands Rests the Bond of the Five Countries Under the Great Sun, Daryoush Siroosi, is dying. He will soon walk amidst the sands.*
> *Come home, Your Highness.*

She stared into the fire. They had left the monastery a few days earlier. Going to the opposite end of Kalyazin simply because Nadya wanted to had been reason enough for Parijahan; it meant being far, far away from Akola.

Rashid was asleep, his head in her lap, her fingers woven through his dark hair. Nadya was by turns morose and strangely focused on something she and Malachiasz spent hours each day discussing. Parijahan had long since stopped hearing the soft sounds of Malachiasz's and Nadya's voices as they bickered in the odd back and forth of Tranavian and Kalyazi they had a tendency to drop into when they were talking. Parijahan didn't think either of them noticed they were doing it. They would talk in one language until one of them hit a wall that the other's language didn't allow them to pass and they would switch to their own and continue.

Her father was dying.

*Come home.*

She was supposed to feel sad, but mostly she was terrified at what that meant with her so far from Akola.

She startled when Malachiasz sat down next to her.

"Is Nadya asleep?" she asked.

He nodded. "Have you told Rashid?"

"I can't tell Rashid."

Malachiasz lifted an eyebrow.

"Yanzin Zadar has been waiting for Paalmidesh to show weakness for decades. They've been trying to topple the Paalmideshi Travash for as long as I can remember. I cannot trust him with this."

"Oh." He set his chin in his hands. "I love hearing that another country's politics are as messed up as Tranavia's."

"I have a hard time believing anything can be worse than Tranavia."

"How's that whole five-kingdom-unification thing going?"

Parijahan was quiet.

"See, I knew that would be a bad idea. At least two kings are manageable."

"If only the Five Fathers had asked you centuries ago, you could have given them your stunning political advice."

"It *is* a shame that I was not consulted."

Parijahan rolled her eyes. "You're good at politics, at least."

"What an accusation."

"Not a baseless one."

"I'm merely good at being patient. And it's a game." He was quiet, then allowed, "And I am good at the game."

He was understating his capabilities. "Ugh. You handle this, then."

"Absolutely not. I was under the impression that you and Rashid were not too concerned with your country of origin's particular squabbles," Malachiasz said.

"I mean, I don't know. Yanzin Zadar has the right to be upset at Paalmidesh; we haven't exactly been kind to them. And Rashid . . . he's said it doesn't bother him."

"Ah, he *says* that."

"Don't you dare, Malachiasz Czechowicz, you horrible boy."

Malachiasz laughed softly.

"He'll tell me to go back," she said. "He'll tell me to do the right thing because he's so damn noble."

Malachiasz drew one knee up to his chest, wrapping his arms around it.

"I can't do it, Malachiasz. I thought they would disown me for leaving. I was prepared for *that* reality, not this one."

He rested his head on his knee, thinking. Every so often, a part of him would shiver, like he wasn't totally in the same realm of existence as everyone else. She had known from the beginning what he was; he had done a terrifically bad job of hiding that he was a Vulture when he was desperate and alone in an enemy kingdom. That aspect of him never bothered her;

frankly it was the lovely, gentle Tranavian boy that always made her more wary.

But it was the lovely, gentle Tranavian boy who always listened when she complained and gave such devastatingly good advice.

He glanced pointedly at Rashid, but Parijahan waved him off. "He's not going to wake up."

"You're going to have to tell him. You're going to have to tell them both, honestly."

That was exactly what she didn't want to do.

"What would happen if you stayed here?" he asked.

"I don't know," she said. "I'm the heir to a Travash. The other two high Travash will put forward their bids for the throne. A council comprised of nobles from all the houses in Akola will decide who will be the next ruler. Yanzin Zadar will likely try to topple the system. Siroosi has held Akola for a very long time. It would be . . . dishonorable of me to abandon it and let it fall into the hands of a different house."

"But you," Malachiasz said, his words careful, "are not exactly honorable."

She shot him a wry look. "Well, *you* know that."

He grinned at her.

"You should be cautious," she said. "I have a bad feeling about all of this."

"Surely my involvement is due cause for said bad feeling," he remarked.

Yes and no. What he had done in Tranavia had been a betrayal, but she wouldn't have been so angry if he had told her from the beginning what he was planning. Grand schemes for divinity to topple gods were all well and good; Parijahan *hated* being lied to. It was part of what made her an absolutely terrible *prasīt*.

"You and Nadya are a dangerous combination," she said.

He gave a soft smile, minus his usual sharp bitterness. The feral animal that he let settle under his skin absent.

*Blessed mother, he's in love with her.* She knew this boy well enough to know that could only spell disaster.

"There was a lot of magic in the sanctuary that night and I'm not so sure we all realize what we've done."

Parijahan scoffed. He smiled ruefully.

"My own plans included."

An eye opened at his temple as if to confirm it.

"Does that hurt?"

"Yep," he said blithely. "Pretty much always! I am in constant pain."

She groaned, a laugh escaping. She rested her free hand over his. As terrible as he was, he was her friend and she didn't want to see him so damaged.

"I miscalculated," he said, shrugging. "It happens."

Parijahan didn't believe him. Though she did wish he had a more obvious tell to his lying. He hadn't miscalculated at all. The magic that he and Nadya worked with was unfathomable to Parijahan, and she didn't particularly care to know it. Akola had its own mages who only stayed out of the conflict between Kalyazin and Tranavia because few people even knew of them. They lived in the deep deserts and only rarely came into the cities to trade.

"Did you really think you would be able to kill a god and topple a divine empire just like that?" She snapped her fingers.

"I was thinking too simply, you're right. I have the power, but I don't know how to use it. I'm worried if I do that will be the end of me."

"But if you had to use that power to save Tranavia?"

He was quiet for a very long time, picking absently at the

skin around his thumbnail. "Then that would be the end of Malachiasz Czechowicz," he finally said.

Parijahan let out a soft breath.

"It's a mess. I may be idealistic, but I'm not so delusional as to think that whatever Nadya has planned is going to bring a peaceful end to this conflict." He smiled, but it was sad.

"Then why are you helping her?"

"Because I want to help. Because I *am* too damn idealistic and I have to let myself hope that one of us can fix this mess of a world or I'm going to drag myself under the weight of my own desperate pessimism." He shrugged. "Because I'm worried about her."

"If you hurt her like you did before, I'll kill you before she gets the chance," Parijahan said.

"You, I am truly terrified of," he replied.

"You should be just as scared of her."

"It's not fear," he murmured. "That's not the right word for it. But maybe it should be? She told me some disturbing things her church has said about her."

"Which you're going to use in an argument on theological morality, I'm sure," Parijahan said dryly.

"The fighting is half the fun. And you're only changing the subject because you don't want to address that letter."

She scowled. "I don't know what to do," she said.

"So, you're going to ignore it, and hope it goes away?"

"It's been working well thus far."

"Parj . . ."

She didn't want him to use that tone with her. He had no right to judge. She smoothed Rashid's hair, stalling. Her leg was asleep.

"I'm doing nothing because Nadya needs my help. I'm not leaving her with you."

"Fair," he acknowledged. "But . . . he's your father."

The wounded confusion in his voice was distressingly genuine. Parijahan shot him a desperate look.

"Some of us don't have those," he continued quietly.

He was right. But it was so much more complicated than he knew. She had said things that could never be unsaid, had done things that would never be forgiven.

She had thought her Travash would send people to kill her, not quietly beg her to return.

She closed her eyes. Malachiasz rested his head against her shoulder.

"Some of us make our own families," Parijahan said. "Not sure where I went wrong that mine has a monster boy in it, but there it is."

Malachiasz snorted.

A long silence fell over them. Malachiasz eventually got up, but only to stoke the fire and gently gather Nadya up and take her into the tent so she wouldn't freeze. She looked small in his arms, his long black hair mingling with her white-blond strands as he dipped his face down close to hers. Parijahan heard the soft muffle of their voices. He came back outside and sat down next to her.

"Go to sleep. I'll keep watch."

"I don't want to rule Akola," she said blankly, staring into the fire. "If I stay here, I don't have to." She buried her face against his shoulder.

He wrapped an arm around her. Her terrible, powerful friend. She never would have guessed when she'd fled her home that she would meet the Black Vulture of Tranavia in a tiny Kalyazi village, an anxious mess of a boy with Kalyazi soldiers on his heels. She didn't want to go back. She couldn't.

# interlude vi

Magic drawn from the saints was so terribly imperfect, and that was what the Tranavians just could not understand. With their heretical magic that made things so easy, they couldn't comprehend magic that took *work*. Serefin had watched with growing confusion on his face as Katya dumped out most of her pack and began riffling through it.

"Are those—" He picked up a handful of mushrooms. "—blood and bone, why do you have *czaczepki towcim*?"

"Only clerics have true magic," Katya said, taking out a small ceramic bowl and crushing some diviner's sage into it. "Be a dear and use your blasphemous power to light this, please?"

He frowned. There was a beat of silence.

"Sorry, have I not made it clear? The gods and I don't always get on. I don't give a rat's ass how you lot get your magic, but my opinion doesn't matter, only that of my father and the church."

They had moved into one of the burned-out shells of a home. Katya's heart ached to see such destruction, especially by something that hadn't bothered Kalyazi villagers in decades. Kalyazin had always had its monsters. They lurked in the corners, the *domovoi* kept their homes, the *bannik* kept the bathhouses, and the *dvorovoi* the stables. But the monsters that did true harm—the *zhir'oten*, the *kashyvhes*, the *drekavac*—those had not been seen in a very long time. And they had risen.

Velyos had once been the god of the underworld and the forests and all the monsters that dwelled there. When he was set free, everything else woke up with him. Kalyazin had finally struggled out of its place of darkness and monsters and now they were being pulled back under. Katya had a terrible feeling that this horror was irreversible. Even if Serefin managed to break out of Velyos' grip, the darkness was here to stay.

Serefin cut his thumb on a razor in his sleeve and lit her bowl. She offered him a mushroom. "You can come with me."

He scowled. "I've had enough divine horrors for a lifetime, thank you."

"I have a hard time believing you would turn your nose up at some light hallucinogens."

"You don't know me at all, dear." He had a flask propped up against his thigh. He conceded, "If blood magic could be augmented with drugs, the Vultures would have figured out how *long* before now. Recreational is another matter entirely."

She shrugged. "Suit yourself." She held it out to Ostyia who hesitated before shaking her head.

"Blood magic is enough for me," Ostyia said quietly.

"Bleed a little more on the sage," Katya told Serefin. "I'll use that to track the Black Vulture."

Serefin shifted nervously. *Silly heretics, so uncertain when confronted with magic they do not understand,* she thought. Whatever she was given from Svoyatovi Vladislav Batishchev would be enough to find the Black Vulture. But she would need to do other rituals to have enough power to kill a Vulture, especially one as powerful as him.

Clerics could use power at any time. People like Katya, who called on saints, had to do lengthy, extensive rituals to gain a scrap of magic. They were good for hunting, good for single encounters, but bad for the battlefield. The magic took too much preparation with very little to speak of as a reward. Katya didn't mind; she couldn't fathom living with power like a cleric, constantly present and *there.*

"First Pelageya, now her, what is with you Kalyazi?" Kacper muttered.

"You've met Pelageya?" Katya cried, incredulous.

"She's my mother's advisor," Serefin said with a frown.

"If witches had an all-mother, she would be Pelageya," Katya said. "*I've* met Pelageya. She's one of the last witches left. Well, she's mostly considered a myth, so the church doesn't try too hard to root her out." It made sense Pelageya would have been in Tranavia all this time; they would be much kinder to witches.

Serefin eyed Katya warily. Or, at least, she thought he did. It was disconcerting, how she couldn't tell what he was looking at through his ghostly eyes. *He* was disconcerting. She didn't understand how a king had been dragged into what sounded like utterly Kalyazi business. How had he been taken by a banished god who had slumbered for a millennia? Was this the cleric's fault? Or had Serefin been singled out for this long ago and there was no stopping it?

Katya did so enjoy a good existential contemplation every now and again.

"It sounds like you don't have a high opinion of the church," Serefin remarked.

"I love the church, but I don't *like* the church," Katya said. "It's complicated."

"Apparently."

"It sounds like *you* don't have a very good relationship with your family," Katya noted with an eyebrow lift.

"I've killed my father and I'm planning to kill my brother," Serefin replied. "I can't imagine what you're referring to."

She fanned some of the smoke into her face, inhaling deeply, before picking up one of the mushrooms. "I'll be right back," she said with a wry grin before popping it into her mouth.

The effects were relatively sudden. And Katya fell.

# 31

## NADEZHDA

## LAPTEVA

*Grigoriy Rogov was a monk who heard the voices of the fallen gods. He was poisoned by a brother at his monastery.*
—The Books of Innokentiy

Malachiasz spent more and more time poring over his spell book. It would almost be a return to normalcy—he had always been bleeding over it before—but there was something in the way he curled over it, staying away from everyone in the evenings when they camped, that worried Nadya. But she couldn't quite convince herself he was plotting to betray them all because he wouldn't be so damn obvious about it. And whenever she went over and poked her chin against his shoulder, he would do his best to explain what he was doing—stringing together spells that would get them through the forest in one piece—not hide it away. Some nights he would ignore the book, sitting folded up at the edge of the fire, sewing

the back of his jacket where his wings had torn through it. Rashid loudly judged his stitching.

He had refused to explain what he had seen of her power in the sanctuary, and she wondered if he knew more than he was letting on. If he knew of the stories of where they were going. But as smart as Malachiasz was, she found it hard to believe that a boy from Tranavia would know of this place. That he would know of Evdokiya Dobronravova, who made the pilgrimage to Bolagvoy but was devoured by Tachilvnik along the way. She was torn to pieces by her own deteriorating mind and flowers grew over her bones.

Surely he didn't know that was the fate Nadya had for him.

They had been traveling for weeks and still had farther to go before they reached the point where the Dozvlatovya Forest became Tachilvnik. The impassible reach. The piece of Kalyazin fully given over to monsters. No one who walked into this part of the forest ever walked out, but it was the fastest way to the monastery. If they survived, they would be there in half the time. But it was a pretty big *if*.

Parijahan had been acting strange and Nadya wasn't sure if she should say anything about *that*, either. She was worried that she had been so wrapped up in her own problems that she hadn't noticed something. Maybe Parijahan had been acting off for a while. Maybe Malachiasz had been growing steadily more anxious. And maybe Nadya hadn't noticed any of it.

Losing Kostya was hard, but it would be worse if the ache of his loss caused her to push away the friends she had left. She couldn't bear to lose Parijahan or Rashid. And Malachiasz . . . well . . . it didn't really matter what her heart thought.

Parijahan and Malachiasz were whispering, the jagged tones of their voices finding her ears. Eventually Malachiasz broke away and stalked off. Nadya frowned. Parijahan had her arms crossed over her chest and was furiously ignoring the looks from Nadya and Rashid.

Nadya moved into the trees to follow Malachiasz. He wasn't trying to be subtle and it was easy to find his tall frame as it slipped through the trees. He was on edge when she found him, standing at the shore of a riverbed, gazing down at the water, somehow still flowing despite the freezing cold.

"I don't want to talk about it," he said as she approached.

Nadya scowled. He glanced at her. His eyes softened.

"It's nothing . . ." He trailed off and waved a hand.

"Evil?" she offered.

He laughed. "Is that the word for it?"

"For you? Most certainly, Malachiasz."

His breath still hitched when she used his name, and she tried to use it as much as she could. She wondered if the reminders helped, if there was any point in reminding him of the fragile anchor tying him to his humanity. She decided, ultimately, that it didn't particularly matter if it *didn't* help, it was still something she could do for the time that was left.

And it was comforting to hear that he and Parijahan were fighting about something benign.

"Well," she finally said, "I'm here if you do want to talk about it."

"Does it ever bother you?" he asked. "Not knowing where you're from and who your family is?"

Nadya couldn't tell if this was related to anything or not. She knew it bothered him that his childhood memories had been stripped away. As much as he *liked* the monster he was, there would always be a seed of resentment for how he had become that way.

She shrugged. Frankly, she never thought about it. Her sense of belonging had always been firmly grounded within the monastery walls. It wasn't until she had started clashing with so many of her faith that she found herself wavering. She no longer knew where she belonged. She would never be able to remain within a monastery's walls again—she had seen and done too much—and the thought terrified her.

She had been quiet for too long. She wasn't usually the thoughtful one. Malachiasz shot her a curious look.

"No," she said quietly. "It bothers me more that I don't think I fit anymore with those I thought of as family."

A pause of puzzlement, before an infuriatingly smug light flickered in his eyes. "Because I've finally convinced you that I'm right?" he asked, falsely innocent.

"You're not even a little bit right," she snapped.

It wasn't that he was right and she was wrong. It was that he had pointed out discrepancies she couldn't account for. Nadya couldn't rationalize the things she had seen in Tranavia.

She returned his smile with a glare and shoved her hands deep into the pockets of her coat.

"I want to know what made me so worthless that I was easily thrown away," he finally whispered.

Nadya's heart splintered. "I thought Tranavians believed being chosen for the Vultures was an honor."

"It *is*. But . . ." He shook his head.

How long until the little things he didn't say became another web of lies? How much could she overlook before she came to regret it? What *had* he done that he was not telling her? She wondered if Marzenya knew, if that was being kept from her as well. She didn't understand why she had to be in the dark. She wanted to *help*.

Nadya had received some further instruction from Marzenya. A dedicated spot to go to. Her instincts had pushed her to the right place, but Marzenya made it sound like she wanted Nadya for so much more.

And maybe the girl trapped in Tranavia would have faltered a bit at that shifting of her destiny. Maybe the girl who had been trapped in the dark heart of the monster's den might have some doubts about Marzenya's intentions, but losing the voice of the gods—losing *everything*—had changed something within Nadya. She couldn't lose everything. She couldn't lose the voice of the gods. She wouldn't be rendered *useless*. But, oh, she was angry at Marzenya and if this didn't work she didn't know where that would leave her.

"I don't know," he finally said. "I don't like these woods."

"You? Not know something? Impossible."

"I'm going to push you into this river."

"I can't swim!"

"That's a shame. I guess you'll die."

He tensed suddenly, turning to gaze into the trees.

"Nadya?" he murmured, eyes growing glassy.

The hairs on the back of her neck stood up.

"When were we supposed to reach Tachilvnik?" Malachiasz asked.

"A week or so. We're still a ways south," Nadya said.

He made a thoughtful humming sound.

"And from there it becomes the forest that only the divine can pass through. Tranavia has lakes, we have forests."

He didn't react, still peering through the gaps in the trees. Though it was midday, they were so deep into the forest that little sun passed through the branches of the trees. With their whole world permanently frozen in the middle of winter, it made everything all the more bleak.

Nadya wanted her prayer beads. She had relegated them

to a pouch in her pack; only Marzenya's bead remained in her pocket. She rolled it through her fingers, wishing she could speak with Vaclav.

A biting chill cut through her, the air of a deep winter. She slowly pulled the bead out of her pocket. The pad of her finger ran across the carving of a skull, only one facet of her goddess's domain. Death. Magic. Winter.

*Winter.*

Pelageya had told her divine retribution on Tranavia would not be so obvious, that the winter was part of it. But the winter was killing Kalyazin as well. What was Marzenya hiding?

"There's something watching us," Malachiasz said, his voice tangled at the edges. He reached for his blade and spell book.

"Blood mage, not Vulture," she said absently.

He rolled his eyes, but they remained clear.

"The things that dwell in this forest are not going to appreciate our trespassing." She could feel it, too, something old and angry watching from the shadows.

She *really* wished she could talk to Vaclav. If it was a *leshy* they were all going to have problems. The guardians of the forests were not known to be particularly friendly.

Malachiasz shivered. He slowly sheathed his dagger and clipped his spell book back to his belt.

"Don't cause undue attention. If it's only watching us, let it," she said. "We need to get through this without drawing them near. Besides, king of monsters, shouldn't they listen to you?"

She received a *look*.

There had been that moment with the *rusałki* and Nadya had been so certain Malachiasz's magic was why they had listened.

What if that had been her?

They waited for the others to catch up, but when they did,

Malachiasz soon wandered off. Nadya didn't bother following this time. She fell into step with Parijahan.

"I'm not going to ask what you and Malachiasz have been snapping at each other about," Nadya said when Parijahan stiffened. "But you can talk to me if you need to, you know that, right?"

"It's nothing. Malachiasz is just being the anxious mess he is."

Nadya lifted an eyebrow. Parijahan smiled at her.

"Besides, I don't want to burden you with my own difficulties while you're dealing with all this," she said.

Nadya didn't want to be spared because she was struggling. She didn't want Parijahan to feel like she had to deal with whatever this was alone simply because Nadya's life had crumbled to pieces around her.

She had opened her mouth to say so when unfamiliar magic slammed into her. Her breath caught. The magic was almost divine. Something crashed nearby, a fight breaking out. Nadya and Parijahan exchanged a glance as Rashid took off in the direction of the commotion.

Malachiasz had a tall, dark-haired girl pinned to the ground. Nadya almost got a question out before someone moved at her elbow and she lashed out instinctively.

Punching one king of Tranavia in the face. He took a staggered step back, swearing and lifting his hands.

Shock melted into relief. *"Serefin?"*

He blinked at her, patted her mildly on the head, and then was very suddenly focused on Malachiasz and the girl behind Nadya. She turned, drawing her *voryen* and holding it loosely.

"Who are *you, towy wilockna*?" Malachiasz hissed. "And what do you think you are doing with those teeth?"

The girl's eyes flashed and she spat something at Malachiasz that Nadya couldn't quite catch, though she recognized Kal-yazi. Malachiasz laughed darkly.

"Who has lied to you?" he asked, voice a low tangle. One hand against her sternum, the other braced an iron claw against her throat. His eyes were murky, seconds from filling with black. "Did they tell you that you would have some secret magic? Take you into a dark room and whisper in a language you did not know until you felt *different*? Did they tell you that you were special, hand you a magic blade? Tell you that you were oh so prepared to kill someone like me?"

Nadya caught Serefin's hand going to the blade at his belt. She edged closer to Malachiasz.

The girl was breathing hard, but a cold smile tugged at her mouth.

Malachiasz grinned back, teeth iron. "You think you're a Vulture hunter, little wolf? Did you think those teeth harvested from my kind made you special?" He lifted the string of teeth around the girl's neck with an iron claw. "Can I tell you a se-cret?" His sick smile tugged farther at his mouth. "I know every tooth on this string and every Vulture you have stolen from still lives. All you are is a girl with no magic and a dull blade and a string of teeth."

*That's enough of that,* Nadya thought, tipping her *voryen* under his chin. "You of all people should know not to underestimate a girl with a blade." She tapped the flat against his cheek. "Let her up, you've made your point."

He let the girl scramble to her feet. He rested his elbows on his knees, hands tipped with iron claws remaining menac-ingly visible.

She was tall, with refined features as though cut from glass. She wore a Kalyazi military jacket in deep navy and had a *voryen* gripped tight in one fist; her sharp green eyes were strangely dilated. What odd new companion had Serefin picked up? And what was he doing here?

"Can—can I see that?" she asked, holding her hand out for the dagger. The girl clearly thought it could harm Malachiasz. Was it another relic?

The girl's gaze left Malachiasz's briefly, her eyes narrowing on Nadya's outstretched hand. She glanced at Serefin wryly.

His eyebrows lifted; he leaned back against a tree. What was *Serefin* doing with a Vulture hunter who held herself with the clear airs of a noble?

"I took every tooth myself," she said to Malachiasz.

"Do you think our teeth don't grow back?" Malachiasz retorted, his voice treacherously pleasant. "Do you think pulling a tooth from our mouths will do some irreparable harm?"

"They were dead when I took them," the girl snapped.

"Darling, we are very good at surviving."

She cocked her head. Her posture was incredibly relaxed for someone who had just been thrown to the ground by the Black Vulture.

"You're with him?" she asked Nadya.

Nadya rested her hand in Malachiasz's hair. That strange spark of magic lit under her fingers but she ignored it. "I'm the one who's keeping him from ripping your throat out, yes."

"Easy," Serefin said, his voice low.

"Let me see the blade," Nadya said, harder this time.

The girl laughed. "You don't *order* me."

"Nadya," Serefin broke in wearily, "might I introduce one *Tsarevna* Yekaterina Vodyanova?"

All the blood drained from Nadya's face. *What?*

"Katya," Serefin continued, "that is Nadezhda Lapteva, your cleric. Please never make me introduce two Kalyazi to each other ever again. I'm going to go nurse my wounded pride."

The *tsarevna* looked smug. She flipped her *voryen* over and handed it hilt first to Nadya, who took it, dazed. The future ruler of Kalyazin was standing in front of her and she was traveling with the Black Vulture. There was no way to spin that as a good thing. But, as Nadya gave it more thought, she realized being around Serefin had desensitized her to the idea of royalty. She might as well act like she wasn't rattled by this turn of events.

"Did you think this would kill him?" Nadya tapped the flat of the blade against Malachiasz's cheek. "Anything?"

"I think—"

"No?"

"I think you have to use it the other way," Malachiasz offered helpfully. He mimed being stabbed.

Nadya snorted softly. They both knew that wasn't true. Her bone relic hurt him by just being near him. This was nothing more than an average blade. She handed it to Malachiasz.

He shifted off his heels, sitting down. His eyes cleared, claws receding except for one, which he used to slice open his forearm. Katya winced. He rifled through his spell book for a few seconds before tearing out a page and wrapping the dagger in it. The paper blew into ash in his hands. He flipped it in the air, catching it by the tip and offering it to the *tsarevna*.

"If you'd like to test it, you can stab me. I'd survive but you would feel very good doing it, *Wécz Joczocyść*," he said.

She bared her teeth at him. He tossed the *voryen* at her. She caught it by the hilt.

"Well," Malachiasz continued, "this is all a nice little coincidence, isn't it?"

"Shut up, Malachiasz," Nadya said.

Malachiasz's single lifted eyebrow was turned on her, and a shiver of fear warned her that she might be treading too far.

But he remained seated, legs casually stretched out. He leaned back on his hands, content to watch this all play out.

"What are you doing out here?" she asked Serefin, hyper aware of the *tsarevna* watching her. Eyeing the hand she had resting in Malachiasz's hair, the bone she was rolling between fingertips.

Serefin's eye looked otherworldly, the other covered with a black patch; he looked terrible.

"He's got an ancient god rattling in his head and we're trying to break him free," Katya answered for him.

"I'm sorry, how are you involved?" Nadya was baffled at what the *tsarevna*'s role was in all of this. How did Serefin cross paths with her? Weren't they at *war*?

Though, she supposed the same could be said about her and Malachiasz; both symbols for oppositional ideologies yet here together all the same.

Katya grinned. "I know a great deal about ancient gods."

Nadya's heart leapt to her throat. Could Katya help her? Would she know what all the cryptic messages Nadya had been getting meant? Would she *want* to help Nadya, knowing she was with the Black Vulture? Nadya wouldn't put it past her for wanting nothing to do with a tainted cleric.

"Where are you going?" she asked.

"Tzanelivki," Serefin said. He rubbed at his eye absently.

"That's where we're going," Malachiasz said, sounding confused. At Nadya's puzzlement he clarified, "Tachilvnik." No longer content to watch, he finally got to his feet. The *tsarevna* tensed as he straightened to his full height.

"We all need to go to the same damn place, apparently," Malachiasz said acidly. "How fortuitous."

Serefin's eyes narrowed. "I haven't forgotten what you did," he said, voice low.

"I would be incredibly disappointed if you had. I worked *very* hard to put all that into place and you had to go and ruin it by surviving."

"Blood and bone, I am so sorry to have foiled treason. Really, it's quite a shame. What Tranavia really needs is to be ruled by the worst Black Vulture we've ever had."

A smile flickered at Malachiasz's mouth. "Tranavia has survived this long because I am the worst. Don't fool yourself."

There was a ringing in Nadya's ears that she couldn't shake. All the weird little quirks that Serefin had that had reminded her of Malachiasz when she was in Grazyk suddenly became frighteningly clear. Watching them face off, the resemblance in their profiles was too close to be a coincidence. Serefin's eyes—before all of this—had been the same icy pale as Malachiasz's. They had similar, fine-boned features. Malachiasz was a wasted, slighter shadow to Serefin, but the resemblance was striking. *One boy cast from darkness and the other cast from gold.*

*Oh, gods.*

# 32

## SEREFIN
## MELESKI

*He lies beneath the waves. Deep water. Dark water. Zvezdan's twisted hands hold between them an army, should he ever think to look up and listen to the drowned priests calling for his grace.*

—The Books of Innokentiy

"You come here, you have the Kalyazi *tsarevna* in tow, who just happens to hunt Vultures—" Malachiasz leveled an annoyed look at Serefin that said *nice try*. "—what are you up to, *moje kóczk*?"

Serefin shuddered at Malachiasz's biting tone.

Katya had dragged Nadya off and was talking with her intently. Kacper looked like he wanted to kill Malachiasz himself. He was sitting on a fallen tree next to Ostyia, who clearly *really* wanted to know what Katya and Nadya were talking about, but after a few minutes got up to talk to the Akolan pair.

"What am *I* up to?" Serefin repeated. "Novel for you of all people to ask me that."

Malachiasz rolled his eyes.

"Especially when I should be asking the same of you."

Malachiasz waved vaguely toward where Nadya stood. As Serefin watched, lightly horrified, a cluster of eyes—pitch-black—blinked open across his cheek. Malachiasz didn't react as his body roiled and shifted. But there was a shiver at his edges that made Serefin think he wasn't really seeing *all* of him. He slowly tugged the patch off his eye.

"You're a mess, aren't you?" he murmured.

Chaos given form. Malachiasz was hiding what he truly was behind a mask that had grown flimsy. The horror was so much more and with his lost eye he could see *everything*. Maybe Malachiasz really had managed to become close to godlike. Serefin had vastly underestimated what he was up against.

Malachiasz frowned, puzzled.

"And what have you done with all this power?"

A fracture in Malachiasz's expression. "I . . . don't know."

*Lying, he's lying.*

*"Of course he's lying. He's built an empire on vulnerability,"* Velyos noted.

*You know what he is, then?*

*"Gaining the power of a god and knowing how to use it are two very different things,"* Velyos replied.

Serefin tucked that thought away. He tied the patch back over his eye.

"You look abysmal," he said flatly.

Malachiasz grinned. "So do you. Who's the god?"

"I don't want to talk about this with you."

"I am flattered that you think I'm going to sabotage you."

Serefin huffed. "What have you spent the last year doing if not sabotaging me?"

Malachiasz's posture was languid but betrayed by his fingers picking at the skin around his cuticles. Serefin blinked, jarred a little. It was an anxious habit of his mother's.

*He really is my brother,* he thought, a sinking feeling pulling him under.

"A question better served for you to answer," Malachiasz replied. "My memory is foggy at best."

*More lies.*

"It's a long way to Tzanelivki," Malachiasz continued. "And you're a long way from home. In whose hands did you leave the throne?"

The needling edge in Malachiasz's voice raised Serefin's hackles. How did he *know* what had happened?

"Right. You didn't."

He had left it in his mother's—blood and bone, *their* mother's—hands, but that wasn't a worthy point to argue here.

"And what would you have done?" Serefin asked.

"Killed Ruminski. Immediately. Take out the leader and the rats will scatter."

"Haven't we seen enough death?"

Malachiasz laughed. "We haven't even gotten started."

*No, they most certainly had not.*

"How did you know all of that?"

"I'm the Black Vulture. I still have my order."

"Do you?"

A flicker. "Well, mostly," he allowed.

"What did you do with Żaneta?"

"As far as I'm aware, she is in the Salt Mines where she belongs as she is a member of *my* order."

Serefin ground his teeth. "You withheld her on purpose."

"Did you think I'd make things easy for you? After your hand in so thoroughly destroying my plans? I held out something Nadya would want more and she took it."

"Because she's *so easy* to manipulate."

Again, a crack. "She . . . cares," he finally said.

"Not enough to help me keep my throne."

"Why would you expect her to choose a Tranavian when she can save someone from Kalyazin?" But Malachiasz frowned. "It doesn't matter. Żaneta took to the changes poorly. It happens. It's best for her to remain in the Salt Mines until she's adapted, and she *will* adapt, she just needs time."

The admission was surprising and almost sounded like Malachiasz was trying to help.

Serefin had wondered what happened down in the Salt Mines. He didn't really want the grim details, but this eased his mind. At least now he knew the whole thing had been as doomed from the start as he'd suspected.

He stepped closer to Malachiasz, words leaving his lips unbidden. The other boy blinked, like he wanted to step away, but held his ground. "You know what she's going to do, don't you?"

Malachiasz tilted his head. "Why, do you?"

"What does that goddess of hers want, Malachiasz?" Serefin didn't know what he was saying. What was *happening* to him? "Did you think she would stop after Grazyk? Or does she want all of Tranavia to kneel?"

Malachiasz scowled, but his face paled.

"What will that precious cleric of yours do at the whim of her goddess?"

Malachiasz swallowed hard, ice in his eyes. "I don't think it's that simple." He stepped away from Serefin. And Serefin, with a shudder, was let go.

Nadya moved away from Katya, her face drawn. The *tsarevna* went to speak to a very miserable Milomir—he nodded and disappeared into the trees—and she bounded over, cheerful.

"Enough wasting time?" she asked.

"Where's he going?" Serefin asked.

"Milomir won't be traveling with us any farther."

"This party has *four* Tranavians," Kacper pointed out.

"And one cleric," Katya said brightly.

As if that was a worthy exchange. Nadya shifted uncomfortably. She exchanged a glance with Malachiasz, unspoken words passing between them.

It hadn't been Serefin who had spoken of Nadya, but the words echoed in his head. What *was* she doing? He didn't like that they were going to the same place because now it appeared as though they were being *led* to the same place, and Serefin could not go where Velyos wished him to go.

*But what if it means stopping Nadya? Stopping Malachiasz?*

He might not have a choice.

The itching in Serefin's head was only getting worse. He didn't have a great deal of time to make it to Tzanelivki before he lost what little will he had left.

And if he lost that, what would be done with him? He needed more information, and he needed to know what Nadya was planning. But Malachiasz was keeping Nadya away from him whenever he could, and when Malachiasz wasn't with her, the *tsarevna* was, and she was just as bad.

So Serefin stuck close to Ostyia and Kacper, ignored how much Ostyia flirted with Katya, and let Kacper do his very best to convince him they were going to get out of this in one piece.

There was some awkwardness that Serefin and Kacper hadn't figured out how to navigate yet. Something hanging over them that kept them *apart*. For Serefin, it was the inevitable—he was probably going to die. It didn't make him feel like he should give in to the shifting spark he had for Kacper, when all he wanted to do was exactly that. He didn't know what was holding the other boy back, though. Perhaps the same thing from a different angle.

Kalyazi forests were dark, the underbrush thick and hard to navigate. They lost the road not long after they ventured into Dozvlatovya. They still had deeper to go, so much further to fall, and they were always being watched. Serefin could feel it and Malachiasz clearly could too; his hands and arms were constantly bleeding as he held various protection spells in place. Serefin wasn't entirely sure how he was conscious with that much blood loss.

Nadya was different than she was in Grazyk, but Serefin couldn't really place how. Was it the same tension that he was feeling? The same heavy inevitability that they were damned hanging over them? That regardless of where they went and what they did, this was so far out of their control that it would only end in disaster. She was constantly bickering with Malachiasz, but only ever about trivialities. Serefin had a feeling they would all know when those two fought about something important.

It took a few days of travel before Serefin was finally able to get Nadya alone. Malachiasz had gone off to find water that they could boil to drink. None of them wanted to risk a fire in the forest, but most nights it meant the difference between survival and a slow death.

Serefin dropped to the ground beside Nadya. She was carefully stringing wooden beads onto a cord, but every so often she would pull them all off and start over. She chewed on her lower lip as she worked.

"He's lying, you know," Serefin said.

"I know." Nadya didn't look up.

Serefin glanced sidelong at her; she returned the look before going back to her work.

How to explain that he could *see* things. Things that didn't make sense, things that couldn't be real. How did he explain that he just *knew* every other word out of Malachiasz's mouth was a lie, even the earnest ones—especially those. How did he explain that he could just *tell*? Malachiasz remembered every single damn thing since fleeing the cathedral. He absolutely knew what he had done; he simply didn't want to admit any of it to Nadya. Why bring to light the fact that their relationship balanced on fraying threads?

"He remembers," Serefin said simply.

Nadya tensed. Her fingers paused in their work. She tugged the beads off the cord, rearranged two, and strung them back on. Strung on a new bead and tied three knots in between that and the next one. She worked in silence for a long time before she spoke.

"You don't know that," she said quietly.

"Nadya, I do."

Her dark eyes were cold. Why did she want to trust him *that much*? After what he had done to her?

"Say he *is* lying," she said, "what does it matter? It's a fairly safe assumption that everything he says is a lie."

"So why do you keep him around?"

"I need him to get to Bolagvoy. Neither of us are getting there without him."

"Do you know that for certain?"

"Serefin, we're both acting on myth and hope alone. If the

stories say that mortals cannot pass through the forest, I'm inclined to believe it. We need someone who is *more,* and that someone is, unfortunately, him."

"Could be me," he murmured, touching the corner of one eye.

She lifted an eyebrow. "Do you want to risk that?"

*Risk?*

Interesting, how there was a name for that place in Kalyazi and Tranavian and it didn't mean the same thing in either language. Interesting, how they needed a monster to get anywhere.

"Also," she said, "nothing has *happened.*"

"I really don't think that should be your metric for how harmless you think him. Because I don't think that's true at all. There was a massacre at Kartevka," he said. "A lot of Kalyazi died and a lot of relics were stolen."

Serefin had the sudden acute awareness he wasn't acting wholly on his own. That other presence was suddenly very *close.* The words were still Serefin's but there was something else nudging him along. Something that liked it very much when Nadya looked up, a fracture in her calm.

"Not good," she allowed. "But still nothing at the levels he implied he was capable of, no?"

"You'd sacrifice your people for him?"

"No," she said shortly. "I'm willing to be pragmatic about him. That's different."

Serefin couldn't really see how it was different at all.

She sighed. "I was never under any assumption that he didn't commit atrocities during those months. I should have been clearer, Serefin, he has not yet declared war on the gods, which suggests he's not quite at the capacity he would like."

"Having the power of a god and knowing what to do with it are two very different things," Serefin said, quoting Velyos.

Nadya blinked. "What?"

She had not seen what Serefin had of Malachiasz. Serefin had a feeling that even at his worst, Malachiasz was still going to appear human. That had not been what Serefin had seen when he had let his altered vision take in his younger brother.

"What are you implying, Serefin?"

"I'm *implying* that you're thinking too simply." Serefin had been shoved backward, his words no longer his. "You are trapped in a very limited perspective where you trust what is in front of you far too much. You have your gods, but what if they're simply beings with power that have figured out what to *do* with all that power?"

She was staring. This was not something he knew anything about, nor had he given her reason to believe he did. He almost certainly sounded completely out of his mind.

"We think about power too simply," he continued, because he had to, because this *wasn't him speaking*. "What if it isn't only blood magic and whatever your power is—"

"Divine magic," she said quietly.

"Yes, that. What if there was more to it?"

Her dark eyebrows tugged down. She looked at the half-strung strand of beads and flexed the fingers of her left hand, the skin strangely stained.

"What if the gods you worship aren't gods at all?" he murmured, quoting Pelageya's words from a lifetime ago. "What if it all comes down to *power*?" Serefin—*not Serefin*—asked.

"Keep going," she said, but her voice trembled.

"Divine power, blood magic, witch magic, then more, then further. Monsters, beings who have figured out how to use their power to transcend paltry mortal bonds, further still—"

"Gods," she finished quietly.

"Gods," he repeated. "So if one has that kind of power, but

doesn't know yet how to use it . . ." He trailed off. Malachiasz had appeared at the edges of the camp, vaguely frustrated.

Nadya stared at him without blinking.

Serefin *had* to come back to himself. But he didn't know how. And he wondered if this was the beginning of the end.

If he lost control so utterly, there would be no bringing himself back. The being—whatever it was—would have him totally.

She turned back, searching his uncovered eye. "Who is the god that has you?"

"Velyos." And when he went to tell her about the other one, he found he could not. Something forced his hand, kept him from speaking. The words died in his throat.

She didn't notice his struggle. She nodded once, her expression never changing. "Of course," she whispered, her voice strangely dispassionate. "Don't worry about Malachiasz. Soon he won't be a problem for anyone."

There was something primal about the forest they passed through now. It was locked in winter, but this was a forest *always* locked in winter. Perpetually dim—the trees here had needles, not leaves, and they didn't give those up for the cold. They created canopies of darkness that they were forced to walk through, even as *something* lurked at the edges of their awareness. It was lying in wait, the slow build of a creature that had slumbered for millennia waking up.

Serefin's little band of misfits had been well enough prepared for a journey this long, and he was relieved to find that Nadya knew how to travel through a forest like this.

But knowing that it was *normal* for it to be so dark all the time didn't make it less terrifying. Knowing that they were moving into a part of the world that was ancient, that still dwelled at the twilight edges of consciousness and was rarely disturbed by mortal steps, didn't make it less unnerving.

The deeper in they traveled, the older and larger everything grew, the trees that had clustered before looming huge and impenetrable.

*"It will be like a flaying of the mind. How will you stop it, young king, young mage? How will you stop from losing everything?"*

With every passing day, Serefin fractured a little further. And the other being—that other horrible voice—took a little more of him. And Velyos flayed off a little more of his soul.

Serefin wasn't going to survive this.

Malachiasz fell into step beside him. As much as Serefin wanted to avoid him completely, it was impossible.

"You must think us all fantastically naive," Serefin observed, using a stick to poke at the ground as he walked. "As if you're only here to be good and useful."

"Do you think there's any point to holding knives at each other's backs?" Malachiasz replied mildly. "This forest is going to kill us all long before we get the chance to kill each other."

Serefin shuddered. Malachiasz dabbed absently at the corner of his mouth, fingers coming away wet with blood. He frowned. His movements were almost imperceptibly shaky, tiny stutters that Serefin sensed were ripples of chaos he was doing everything to hide as he fell apart.

"And we both want what's best for Tranavia," Malachiasz continued as if the blood had never happened. How Tranavian.

"Are you offering me a truce?"

"Not in so many words, no." His voice was delicate with distaste.

"You had me *murdered.*"

He grinned. "*I did nothing but suggest that Izak would need a powerful mage for the spell.*"

A pang struck through Serefin's chest. His father had chosen him to die. He was never going to be good enough for his father; Izak had taken the out to get rid of him the first moment he could.

"You could do perfectly well for Tranavia," Malachiasz continued. "Current decisions notwithstanding. I could be convinced to let go of some of my previous plans."

"I have a Kalyazi god trying to tear me apart from the inside out," Serefin replied wryly, "there was ultimately only a singular course of action." There was something oddly heartening about Malachiasz admitting that maybe he didn't need both thrones. It didn't change anything, Serefin was still set on his path, but the confirmation that the Black Vulture could, in fact, make a mistake was nice.

Malachiasz made a thoughtful sound. "The same god that brought you back?"

Serefin nodded.

"Interesting."

"Not particularly. He's spent a lot of time telling me I wasn't his first choice. Nadya was, but circumstance made her unavailable."

Malachiasz eyed where Nadya was walking with the *tsarevna* farther ahead.

"What is she planning, Malachiasz?"

"Transcendence, of a sort," he said. "But I don't think she realizes it. Don't worry. I have Tranavia's best interest at heart, Serefin, I always do."

*Sure. You only instigated a coup that's causing us to crumble. Tranavia's best interest, indeed.*

"I think we should be glad the god took you and not Nadya," Malachiasz murmured.

Serefin shot him an incredulous look, but Malachiasz's gaze was faraway.

"She's dangerous enough on her own."

# 33

## NADEZHDA

## LAPTEVA

**Svoyatova Valeriya Zolotova:** *A cleric of Omunitsa, she drowned in a flood sent by her goddess to wipe out the ancient city of Tokhvoloshnik.*

—Vasiliev's Book of Saints

The conversation with Serefin left Nadya shaken. Obviously Malachiasz was lying. That wasn't it. But the suggestion that, oh, no, Malachiasz had very much accomplished what he had wanted, he simply didn't know how to handle it—Nadya didn't know what to do with that.

Malachiasz had relics. Malachiasz had slaughtered her people. Magic was changing.

She had nearly finished with her prayer beads. It was hard to remember the order of the beads, and as she worked at them every evening—while those around her argued about whether to risk a fire, while Malachiasz sat curled over his spell book in a way that was suspicious—she didn't really know if it mattered if she got the order right.

Or perhaps it would make all the difference. What if there truly was a hierarchy that Nadya was ignoring? One she'd never even known about?

And she still couldn't shake the feeling that there was a bead missing, but whose? Every time she counted twenty.

"Of course the church didn't want you to know about the fallen gods," Katya said as Nadya sat next to her one evening. "They don't want anyone to know. People get curious; people would try to wake them up."

"It's more they didn't want *me* to know," Nadya said, frowning.

Katya scoffed. "What makes you so spe—" She broke off. "Oh."

Was that what it came down to? The church was afraid that Nadya would communicate with the others, the ones outside the pantheon? Technically, she already had. She supposed their fear was justified; the first thing she had done once she had spoken with one of the fallen gods was to set him free. But she wouldn't be so easily swayed again.

Except she knew that didn't matter.

"What are you doing all the way out here?" Nadya asked instead.

"Avoiding my father, mostly," Katya said with a frown. "And trying to keep that boy from unleashing the monster that's in his head."

"Technically, I freed Velyos," Nadya said.

"I can't believe no one ever told you who he was."

Everyone thought it better to protect her, to shelter her, then throw her to the wolves.

"It's not really Velyos that's the problem," Katya continued.

"It's the implication that Velyos can lead to those who are older."

Malachiasz sat down next to Nadya. Katya hesitated, but kept speaking.

"And the other fallen, well, they're bad, but we've survived worse."

"But there are gods older than that?" Nadya asked.

Katya nodded. "I've never found anything but whispers. Most of their names have been banished from memory. But there is one . . . Chyrnog. Entropy. So few remember him and that is exactly how he wished it."

Malachiasz was tense at Nadya's side.

"And maybe I'm being overly cautious—there's no proof that an elder being has stirred—but I can't help but feel like this is the start of a much greater disaster. There are many things the church has wrong," Katya said. "And, gods, I never thought I'd say *that* to the cleric, but you don't seem held particularly strongly under their sway."

Nadya elbowed Malachiasz hard before he could say something smug.

"What else does the church have wrong? Magic?" Nadya asked, lifting her arm and threatening to elbow him again. He was like a dog straining at his leash; she could feel how much he wanted to break into the conversation.

"Oh, absolutely." Katya vaguely explained the magic she had access to, casting Malachiasz distrusting glances the whole time.

It made sense: the rituals, the prayers to call on saints for spells. It clearly came from an understanding of divine magic, only altered for those not strictly touched by the gods. "And the church accepts this?" Nadya asked, turning over a small icon Katya handed her.

"No," Katya replied. "It's bleedingly occult. Saints aren't gods, so the magic isn't holy."

Malachiasz groaned, tipping backward and draping an arm over his eyes. "Not more theology."

"No one is talking to you," Nadya pointed out. She turned back to Katya, confused. "How, then?"

"How does the *tsarevna* use occult magic without being hanged for it?" Katya asked dryly. "The church looks the other way when it comes to the *Voldah Gorovni*. Something needs to kill the abominations."

Nadya ignored Malachiasz's little scoff.

"It's hardly safe Kalyazi magic," Katya allowed.

"So anyone caught using it who was not *Voldah Gorovni* would be hanged."

Katya nodded, unperturbed and unaware of the *look* Malachiasz was shooting Nadya from his vantage point on the ground. She covered his face with her hand and pushed it to one side.

"But how long has this magic been used?"

"It's old, old magic."

Nadya frowned. That didn't make sense. She had been taught that there was only divine magic—only that was acceptable. Malachiasz sat back up, reaching over and pulling the glove off Nadya's left hand. Katya's face changed almost imperceptibly, a shock she kept carefully masked. Nadya's hand was that of a monster's, twisted and corrupt. She drew it close to her chest, suddenly deeply ashamed. What was he doing?

"Wait," Katya said, tugging at Nadya's hand and uncurling her fingers. "That's Velyos' symbol."

Nadya nodded, biting her lip. It had been so *stupid*, what she had done, but there hadn't been any other way.

"I woke it up," Nadya said. The darkness. This power she was avoiding. She had blamed losing control of her magic on the relic, on touching a god, but it wasn't Krsnik's power—she had used that before, she knew the shape of it. This was something else.

Like dark magic of her own.

"Kostya said the church feared I would be corrupted. They knew there was something wrong with me from the beginning," she whispered. She was going to cry.

What if she had never been the hope Kalyazin needed to survive? What if she was only ever going to be its destruction? So easily she had fallen for the enemy; so easily she had turned to darker magic to see her end goal. What if she had never been divinely blessed, but rather a creature of dark power? Where was Marzenya in all of this? Where was she *now*? Nadya reached for her and got no answer. Despair flooded her.

"There's nothing wrong with you, *towy dżimyka*," Malachiasz murmured, taking her hand. Her heart wrenched painfully. She didn't deserve his kindness. Using him as he'd used her was a novel idea at first, but it hadn't quite factored in how much she cared for this awful boy.

Katya wasn't as certain as Malachiasz. She tugged her braid around one shoulder and was absently unraveling it and re-braiding it, long fingers working fast.

"You think that's connected with the fallen gods?" Katya asked Malachiasz.

He shook his head slowly. "The others, perhaps."

Nadya let out a tiny, strangled whimper. He had to be wrong. He had spoken of her power in terms of divinity, not eldritch horrors like his own magic had become.

"It's hard to know," he continued. "It's not like there's a wealth of others using magic this way that we can compare it to."

Katya frowned, eyeing Malachiasz appraisingly, like she was seeing *him* for the first time. She was seeing the boy who liked puzzles, not the Black Vulture. It wouldn't last. Even as they sat on the underbrush with the weight of the forest bearing down on them, Nadya could feel a tense thread of hatred strung between Malachiasz and Katya.

He slid his index finger down Nadya's before pressing his knuckle against her palm. She shivered.

"Magic is changing," Nadya said softly.

"Is this why you're here?" Katya asked.

Nadya nodded slowly. She caught the twitch of Malachiasz's eyebrows. She was hardly lying. She was here to figure out what had happened to her magic . . . and do something that would finish off this war once and for all.

"Divinity corrupts," Malachiasz murmured. "We are not made to hold this much power without it twisting us."

He shivered, clusters of eyes opening on visible skin. It was quite a statement.

"But you think this is *my* power."

He said nothing, just lifted his eyebrows, a gentle entreaty for her to understand. But she didn't want to. She didn't want to confront the idea that there was possibly some other reason the church she had trusted so much was so afraid of her, so quick to assume she would falter. If divinity was a thing of monstrosity, truly, then what did it all make *her*?

Katya watched Serefin where he stood on the other side of the camp, talking to Ostyia and Rashid. "You freed Velyos?"

"Yes," Nadya said, grateful for the focus to pull away from her.

"Then why does he have Serefin?"

Now that was a question.

Nadya didn't want to talk about this anymore. She was terrified that Serefin might fail at breaking himself out of the very thing Nadya was trying to get back for herself.

"What would that other one do?" Malachiasz asked. "If it were set free? The older one, I mean."

"Devour the sun," Katya said bluntly.

And if Malachiasz was lying maybe he already knew, divine creature that he was, but he only looked curious. Nadya didn't like the clear providence leading them all to the same place. She especially didn't like that the Tranavians had a word for Bolagvoy as well; it meant something very different to them. *Gods' seat*, it meant in Kalyazi. *Wellspring.*

In Tranavian it meant *hellmouth.*

How dare Marzenya be silent with her *now*?

Katya and Malachiasz gave each other wide berths as they traveled. Malachiasz was erratic, growing more visibly nervous each day, and Katya had noticed. It was hard not to, the way his pale fingers were consistently red and bleeding because he wouldn't stop picking at them, nails chewed down to slivers.

It was strange, to have another Kalyazi to travel with who wasn't from a monastery. Katya was shockingly irreverent, even by Nadya's standards, and she got on surprisingly well with Serefin. To the point where, as the days turned into weeks, Nadya was fairly certain they were *friends*. It was bizarre.

Ultimately, though, all of this felt transient. The days that passed felt unreal. They were here, in this place, by fate and circumstance alone, and when the spell was broken they would turn on one another. Malachiasz and Serefin were the enemy, no amount of careful friendship was going to change that. The way Malachiasz would catch her fingers with his as they walked—careful, fleeting touches—didn't matter, their time was limited and fast running out. She couldn't think about it. She didn't think about it.

They came upon a clearing, unnatural in how the massive

trees broke into a circle. Within the clearing was a series of immense statues, and Malachiasz grew tense beside her. She glanced up at him at the same time he looked down at her. His pale eyes were unfathomable.

She didn't like when his face was so hard to read.

Her breath caught. The eyes of the gods were turning toward her once more and she could *feel it*.

There were forty statues in a ring around the clearing.

"Oh, this isn't strange at all," Rashid said as the rest of the group caught up.

Kacper took Serefin's arm, yanking him back into the woods. Ostyia followed. Parijahan watched Malachiasz with the same careful wariness that Nadya was feeling. Katya stepped up beside Nadya, curious.

What would it be like, to be a casual observer of the divine and the occult like Katya? None of this would ever truly touch her. She would continue with her place of power and her necklace of Vulture teeth and all this divine madness would spin around her.

Some of the statues appeared older than others. While Nadya had never seen any of the figures in the statues—strange, eldritch, bizarre figures—she recognized half of them intrinsically. That High Twenty of the pantheon. They had found something *very* old.

Malachiasz's pale gaze was on her as she took the first step past the boundary holding them back. It struck her immediately, the presence within the clearing, the war that was being fought around them without anyone knowing.

*Gods, we started something terrible,* she thought, spinning in a slow circle, taking in each statue.

She knew twenty of the statues. Each monstrous figure. Each sharp tooth and extra limb. Each body twisted into unreality. Each face made incomprehensible. And one she knew better than the rest.

She wanted to burn this image from her brain. The teeth that lined down a lithe body—barely human—the elegant, curling horns. The eight unblinking eyes, unfathomable in their carved stillness. The skeletal upper body.

Death and magic and winter.

*Death.*

Eighteen years Nadya had lived with this goddess speaking to her, through her. Eighteen years and finally Nadya understood what she was dealing with.

Nadya was very small and very young and very insignificant in the face of this being who had claimed her soul.

*Our lady of death and magic.*

Marzenya was, of course, silent.

Nadya had tried to be the hand of death her goddess desired, but she kept faltering, failing. It wasn't even a matter of compassion; Nadya simply had too much doubt.

That wasn't even remotely all the horror Nadya had to confront as she cracked. She was not made to witness this. She was not supposed to *know.*

There were twenty more to contend with. These were the ones where time had eroded the figures. These bordered on something that Nadya's brain couldn't quite find words for; her eyes wanted to skip past them, she didn't want to consider them. But she felt a pull; she was drawn to them. And above it all there was the thought that had been haunting her for months:

*What if the gods aren't gods at all?* Fallen and eldritch and *mad.*

What were they doing?

"Nadya." Malachiasz's soft rasp ripped her from her thoughts. She was having trouble getting air. His hand was at the small of her back. He cupped his other hand against her face, shielding her eyes from the statues as he turned her to him. "Come back down, *towy dżimyka*," he whispered.

"Malachiasz?"

He shivered at the sound of his name. She watched his face, watched as he took in each statue.

"It's a lot of power," he said contemplatively. "Each statue, the smallest of tastes."

His mask was slipping.

It was pieces at first, easy to miss because it had been happening for months; she had grown used to the eyes blinking open from his skin, the decay that ate at him, the mouths and strange teeth. But over time his edges had grown shadowy. What she had seen of him in the Salt Mines—that shifting, chaotic horror—wasn't even the worst of it.

Serefin was right.

Malachiasz had all that power at his fingertips. And Nadya wasn't so sure that he didn't know what to do with it. She couldn't believe that he wasn't capable of harnessing the nightmare he had become.

His mask fell back into place when he looked down at Nadya. Just a boy, Tranavian, beautiful, lonely.

"Are you all right?" he asked.

She pressed her face against his chest. His arms wrapped around her, one hand cradling the back of her head. She needed to breathe—all the air had been sucked out of the clearing and she would die here, in the center of this circle, surrounded by gods and not gods and *what if these gods we worship aren't gods at all?*

What if?

What if that wasn't the right question? So what if the gods, as they were, were something else? So what if they had ascended to this state from something lesser? They were there. That wasn't the thing that immediately made Nadya want to flee.

It was the other twenty.

The fallen, the lost. What had happened there, and what would happen if they were to rise? And what was *she* that she felt some draw to—not even the fallen, but the older ones? The ones created from a void so complete and deep that it had been forgotten because to remember was to go mad.

Divinity and an unknowable darkness.

"There are more here than I thought your pantheon held," Malachiasz said thoughtfully. His sharp chin rested on top of her head.

"Do you suppose we'll meet the people who carved these?" Katya asked, moving up to the statue that Nadya somehow *knew* was Bozidarka. The figure had holes in her palms, her spine visible through a cavernous torso. The face had no eyes, only empty sockets, including one in her forehead. Nadya's forehead itched. "Not the *original* people, but surely someone tends these?"

"There's no one here," Nadya said. This place was not made for mortals. There were stories of clerics who had made this journey, surviving in the Bolagvoy monastery for months in solitude before clawing their way free from the forest. Mere folklore. No one ever made it out.

Katya snorted. "Well, I suppose I get to tell my priest back in Komyazalov 'I told you so.'"

Malachiasz tugged on a piece of bone in his hair. "Does this mean *I'm* right?"

"No."

He waved erratically to the primordial twenty. Nadya eyed them, shivering as her palm ached and the sudden desire to move closer to them rushed through her. She turned back to him. He stared at something just past her, his face deathly pale.

"We're not alone," he said, voice low.

Katya's head whipped around and she swore.

Malachiasz rolled his sleeves up, reaching for the knife at his belt. Mage, not Vulture. That made Nadya feel only marginally better. She tugged her bone *voryen* from her belt. Malachiasz nodded slowly.

"The relic will do you well here," he said.

Katya's eyes narrowed.

Nadya reached for her necklace. She had finished restringing it and her fingers found Marzenya's bead. Despite everything, she still turned to her goddess first.

*Just . . . please.*

Nadya got no answers and no magic. Only silence. Just the expectancy of complete dedication. Nadya had to go this alone. She chewed on her lip, watching Malachiasz. She had no idea what she would find when she turned, but she didn't like anything that made Malachiasz nervous.

"*Litkiniczki,*" he murmured.

*Lichni'voda,* her brain supplied in Kalyazi.

Bad luck. Dark omen.

Except not the concept. The creature.

"Move very slowly," he said quietly. "Though it doesn't matter. It sees us. I see it."

There were regular Kalyazi portents, small ones, simple ones. Little creatures that spelled out small disasters when they were seen. But the big ones, the monsters, if you survived an encounter with *Lichni'voda,* you would have all the bad luck of the omen to follow you.

Blood trickled down Malachiasz's forearms. Nadya heard Parijahan call out to them, but Malachiasz held a hand out.

"Don't pass the threshold," he said, his voice only just loud enough for them to hear.

If the *Lichni'voda* didn't see them, the portent would not follow.

Only Nadya, Malachiasz, and Katya were caught by its eye. Parijahan ducked out enough to see what Malachiasz was staring at. She moved back around the statue, eyes wide.

They were in trouble.

"All right," Malachiasz said gently. "There's no saving any of us from this, so we might as well kill it, yes?" He moved closer to Nadya, ducking his head and kissing her.

His hand was bloody and it smeared against her chin as he lifted her face to his. It was a desperate thing, messy and scared. She could feel his heart beating fast in his chest. He was panicking but trying to keep calm for her sake, but he didn't need to, she understood the gravity of the situation.

Killing the thing wasn't the problem.

There had been a part of her that thought all of this fear of the forest was unnecessary. That what they would be up against would be easily dealt with. Serefin was a powerful mage. Malachiasz was the Black Vulture, the king of monsters. And as much as she doubted it, Nadya had power of her own.

She hadn't expected something so far out of myth and legend that there were no stories on how, exactly, it might be killed. Something that would have further consequences than whatever this encounter wrought.

They were doomed and it would be a very real and unavoidable thing.

"It's fine," she murmured, "where is it?"

His gaze flicked over her shoulder. "Just watching."

"Do you think we can wait it out? The damage is done."

"I'd rather not do that," Katya said.

He winced. It wasn't something Nadya wanted to consider, either, not when they were in a place so very dangerous, not when the scope of the bad luck could be incredibly deadly. And it was on both of them *together*. It was on the godsdamned *tsarevna* of Kalyazin.

"Why didn't we let Serefin walk in here instead?" Malachiasz muttered.

Nadya laughed, panicked and grating. "You're horrible." She leaned up on her toes, kissing him once more. The alignment of her world shifted ever so slightly on its axis. The awareness that this spelled out a Before and an After. That *Lichni'voda* were things of myth and that myth had descended upon them.

"Maybe the Vulture, not the mage," she offered.

A half smile caught at his mouth and it made Nadya ache. She took a step back, glancing at Katya.

"I'd keep back at first," she said.

Malachiasz's pale eyes flickered between her and where the thing was behind her. His pupils dilated, covering his colorless irises. His posture shifted almost imperceptibly, until the roiling chaos started to shudder through him. Claws extending out of his nail beds, iron spikes jutting from his skin, but more, worse because he was so much more and so much worse now. He glanced at one of the clearing's statues.

His mask dropped and he moved too fast for her eyes to track as he swept past her.

Her own power was buried deep, but she could find it. If Marzenya would not speak to her—or could not—fine, *fine*. But she wasn't going to die here, and they were dealing with something far older than Kalyazin's normal monsters.

She pressed her fingers against the scar, feeling the sharp

ache of power. *Her power. Waiting to be claimed, the shape of it strange and unformed and so very old.*

The *Lichni'voda* was almost human in figure but wrapped in shadows. A single, black, unblinking eye sat in the center of its face. The nose caved in like that of a skull. A mouthful of razor teeth.

And the *sounds* it made scraped at her ears. Nadya wanted to flee.

But she could feel the creature's power. The tricks of luck, turning it sour, causing Malachiasz's magic to not work the way he was used to.

Malachiasz's frustration was rising as the thing circled him and his own magic never hit its mark. Nadya ran her fingers over her necklace.

There was a hierarchy to things. Clerics were high up on that hierarchy but it had been made very clear to her that she was not *just* a cleric. There was some other power that was waiting for Nadya to open the door. She had been knocking, she kept knocking, but she hadn't been able to open it.

Nadya took in the clearing. She eyed each statue until something sharp went flying past her ear, pulling her attention back to the creature. But she had the time she needed. She knew what she had to do as she pulled Marzenya's bead to the bottom of her necklace. *What if the gods you worship aren't gods at all?*

What if that didn't matter one single godsdamned bit?

What if that was never the question?

What if the question was: What if there was a girl who could call down the magic of the divine and dredge up the power of the dark, and sift through the magic of the forests?

What if it was all about magic, in its singular essence?

It wasn't about how Nadya got to it. It was that she was

able to touch it without being obliterated. That she was able to combine divinity and darkness to kill a king and maybe *maybe* stop something bigger. Old and eldritch and *mad*.

*Divinity tastes like copper and ashes,* she thought idly.

It was more than she had ever anticipated.

Nadya opened the door.

# 34

## SEREFIN

## MELESKI

*Three crowns for the brows of Cvjetko, for the wolf, the bear, the fox. For his claws are sharp and his teeth are many and he chews and he gnaws and he howls.*

—The Letters of Włodzimierz

As soon as the clearing had come within view, Serefin's vision had been blinded. Nothing but a searing, agonizing white. He could feel blood trickling from his eyes. The patch on his left eye was suddenly painful—if he kept it on for a second longer it was going to scorch through his skull. He ripped the patch off and nearly dropped like a stone. He let out one strangled cry before Kacper pushed his face away and pulled him back, deeper into the forest.

What he had seen was being burned into his mind where it would live and form and take him over until it clawed out the core of him and left nothing behind.

They were dealing with powers so much more ancient and vast than they could comprehend. Serefin had always known, but it had been all too easy to ignore.

"Serefin," Kacper murmured. He was careful as he took him by the shoulders and pushed him to the ground.

Serefin covered his eyes, whimpering when Kacper pulled his hands away.

"You're going to hurt yourself," he said gently. He sounded scared and confused.

Serefin blinked hard, granting himself a few seconds of vision. His hands were bloody, the red caked underneath his fingernails. He reached up to his face and found the gashes left by his nails.

He shut his eyes.

"He's getting worse," Ostyia said.

"You've stopped flirting with the enemy long enough to notice?" Kacper snapped back.

"Hey, hey," Serefin said, holding out a hand. "Stop." It was hard to speak; the pain in his head was piercing.

The clearing had not only been a forgotten collection of ancient statues. Souls had been slaughtered in that circle. Thousands of sacrifices made. It hadn't been underbrush their boots had crunched over, but ancient bones scattered at the edges.

"We have to stop this," Serefin said.

"We have to figure out how to get *you* out of this!" Ostyia replied. Her hands were on his face, gentle as she traced the gashes. "You just tried to take your own eyes out. You can't tell me you're all right, Serefin."

"I'm *not*," he snapped. "Clearly I'm *not*. Take my hands," he said to Kacper, the urge to scratch at his eyes overwhelming him.

Kacper's warm hands wrapped around his, calm and sure.

"All right," Serefin said, his voice sounding strangely more even than he felt. "I need you to knock me unconscious."

Kacper let out a strangled sound. An inhuman scream tore through the woods from the direction of the clearing. Ostyia started to get up.

"No. The others can handle it," Serefin said through his teeth. "Malachiasz is in there, they're fine."

"I don't think—"

"Both of you *stop*. Stop trying to figure this out. Stop trying to fix it yourselves, you're never going to be able to and you'll make things worse."

Through the blood fogging his vision he saw Kacper's face fall and his guilt was immediate. *Of course* they wanted to help. He was in pain and something was obviously wrong. But they were blood mages; they were Tranavian. They had no idea what was going on. *He* had no idea what was going on.

He hissed as something tugged on his chest, trying to pull him back into the clearing. He couldn't put to words the things he had seen there. He had expected monsters. He had expected things like Velyos—terrifying, powerful, but forms he was able to rationalize, comprised of parts his brain knew how to handle.

But *those statues*. The human brain was not made to see those things; mortals weren't meant to *know*. It was supposed to be about power. Beings of vast power. But what happened to something when they had that much power? How far would a person be mutated with that kind of magic churning in their blood?

Kacper's grip on his hands tightened. Had he tried to move?

*"So you see, finally, don't you?"* It was the *voice*. Serefin almost wished for Velyos. This voice with no name and Velyos, rattling in his brain, both clamoring for his attention. His nerves were frayed to a snapping point.

*"You see what you are trying to fight. But you don't have to. You don't have to fight me. You don't have to fight Velyos. It would be so easy, so quiet, to fall. It's such an easy thing, to let yourself be taken under. Burial requires no action, merely acceptance."*

Serefin clenched his jaw, catching a piece of skin between his teeth. Blood flooded his mouth, dripped down his chin.

"Serefin?" Ostyia's voice hitched with desperation. He didn't know how to tell them that he was probably fine because these gods still needed him.

He didn't know what would happen when he finally outlived his usefulness.

*"You all fight. Those of you from that grain of sand you call a country. Those of you who spill your blood for a taste of what we could give you in full. You will give up soon."*

Serefin wheezed for a long, painful breath, and he almost agreed. Anything to make this stop.

But his hands were given a tight squeeze, and he became aware of Kacper's hands still clutching his, keeping them from his face.

*You haven't broken me yet.*

The voice laughed darkly. *"If I had wanted to break you, I would never have given you the opportunity to fight back. You're so close. I'm almost done with you. But if you don't prove strong enough to look upon the faces of those who are so much better than you . . ."* The voice trailed off.

Point made.

Serefin's head pounded and the horrors in the clearing grew dim enough to shove away. He shuddered, his muscles going liquid in his body. He slumped forward, Kacper only barely catching him as he dropped out of consciousness.

"What happened to you?"

When Serefin woke up it was dark outside. He couldn't *feel* the clearing nearby, which he hoped meant that they had moved far from it while he was unconscious.

He groaned, moving to press his hands against his aching eyes.

Nadya caught his arms. "I wouldn't do that if I were you."

He went limp, letting her drop them back down. "How bad is it?"

"You look like you got into a fight with a very angry cat," she said, cheerful in a way that implied she was trying to cover something of her own. She mimicked dragging both hands down her face.

He laughed even though it hurt.

"Have you ever thought that maybe we're doing the wrong thing by being here?"

He worked himself up to a sitting position; it was mild agony to do so. "I don't have any choice," he murmured. He had no doubt that if he had ignored Velyos and the other one completely, he would be shredded and his pieces tossed aside.

She wrapped her arms around her knees. "I wish I'd never been given that pendant. None of this would be happening if not for me."

"I would be dead, though, so I can't really fault you for it," Serefin pointed out.

"You're probably the only one." There was a moroseness to her voice that didn't sit right. "Do you think anything will ever change?"

Nadya wanted assurance that they would be all right, and Serefin had to believe that from this chaos there might be a chance for peace. Plus, he and Katya hadn't murdered each other yet, always a good sign.

But he didn't know what was happening in Tranavia and it was eating him up inside. He wasn't naive enough to think that his throne hadn't been wrested away in his absence.

"I don't know."

She exhaled slowly. "Velyos wants you to wake up the other sleeping gods, is there anything else?"

*There's the nameless one who wants Malachiasz dead, and I don't know what else he wants but it will ruin you.* And he tried so hard to tell her, because he didn't want to actively betray this girl, but just like before the words refused to pass his lips. The nameless one demanded his silence. If the sleeping gods woke, they were all lost. If Malachiasz managed to topple this divine empire, they were lost. Serefin had to at least try to save Tranavia.

He shook his head. Her eyes narrowed, but she relented with a nod.

"I want your gods to leave me alone," he said.

"You don't want the power they can give you?"

"If there was power at the end of this, maybe I could be convinced," he said dryly. All he had were moths and stars and the knowledge that he was different than before. But he didn't *want* to be. He wanted to be Serefin again—except Serefin kissing the beautiful Tranavian boy who wanted him, Serefin who knew what it was his country needed and how to keep his throne, Serefin who could be a *good* king—not Serefin with all this horrific stuff tacked on.

Nadya gently touched his head, oddly comforting, before she got up and walked over to where Parijahan was sitting. The Akolan girl had looked more and more bleak the longer they traveled. Serefin couldn't really figure out what was going on there.

"Well, now that you aren't trying to claw off your own face," Ostyia said as she took the spot Nadya left behind, a knowing grin at her lips. "Kacper?"

"Stop."

Her grin widened. "I knew it."

He groaned, leaning his head against her shoulder.

"I have been waiting years for you to notice," she said.

"*Stop*," he pleaded.

"I thought you were getting somewhere when you promoted him but *no*, you were only being friendly! How was I ever supposed to say, 'Hey, Serefin, that soldier you just promoted to your glamorous royal circle is head over heels in love with you but you're too royal to notice.'"

He sighed.

"I'm glad you figured it out." She waved Kacper over. He handed Serefin a tin mug of tea.

"What on earth . . ."

"We're going to be here for a while," Kacper said. "Malachiasz doesn't know what he's doing."

"It's complicated!" Malachiasz called from across the clearing. Nadya had somehow worked her way onto his lap and was studying his spell book with him, his head tucked against her shoulder. Regardless of what Serefin thought of Malachiasz he found that his chest ached as he watched them.

He turned his attention back to the cup of tea. "Did you . . . did you pack this? Did you just have this with you?" Serefin moved for Kacper's pack behind them. "What *else* do you have in there? Did you fit the royal kitchens?"

Kacper laughed and shoved Serefin away. "Blood and bone, I wish. My greatest regret is learning how it is you people eat."

"It's better than peasant fare," Serefin said solemnly.

"It sure is," Kacper agreed.

Serefin frowned. "Kacper, this is very important."

Kacper lifted his eyebrows.

"Do you have *alcohol in there*?"

"You drink that first. I might have something."

"You are too good to me."

"*That* is very true."

As Serefin sipped at the tea, Kacper did what he could with the cuts on Serefin's face. If they got infected Serefin would be in a whole new world of trouble.

"Are you going to tell us what's going on?" Kacper asked.

Serefin took a drink to avoid answering right away. He was still struggling to figure it out and apparently he wasn't allowed to tell anyone about this second god. Panic needled at him.

Nadya and Malachiasz were arguing about something across the clearing, but Serefin couldn't hear them well enough to make out what.

"I'm just trying to get rid of any divine nonsense," he said.

"And then?"

"What do you mean?"

Kacper leaned back on his heels. Serefin sighed.

"I have to survive this first."

"I am *not* going back to Grazyk if I have to suffer Ruminski's court," Ostyia complained.

Serefin rolled his eyes, but he couldn't laugh at her words. If he didn't survive this, there might not be a court in Grazyk to return to. There might not be much left of Tranavia at all.

Katya moved over to where the three of them sat. Ostyia shifted over slightly and the *tsarevna* sat down between her and Serefin. Her dark hair was wild and tangled around her head.

She sighed and put her chin in her hands, eyeing Nadya and Malachiasz.

"Does he have your relics?" Serefin asked.

"I don't know. But she has a relic that can kill him."

Serefin straightened, earning a sound of protest from Kacper. "What?"

"Svoyatova Aleksandra Mozhayeva's shin bone—"

"Blood and bone, you people are morbid," Kacper said.

Katya shrugged. "I can't imagine where she got it, but if there was anything that could kill a Vulture of his power, it's that." She leaned back on her hands. "Neither of them are what I expected."

Everything was easier when Serefin thought of the boy on a throne of bones watching as Izak Meleski tortured the son he had murdered hours before. It was easier when Serefin only knew Malachiasz as the Black Vulture, cruel smile and cold words and plans for treason.

He didn't want to confront the teenage boy across the camp, grinning brightly at the Kalyazi girl sitting next to him.

"If I can get that dagger, all we'll need is the right moment to strike."

# 35

## NADEZHDA

## LAPTEVA

**Svoyatovi Sergei Volkakov:** *Even when his hands were cut off and his tongue cut out by Tranavians, Svoyatovi Sergei did not rest and brought a mountain down upon the heretics.*
—Vasiliev's Book of Saints

"This isn't going to be pretty." Malachiasz was eyeing the border.

It was only more forest. Nadya could feel it, the place where the forest went from mortal to divine. Their map had been surprisingly accurate, though even if it hadn't been, there was no missing the power emanating just out of reach.

"What if you just walk into it?" he asked.

She looked up at him. She was sitting on the ground, his spell book in her lap. She couldn't read much of it—his handwriting was far too messy. She was mostly searching for the sketches tucked between the pages, hidden

amidst the spells. He pretended like he didn't know what she was doing.

"Do you want to test that?"

"No, I'm only—"

"I don't think anything would happen, if that's what you're asking. I don't think any of us would be struck down the second we stepped past the border."

He tied his hair back as he considered the magic.

"My guess is anyone who walks into it will end up turned around and back in the regular forest," she said, continuing to flip through his spell book. She found a lovely profile sketch of Parijahan, whose expression made it clear she knew he was drawing her. "Or torn apart by monsters."

Malachiasz made an appreciative noise. "Sound theories."

"Ooh, high praise."

He rolled his eyes. "Do you think I could just wander into it?"

"Yes. You have to figure out how *we* can walk into it with you." Maybe not *with* him. Nadya wasn't entirely sure just when the forest would claim him. She wondered if it had already started. If his slight, anxious trembling wasn't so benign. She gently pushed those thoughts away, he was nervous, that was all, it was going to be a complicated spell.

"Give me the spell I dog-eared."

"You monster." She flipped to the marked page but didn't tear it out, instead handing the book to him. "I'll not have your devil magic."

"Just your own," he said, voice prim. "You're in a good mood," he noted.

Maybe she was tired. It was so *exhausting* feeling things all of the time. The dark omen hung over them, right at the beginning of the end, and she didn't want to think about it. Only he could ferry them across the border, and it would destroy him. She had led him by the hand to his destruction, holding the promise of absolution before him that—regardless of his lack of remorse—he desired.

"I used enough power in the clearing that I should be dead . . . I'm mostly trying to forget about it," she replied.

Malachiasz ripped the spell from his book before handing it back to her. His forearm was sluggishly bleeding and he used his fingers to sketch blood onto the page. He placed the spell into the open air. A shiver, a crack, a shattering of the vision of the woods before. A high, black wall appeared.

She whistled low, tilting her head back to gaze up at it.

"If you'd like to test your theory . . ." He gestured dramatically.

Slamming face-first into a wall wasn't something she particularly wanted to do. She glared at him.

"I think you're right, though—"

"Oh, I love hearing that. You should make a habit of saying that."

"—it was merely undetectable. If someone unwittingly stumbled in here they would be turned back home."

"Or monsters."

"Nadya, we're going to see plenty of those without you invoking them so cheerfully."

She shrugged. They were doomed to die anyway. Might as well make it interesting. Uncertainty passed over his face. "We'll get out of that," he said softly.

"We won't, the omen is set, but please continue being so delightfully optimistic, it's a good look on you."

He sighed as he wiped his hands and forearm off. He lightly touched his fingers to the wall. Dozens of inky black eyes snapped open along his arm, up his neck, across his face. He yanked his hand back, letting out a low hiss through his teeth.

"Is this going to be worth it?" he whispered.

*Worth showing Tranavia that they won't be able to raze Kalyazi with their magic any longer?* Nadya considered. *Worth ending this war? Worth winning back the favor of the gods?*

*Yes.*

But she didn't think he was talking to her. Nadya met his icy pale eyes and nodded.

"Can we wait until morning? I would rather not open this now."

His unease was telling. But it was growing dark and Nadya understood. Her quips about monsters edged too close to the truth. She didn't know what they were going to face on the other side, the monsters here were bad enough, and truthfully . . . she didn't want to lose Malachiasz just yet.

She handed him his spell book. He clipped it to his belt before folding himself up next to her. He took her scarred hand. The blackened veins hadn't spread farther, but they looked like death. He carefully traced the scar with an index finger. He had been so enamored with it since that moment at the monastery and she *still* wasn't entirely certain what that had been. But it didn't hurt so much anymore, not since the clearing. Maybe the constant ache truly was her rejection of the power. Maybe using it wouldn't hurt her. But . . . she didn't know if she really believed that.

"There were a lot of statues in that clearing," he commented.

Nadya was *not* ready to have this conversation.

"There were," she allowed. Likely he was right. There must be some kind of ascension the Kalyazi did not discuss—if they even knew. "If you're smug about one single thing, I'm shutting this conversation down," she said before he could continue.

He looked only a little smug.

"You said yourself that spell didn't do what you thought," she said. "*You're* not in that clearing."

"But could I be? We don't know where those came from."

"But what does that matter?"

"Because you ascribe so much importance to twenty—but only twenty—of the beings in that clearing. What of the others?"

"Somewhere along the way the Church must have . . ."

"This isn't a matter of apocryphal material, Nadya."

She leaned back on her hands, her fingers catching his. He wove their fingers together as he looked up at the wall. Her face grew warm.

"I don't think we're approaching this from the right direction," she mused.

"*We?*"

Her face flushed hotter. Gods, she hated him. "*Fine, Malachiasz.* You had a fucking point about the intersections of power and godhood."

He grinned so brightly that it felt like she had been punched in the chest. It had been so long since she'd seen him smile like that.

"That's all I wanted, thank you."

"Don't get used to this. You're wrong about that intersection undermining the concept of godhood."

"Why do you think the others have been kicked from your pantheon?"

That, she didn't know. Clearly knowledge of those gods and what had happened to them existed. Katya knew bits and pieces—not enough, by any means, mere fragments—but it had been held back from Nadya because, what, the Church feared she would seek them out? Why would she be led to do that? If she had never been given the pendant trapping Velyos, she never would have known about these others.

Unless . . . this meeting was inevitable.

She contemplated her hand. "I don't think this changes anything."

Malachiasz let out a breathless laugh. "You're so *stubborn*. How can this not change anything?"

"The gods are still there. I can still talk to them."

Malachiasz made a face. She rolled her eyes—yes, that wasn't wholly true, but even if they wouldn't speak to her directly, they were *there*.

"So, what you did in the clearing? What was that?"

She had ripped the monster into oblivion with nothing but her power.

"I don't know," she said.

"Two displays of a stunning amount of magic. I wonder if you could always cast like this but were holding yourself back."

"For good reason! I can't control this!" She had killed so many people in a moment of divine, what, bliss? She tried to not remember how *good* it felt to use that much power, even if it was completely out of her control. "I don't know what I am. I thought . . ." She didn't know what she thought. If she could *always* cast like this then she should have ended the war a long time ago. But it wasn't about that. It wasn't about which side of this damned war had more power to throw around—if that was the case Tranavia would have ended it years ago.

Malachiasz was quiet. His long fingers slowly found the pins holding her braid coiled around her head, tugging them free. Her hair fell in pale waves around her shoulders. He ran a strand through his fingers.

"Nadezhda Lapteva," he said contemplatively.

She shivered, hearing something in his voice that she couldn't place. She was going to betray him. It wasn't a matter of what her heart wanted anymore—and a tiny part of her *did* want him to hurt for what he had done.

"I told you, once, that you could make this world or tear it to pieces," he said quietly. "That's still true."

"Things were supposed to change," she said. "But you . . ."

"I did what I thought was necessary," he replied. "And that didn't change much, either."

She lifted an eyebrow. *Lying.*

"You have extra eyes opening up on you at all times, Malachiasz, you can't really say not much changed."

His smile was mournful. "To be perfectly honest, that clearing terrified me. If your twenty can work through you, those can as well."

"You think they'll try to use me?" *Is that why everyone has been lying to me?*

He nodded.

"The gods can't technically force a mortal's actions."

"Can't or don't for some ethical code half the others may not care about?"

Nadya frowned.

He tilted her chin up. "And what could those others do with you? Now that we've seen what you're capable of?"

"I can't even get the twenty who spoke to me before to acknowledge me," she said dryly. "I doubt I've caught the attention of those older and more primal."

He did not look convinced. In fairness, she *had* caught the attention of one older and more primal already. But she had forced that meeting into fruition. Would it have happened at all had she not been in such a desperate place?

"Nadya, you're like a beacon with all that power. I was drawn back to you across Tranavia even when I was . . ."

"Like that?" she offered.

"Like that," he repeated.

"Completely out of your mind? Totally insane? A barely coherent, soulless monster?"

"All right, I get it."

"You're still all those things."

"Thank you."

"That's how you could talk to me, though. Intersections of divinity."

"I can't figure out if it was a product of you stealing and binding my magic with yours, or simply because I am pulled to what you are. I wouldn't be so sure that you haven't caught the attention of older, far more dangerous gods."

A chill of fear gripped her. She curled her knees up, wrapping her arms around them. His fear wasn't something she had considered, but it was a valid one.

"And . . ." He paused, shaking his head. "Your power is terrifying, Nadya."

"At the monastery—"

"At the monastery I wanted to see if you were drawing from some fallen god and you're not. You're not drawing from anything, whatever Pelageya says. But what you have feels . . ." He paused, searching for the right word. "Ancient."

She stared at him wordlessly.

"When we go past the wall, I don't know what you're going to be opening yourself up to," he finished.

"No, but you'll finally get a taste of the power you crave," she snapped, knowing she only said it because he was scaring her.

"That's not why I'm here and you know it." He bristled, something dangerous and erratic sparking in his voice.

"Playacting emotion isn't going to work again, you know that, right?"

He sighed and tilted his head back. "Nadezhda Lapteva." His tone was a little bit chaotic monster, a little bit melancholy boy.

"How much of this is ulterior motive?"

Too fast and too suddenly he had her face between his hands. His touch was gentle, but oh, he made it too easy to remember how swiftly he could kill her. How quickly iron claws could embed in her skull.

"You stupid, infuriating, *clever* girl," he murmured. "I want to *help you*."

"Insults are definitely the way to get your point across. Keep going, you're doing marvelously."

He let out a frustrated groan and rested his forehead against hers. "You need my help," he finally said. "I'm helping. It's not enough, but I'm trying."

"None of it is enough," she said softly. "I know you're lying to me."

"Am I?" he asked carefully.

"I was in that clearing, too, Malachiasz," she said. "I know what I saw. Your mask did not hold up when confronted by other *beings of power*."

"And what do you think you saw?"

"I don't know," she said, taking his face in her hands in turn and studying his features, sharp cheekbones and long eyelashes. The flickers and shifts had become mundane despite the horror. But her mortal brain didn't like to remember how he had looked in the clearing; it skipped over it entirely.

What had all that power done to him? Aside from turning him into a monster made of pure chaos. Was he still mortal?

And if what he said about her own magic was true . . . what was she?

"Can you be killed?"

"Are you going to try? It's been a while since you've held a knife to my throat."

She slid her hand down until it was wrapped around his throat. She lightly pressed her thumb against his windpipe. He shivered.

"Would cutting your throat even kill you?"

"It depends on how you went about it," he said, a little breathlessly.

She released the pressure, but kept her hand on his throat a few seconds longer, until she finally shifted, weaving her fingers into the hair at the nape of his neck.

"You're trying to ask me something," he said.

"Are you immortal?"

He blinked. "Blood and bone, I hope not. I don't *think* so."

"You've said there are Vultures who are ancient."

"There are. I'm the Black Vulture, though. Someone's going to kill me eventually for the throne."

He said it so matter-of-factly. Not like he didn't care, but more like it was an inevitability. It broke her heart.

"But all this power must have an inverse effect on you."

He shot her a dry look. His body was constantly twisting in on itself—chaos made form. Wasn't that inverse enough? She realized he was hiding a lot of pain from her, and she waited to feel triumphant—didn't he deserve that for what he had done? But she didn't. He was just a boy who hurt.

She drew his head closer until her forehead rested against his.

"I don't regret what I did," he said. "But I do regret that it took so many lies. You weren't supposed to be so brilliant. I wasn't supposed to care."

"You care far too much about everything. It is, unfortunately, part of your charm."

This was going to kill her. This, right here, this beautiful boy and his monstrous power and his lies and the knowledge that nothing mattered, they would always betray each other in the end.

She didn't know how to contain the tangled mess of everything she was feeling. The wanting and the revulsion and the hatred and the hurt. And, gods, the overwhelming guilt. She had lost so much, her family, her faith, Kostya. And she was still trying to hold on to this boy who was at the heart of so much of her pain even as she prepared to ruin him.

Malachiasz gently kissed her forehead, then went to see who was going to take first watch, yawning.

Nadya stared up at the black wall.

*Did you know about Velyos and Serefin?*

"Of course I did."

*Do I stop him, too? What if he can't break himself free? What if he does what Velyos wants?*

Marzenya wasn't particularly forthcoming. Nadya hated that if she had a question about something important, she would likely be ignored or receive something vague in return.

"*If you do as I command, you will not have to worry about that boy.*"

Nadya frowned, unable to respond as Malachiasz returned. He grinned at her, loose-limbed and sleepy, before collapsing into a boneless pile of boy beside her.

She laughed. "You're not sleeping out here, you'll freeze to death. Come on, into the tent."

"Only if you come with me," he mumbled.

She tensed. He opened one eye, looking up at her with a wickedly mischievous glint. That would not be keeping her distance. That would be throwing away entirely the haphazard, messy shield she had been attempting to build the whole journey.

That would be acknowledging they didn't have much time left.

*Was it this hard for him?* she wondered, wavering. What if she told him? Right now, what if she told him that the moment that wall dropped he was likely going to die. Gave him some kind of warning so he might see the other side of this. It would be so easy to save him. She was so numb to the idea of his destruction that sometimes she doubted it would actually happen, until she realized she was only lying to herself in order to keep going.

"You're a nightmare. I'm exhausted. Come on."

He followed her until she had another boy pile at her feet inside the tent. She draped a blanket over him, rolling her eyes. He mumbled something incomprehensible but vaguely thankful. And then he pulled out the backs of her knees and yanked her down next to him. She stifled a surprised yelp as he firmly kissed her forehead before burying his face in her hair.

"I actually sleep when you're near," he murmured. "And I'm so tired."

She let the hairline fracture in her heart split as she shifted into a more comfortable position and tugged the blanket and furs over them both.

*Tell him the truth.*

What could he have been if he had never been taken by the Vultures? She wondered, sometimes, if he would have been better, or if it was this trauma that made him so gentle toward the people he cared about. She couldn't fool herself about the other pieces: the cruelty, the coldness, the calculated plotting. But the exhausted boy with the devastating grin who only wanted the girl he cared about close so he could sleep through the night?

Nadya was actively damning herself for that boy.

She twined her fingers in his hair. His eyes were closed and she traced his features, pressing her thumb against his lips.

"Thank you," he mumbled.

"For what?"

"Coming back. No one's ever done that."

She swallowed down a threatening rush of tears. "This will work out, right, Malachiasz?" she whispered.

He made a sleepy affirmative noise.

But he was Tranavian, a blood mage, and the *Black Vulture* for gods' sake, and she was Kalyazi, a peasant, the cleric.

Nothing would work out at all.

# interlude vii

Katya waited until the others had all gone to sleep before she made her move. She had grown frustrated, thinking it impossible to kill the Black Vulture, but seeing the relic in the cleric's hands had changed everything.

She knew Svoyatova Aleksandra Mozhayeva's shin bone. She knew what that blade could do. She just wasn't sure how to get her hands on it without the cleric knowing.

Someone sat down beside her. Katya tensed.

"Frankly, I don't trust you out here alone," Kacper said.

"If I haven't murdered your dear king yet, why would I do it now?" she said, riffling through her pack. She would need magic to sneak into the tent and get the *voryen* without the cleric—or worse, that Vulture—waking up.

"A strategist would know to wait."

She grinned. "All my reports say you're the one to watch."

He grunted. "Why is that?"

"The girl is a noble. Hanging around the king is a rebellion. She's a powerful mage, but there are a lot of those in Tranavia. *You* are more complicated."

"I assure you, you are definitely overthinking it," he replied.

"I'm not so sure I am."

"Is that what this is about? Reconnaissance."

"That would only be useful if they listened to me," Katya said. "They do not."

Kacper made a thoughtful, if vaguely disbelieving grunt. "They're all just plotting on how best to destroy the others," he said. "The cleric, the Vulture, Serefin, that Akolan girl."

"But not Rashid?"

"Rashid does whatever Parijahan wishes him to," Kacper said. "She's close with the Vulture, so that could be dangerous."

She hadn't noticed any of this. He *was* the one to keep an eye on.

"What are you doing?" he asked.

Suddenly a wailing pierced the air. Kacper's hand moved for his spell book. Katya remained seated. She held out a hand, keeping the Tranavian boy still.

"Wait," she whispered.

The wails were fevered, panicked, morphing into screams so terrified they rattled down to Katya's bones. She hated this place, regretted ever coming here.

"*Deravich*," she murmured.

"What?"

"A monster borne of the dead. Of those who have died in trauma. Keep quiet. If it doesn't notice us, we'll be fine."

She had been in that clearing with the *Lichni'voda*. She had seen the inhuman monster the Black Vulture truly was and the kind of power the cleric held within her. She had been marked along with them. It didn't do her any good to worry about it, but she wished she hadn't been so curious.

The wails quieted. Katya sighed.

"We aren't welcome here," Kacper said.

"Not even a little bit."

She took a small vial from her bag. She only needed a bit of magic—and to go into a light stupor to contact a saint. Hopefully this would do the job.

"Can you keep watch for me for a few minutes?" she asked Kacper.

She didn't wait for him to respond before she downed the acidic liquid and moved to slip into the tent.

The next moment she was aware of, she was back outside with the bone *voryen* in her hands, breathing hard. She couldn't shake the feeling that—while she had succeeded—the Vulture *knew*. She didn't think he had woken up but everything was always so fuzzy when she used magic. The world's edges dimmed and colors were wrong. It was a dangerous state to be in, because she was never entirely sure of just what she was doing.

But she had what she needed. Hopefully the cleric would be too distracted to ever realize it was missing.

# 36

## NADEZHDA

## LAPTEVA

*She dances in the swamp, Zlatana does, waiting for wanderers to hear her merriment. Waiting to pull them to Dziwożona for her bargain with the hag feeds her well.*

—The Books of Innokentiy

Nadya woke to screaming.

Malachiasz was out of the tent before Nadya even had time to register what had woken her. She stumbled after him, bleary-eyed and still feeling his warmth against her skin before the blistering cold shocked her awake.

The second she was outside of the tent Nadya *felt* it.

They already had the attention of the fallen gods. She had thought Velyos was something else at first—he'd told her he wasn't a god, and stupidly she had taken that at face value. Serefin had been dealing with Velyos' touch upon him and Nadya could feel that. But here there was something else, dark, deep, harder to place, harder for

her to pinpoint—and this newfound power of hers was tapped into a thread of divinity that meant she was *always* feeling something. This was different. This was another god.

Malachiasz held an arm out, stopping Nadya from coming any farther. She clutched her hand over her mouth.

"We are dealing with powers far outside our comprehension," he murmured. "Is this Velyos?"

It didn't feel like Velyos; there was no need to worry them further. "I think so."

Serefin's body wracked with seizures and blood fell from his eyes. Nadya grasped for her necklace, catching Marzenya's bead.

*I have to help him,* she prayed.

*"He is far past our help, child,"* Marzenya replied.

Nadya didn't want to take no for an answer. She slid to the ground where Kacper was holding Serefin down to keep him from clawing at his eyes.

"I need cloth," she said. Malachiasz blinked at her before going for his coat and returning with a cloth he used to clean blood off his hands—it had not been used, thankfully.

Nadya moved closer, careful to avoid Serefin's thrashing, remembering the incident on the boat, his bleeding eyes. She moved behind him, catching the back of his head before it slammed into the ground.

"All right, you glorious fool," she murmured as she tied the cloth tight over his eyes. "You're going to be all right. Fight it if you must but there's no shame in giving up," she whispered, her mouth close to his ear. She stroked his hair back from his forehead. "Let me see what we're dealing with." She slid her palm over his forehead, closing her eyes.

She took one horrifying glimpse. Something old and foul had grasped onto Serefin's soul and was holding on tight. Nadya could do nothing, frozen in place at the foot of an immense stone temple as a massive hand crept through the door. Another hand followed until dozens of hands were all clawing to escape.

Her eyes flew open, her hand moving away from Serefin's forehead. This was not a connection she could break. She looked up to where Malachiasz was standing nearby and shook her head.

"What is it?" Kacper asked, desperation filling his voice.

"Something ancient." She shifted off her heels, sitting down with Serefin's head in her lap. "If he doesn't break this thing with Velyos, it's going to devour him." But even as she spoke, she was certain this wasn't Velyos. But she didn't know who it was, and that terrified her.

*What has happened to him?*

"What do we do?" Ostyia asked, panicked.

Malachiasz rubbed at his jaw, the dark look on his face uncomfortable.

"Has he given the impression that he knows how to break this?" he asked Kacper.

"Barely."

*What does he want?* she asked Marzenya.

*"What do you think, child? We banished him a long time ago. What else could he possibly want?"*

*Revenge.*

*"Even so."*

"The ruins—" Katya started.

"He *wants* Serefin here," Nadya snapped, cutting her off. "How do we know that pushing him closer isn't going to set off exactly what he wants?"

Nadya shivered. She hadn't grabbed her coat in her dash outside. Malachiasz shrugged out of his and draped it over her shoulders, crouching next to her.

"There's nothing to do but keep moving," he said. "We can only hope our current trajectory is the right one."

Nadya nodded, frowning. Acting off myths and hope. It was flimsy at best and the only thing they had. It was too late to turn around. She got to her feet and Kacper took her spot, placing Serefin's head in his lap with gentle hands. "Don't wake him," she said. "We can wait."

"This never would have happened if you hadn't interfered with Tranavia," Ostyia snapped.

"This happened because your last king and *he*—" She pointed at Malachiasz, who had the decency to look miserable. "—toyed with powers they did not understand. I had nothing to do with this. I want to help him. We help him by continuing forward."

It took more blood than Nadya thought Malachiasz could physically spill. She kept waiting for him to pass out but he just kept feeding blood into the spell, his features roiling, the mask crumbling and falling away as he stood at the feet of divinity and it stripped him raw and showed the world what, exactly, he had become.

He ended up on his knees, head bowed and shaking, and Nadya briefly worried this was the end of him before that terrible, brilliant, monstrous boy struggled back to his feet and slammed his hand against the black wall.

And the entire thing shattered like a pane of glass.

He wavered on his feet as the magic fell away and ancient power rushed past them in a torrent that even those who did not touch magic regularly would feel burn into their skin.

Malachiasz's mask did not return, and his head twitched, talon tipped fingers fluttering at his side.

*Oh.* The forest was already gnawing at his mind. That was it, then. He was gone. So easy, ultimately. So much easier than twisting the knife herself.

*No less painful,* she considered, her chest tight.

She waved the rest of them back and away as she stepped toward Malachiasz, reaching for her well of power. His head snapped up as she approached and he stared at her with black, unfathomable eyes.

"*Dozleyena, sterevyani bolen,*" she said, holding a hand out. "You're going to come back down from that, right, Malachiasz?"

A shudder at the sound of his name on her tongue. A sharp breath hissed between iron teeth. Fear settled deep in Nadya's core, different than when she was in the Salt Mines. She could no longer feel the scraps of his coherency.

That thread that tied them together was something animalistic and harsh. Something powerful and basely cruel.

He shifted on his feet and Nadya jolted, almost bolting in fear. He took one step closer to her. Blinked onyx eyes—so many of them, sliding across his features in a way that made her stomach turn. It was the horror of the Salt Mines taken further as the little pieces of Malachiasz still holding on were swept away.

Then he vanished into the forest.

"Fuck," Nadya muttered, staring at the spot within the trees where he had disappeared.

She had shoved him right over the edge to ruin.

# SEREFIN

# MELESKI

Serefin only lasted for a few seconds without the cloth tied over his eyes. He had lost the left one entirely, and the right wavered so badly that he could only go a few steps toward Nadya without wanting to vomit from the horrors clawing at his vision. His head pounded with nearly blinding pain as he slowly moved to where the wall of magic had fallen.

"Do you think we've unleashed something by doing that?" he asked amiably, peering at what little he could see through the thin fabric.

Nadya swallowed hard. "I didn't even think of that," she whispered.

Malachiasz was gone, not much of a surprise to Serefin, but Nadya had paled considerably. Did she really think he was whole enough to help them?

"He . . ." she started and stopped, her voice wavering dangerously. "He was so normal before. I didn't think . . ."

Serefin very carefully put a hand on her shoulder—carefully, since he really couldn't see where it was—and squeezed gently. She reached up and put her hand over his.

"You're in bad shape, too," she said.

He shrugged, mostly to mask his sheer terror. He was decidedly not well, but what could he really do about it?

*"You're going to let the rest out,"* Velyos hissed. *"Leave everything else to me. Those two will tear each other apart and finish our jobs for us."*

*I'm going to drive you out.*

*"I will very much enjoy seeing you try. Help me and you'll get your chance to kill that creature."*

*Can he be killed?*

*"Dear boy, anything can be killed. Even gods."*

He glanced at Katya, whose features had stayed smooth and oddly unworried.

It wouldn't be a long journey to the temple at the base of the mountains. Nadya had estimated at most a week. But a lot could happen once they stepped past the border keeping all that divine madness in check.

Kacper moved closer to Serefin and gingerly wrapped his arm around Serefin's waist.

"You need help," he murmured in his ear. He skimmed his nose against Serefin's cheek. "Let me help."

He leaned into Kacper, nodding wearily. "They're—he's taking me over," he said. Nadya tensed at his other side. "If I start sounding odd, or if I . . . do something and it's clear it's not . . . well, not *me,* then—knock me out. It's horrible when I'm asleep, but it might be easier to handle me."

"Serefin . . ." Nadya murmured.

"Nothing to be done," Serefin said, falsely cheerful. "Should we be off?"

Nadya tucked a lock of hair behind her ear. She hadn't braided it and it hung loose around her shoulders. She picked up Malachiasz's spell book from where it was lying on the ground, staring at it before handing it to Parijahan. Rashid pulled her into an embrace.

"It broke him," Serefin heard her say. "I wouldn't have asked if I'd really thought . . ."

Rashid kissed the side of her head. "He was already broken. He wanted to help. He gave us that."

She nodded, stepping back and wiping quickly at her eyes. She turned to Serefin. "Let's go."

Kacper took his hand. "Just trust me," Kacper murmured. "We'll get to the other side of this like we have everything else."

Kacper nudged his forehead against Serefin's temple and their lips met in a whisper of a kiss. Serefin reached back and made sure the blindfold was firmly tied against his head, and Kacper tugged him forward.

# 37

## NADEZHDA

## LAPTEVA

*A knife twisted in the gut of the divine as he waits and he watches and he knows that they will fall, they always fall, nothing is eternal except for the darkness.*

—The Volokhtaznikon

One second, Nadya was with the others, picking their way through a forest that had not been trespassed in hundreds of years. The next, she was completely alone.

Panic seared through her as the silence suddenly became unbearably loud in her ears. It was hard not to notice the absence of Serefin's awkward steps as he struggled with only Kacper's hand to guide him. She turned slowly, afraid of what she might find behind her.

There was nothing.

Nadya clutched at her prayer beads. Should she continue alone? Should she try to find the others? There was

no telling what the forest was going to do to them before it allowed them to their destination—*if* it allowed them there.

Would having Malachiasz for a little longer have saved them from the toying of the wood, or was this inevitable?

*What am I supposed to do?*

*"You keep going."*

Marzenya's presence was stronger and more terrifying here. Something about it, about her, felt . . . different. Nadya didn't know what to make of it. But her goddess was right.

She had to keep going.

Here the trees were vast, a single one wouldn't fit in the width of the sanctuary at the monastery where she had grown up. Unfathomably large. It was perpetually dark, perpetually cold, and Nadya felt strange. There was a distracting humming in her blood.

She could feel where she needed to go, but couldn't bring herself to step forward. What if she was meant to search for the others?

*They can handle themselves,* she thought, though that wasn't even a little bit true. Serefin was a wreck, only barely in control of himself. And Parijahan and Rashid had no magic in a place where magic was everywhere.

A pang of worry stabbed at her, but her decision was made. She had to continue and pray the others would be fine.

Pray they didn't happen upon Malachiasz.

Pray she didn't, either.

Nadya tucked Malachiasz's coat closer around her, rolling the too-long sleeves back. It smelled like him again, but it was a cold comfort.

He had only been trying to *help* and it had broken what little he had left.

*Was this part of the curse?* The dark omen upon them was

going to strike eventually. But no. She had known pressing past that wall of magic would tear him to pieces and she had asked it of him anyway.

*"Do you want it to be? Would that make it easier to bear?"*

Nadya sighed.

*"He is not what should concern you. You have far greater things to deal with than that worm."*

*I really feel like your insults for him could be better.*

*"Be grateful he still lives, child,"* Marzenya replied dryly.

Nadya smiled slightly. It was almost like a conversation she would have had with Marzenya before. She missed the rest of the pantheon, but having Marzenya back was enough. Almost. The difference in Marzenya was troubling, though. Always a little cold, a little cruel, but Marzenya did not control secrets— those were for Vaclav. Her words had a dispassionate bite to them, like she was talking to a stranger, not a girl she had spoken to her whole short life.

But her smile fell away. He wouldn't live for much longer, though, would he?

It was oppressive, how the forest lived and breathed and wanted Nadya *out*. The underbrush was thick and difficult to navigate, full of leaves chewed by worms and bleached bones, and she had to completely reroute her path to go around the massive trees. Everything smelled of damp and decay, cut through by the bitter sharpness of cold.

It didn't take long for Nadya's weariness to slow her steps and her loneliness to latch itself around her heart. It was hard to see the end of this and believe anything would be better.

Was losing track of Serefin another failure? If he faltered, Nadya and the rest of the world would be lost. She couldn't lie to herself—she knew, deep down, what would happen to her if the fallen gods were set free. They would take her and she wouldn't be strong enough to fight back.

Maybe she should try to find him instead.

*"Keep going."*

She chewed on her lip, staring up at the dark canopy of leaves covering the sky. She missed the sun; she had been in the darkness for too long.

She pushed into a clearing. Malachiasz lounged in the low-slung branches of a tree, casually picking at his fingernails. Something twinged in Nadya's chest. This was the Malachiasz from the night in the cathedral. Kohl lining pale eyes, making them even more colorless and strange, black hair tangled with golden beads and bits of bone.

He was wearing the clothes he had disappeared in. A black tunic and black leggings. And there was a cruel, detached look in his eyes as he gazed down at her.

She couldn't tell if he was really there.

"Where do you think this is going to go, truly?" he drawled.

"What?"

He waved a hand. "All of this. The temple, the gods, that business with Serefin. What's all this to do?"

"To stop the war," she said evenly. "Serefin has to break free from Velyos. I need answers. Marzenya—"

"The bitch who bosses you around."

Nadya froze. "I'm sorry?"

"You heard me," he said slowly. A smile tugged at his mouth as he dropped to the ground, his movements as elegant as ever. "You don't need them but you also don't listen to reason so there's really no point in any of this. You'll remain irrational, this war will continue, nothing will change."

"What are you talking about?"

"Give up, little cleric. You lost. You killed the king of Tranavia and nothing changed, except your petty gods cast you out because you dared think for yourself. Kalyazin is never going to win. They are underpowered and incapable of matching the blood magic that a Tranavian *child* could cast."

She took a step back as he inched closer, eyeing her like a predator. Her back hit a tree and she was trapped.

He placed his hand against the tree—iron claws long and sharp, tapping the space next to her head. He leaned in close. "I was right and I always will be. You are nothing but a girl with a blade."

He was a breath away and she could taste something *off* in the air. Her heart tripped over itself in terrified, erratic beats that she couldn't explain, because even at his worst—tearing out hearts and eating them in front of her—he never kicked off such a primal instinct of fear within her before. She never thought he would truly kill her, except here . . . she wasn't so sure.

His sleeve slid back ever so slightly. Nadya glanced from his arm to his face. She trailed the sharp thumbnail of her left hand against his cheek, a cut opening and dripping blood.

"You would doom us all," she whispered, "for the sake of your vendetta. But, of course, you do know everything, Malachiasz Czechowicz—" She waited. "Like you know to never underestimate a girl with a blade."

She reached for her bone *voryen*, panic settling between her ribs when she discovered it gone. Her fingers closed over one of her other blades and she tugged it from its sheath, holding it loosely.

A beat of hesitation—*if she were wrong*—no, if she were wrong, he would be fine.

She slid the blade through his ribs and into his heart.

Blood poured over her hands, warm and not his *not his*. She was right—she had to be right.

The eyes of the *Telich'nevyi* went white, shock and confusion twisting its face. It grasped the hilt of her blade, letting out a small, pained gasp that sounded like *him* and Nadya closed her eyes because she couldn't watch this. *It's not him, it only stole his face.*

It crumpled to the ground at her feet. She shuddered, standing in the clearing with blood on her hands, forcing her nerves to settle before she moved, nudging at the body with the toe of her boot.

"Nadya?"

She whirled, *voryen* raised. Malachiasz was staring past her at the body at her feet. Nadya wasn't sure it was possible for him to look paler than he did right then. She supposed stumbling upon one's own dead body would be alarming. But, oh, gods, it was really him. Was it really him? Or was this another one?

*Telich'nevyi* were also straight out of Kalyazi myth. Shape shifters who only needed a single strand of hair from someone's head to copy them so completely that their loved ones would never know.

"Give it a moment, it'll change," she said softly, any louder and her voice would crack, because this one *might* actually be Malachiasz.

"Did you kill it?" His voice sounded off.

"I did."

"Did it look like that?" Smaller, now.

"It did." She was starting to tremble. She had stabbed him. Not him, but him still. He acted like that normally, it wasn't his behavior that had tipped her off at all. It was a guess, a lucky guess.

"Oh." More a strangled exhale than an actual word.

She wiped the blood off her hands, searching through the underbrush for something to wipe off her blade.

"How did you, uh, h-how—"

"How did I know I wasn't killing you?"

He swallowed hard and nodded.

*I didn't, gods, I really didn't.* She stared at him. He grew even paler.

"Nadya," he said quietly, desperation in his voice.

She shook her head. "It—it didn't get your eyes right. And you do this weird little shudder when you hear your name, it didn't do that, either."

He couldn't pull his eyes away from the body. It still looked like him. She turned his face, fingers skimming over the spot on his cheek she had cut open on the *Telich'nevyi*.

"This place wants us to destroy each other," she said. She kissed him, a gentle, quieting touch. "We can't let it." How easy it was to lie to him.

His hand was at her waist, trembling as his fingers dug into the fabric of her jacket—his jacket. She turned to go, but when she took a step and his hand slipped from hers, her heart dropped. She turned. She was alone.

"Shit," she swore.

## SEREFIN

## MELESKI

The voices had become incessant. The ones he was supposed to wake growing louder with each step. Their voices adding to the other two that rattled in the back of his head, growing to a fever pitch, a cacophony, insufferable. He lost track of how many voices there were, they lost anything that might make them distinct as they merged with one another in an awful chorus.

He didn't think he could fight this much longer. The best thing to do would be to obey and hope he survived to see the end of it.

His eyes hurt. Kacper's hand clasped around his was a warm and solid comfort even though he could feel his rapid pulse and knew he was terrified.

Kacper was leading him in the wrong direction. He knew where he needed to go; knew where it was the fallen ones slept. Serefin jerked his hand away. The second he did, he was alone.

"Wait!" he said, stepping forward as if he could pull Kacper back from wherever he had gone, but there was nothing but dark forest around him.

His breath came hard and fast. He reached back with shaking hands and untied the cloth around his eyes.

The nightmare came to life around him.

He stood in the center of a graveyard of giants, their vast bones scattered and creating a forest of white. The moths kicked up in a frenzy around him, but they were unnatural. Marked, black and white with skulls on their wings.

Serefin pressed his hands to his eyes. They came away bloody. He tried not to panic because if he panicked he would do something stupid and if he did something stupid he was lost. He needed to think.

*He needed to wake those who were sleeping.*

No. He was here to break this off. He needed to keep going because that was the only way to cut Velyos and the rest off.

Velyos urged him on, through the graveyard of bone. He walked past skulls the size of the great hall in Grazyk. Some were almost human, except there were too many eye sockets, the shapes wrong, the jawbones too long. Some were like animal skulls: deer, wolves, rats, snakes, and one that looked terrifyingly like the skull of a dragon.

Glittering spiderwebs covered empty sockets. One of Serefin's moths was trapped in a web and he watched in horror as a spider the size of a wolf crept out from within the recesses of the skull to devour it.

*When I died, you showed me visions of what could happen to this world, didn't you?* he asked cautiously. Grazyk burning. Kalyazin a barren wasteland. Blood raining from the sky. But what would be the catalyst for that kind of apocalypse? Inaction? Continued war?

"*I did,*" Velyos said. "*You are but one veil away from my domain. One side step and you are there.*"

*Where am I now?*

"*This is also mine, if mine in a different form. You have exceptional power, Tranavian, but you feed on a whisper of magic. The girl drinks in so much more.*"

*And Malachiasz?*

There was silence as Serefin continued on, bones crunching underneath his boots.

"*He has the power of a god,*" Velyos finally said. "*And that is why he must die.*"

Something close to sorrow filled Serefin. He kept remembering the boy with the mess of black hair standing in the servants' hall, tears streaking his cheeks, terrified of his power. Kept thinking of his brother walking beside him and offering a truce. He didn't know if he could do it in the end.

"*If you want to avoid what I showed you, you must continue. I have been putting the pieces into place for so long and I have lost many along the way. But finally I have found the pieces that will move in the correct directions and we are so close, you see, so close to real change.*"

Serefin paused. During the year of Velyos rattling in his brain, the being had grown coherent. Far more coherent than when he had spoken to him after he had been killed. Velyos was growing stronger. Each step west had given him strength.

Serefin only wanted his eyes to stop hurting, to stop bleeding. He wanted his throne back. He wanted to save Tranavia.

He wanted to sleep.

He wasn't so sure he was strong enough to break this off.

*How do I wake the others?* Better to avoid it, he thought. He tried to take a step away from where Velyos wished him to go and could not. The only way out was to see this to the end.

*"You'll know. It will be easy; you are nearly there. You already started the process and didn't even know it! Mortals, so fleeting so fast but when you are nudged in the proper directions you charge headlong into the abyss without a second glance and that is good, so good. Wonderful that now the song can continue.*

*"It was broken, you see. Long, long ago. There was a note, here and there, but the song needs to play to its end and we are so close, a few more instruments, a little more exquisite torture and we will have it."*

Panic clawed at his chest. When he took a step forward the crunch of bone sounded too loud in his ears.

*"I wanted the four. I wanted all of them, you see. Because, oh, the things I could make right if I had the girl and the monster and the prince and the queen. But I will make do. I am resourceful. You have been so very useful to me, young prince turned king turned instrument and omen. We are so close. So close to a beginning, so close to a reckoning."*

*Against the other Kalyazi gods?* Serefin tried to put reason to Velyos' words.

*"Who else?"*

# interlude viii

## KACPER

## NEIBORSKI

Serefin was gone.

Again.

He had lost Serefin *again*.

Not only that, but he had lost all the others. Damn the Kalyazi, he wasn't concerned with her, but *Ostyia* was out there somewhere alone. He had to keep calm but all he wanted to do was flee this bloody forest, go back to Tranavia, and pretend like none of this had ever happened. He had never been assigned to the prince's company. He had never gotten into a fight with Ostyia because she had teased him about his crush on Serefin in front of the other soldiers. He had never been promoted into Serefin's inner circle.

None of this madness had ever happened.

He was just a boy from the country. He wasn't made for this. Royalty and Vultures and divine nonsense. He

was good at blood magic but there were plenty who were better. And blood magic was so basic, so *normal*. Whatever this was wasn't normal.

Blood and bone, he hoped Serefin was all right, but he had a sinking feeling deep in the pit of his stomach that something very bad was about to happen and there was nothing he could do to stop it. He hadn't been able to stop Serefin from leaving. He could do nothing to help Serefin as these *beings* tried to rip him apart, could only watch in horror as his eyes bled and he tried to claw them out even if he had to go through his own skull to do it.

Kacper wished he had never left home. Taken over the farm from his sister. Did his duty at the front and returned the instant his contract had ended. But he had to meet a ridiculous prince with pale eyes and a grin that could light up a room full of soldiers who were tired and only wanted to go home.

A boy who drank too much and it made him too trusting. Who would lie on the floor of his tent and complain to Kacper about how at least at the front he could be *Serefin*, when at home he had to be quiet and fade into the background to escape his father's notice.

Kacper didn't know if he could survive losing Serefin. He had pushed his star into the prince's orbit and it would be cataclysmic to try to get out of it. He had done the one thing he had always been told to never do and fallen in love far above his station.

He found Serefin's brilliance blinding at times. Kacper had seen him win battles on strategy alone, ones where they were outnumbered and underpowered. Serefin was clever; he knew how to twist scenarios into his favor. And watching everything fall apart around Serefin was killing him.

He took in his surroundings. Everything was starting to

look the same and the little light there was left was starting to fade.

*I won't survive a night out here,* Kacper thought, fear taking him in its hold.

Something snapped nearby. Kacper whirled, hand falling to his spell book. He usually favored a blade—Ostyia and Serefin were better mages and it was wiser to have someone who could act without magic. But here a blade was going to be useless against whatever Kalyazi horror the forest decided to spit out at him.

Was this a test? Or was this ancient forest merely toying with them because it could? Because they had walked into the mouth of hell and now they were at its mercy.

Tranavia had stories about this place that they had all ignored because Serefin was being forced to come here.

And they were going to die because of it.

# PARIJAHAN

## SIROOSI

Parijahan skirted the edges of a swamp. She kept hearing things, whispers, words that sometimes sounded like they were Kalyazi, sometimes Tranavian, but sometimes she heard Paalmideshi and the sound made her want to cry.

What was she doing?

She was alone. She hadn't been particularly surprised when she'd looked up and the others were gone. Including Rashid— and she hadn't been without him at her side in a very long time. His absence was a thorn in her heart.

*Please survive this,* she prayed, even though her gods were very far away and the ones of Kalyazin did not care for her. Here she walked in the realm of gods that did not belong to her and it was ironic, really, how her cowardice had taken her this far.

How much farther still before she finally stopped running?

She dropped her pack and sat down at the edge of the swamp. She couldn't pass that. She could not play this game that the others *could*. All she had were a handful of weapons and her own wits and she worried those wits would not be enough here.

The letter was still at the bottom of her pack. She had tried not to think about it. Had tried to work out what she was supposed to do with Malachiasz, but his help could only extend so far and he, strangely, wanted her to do the right thing.

A puzzle, that boy.

The right thing would mean facing her family. Testing a fragile peace that had only been won by her fleeing the palace in the night and never crossing the Akolan border again. It would mean handing herself over to a family that was more likely to execute her than to welcome her and hand her the Travash. She didn't even *want* the Travash.

But not taking it meant condemning Akola to a civil war that had been churning at its edges for decades. She had to choose herself or her country.

And being around people like Nadya and Malachiasz made everything so much worse because both would die so quickly for their countries and Parijahan just could not force herself to feel the same. Maybe she was selfish. But she couldn't be like the friends she had made in this cold and bitter land.

Something splashed nearby and Parijahan tensed. She had

foolishly walked in here thinking that she would at least have the safety of her companions to rest on in this place of magic.

She dug into her pack, taking out the letter. She read it again, though the words were burned into her brain.

Crumpling up the letter, she threw it into the murky swamp water before she could change her mind. The water bled over it, making the ink run. She stood up. She had to find the others.

# 38

## NADEZHDA LAPTEVA

*The world they wish is broken bones and blood—always blood.*

—The Volokhtaznikon

In the ruins of Bolagvoy there was an altar and a well and a place where those before her had come to petition for lost rites. She had thought she would be going to the altar to beg forgiveness for her sins and a return to what she knew.

But she was to go to taste divinity instead.

Nadya refused to sleep. She kept walking, even as night fell. Even as it grew so dark around her that she could barely see. Even as her body began to flag from exhaustion. She had this one thing to do, and then she would have answers. She might be forgiven. She might find peace. Something, *anything* might change.

The undergrowth crunched beneath her boots, Marzenya pulling her toward the heart of the forest, toward

the mountains. What was she, after all, if nothing but a vessel for the gods' will? What other purpose did she have? What else was there?

Nothing and nothing and nothing.

And so she kept going. Every time she closed her eyes, all she saw in the dark against the backs of her eyelids was her blade being plunged into Malachiasz's chest. The betrayal in his eyes before they had gone dim, dark, silent.

She had done it with so little hesitation.

What else might she do to him? How little was he worth to her, truly?

He was everything; he was nothing. She was torn apart in a thousand directions but there was only one and it was *forward*. There was nothing else but this.

But the blood on her hands, warm and his—except it had been a monster. But *he* was a monster. And how long until he turned on her like that, and she was forced to act?

She couldn't do that again. She could never do that again.

But she did not know what this future would hold and they had been cursed. Maybe that was the worst of it. Or maybe the worst was to come.

The monsters left her alone, as if held back by a greater hand. But she saw them in passing. A *leshy* as it sat on a stone altar and watched her go. A bear, massive and primal, lumbering through the woods just past her, moving in the same direction. Toward the mountain, ever closer to the mountain.

Nothing else mattered but getting to the mountain.

The seat of the gods. The well of divinity.

Hellmouth.

Nadya swallowed that fear because it was Tranavian in origin and it did not belong to her. She was Kalyazi and divinely touched and maybe that didn't *matter*, but she had to try.

She would crawl back to her goddess.

She had broken the boy she loved. Stabbed him in the heart. He was out there, more monster than anything else, and she left him to that, because there were greater things still to come.

But she would have to make it there first. All she could do was put one foot in front of the other and keep going.

# SEREFIN

# MELESKI

It was devouring him.

Somehow he had reached the place he was meant to be; the tug at his chest had quieted. And when he blinked his eyes, he would be in a forest, grim and dark, and then everything would blur and bones would be strewn as far as the eye could see.

And so he sat down because he was so very tired. He had fought for so long. He wanted to sleep. Surely it would be fine if he slept. Nothing would harm him—they needed him, he was needed to wake those that were sleeping.

He lay down.

And the forest, it hungered. It knew what had stepped inside it, knew those great powers that dwelt within and around and in between and underneath its trees had great plans for the little insects that were scurrying around while it watched.

Serefin did not know how he could *feel* the forest. He closed his eyes. He did not notice as moss started to grow over his hand, as the roots of the trees began to wrap over his legs and pin him lower and lower into the soft earth. Suddenly he could feel the hunger of everything around him. The clawing, cloying hunger turning Malachiasz inside and out. This ache that settled at the core of every being who called itself a god, who called itself older than the very earth, this desire to be needed and wanted and to *do* when they were so very far away and could do nothing but suggest and whittle and be patient.

The moss crept farther up Serefin's arm.

It was this hunger that began to chew Serefin up inside. It was not natural to him; he did not want it. But for a second, he understood what it was to be Nadya, someone accepting of their place in this scope of power that was all too vast to comprehend.

And he understood what it was to be Malachiasz, who clawed for more and tried to set all the pieces right only to watch them topple. Who fought his way into becoming something so far past mortal and know that ache and keep wanting, keep reaching, and keep watching everything fall to the ground, hoping if he only made it a little farther, everything would be all right.

He could feel Kacper and his panic and bewilderment and an unflagging love for Serefin that he could not comprehend deserving. And Parijahan—*the queen*—quieting herself from the song. Turning her back and making a choice. A discordant note rattling through him, painful. The *tsarevna* who walked the forest with a strange calm the others did not have. Who knew this place would not touch her because she knew the moment of her own death and this was not it.

He sank farther.

Wasn't he supposed to be fighting something?

He was Serefin Meleski and the fight was all he had because the forest was taking everything else—Velyos was taking and taking, with his long pale fingers and fathomless eyes blinking out from the skull of a deer. As he dissected Serefin into use-able parts and pushed him farther and farther down until the trees grew over him and he was nothing and everything and this was happening again, *how was this happening again?*

He was too tired to fight. He let it happen.

It was the giving up that was key. It wasn't some radical, dramatic act, waking up those who had slept for thousands of years. All it took was resignation. All it took was one boy say-ing he'd had enough and laying everything down.

Letting the forest take him apart.

He didn't know if he would be put back together, in the end, if there was an end, if *anything* would ever end or if this would go on and on and he would feed this forest for eternity.

*"You are deeply melodramatic, I hope you know that."*

A flicker in his awareness. Serefin was still half-scattered, many disparate parts thrown to the wind, barely the shape of a boy remaining.

*"You cannot sleep through the turning of the age,"* Velyos said. *"Sweet as that might sound. Get up, king of Tranavia, king of gold, king of blood, king of moths, there is so much more to be done."*

But the first steps had been taken. The forest shivered as those it had held within its grasp for so very, very long began to blink awake.

There was Velyos, finally clawing his way to the sun after centuries. He had woken up bound, aware yet trapped. And now he was free to take his revenge on those who had bound him. The god of the underworld and of rivers and of tricks.

And Cvjetko, who had been at Velyos' side when they had made the final reach for Peloyin's and Marzenya's thrones. For their crowns made of earth and bone and blood. A god of three heads and three beings and three elements that did not coex-ist but lived in a constant churning storm.

Zlatana, of the swamps and the undergrowth and the monsters that dwelled in the darkened corners of the untamed world. So angry for having been trapped for so long for so very little.

Zvezdan, of the darkness of the waters.

Ljubica, of eternal tears. Tears and mourning and anguish and darkness, darkness, darkness.

And . . . Chyrnog, the last and of a very different kind of darkness.

Serefin was puzzled. There were more here than he had thought.

*"Five minor, in the grand scope of things. We who are under those who are above, or, in this case, below,"* Velyos said slyly. *"Chyrnog is the greatest, the oldest, he has been asleep the longest. He is the one who will turn this world over and make it anew. He is the one who will help you on the second part of your quest, young king. He will give you your crown back."*

Serefin felt something horrific begin to stir.

And, not for the first time, he wondered if, perhaps, he had made a terrible mistake.

Serefin was pulled under.

# 39

*It would be too easy to muse that these circumstances have been misinterpreted over time. That magic is a simple matter of divine connection between mortal and god would be a risky assumption to make. For what of Tasha Savrasova, who was touched by none of the gods—her form twisted into something resembling Tranavia's Vultures—and yet held divinity within her palms? What of her?*
—The Letters of Włodzimierz

When Nadya made it to the doors of Bolagvoy, it was as if she had walked the forest alone for years. She had lived a day and an eternity all at once. The building was made of wood, dramatic and massive with wide onion domes. It had stood since the beginning of time, and it would continue to stand long after everything fell away.

"My child, you have come so far." Marzenya's voice was very close. "So much farther than any other mortal I have

*blessed. I knew you would change everything; you would fix this broken world."*

Nadya swallowed. The inside of the church was bright. At the base of the mountain, the trees could not block out the sun so easily. Icons framed the doorway. Every saint that had ever been had a place within these walls. Overgrowth crept along the floor, climbing the walls, lush and green.

It was beautiful but the feeling here was distorted, unholy, as if she would blink and see something very different, but she wasn't sure what.

*What am I supposed to do now?* Nadya asked. *I only want to understand. If I'm so special, so different, why have I been treated like this?*

*"Oh, child, you didn't know?"*

Nadya had started toward the sanctuary doors, but she stopped, not recognizing the tone in Marzenya's voice. *Know what?*

*"We never turned away, child. Did you think the boy who forged the veil to cut his country off from our touch would stop there?"*

Nadya went cold. Her hand tightened into a fist. That couldn't be right.

*What?*

*"The boy who treads at the edges of our realm, who has the power to cross over but not the knowledge, the boy who hopes to become something greater than he is meant to be. Did you think he would leave you alone to live your life at our whims? Did you think you had not given up something great by choosing him?"*

Nadya shook her head. Malachiasz wouldn't have done that to her. They had their differences, fundamental oppositions, but he had only ever treated her belief in the gods with a kind of cautious—if derisive—respect.

Yet it made too much terrible sense. Of course he had been hiding something like this. Her gods would not abandon her.

But that didn't explain everything. What was *she*?

*"You were always meant to be divinely blessed,"* Marzenya said. *"Does the rest matter?"*

Yes, yes it mattered. She had thought she was a simple cleric but she was something so much more and it was terrifying.

*What do you need me to do?*

*"If I asked you to kill the boy, well and truly, would you?"* Marzenya sounded curious.

Nadya faltered. She bit her lower lip, tears springing to her eyes. Even though a monster like him did not deserve her tears.

*Are you asking me to choose?* Nadya asked. She stood beneath the sun piercing through the windows, trembling under the weight of divinity. *Are you asking me to choose you or him?*

*"Yes."*

Kostya—her Kostya—had given her the same ultimatum, that this would not be able to continue forever. Nadya would have to make a decision between Malachiasz and her devotion to her gods. He was a sin she could not ignore.

Nadya closed her eyes. She thought of Malachiasz's vibrant grin, dimmed by the darkness he held close. The warmth of him next to her, the way his hand cradled the back of her head when he held her. His pure delight every time he made an absolutely terrible joke.

A ridiculous boy from Tranavia who couldn't sleep and wanted her close.

Nadya put her hand on the door.

They were cursed, thrown together by chance in Kalyazin, drawn together by circumstance but fated for opposite paths.

She thought of his pale eyes shuttered with cruelty. The roiling chaos of his body and features. His shattered mind. His desire for something that would destroy her world because he thought it was right.

But she was Kalyazi, and there was more to this world than the boy she loved in it.

Nadya shoved the door open.

Marzenya's approval washed over her. In front of her was a set of stairs. She frowned, uncertain where they would lead.

The stairs descended into darkness and impossibly far down and everything hummed in a way that felt familiar but Nadya couldn't place it outside an itch just underneath her skin, a horror, a vague unease. She didn't know how much time had passed—her shallow breaths and the walls that seemed to be slowly closing her in were her only marker—before she arrived in a stone temple. Covering the floor were luminescent white flowers, bathing the room in a soft, eerie glow. She brushed her hand over one and it curled in on itself, opening only after she stepped away.

At the far reaches of the room was a deep pool carved into the ground. Everything about this place felt so much older than the ruin above. This was ancient power. She could see the footsteps of those who had come before her to this place. Most had died here, their bones scattered amidst the flowers. A rib cage housed a cluster of vines that wrapped around each bone and sprouted into pale blooms.

She moved closer to the well.

"*You wanted answers,*" Marzenya said. "*It is time. There is only one way to get them. And with those answers I need you to do something for me.*"

*Anything,* Nadya said in a rush. She had been desperate for this for so long. She knelt at the edge of the pool, running her fingers over the symbols carved into the stone.

Water would have been too simple, made too much sense.

It was filled with blood.

Nadya choked back a sob.

She held her hand over the pool. This was what she had come for, this was what she wanted. But, at what cost? What would this take from her?

What did she have left to lose?

*Anything,* she repeated. *I would do anything.*

And she shifted, dipping her foot into the pool of blood. It was sickeningly warm and she swallowed back the bile that surged in her throat. There were steps at the edge of the pool. How many before her had done this? Where would this lead?

Before she could go on, something shook the very foundation of the mountain. Marzenya's alarm struck her. The goddess turned away from her and toward something else.

*"What has that boy done?"* her goddess hissed.

Nadya's stomach flipped. Serefin or Malachiasz? It was impossible to know and she had to keep going.

She slid into the pool to her calves and stood, taking one shaking step down. The blood was at her hips, soaking into the fabric of her dress. She hastily tugged Malachiasz's jacket off. She brought it to her face, catching the faded scent of him, before she tossed it to the corner of the room. She couldn't bear the thought of ruining it. Nadya skimmed her hand over the surface. She took another step, the blood at her chest. The next step would take her under. She hesitated. The rumpled jacket in the corner sent a pang through her.

What if this was the wrong choice?

But Nadya had been touched by the gods, *chosen* for this.

She took a deep breath and dropped, letting the pool of blood swallow her whole.

*"And so the little bird risks oblivion."*
This was obliteration.
This was what it was to be pulled apart and cast out against the fabric of time. To hear the song that denoted the present but *see* it all before her. To see it play on and on and on.
Here, then, were her answers, of a sort, in a way that was an assault unlike the careful fragmented pieces she had picked up along the way. A hierarchy of power that could be broken into, torn down, *changed*. The gods were real—they *existed*— but beings of benevolence? Hardly. They could manipulate this great song outside of the mortal realm, but they could not press past the boundary that separated *them* and mortality. And some were kind and some were cruel and they fought amongst themselves. Yet still, they held a careful alliance and only one single rule was to be followed: they could watch, they could suggest, but they were not to directly influence the course of mortality.
Magic was an unwieldy beast, not to be tamed, but there were those who were capable. And there were those who could twist magic to their will in small ways. Mortal, powerful, imbued with magic.
But what of those who could stand between realities; who would walk from one side to the other, shifting themselves into beings of coherence amidst the madness as they nudged the mortal realm along its path. They watched. They waited. They ferried the mortals along like ants. What had they been, once? Mortal or magic or something in between? Fallen gods or humans who had broken past a certain point of transcendence?

That, in the end, was not the great mystery it might have seemed a year ago.

Gods were gods were gods and it wasn't a grand question because, yes, a mortal could make that ascension but at what cost? The few that survived were so altered, it was like they had never been mortal at all.

Could you kill a god?

Anything could be killed.

And underneath it all was the song of the darkness. Underneath that careful hierarchy was a vast ocean of power that churned and held within it creatures ancient and unfathomable. And she knelt at the edge of that place and contemplated just what it meant that she wanted to dip into that ocean of power and take it all for herself—that somehow she felt as if she already had.

She was everything and nothing and yet the scar on her palm twinged just once, an answer to that discordant call. And she let herself reach down. She let herself touch the surface of that dark water.

The space she was in shifted, no longer a song, and Nadya woke up in a dim room where blood dripped from the walls and the stone floor was dusted with snow. She shivered, wrapping her arms around herself. Before her were rows and rows of strange jars and different pieces of bone, like an apothecary's shop—or a witch's workroom.

"Magic is changing."

Nadya jumped. A young girl was alongside her, eyeing the shelves of jars. She had strange, wide-set features and a long black braid that brushed the ground by her bare feet. She picked up one of the jars.

"The world is changing, but that's how the world works.

Magic, though, magic is supposed to flow in only one direction, and that is no longer a truth."

Nadya frowned. "I have a friend who would say it's all the same."

"In essence, it is," the girl agreed. "Are you not proof of that?"

"Am I?" Nadya asked desperately. "What is all this?"

"Bits and pieces of everything and anything. There are things happening now. A shifting in the world caused by so many little disasters, so many choices compounding to bring us to this point. The divine and the heretical are combined to twist a boy into the semblance of a god."

Nadya took in a sharp breath.

"Impossible before, possible now. Don't act surprised, you knew what he was studying. Your people study it in secret as well. A girl who had darkness locked away, what will you do now that it's woken up?"

This girl was familiar, but Nadya had no idea why. She didn't even know if the girl was real. Nadya drew her hand close.

"An abomination, and yet . . ." She paused thoughtfully. "Maybe something more. To be both is impossible. Both is oil and water and yet that boy. And yet *you*." The girl picked up a jar trapped in a perpetual state of a drop of blood falling into milk, the colors still separated. "This is what you want."

But Nadya was drawn to a silver jar with a string of teeth tied around its neck. She picked it up, aware of the girl watching her.

"What will I find?" she whispered.

"What are you looking for?"

"I want to know what I am."

The girl shrugged.

Nadya carefully opened the jar. She got what she wished.

A girl. Like any other. A girl who could hold power that would doom another mortal. A peasant girl from a monastery deep in the mountains of Kalyazin. A girl who had known loneliness and hunger and war. A girl who had lost and loved and wondered.

A girl who had doubted.

Everything and nothing.

But these were things she already knew. She let out a frustrated sound.

"Give it a moment," the girl said.

That ocean, that well, that vast roiling chaos of power. Eldritch and darkness and madness. There was another twinge of acknowledgment from the scar on her palm. A thrill of confirmation.

She capped the jar, putting it back on the shelf.

"You're not asking the right questions," the girl observed. "You know who—and what—you are. That never changed."

"Then what *did*?"

Something had changed. Something had led her down this path toward destruction where she had ruined so much under the guise of trying to do right.

The girl cupped Nadya's face in one hand. "Maybe you were never meant to save the world, daughter of death, maybe you *are* doing exactly what you were supposed to. You danced on the edge of darkness and light and you fell. You were always going to fall. The darkness was always going to have you. There has never been any escape from it. It was exactly what you were born for."

That couldn't be possible. The girl wordlessly handed Nadya the other jar.

"This won't destroy Tranavia, will it?"

"I told you," the girl said, "destruction is not my intent."

Nadya let the jar fall from her fingers, watching the glass shatter into crystals. Myth and hope and faith.

# 40

## NADEZHDA

## LAPTEVA

*This world awaits a turning, a revolt, a reckoning. It has churned and spat and twisted itself into something that is so different from the plan the first ones, the old ones, the dead ones wished it to be. Do not assume that plan was good and just. Never assume kindness. Assume oblivion.*

—The Volokhtaznikon

With a hard yank, Nadya surfaced, choking and gasping for air. Malachiasz pulled her out of the pool, panic shot through his voice as he repeated her name over and over.

"It's fine," she said, spitting out a mouthful of blood, wiping it out of her eyes. "I'm fine." She hesitated before looking up to where he crouched before her.

He was half gone. The mask had been shredded away but he had grasped onto pieces of it. His black hair was wild, his features fluid. Black horns spiraled back into his hair. But his eyes were pale blue, and he gently pushed

her blood-soaked hair out of her face and wiped the blood from her skin.

"What did you do?" he murmured.

Nadya shook her head, wordless. She had given him up. She had chosen Marzenya. How was he here and mostly whole?

He studied her face and she was terrified that if he looked too close he was going to see. He would know what she had done.

She grabbed his face and kissed him hard. It was meant to distract him, but then he made a *sound* and heat burned all the way to Nadya's core. She wanted this, wanted him. How many lies had she told herself as she pushed him away?

He kissed her back with the same kind of desperate hunger she was feeling. She shifted closer, straddling his hips and tangling her hands into his hair.

"Nadya," he groaned. "This is a bad time."

"Shut. *Up*. Malachiasz," she said between breathless kisses. She didn't know if she was kissing him out of regret, if this was goodbye, or if this was a reminder that no matter how hard she tried she couldn't pull herself away from this terrible, beautiful Tranavian boy.

She didn't want it to be any of those things. She had chosen Marzenya because she had to. But she loved Malachiasz, terribly, painfully, desperately, and what if she had chosen wrong?

His hand cupping her face turned hard, grasping her jaw, breaking off the kiss as he turned her head roughly to one side, kissing her jaw, her throat. When his sharp teeth grazed against her collarbone she gasped, her fingers curling against the back of his head. His other hand trailed down her spine before flattening against the small of her back, pulling her as close as possible.

There were too many layers of clothing between them. Nadya

grasped one of his spiraling black horns and used it to yank his head back so she could kiss him again, tugging his lower lip between her teeth, hearing the groan that broke from his chest. He leaned back on one elbow as she shifted her weight against him. The white flowers covering the floor curled away from their movements. Every place he touched burned long after his hands roved on; the pressure of his mouth exquisite torture.

His hand gathered up her skirt to grip her thigh and she was too far gone to be mortified by the whimper that escaped her and the way her hips ground down onto his. Kissing him deeper, his lips parted as he followed her lead, as she slid her hands under the hem of his shirt and traced the lines of his body, his skin hot beneath her hands.

He froze. Nadya kissed his cheek, the bridge of his nose, the tattoos on his forehead, before she realized he had gone still against her. She leaned back slightly.

His pale eyes narrowed, his edges sharpened, but somehow it didn't feel like he was looking at her. "Nadya," he whispered, panic lacing his voice, "what did you do?"

"I—"

"*What did you do?*" He grabbed her upper arms, his grip hard enough to hurt.

She closed her eyes, the tears threatening to flood her. She didn't know what she had done. She had simply followed her goddess's orders. She had chosen her goddess.

"I did what I had to," she whispered.

Abruptly, she was dumped from his lap as he scrambled to his feet. Panic was causing his features to shift swiftly and chaotically to the point where it looked painful, until it tapered down, disappearing, and all that stood before her was a lanky teenage boy, broken and lost.

"No," he whispered. "She's taking it all. She's taking everything."

*What did I do?*

*"The profaned magic will never be cast again,"* Marzenya said, sounding smug. *"How can they use what they do not remember?"*

The bottom of the world fell out. *Oh.* She carefully got to her feet, afraid of what Malachiasz might do. She had broken something in the fabric of the universe. She had pulled the knowledge of blood magic away from Tranavia.

She had changed the world.

She had done the one thing that might end the war.

*But at what cost?*

Malachiasz was laughing. It was a horrible, panicked sound, his eyes bleeding, darkening to onyx. His posture shifted and all Nadya's will to fight bled away as she faced the Black Vulture.

"No, oh, no, it's not that easy," he said. "Clever, though, clever girl," he spat. "An eye for an eye. Betrayal serves itself, I see."

He took a step closer. She took a step back, but the pool of blood was close and she did not want to fall under its magic once more.

"Blood and bone, I underestimated you," he said, voice tangled and dark. "A mistake I will not make again."

"Malachiasz, please, I—"

"You've done enough," he said through iron teeth, grasping her jaw in one hand, pulling her closer. His eyes flickered pale for a heartbeat and the aching betrayal there broke her heart.

"You thought that would finish things, did you? No more *devil magic.*"

She closed her eyes. She hadn't known that *this* would happen, but she had known that bringing him here would break him. That this would break Tranavia. She had gotten exactly what she wished.

"All this time," he murmured. "This was the game you were playing. You weren't looking for answers at all. You needed me so you could stab me in the back."

"Like you did to *me*," she snapped. She would not let him forget what he had done to her *first*.

"This is about *revenge*?" He sounded incredulous.

It wasn't. It was never about revenge.

"Would that make it easier?" she asked softly.

He stared at her, hurt and angry. She couldn't stop the tears from rolling down her cheeks.

"Would it make it easier to cast me as the villain who only wanted to hurt you as you'd hurt me? If you were only the nightmare in my dreams? If this was just a game I was playing so I could twist the knife a little harder? You know none of that is true."

"Nadezhda, stop," he said.

"You know that I will always choose my goddess and my country and you will always choose your Vultures and Tranavia."

"*Nadya.*"

Her goddess had lied to her, deceived her, had made her believe she was nothing without her—and it wasn't true. Yet Nadya could not turn her back on the one thing she had always believed in.

"Tell me you didn't mean for this to happen," he said beseechingly. "Tell me you weren't planning this the whole time."

She remained silent.

He let out a choked breath and let go of her. One of his hands went to his hair, unknotting a piece of bone that was tied in the strands. He worked quickly and efficiently until he had a pile of bones in his palm.

"Well played, *towy dżimyka*," he said, "but you and I are so very different and you forgot to keep your eyes forward. You forgot that this game would continue. Was it supposed to touch me as well?"

"Malachiasz . . ."

"Take away all I had? The only thing that has ever made this worthless life even a little bit useful?" He rolled a piece of spine between his fingers. "I am *so far past that.*"

Each of his words was a blow.

"I am so much more," he whispered, as though his heart were splintering. Then, colder, "I'm a god. As admirably as you have played this game, you've lost. Because of course I would help, of course this is how this would end. You brought me right where I wanted to be."

And she was too numb for shock because his words were inevitable. Betrayal was inevitable. That was all they really had between them—the willingness to betray one another to push their own ideals further. She had been a fool to believe it might be anything more.

She had twisted a web around him, but she had never been set free from the tangle he had caught her up in and he had used that. She had let him.

He crushed the bones between his hands. The monstrous godlike being he had become given form. His edges started to shiver.

Nadya thought fast. There were beings with more power and they existed just outside this realm. She heard the doors slam upstairs, but it was too late, she had stepped backward, back into the pool of blood. Back into oblivion.

# SEREFIN

# MELESKI

Serefin spat out a mouthful of dirt. He struggled to his feet, his head spinning.

*"You're not finished, boy,"* that voice hissed. Chyrnog. *"There is still more for you to do. They're at the temple. I want the boy."*

Serefin groaned, pressing his hands against his forehead. What had he done? And the gods were still here, he hadn't been let go.

Chyrnog laughed. *"Did you think you were ever going to be free? No. This is your fate. You gave up. You fell. You belong to us."*

Serefin tried to fight. He tried to take control of . . . something. But he had nothing left to fight with. He started walking but it was barely of his own accord.

Soon he could sleep.

He must rid Tranavia of the traitor, stopping him before he set into motion something cataclysmic. Just one more thing to do.

The problem was, Serefin wasn't really the one walking. Yet still he moved through the forest—it, thankfully, looked like a perfectly average forest, but who knew how long that would last.

Serefin didn't have control. The gods had him completely.

"No," he said into the silence, trying to force his legs to stop, trying to regain *some* kind of control. "No. I won't let you do this."

There was a long silence. The forest was eerily quiet.

*"Fine. Work for your salvation."*

There was a strange buzzing in the back of his head, the

feeling of something wrong, which was ridiculous because of course something was wrong, *everything* was wrong. This was the world thrown from its gentle and precarious balance. This was something changing so astronomically that even as it brushed against Serefin, he felt it. Even though it did not touch him completely.

Even though he was spared.

It was terrible, whatever it was. None of them should have come to this place.

The forest spat out Kacper and the *tsarevna*. Kacper landed heavily at Serefin's feet, blood dripping from his nose, covering his hands.

Serefin wanted to collapse with relief. "Kacper," he breathed, dropping to his knees in front of him.

Kacper looked dazed, staring through Serefin. He blinked, his dark eyes clearing only so slightly. "Serefin?"

Serefin put his hands on either side of Kacper's face, tracing the shell of his ears, index finger moving to skim over a cut that ran down his cheek. He almost sobbed. *What had happened to him?*

Did he even want to know?

"We have to get out of here, Serefin," Kacper said, hands grasping for him, fingers catching in his shirt and pulling him closer. "This place is evil. We have to get out. I lost . . ." He shook his head slowly. "I can't remember. I can't remember what I lost, but it feels important and it's *gone* and I don't even know what it was."

Serefin stared at Kacper, eyes wide. Or, he tried to. His one eye was so far in a different reality that it wasn't even registering Kacper in front of him. But he still held on to the other. He hadn't lost his right eye.

"Can't you feel it?" Kacper asked desperately.

Serefin nodded, but he had no idea what it had been. Kacper choked on a sob and Serefin pulled him closer, burying his face against his neck. Kacper's shuddering breaths shook him as he clutched at Serefin.

"I'm not finished here," Serefin murmured against Kacper's neck. He kissed it. "There's one more thing I have to do." He let go of Kacper to reach for his spell book, looking up at Katya where she stood dazed. There was a long trio of cuts down her cheek, and her right leg was covered with blood. "Can you find Ostyia? Gods, the Akolans, too, they don't deserve to be left behind. Here, I have a spell so we don't lose track of each other." He tore it out of his spell book and held it out for Kacper.

Kacper stared at his hand.

"What are you doing? It's simple, I promise."

"Serefin . . ."

Something in Kacper's voice made Serefin go cold. He couldn't put a name to it, the blind panic mixed with blank confusion.

"What am I supposed to do with that?" Kacper asked carefully, delicately, like he was trying not to offend Serefin but also like he *knew* that he should know exactly what to do.

"What do you mean? You know what to do."

But Kacper was shaking his head slowly. He skittered back from Serefin and did not take the page. "I-I know where the temple is. I'll find the others and meet you there."

"Kacper?"

Kacper had already gotten to his feet and disappeared into the trees. Serefin slowly crumpled the piece of paper in his fist, dread making a home in his chest.

*What happened?*

He met Katya's eyes. She was holding a long dagger of bone in her hands.

"I think," she said quietly, "we're all going to die here."

Serefin wheezed out a laugh.

She flipped the blade in her hand and held it out to Serefin, hilt-first. "Can you kill him? Whatever that was, there's more to come."

Serefin took the *voryen*. The hilt warmed in his hands. He could feel the soft thrum of power within the bone.

They had all been waiting with their knives at one another's backs. It was time to plunge the dagger home.

# 41

## NADEZHDA

## LAPTEVA

*A bone broken under the weight of a thousand roiling worms, desperate for purchase, frantic for light. To hunger, to devour, to consume.*

—The Volokhtaznikon

Nadya was not meant to be here. Creature of magic that she was, she was not meant to walk this realm. She was supposed to remain firmly in the mortal world; oblivion was not supposed to be a lasting state. But she had to stop Malachiasz.

Here was the next step in his grand plan turned into reality. The bones in his hair she'd chosen not to think about were the magic she'd felt the whole time. Relics he had stolen from her people because he had known it would take a little more magic to get to the place he wanted.

He had lied *again*. And again she had believed him because she had so truly wanted to believe that what he

had done had not fully worked; that he would not be able to put the chaos he desired into motion. That he had *become* chaos.

It was all a lie. He had known, the whole time, what he needed to do, where he needed to be.

He hadn't wanted to help. He'd known that this was exactly where he could get to the gods he wanted to destroy. She had been strung along *again*.

Betrayal serves itself.

She was a fool. Here, perhaps, was the curse laid upon them by that creature in the clearing. Or it was just their thousands of lies catching up with them.

She had known not to trust him, but she had accepted his lies all the same. But what had she wrenched from him in return?

Maybe he would never forgive her. Maybe she didn't deserve to be forgiven. Maybe this was the line that neither of them would be able to cross. It had to come eventually.

This was never meant to last.

Where she was now was an overlay on the world Nadya knew, this world of gods and monsters. She pulled herself out of the pool and found everything slightly askew. The stone temple had become carved of bone. The flowers were crumpled black stains on the ground, crawling with maggots. When she took the stairs back up, the wooden church was made of polished marble and the stairs ascended up into the mountains.

It was a sick bit of irony, a cruel turn of the knife in her heart. She didn't need to count the stairs that twisted up into the mountains, she knew.

Seven thousand.

Seven thousand stairs to take her to where the boy she loved was doing his best to destroy the gods she had dedicated her life to. Like the seven thousand stairs that led from the monastery she used to call home down to the base of the mountain.

She pulled her *voryen* from its sheath and started up.

If she had known how this would end, would she still have gone through with it? She didn't know the answer to that question. Whatever they had between them must end here.

They had betrayed one another.

And the entire world would suffer for it.

But Marzenya had lied to her as well, hadn't trusted her. *Everyone* had lied to Nadya.

The ground shook treacherously. Nadya had lived her whole life in the mountains and she knew how terrible, how *fast* an avalanche could come. She paused in her ascension, waiting to see if this was where she would meet her end or if she had a little time.

A few errant chunks of snow skittered across the steps in front of her.

But the tremors continued. Each one gave her pause, each one made her wonder if this was it. Surely this wasn't Malachiasz's doing. He didn't work in massive, broad strokes of power, that wasn't—

Well, that wasn't *Malachiasz,* but she didn't know how this god of chaos given form would act.

The tremors couldn't stop her. She had run up those seven thousand steps at the monastery before. She could do it again if she had to.

Gone were her doubts that he could not do this; that he had underestimated his own capabilities and could not see this destruction through. She didn't know how she would stop this, how she *could* stop this. She did not have the power of a god. She was only a girl with some magic and a blade.

But a girl he consistently underestimated.

She kept climbing, climbing, climbing as the mountain shuddered around her, as the world started to fracture. Something else had woken up. Hers was not the only cataclysm to have started here, and the thought terrified her.

Serefin had failed. A part of her always knew he would. And maybe she could have stopped him, or maybe that would have further doomed the world.

But Serefin was the one whom *Nadya* underestimated. Serefin, the drunkard, the reluctant king who *ran* before trying to fix his mess of a kingdom. He had been caught in the web of a god she had set free and she had been too caught up in her own miseries to realize that maybe *maybe* she should have helped him first.

It was too late. Thunderous cracks sounded around her; something was crumbling within this mountain. Something unforgiving and furious had been unleashed. The consequences of her actions, of Malachiasz's, of Serefin's, all one glorious nightmare. What would she find when she reached the top? How would she get back to her own realm of existence?

Would Malachiasz come with her? Or was this where he existed forever, now? Did she even want him to return with her?

Nadya felt strange. She did not belong here. Or maybe she had changed something within herself and *those* consequences were still to come.

Her hand no longer hurt. The scar had blackened her hand, like she had dipped it in ink. Her fingernails were sharp—not unlike Malachiasz's iron claws, they were unnatural in their sharpness. But the darkness had stopped seeping out over her. It trailed a little up her forearm before it disappeared and came to a halt.

"You fucked up."

Nadya froze. There was a figure sitting on the stairs.

Human-sized, but even sitting Nadya could tell they were very tall. Their long hair was void-like, with stars twinkling in the depths, and their voice sounded impossibly sad. It made Nadya want to lie down and give up right then and there.

Nadya closed her left hand into a fist. The figure looked up at her through their hair—their eyes were similar voids.

"They wanted you to be perfect. You weren't." The figure shrugged. "Now you have a war of magic raging inside of you. It must hurt."

Nadya shook her head. "Not too badly."

"They won't let you go, though." The figure cocked their head. "That's the odd thing." They closed their eyes, smiling slightly. "That's what happens when your magic comes from the same place as mine, I suppose. They locked me up, and those like me, you know. They don't like when magic doesn't fit their immutable rules."

A chunk of ice tumbled past and when Nadya went to move around the figure—there was *no time*—they put a hand out to stop her.

"My name is Ljubica," they said. "You and I will be seeing a lot of each other in the future. Someone has to answer your questions, no? Hold fast to your mortality, little cleric—yes, still a cleric after all this, but perhaps bound to a different sort of god—because it's the one thing you do not want to lose."

They disappeared into smoke. Nadya frowned. She clutched her hand to her chest, urgency building inside her. She had to keep moving. The world was shifting underneath her feet, its very fabric altering.

At the top of the stairs was simply more mountain, and so Nadya trudged through the snow as the ground pitched treacherously, the sky a sickly ominous green.

There were bloody footprints in the snow, the feet bare.

Nadya followed them reluctantly, praying she wasn't too late. She would know, wouldn't she? She could feel whispers in the air, the blood she was drenched in drying stiff and uncomfortable against her clothes. Little bits and pieces of her were breaking away with every step.

Through the snow, with the mountain falling down around her, Nadya fell into a blizzard. The heart of a storm, of a war raging around her that she was still too human to see.

Nadya shoved her fingers against the palm of her corrupted hand. Ice froze her eyelashes. There was a well of power within her, eldritch, dark, *mad*. Divine. She still didn't know what that meant, but she was desperate, and she would use it. She dipped into the swirling vortex of power that tasted of poison and copper—copper and ashes—and swept itself over her bones until her blood was on fire. She held out her hand—

—the blizzard froze around her.

And, once more, there were the bloody footprints in the snow. Not much farther to go; not much farther to fall.

Maybe it wasn't about where it came from, or what this meant. She had been lied to for so long, and maybe all she had was herself and this power. Maybe that was all she needed. No more trusting beautiful Tranavian boys with tortured smiles, no more listening to a goddess who gave so very little in return for such ardent devotion.

The snow began falling slower and the footprints were less faint. There was so much blood left behind in the snow, heavy drops of it in a trail to a scene that Nadya wanted to flee from.

Nadya's mind could not wrap itself around what Malachiasz had become. Chaos was a fitting mold for the erratic, anxious boy. It was as though all the shifts from before were amplified tenfold. He was an ever-changing horror—yet still so unlike the horrors he faced, static in their monstrosity.

He wasn't facing down the whole divine empire. They didn't deem him important enough. He was a nuisance. A mortal who had stepped too far and needed to be dealt with. But Nadya knew the god before him.

Death and magic and winter.

*"Child of death, you are exactly where you are supposed to be."*

Nadya was too far away. They seemed so close, but each step she took only pushed them farther away. She couldn't stop him if she couldn't *reason* with him.

But her heart knew they were past reason. Past sheer brute force. She didn't understand why they were so out of reach, why she couldn't touch the hem of Malachiasz's shredded tunic.

No one looked upon the faces of the gods and lived. No one—full stop. Nadya had thought that her dreams of many-jointed monsters with rows and rows of teeth would be as far as she ever reached, condemned to the subconscious wanderings of a tormented experience. But this was real. She had tasted divinity and oblivion and *survived*. She was a cleric of the divine who was born of darkness.

And if she didn't stop Malachiasz, there would be no defense against what Serefin had set into motion. Her gods were all they had left against those Serefin had woken.

Magic churned around her in a storm until suddenly she broke through whatever had caught her in its loop—suddenly *allowed*—and her fingers grasped Malachiasz's arm—

—only to pass through air, his arm gone.

—then there were too *many* limbs because he was ever-changing.

There was nothing of the Vulture boy from Tranavia to cling to. Gone was the renegade blood mage, the advisor to kings, the anxious, ridiculous soul she had tried desperately to save.

*"There is no reasoning with chaos,"* Marzenya said from behind Nadya.

Nadya didn't turn, she didn't need to. The eight fathomless eyes. The skin translucent pale. The ribs of teeth and fingers painted with death.

Her gods were glorified monsters. That was no longer the question. She had moved past that conundrum and on to a new one that she still had no answer for.

Did they care, at all, for those such as her? Or was she only another pawn in their divine madness?

*"Chaos is inevitable. It is a storm that passes eternally through the world. And we have not had chaos in our number in a long, long time."*

The chill of death was at her shoulder, Marzenya's fingertips hovering at her skin, bruises blooming underneath the inch of space the goddess's fingers left even as they did not truly touch her.

*"What a sad creature he is, but strong."*

"You knew," Nadya whispered, horrified. "You knew he would do this."

*"Of course I knew."*

Nadya tried to reach for him but the snarling monster snapped at her, blood pouring from his mouth of jagged, iron nails. Her tears froze on her cheeks, blood dripped from her nose.

"So this was your plan? To bring me here, to use him, to turn the gods away so that . . . what?"

*"The era of heretic magic is over,"* Marzenya hissed. *"The time of the abomination has ended. Sacrifices must be made to reach an ending that speaks of truth."*

Malachiasz fell to one knee. His spine cracked out from his skin. Nadya slammed a hand over her mouth to keep in a sob.

Marzenya's fingers clutched the back of her head, forcing her to watch. Blood dripped underneath each spot the goddess touched on her head. But she could no longer look away as his bones cracked and bent, re-formed only to shatter. As blood fell from his eyes and his eyes and his eyes and there were too many, so many, and it hurt to look, it hurt to see.

She loved him. Even now, even here, even when he had forged the last pieces of his monstrous plan into place with hatred in his heart for her. His betrayal for her betrayal.

He would die here. He had the power of the gods, the knowledge to form it into being, but, oh, he was so young—a child—and they knew how to twist his power of chaos against him. They'd had gods of chaos before and every single one burned out as they would burn Malachiasz out.

He wouldn't survive.

*"You have been so good, so useful to us,"* Marzenya whispered. *"I love you, my daughter."* She brushed a finger over Nadya's cheek, still holding the back of her head. Nadya flinched, her skin parting beneath her goddess's caress.

Nadya turned her face into Marzenya's touch. "And I love you," she whispered, dropping her corrupted hand down from where it rested close to her chest, palm out to Malachiasz.

Marzenya's hand slid down from her head to her back. It would take so little, one errant brush of her deathly cold fingers, for Nadya to die. Her usefulness at an end because for all that she had done, she still asked too many questions. She still doubted too much. She had still fallen in love with a monster.

Can you love a god? No, such things were impossible.

The barest glimmer, a fraction of sharpness in Malachiasz's onyx eyes.

His hands clasped over hers—mortal and eldritch—and his iron claws punched clean through her palms. A starburst of pain that felt distant as she toppled the dark well of magic within her and flooded him with it. He was darkness and eldritch and mad, and, in the end, with a cracked and bitter halo of divinity tainted by an ocean of horrors, so was she.

Marzenya shoved her away as Malachiasz staggered to his feet. A monster—chaos—but sharpened. Coherent. The Black Vulture, and a god in control of the magic churning within him. Only in control because Nadya's dark thrum of power had smoothed the edges of his chaos. A bond broken; a bond reforged.

"Leave us," Nadya spat at him, through a mouthful of blood.

He spared her a brief glance as Marzenya's hold of death grew palpable. And with a twisted smile, he slammed his iron claws into the goddess's chest.

The death of a god was like a star collapsing, crumpling in upon itself until there was nothing left but a supernova—one solitary moment of brilliance before emptiness.

*No.* She had given him power to *flee* to *run* not to do this. Not *this.*

It was over before Nadya had even realized Malachiasz had struck. And all that was left was the snow raging in a blizzard around them and an absolute and utter emptiness.

The other gods were gone. None would risk this god killer's wrath.

Nadya scrambled backward in the snow as Malachiasz turned on her. All she had wanted was to set him free. And all she would get in return for that mercy was death.

# 42

## SEREFIN
## MELESKI

*Their names are lost to time, these gods of chaos, these beings of trickery and deceit and chance. But those who destroyed them live on: Marzenya, Veceslav, Peloyin, and Alena. Striking down those who would strike them down by their sheer nature alone. And so the cycle stretches on, turning, turning.*

—The Books of Innokentiy

Serefin clutched the bone dagger so hard he was afraid the hilt might crack. The scene had left a mark upon him. A monster of shifting parts and sharp teeth and claws destroying the one of ice and snow and death. A god made, a god murdered.

Serefin only had one last thing to do before he could sleep. Gone were all thoughts of returning to Tranavia and reclaiming his throne. Gone were any thoughts of

making it off this mountain. If he just dealt with the monster before him, his younger brother, he could sleep. He could sleep forever.

That sounded fine to Serefin, nice even. A moth fluttered against his shoulder. He brushed it off absently. It returned with more urgency.

He crushed it in his hand. There was no time for that.

"Malachiasz," Serefin called, and his voice sounded wrong in his ears.

The monster turned and slowly, unwillingly, abandoned the cleric where she lay gasping and blood-covered in the snow.

"Come now," Serefin said, voice softer. "I don't know if you've known for long, or if you know at all, or if it takes magically transcending time and space to dredge up memories the Vultures locked away, but we need to talk, you and I. It isn't worth it, turning on her. Well, maybe it is, she *is* the enemy, but you would regret it."

Nadya dropped her head back in the snow, covering her face with her hands.

Malachiasz took a step closer to Serefin. Twisting, roiling, churning, teeth and limbs and chaos and madness until quiet.

Quiet.

Narrowing down, slower and softer, until all that stood before Serefin was a boy, taller than him, younger than him, terrified and confused.

The boy standing in the hallway of Grazyk, tears running down dusty cheeks as it dawned on him exactly what his power meant. Serefin hadn't understood, that day, what he had done. Forcing Malachiasz to reveal his power to that Vulture had damned him. *Serefin* had damned him. And, maybe, the Vultures were where Malachiasz belonged, but if it hadn't been for him, Malachiasz might still have been simply a noble boy raised in Grazyk. Malachiasz might have known they were brothers long before this.

Serefin's heart clenched in his chest. He took a step closer.

"You managed it," Serefin continued. "That grand disturbance against your enemies."

"It's not finished. I'm not finished," Malachiasz said desperately. "That was only one and there are so many—"

"And what happens then?"

Malachiasz blinked. He opened and closed his mouth, licking his cracked and bleeding lips.

"What happens when you topple this divine empire?"

"I make it *better*," Malachiasz said. "I make Tranavia *better*."

"You can't do that," Serefin replied.

The way Malachiasz was staring at him: hurt and anger and such a *deep well of sadness*. He *knew*.

"It's been a long time," Serefin said lightly. "I did miss you."

"Not enough," Malachiasz spat, taking a step back. He pressed his hands to his temples. His features still shifted— eyes blinking open, teeth clawing his skin where no teeth should be, only for it to heal—but this was nothing like that monstrous display of divinity. "Not enough to ever tell me?"

"I didn't know."

"You're a liar."

"I am." Serefin shrugged. "A liar. A murderer. A drunk. You're no better. A liar. A murderer. A monster. What a pair we make. The kings of Tranavia, a pair of good-for-nothing brothers."

Malachiasz flinched like he had been struck. Serefin stepped cautiously, finally making it to the other boy. Malachiasz was anxiously shredding his fingernails, his edges shivering as though he was seconds away from becoming the monster.

Malachiasz swallowed hard. His pale eyes were glassy with tears. "Brother," he murmured.

And it was the broken, hollow emptiness in Malachiasz's voice, the tears running down his bloodstained cheeks, that tore what was left of Serefin to pieces. He wasn't as cruel as he thought. Serefin couldn't do this. The boy standing in front of him wasn't only a traitorous Vulture trying to ruin Serefin's life. He was more than that. Serefin had so little family left, he couldn't kill the brother he had never really known. Malachiasz had made his life an absolute hell and *that* was one thing, but Serefin couldn't repay that with another murder.

Serefin let his hand fall away from the bone dagger at his belt.

"I am most certainly the last person you ever wanted to hear that from," Serefin said. "And, honestly, I could have done better in the little brother area, but—"

He was startled as Malachiasz yanked him into an embrace, his shoulders shaking with sobs. Serefin stood frozen, held captive by how much he had *missed* Malachiasz and how much he loathed and hated him but couldn't stand to see him so broken. He returned the embrace.

The world flashed, warping as Serefin lost control of his left eye. It was a slow bleed, shadows crept into the corner of his vision, and his hand was wrapping around the hilt of the dagger, pulling it from its sheath.

*No. I have given you enough. You have taken enough,* Serefin thought, struggling, trying to drop the blade, trying to get Malachiasz to pull away and *see* what was about to happen so he could at least try to stop it.

But he didn't have control. He was utterly helpless to watch, to feel, as his hand gripped the dagger tight. His other arm embracing Malachiasz in return.

"Goodbye, brother," his mouth whispered into Malachiasz's ear.

A wrenching as he pulled back from Malachiasz. The dagger plunging into Malachiasz's chest. Malachiasz stiffening, his exhale of pain. The warm blood pouring over Serefin's hand.

He took a step back. He was crying. This wasn't what he wanted—he hadn't wanted to kill Malachiasz.

He was dimly aware of Nadya's scream of anguish.

He had to get control. It couldn't end like this. He would not *live* like this. What would be the bloody point?

Every time Velyos or Chyrnog had spoken to him, every time something weird and divine happened, it began the same. His left eye would hurt and start bleeding, his vision would go blurry. His left eye was the problem.

There was no spell to cast, no magic to break this connection. The divine were too strong and Serefin was too mortal. A moth landed over his left eye, forcing it closed. The eye hungered to see and to control Serefin and use him for more killing, more ruin of this world so it could delight in the suffering left in his wake.

He needed it out.

It was an impulse, an irrational, uncontrollable beast. No one was paying attention to him. No one noticed his hands snaking up his face. It wouldn't take much. Eyes were fragile, and this one was weaker than most.

This would end it.

There was a very real danger of bleeding out up here. And there was the equally real danger that Nadya would leave him up here to rot like he deserved.

But he had to get it out.

Cut out the eye, cut off the divine. It was so easy. So simple. If only he had done it before he had come to this hellish place. Before the worst had happened.

Pain was a familiar friend to Serefin. What was a little more pain?

He hesitated. Kept hesitating. That little human instinct that keeps the body from harming itself prodding at him.

But he didn't have control of his left eye.

It wasn't even *his* anymore.

And if it wasn't his, what was it doing in his body? He had to get it out. He had to drive it out.

*He had to dig it out.*

And his fingers were prodding at his eye socket and that little, needling voice—that little, careful instinct—went quiet. It went dark. It let him claw, let him bleed, let him pry and dig until something gave. There was so much blood—*so much blood*—Serefin grew dizzy because even the starburst of pain wasn't enough to knock him out. He had survived too much. The aching agony wasn't enough to shut him down and finally let him sleep. Maybe he would never sleep. Maybe this was his damnation. To claw out his own eye and never sleep, never dream, never know another moment's rest. He had been taken by these gods—*claimed*, and he would never be free.

Something snapped.

It had not wanted to break. Bodies, so fragile, so mortal, but so resilient under pressure. They did not *want* to break. But it broke, it snapped—the piece of flesh that kept his eye grounded in its socket, that let him see, let him feel, broke in two.

And, for the first time in months—*silence*.

Serefin broke the connection with the gods.

His left eye fell to the ground, a chaos of stars.

# 43

### NADEZHDA

### LAPTEVA

*Greedy, he is, Chyrnog, greedy to feast on all he desires.*
*Alena's power rests in the sky and he yearns, he hungers,*
*and if he were to escape, if he were to break past the bonds*
*that bind him, he would devour her.*

—The Volokhtaznikon

Her grief was going to swallow her whole. Her goddess
was gone. She kept reaching for Marzenya and there
was only a void, empty and silent.

She barely saw Serefin through her tears as he approached Malachiasz. Suddenly they were so very close.

The tremor of agony that cut across Malachiasz's face
sent terror deep into her core. He stumbled back from
Serefin and it took Nadya a moment to register the blood
covering his hands. The hilt of a blade buried in Malachiasz's chest.

*No.*

The ground tilted as the rest of Nadya's world tore apart. She scrambled forward as Malachiasz fell to his knees. She was only aware of her surroundings in painful flashes. Tears streaked down Serefin's cheeks as he raked a bloody hand through his hair, glassy, godstouched eyes staring at nothing. The terrible blank of Malachiasz's face. Her own heart pounding in her throat as she panicked.

But Malachiasz was the Black Vulture. She had seen him stabbed before and survive. This would be nothing. He would be fine. It was almost impossible to kill a Vulture, and he was far more.

Nadya's hand neared the hilt of the blade and she *felt* the power it was giving off. She knew this blade. She knew what it was capable of.

A terrible dread spiked within her. She slid to her knees in front of Malachiasz and, gods, there was so much blood and his breathing was shallow and this couldn't be happening *this couldn't be happening.*

"Malachiasz, look at me," she whispered, panicked and shaking. "Stay with me."

His eyes were unfocused and he pitched forward. Nadya only barely caught his shoulders, lowering him to the ground, cradling his head in her lap. She smoothed his hair away from his forehead. Surely she could do something. Her magic could heal. Frantic, she called on it—feeling the immeasurable void with no Marzenya to meet her prayer—and pressed her hand over the wound. Fine. *Fine.* She would use her own power. She was desperate—beyond desperate—this couldn't be *happening.* Surely her magic would comply. Surely that well of power must be worth something.

"Nadya," Malachiasz murmured, the urgency in his voice pulling her attention away. But she knew *she knew* the worst.

It wouldn't work. She had expended the power she had breaking him free from Marzenya; there was nothing more she could do.

Whatever that blade was, whatever power was within it, there was no stopping it. There was poison and magic, and if the blade hadn't done enough damage on its own, the magic and the poison would finish the job soon.

Not this. Not now, not after everything that had happened. She couldn't lose her goddess and *him* all in one terrible blow.

"No," she said fiercely. "You're not going to die on me." *I haven't gotten to apologize for what I did, and you killed my goddess, you unrepentant bastard.*

He gasped for air, his hand reaching up and leaving bloody fingertips against her cheek, over her lips.

"Malachiasz, please," she said, her voice cracking. "About what happened—"

"I love you," he said, cutting her off. "So much. I wanted . . ." He trailed off, face wrenching, blood welling at the corners of his mouth.

"*No,*" she whimpered. She clutched his hand, his fading pulse trapped under his skin.

This wasn't fair. She had been given all this power, and here, when it mattered, she was powerless. She couldn't save him.

"I wanted to show you peace," he finally whispered.

There was nothing left of her heart to break.

He let out a breath but never took another. His pale eyes dimmed, lights blinking out.

Nadya waited for all of this to be one big cosmic joke. For him to laugh at her for being so dramatic. But as his hand clutched in hers went limp, reality began to claw at her.

A terrible, panicked sob broke from her chest. Grief too big for words drowned her. He couldn't be gone, *he couldn't be.* She had worked so hard to get him back, to keep him human—too human, in the end, too mortal.

"No," she whispered, kissing his tattooed fingers. "No, *no,* come back, please come back."

She rested her forehead against his, her tears given less distance to fall. She didn't know what to do. Someone was pulling at her arm and distantly, as if very far away, she could hear someone tell her that they had to go. But she wasn't going to leave Malachiasz, she couldn't.

The beautiful, terrible boy who only wanted, in the end, nothing more than peace.

He couldn't be gone.

"Nadya." Her face was jerked to one side, inches from Parijahan's tearstained face. "We have to go."

She shook her head, digging her fingers into Malachiasz's hair.

Parijahan took Malachiasz's dagger from his hip, stuffing it into her bag next to his spell book. Sorrow broke her features and she reached out, touching his cheek, carefully closing his eyes.

"Goodbye, darling fool," she whispered.

Something deeper cracked with Nadya. "Parj, I *can't.*"

"He wouldn't want you to die here, too."

"We can't just leave him."

The ground shook. Parijahan staggered to her feet. "If we can come back and give him the burial he deserves, I swear to you, we will. But, Nadya, if we stay any longer, we'll be dead. Please, I know it feels impossible, but we have to keep moving. This mountain is going to come down around us and we need to get down now."

If they left they were never going to be able to come back. She had to leave him here.

Nadya nodded very slowly. Do what had to be done. She kissed his still mouth one last time. Took her *voryen* and caught a lock of his hair where a golden bead was threaded through, slicing it off.

"I love you, Malachiasz Czechowicz," she whispered. "And I never told you and now I have to be mad at you forever and I'll never forgive you for that."

She placed her hand on the dagger buried in his chest, but couldn't make herself take the next step. She needed to know what had done this; how the boy who had survived so much had been killed by this. Another sob rattled through her.

Parijahan put her hand over Nadya's and yanked the dagger out.

Her anguish scrambled for something to latch on to and bury itself deep within and it landed on the one who had held the blade that severed the life from Malachiasz's twisted body. Nadya would kill another Tranavian king if she had to, she would keep this damn cycle burning forever.

But he was gone. A pool of blood all that remained of where he had stood.

Nadya didn't remember getting to the bottom of the mountain. Being pulled apart and put back together was catching up to her. She wasn't conscious when the mountain broke in half and her gods finally turned away altogether.

Nadya found herself in a warm, dry bed. It was a dismal comfort as she curled up in a feeble effort to protect herself from the ache of a loss she feared would never release her.

The air felt wrong. Something fundamental had shattered and they would spiral ever faster toward chaos. The loss of the gods—of everything—a tangible weight, a tinge in the world's colors. Everything felt wrong.

The door opened. She heard Parijahan sigh. The bed shifted as the Akolan girl crawled in next to her.

"I know you're awake," she said.

Nadya said nothing. She curled the fingers of her corrupted hand into a fist, tucking it close to her chest.

"And I know you're going to want to stay here forever until you waste away into nothing. I don't want to rush your grief."

"Then don't," Nadya said, finally turning over and sitting up. Parijahan's dark hair was splayed out on the pillow, her eyes tired.

Parijahan opened her mouth to speak, but Nadya held up a hand. "Don't tell me what this has done. Don't tell me how much worse it's gotten, I can't bear it. Where are we?"

"A village outside Dozvlatovya, to the west. It turns out that Tachilvnik is actually a very small stretch of forest when it's not trying to hold you there forever. Nadya, I can feel it, too. The—the *breaking*."

Nadya shook her head. "And Serefin?"

"No one knows. We found Katya and Ostyia—Rashid is mostly fine, he broke his wrist—but not Kacper or Serefin."

Nadya couldn't dredge up any worry for the Tranavian boys. Serefin had killed Malachiasz. Maybe he had died when the mountain crumbled. One less problem to solve.

"Good."

"Nadya . . ."

Nadya dropped her head into her hands. She had never been so totally alone before.

"There's a priest here who wants to speak to you," Parijahan said carefully.

"No."

Parijahan just nodded.

"He died hating me," she said, voice blank.

*He told you he loved you,* she chided herself. But he had only said that because he had known he was dying. There was no healing her betrayal. She stared at a painting of flowers on the wall in front of her but barely saw them. "I did something very bad, Parj, and—"

Parijahan shushed her. "Don't, Nadya, it's not worth it."

Nadya pulled her knees up to her chest and buried her face in her arms, a lump in her throat. She had lost her goddess— lost all of the gods—and the boy she loved, and she didn't know which she was supposed to grieve first, which one was supposed to hurt her more, because right now everything hurt and she couldn't see the point of anything. She had *nothing* left. How quickly had she lost her home, Kostya, Malachiasz, everything *everything*.

"He was terrible, but he was also so very good," Parijahan said. "And you and I both know he wouldn't want you to fade away because he's gone."

"You and I both know he would want to be mourned as dramatically as possible," Nadya said, sniffling.

Parijahan laughed, but it was a broken sound and Nadya couldn't parse the rush of emotion that filled her. Anger, because she had lost *so much* and how dare anyone else be mourning as well. Regret, because Parijahan and Malachiasz were close and Parj had every right to be devastated.

But it all got swept up into the empty blank of her shattered pieces. And Nadya was left with nothing. Memories that would fade but for now she could hold them close. The gentle, earnest way he had been during their journey to the forest—and as much as that had been a part of his game, she knew it had been real, too. His lies were his truths and that was what made him so frustrating. She had hated him and she had loved him and now he was gone.

"What did the priest want?"

"No," Parijahan said. "No, you know what? You're going to throw yourself into something to distract yourself and it's going to kill you. Don't look at me like that, I don't care if that's what you want. You and I are going to stay here and you're going to grieve yourself into oblivion if you must, because I know, Nadya, I know how much you loved him and I'm sorry."

"I lost Marzenya, too," Nadya whispered.

Parijahan sat up very slowly. "What?"

"Malachiasz killed her. He got his wish, he killed a god." Nadya shook her head. "I don't have anything left to fight for. The gods have turned their backs on us and it's my fault. Can you feel it?"

Parijahan shuddered. "I didn't know what that meant."

Nadya closed her eyes, wanting to suffer the void. With a start, she realized she could feel something. It was far older. A spark of something she could reach for and talk to that was not her gods but like them. The fallen gods had been woken up, and what that meant, she didn't know. But what about the darker creatures? What about *her*?

Maybe it wasn't over for her yet.

Or maybe everything would fall apart around her no matter what she did.

All she knew was that she wanted to stay here and disappear forever. No one would ever know the fate of the cleric who had doomed the world. The fate of the girl who had loved the wrong boy and had lost everything because of it.

*"You and I are going to be seeing a lot more of each other in the future,"* Ljubica had said. Nadya let out a slow breath, know-

ing, with sudden piercing certainty, the grand game played by the gods had not yet ended.

Nadya had thought the gods she knew were playing the game, but as she reached further, she found something else that had been unleashed, something that had been pushing its mortal pieces around for a very long time.

That being was winning.

That being was going to destroy everything.

There was a knock on the door. The person on the other side did not wait for Nadya or Parijahan to respond.

"The *tsarevna* demands your presence immediately."

# 44

## SEREFIN

## MELESKI

**Svoyatovy Maksim and Tsezar Belousov:** *Both chosen by the goddess Bozidarka, the brothers prophesied Tranavia's ultimate downfall and Kalyazin's victory over the heretics. Their prophesies were considered apocryphal and discounted when Maksim blinded, then murdered, Tsezar.*
—Vasiliev's Book of Saints

If the mountain had crumbled around him and swallowed him whole, Serefin would have been fine with that. He wasn't entirely sure how he was supposed to live with what he had done.

If he survived.

If the searing pain in his head and the fever that was scrambling his brain didn't kill him first, of course. As it happened, tearing your own eye out with bloody hands was *not* the most advisable of things to do.

But Serefin couldn't feel Velyos. The moths still flut-

tered around him, he would never escape being touched by a god. But the god was *gone* and could not control him anymore. Chyrnog was also gone, and that was . . . concerning, to say the least. He didn't know where they were; he didn't care. He had to get back to Tranavia. He had to go home.

Because something had happened at the top of that mountain and Serefin didn't know what it was, only that it terrified him. Only that he could feel something had changed and he couldn't place just what it was. But there was an ominous dread that refused to let him go and he knew those two things were related.

What had they done?

The whole world felt wrong in a way that Serefin couldn't put to words. Like something had been pulled away from reality; like all color had been dimmed. Maybe it was just *him* and his eyesight, now somehow better and worse than before, but he knew that wasn't it. They had shifted something, *broken* something.

He had lost Ostyia somewhere in that forest, but he had to hope—to trust—she would make it out all right. He couldn't go back to find her. He couldn't go back into that horrific playground of the divine.

At least he had Kacper, but he was acting strange. There were gaps in his memory that kept showing themselves, and Serefin didn't know what they meant.

They kept moving, even as Serefin's fever burned hotter and brighter and his steps grew less steady as he adjusted to officially having only one eye. It was, at least, the one that had always been a little bit clearer. A small mercy.

If he was going to die, he did not want to do it in Kalyazin. He wasn't certain he would have that luxury.

It got to the point where he was too weak to walk and

Kacper had to drag him into a Kalyazi village to find a healer. The only place they could go was the church, where an old priestess was known to have healing powers granted by some saint or other.

There was no time to hide that they were Tranavian. There was no way to mask who Serefin was.

The priestess opened the door to the wooden, rickety church and took one look at the boys, bloodstained and exhausted, before nodding her head and beckoning them inside. Serefin was far past the point of caring about how if he never stepped into a Kalyazi church again it would be too soon, and he let Kacper pull him in.

"What on earth did you do to your face, boy?" the priestess asked as her weathered hands touched his bloodied face, taking in the infected, empty eye socket. How it hadn't killed Serefin yet very well should've been a miracle. "Those scratches on your face will scar, most likely. If you survive," she added.

"Please," Kacper said softly, a plaintive entreaty in his voice.

The woman didn't blink at Kacper's accent. She sighed and nodded and left the room, muttering about collecting instruments and praying the saints would wish to bother with a Tranavian heretic.

Kacper sat down on the bench beside Serefin and tugged his head against his shoulder. Serefin was shivering violently and he had a terrible feeling this might be the end.

"I didn't mean to kill him," he said. "My brother. I didn't . . ."

"Is this the fever talking, or is it you?" Kacper asked.

"It's me."

Kacper nodded. "You're going to make it. And we're going to go back to Tranavia and forget about all of this."

Serefin couldn't do that. He couldn't forget about any of it. Ostyia was still out there—somewhere, he hoped, because he couldn't really consider that she might be dead. His brother's blood was on his hands and he had ripped out his eye to sever a connection with some Kalyazi god that was going to wreak havoc on everything.

And Kacper couldn't remember how to use magic. Serefin didn't know what that meant, either, but it chilled him to his core. Why could he remember and Kacper couldn't?

"You boys should get back to your country," the priestess said as she returned. "Normally I would send you to the garrison to burn for your sins, but blood magic has stopped in Tranavia. Maybe your people have finally seen the error of your ways."

Kacper looked confused. Serefin tried to straighten, the blood draining from his face. This was a dream, this was a fever dream and he had lost coherence from the pain, that's all this was.

"What do you mean?" Serefin asked, trying to only sound a little curious, aware the pain was causing him to slur as if he were drunk. He *wished* he were drunk.

"The front has had a standstill," the woman said. "I suppose you'd not have heard all the way out here. What *are* you doing all the way out here?" she asked, suddenly suspicious.

"If we told you we were spies would you kill us faster?" Kacper said wearily. "The truth is too long and makes little sense."

The priestess waved that away. She eyed them as she mixed a poultice in a small stone bowl. "You lot just stopped using blood magic."

Again, Serefin looked at Kacper for some kind of response, and Kacper only shrugged.

"It's like the Tranavians have finally seen the light," she said contemplatively, "I wonder what changed. Maybe the war will finally end. Do you think your king finally saw the truth of matters?"

Serefin flinched as a wet cloth touched his face. She cleaned his wound as best she could and it hurt more than the steady, aching pulse that had hammered in front of his brain for days now.

"I doubt it," he finally said. "The king has seen too many horrors to ever give up so easily."

The priestess made a disapproving sound but fell silent as she worked.

Serefin's mind raced. Whatever had happened to Kacper had happened to everyone.

Tranavia would never survive without the blood magic that had built it up.

His entire country was about to fall.

# epilogue

## THE BOY LOST

## IN THE DARK

It was different, this time. Darkness was something he was intimately used to; darkness was nothing to him. He had lived and toiled and learned in darkness. This was both more than that and yet something else entirely.

*"I have waited a very long time for you, boy."*

The voice was ageless and unending. It scraped at his insides, shredding him. But he had been torn to pieces before. This was no different. There was no further to fall.

(So he thought, but truly, what was left for him?)

But this was not how it was supposed to be. Because he still had a piece of himself, this time, and he held it close. He was unwilling to lose it again. He was unwilling to drop down into the swamp of pure hatred that was waiting for him, just over the edge.

She had tried to take from him the only thing that had ever mattered, and hatred would burn so easily. So

he waited at the edge, he waited to fall, he waited for this—whatever this was—to become the oblivion he knew it to be. Because that dagger in his chest had done the one thing no one could. But there had been something in that blade, and even while it had severed the threads of his life, it had also done . . . something else.

That voice, that single voice that was not his and did not belong here but whispered whispered *whispered* relentlessly until he thought he would break the last piece of himself between his hands to make it stop.

But he couldn't do that, not yet, something was wrong.

*"Are you not ready to go yet, god killer?"*

He frowned. He had done that, hadn't he? Too little too late.

*"I could keep you here . . ."*

His heart began to lift but he quashed it. That was not the way this worked. Death was death was death, and it was inevitable for him; he had always known it would come for him sooner rather than later. It was not for him to reject.

*"Of course, you have to do a few things for me . . ."*

He had so much more he wanted to do . . . There was so much he had not yet finished. He wasn't *ready*. But, no, no, it was his time. It was his time.

But there was a yearning amidst the hunger. There was want beside the acceptance. He didn't *want* to go. He stepped back—death was not for him to turn away from.

*"Oh, boy, you don't understand. I'm not giving you a choice."*

Malachiasz woke up in the bloodstained snow.

And entropy, the death knell of the world, woke with him.

# ACKNOWLEDGMENTS

I was warned about the second book, I was, but I truly don't think there's a way to be prepared for the singularly specific struggle that comes with it. *Ruthless Gods* tried its very hardest to break me, and 2018 became a bit of a black hole because of it. I'll do my very best to thank everyone who helped me keep my head above water, but I'm certain I'll be as forgetful as I ever am—so if you were around for the chaos that was this last year, thank you.

Thank you to Vicki, who took all my weird ideas without so much as a pause and somehow managed to push me to get weirder.

Thank you, as ever and always, to Thao, the greatest champion and cheerleader, and to the rest of the SDLA team.

Thank you to DJ—sorry I did all that to Serefin, I know he's your favorite. To Meghan, publicist extraordinaire: one day I'll remember to put everything in my calendar. To Jennie, Olga, and the rest of the Wednesday Books team: I feel so honored every day that I get to do this whole book thing with you all. To the library marketing team, you guys rock. And thank you, once again, to Mark for the most metal art for the book covers. Thank you to Anna, who gave *Wicked Saints* the most gloriously striking packaging. Thank you to Melanie, who wrangled all my Polish Żs. And thank you to the Creative Services team for continually leaning in to the Metal Goth Aesthetic— it means so much to this Metal Goth.

My writing process for *Ruthless Gods* was far more solitary than for *Wicked Saints*, but I would have fallen apart if not for R. J. Anderson, R. M. Romero, and Jessica Cooper's early advice. To the Slack group—you know who you are. To Stephanie Garber, Roshani Chokshi, Margaret Rogerson, Robin LaFevers, Adrienne Young, and Rosamund Hodge for your beautiful words and your early support. To Marina, Lane, Tatra, Diana, Dana, Ashely, and Hannah, y'all are still here!

To the Spell Check gang, Margaret Owen, L. L. McKinney, Linsey Miller, Adib Khorram, and Laura Pohl, thanks for the reprieve from the real-life chaos and wild DnD shenanigans.

To Christine, Rory, Claire, and Nicole, this wild journey would be so much dimmer without you four. (Also, Claire, finish your book.)

To all the bloggers who showed *Wicked Saints* so much love, thank you for all you do. I was blown away by your enthusiasm and support, and it meant the absolute world to me. To the booksellers who yelled about it from the beginning—Allison, Sami, Shauna, Kiersten, Jordan, Meghan—you're all wonderful. To the artists who keep taking these weird kids of mine and creating masterpieces, thank you.

To my library family, thanks for suffering me. I know I can be a bit of a hot mess, but you all make the day job such fun.

# ACKNOWLEDGMENTS

To Tim, Kara, Kyle, David, Sadie, and Matt, you guys keep me grounded.

As always, to my family for their unwavering support.

And to everyone else my goldfish brain has forgotten, thank you. Let's keep making weird art.

# Bonus Scenes

## NADEZHDA LAPTEVA

Alone. Again.

This time, Nadya did sit down. She was frustrated and tired and there was blood under her fingernails from the thing that *was not Malachiasz* and she desperately wanted to break. She was not strong enough for this. Better she had stayed in the monastery, been cut down with the rest. Stopping here might mean her death, but she couldn't go any farther.

Something moved in the trees and Nadya contemplated staying where she was and letting whatever happened, happen. But then the last dregs of adrenaline she had remaining shot her to her feet—

—and right into Malachiasz.

If it even was Malachiasz.

The thought made her panic and she shoved away, but not fast enough. He caught her wrist, causing her to wrench her arm painfully in its socket.

"It's only me," he said, his voice soft in a way that gave Nadya pause. A troubling sort of gentleness.

She felt his hand on the side of her face and she froze, not looking at him, because if this was the forest again, she didn't know what she was going to do. He pushed her hair out of her face, hooking his forefinger under her chin and tilting her gaze up to his.

"It's only me," he repeated.

"At the best of times, not necessarily a comfort," she said, her voice strained.

The *Telich'nevyi* had gotten his eyes wrong and the scars on his forearms were missing. She carefully pushed his sleeve up his arm, revealing the messy, pale lines scattered over his skin. It wasn't quite enough proof, but it was something, because his eyes were dark, murky in the way that happened when he was more monster than anything else, and thus not much help.

"Do you want more proof?" he asked. He shifted on his feet, and for a terrifying second she thought he was going to kiss her, which would have mostly just proved it wasn't Malachiasz at all.

She let her fingers hook around his wrist and shook her head. "Only the mage? Not the Vulture?"

He looked wary, but closed his eyes, and when they reopened they were his almost colorless blue. Nadya relaxed a little more.

*How is he still coherent?* But she gently pushed the thought away, choosing to put off the inevitable for a while longer. She tipped forward until her head landed against his chest.

He let out a soft breath, one hand weaving through her hair to cradle the back of her head.

"I'm scared," she whispered, better to admit with her voice muffled against him.

"Ah, and here I thought I was the only one."

She wanted to ask how he was feeling but she didn't want him to suspect that she knew what was probably happening to him. This close, she could feel him shaking. Was she grateful that he was holding on, or was this only going to make the moment when the forest finally tore him to pieces all the more horrible?

It wasn't like she could deny it was happening. When she finally pulled away, she noticed a muscle in his jaw flutter, a tension, control that slipped and a roiling of eyes swept over his skin. He shuddered and spat out a mouthful of blood, lifting a hand at her before she had a chance to say anything.

"Don't bother asking."

She pursed her lips. She did not ask.

"I got turned around," she said, taking in the clearing. "I was being pulled north, I think, but now . . ." She trailed off. She wasn't entirely sure where north was, and the pull that had been so insistent had quieted.

Malachiasz looked thoughtful, but Nadya recalled his sense of direction in the mountains and sighed.

"You have no idea which direction is north, do you?"

He pointed, clearly at random. She couldn't help a smile.

"We should stay here until dawn," he said, peering up at the trees. Everything, already dim before, was starting to grow shadowy, and the thought of being in here in the dark was almost unbearable.

"Should we?"

He looked over at her, something in his expression she had never seen before, and then he groaned and collapsed under the tree where Nadya had crumpled only minutes before. He buried his face in his hands.

"I don't know," he said, voice muffled through his hands. "I can't think."

Nadya chewed on her lower lip.

"My head hurts—everything hurts—and everything feels foggy and I—" he broke off, fingers digging into his hair.

Maybe it would have been better had they remained separated, so she didn't have to *see* him taken apart. Maybe this was exactly what she deserved.

"We'll stay here," she said softly.

He didn't really react to her words. She sat down next to him.

"Why are we doing this?" he asked, voice hoarse, distant in a way that she wasn't sure he was actually asking her, but the question made her go cold anyway.

"You know why," she said softly, but another seed of doubt was driven home.

He tilted, leaning against her. She wove her fingers through his hair, around the chips of bone and beads tied in the strands.

"There's a story that a sister in the monastery told me," she said. "About twelve sisters who were bathing in a lake one day. When they came out to fetch their clothes, a snake was on the twelfth sister's clothes and he demanded she marry him."

"How could the snake talk?"

She flicked his temple. "Be quiet."

"Ow."

"The twelfth sister did not want to marry the snake—"

"Well, it was a snake."

"Malachiasz, were you this insufferable as a child?"

"Sorry," he said, but she almost immediately regretted the question, hating the way his expression fractured. He hadn't had a childhood.

She hesitated, unsure if she should apologize, but he tilted his head back to look at her, lifting his eyebrows.

"You were at a snake wanting a wedding?"

She laughed softly. "Right. And so all the sisters went home. But for three days and nights the snake circled the house, demanding the hand of the twelfth sister. Finally, she went out and married the snake."

"I have a question."

"Shhh." She pressed her hand over his mouth.

"It turned out that at night, the snake became a young man. And the twelfth sister and the snake were very happy, but during the day, the young man was a snake again and returned to the lake. Every evening, the sister would go out and call for her husband and he would come out of the lake—as a man—returning to her for the rest of the night.

"Then, one evening, the mother, thinking to protect her daughter from the snake who had forced himself on her, spied on the daughter, but only heard the first part of the call she used to bring out her husband. The next evening, the mother went out, called the snake out, and cut off his head. The daughter, finding her husband dead, turned into a swan and was never seen again."

Silence stretched between them for a long, drawn out moment.

"Huh," he finally said.

"It's woven into our stories," she said softly. "To keep away from Tranavians, to stay away from monsters."

"Kalyazi stories are extremely bleak," he said with a frown.

"Oh, as if you have better."

He straightened, considered for a heartbeat, and slumped back down against her. "I don't know," he said, sounding puzzled. "It's not like anyone was telling the Vulture recruits stories."

"I find it hard to believe you haven't read any. You read everything."

His expression grew distant, thoughtful.

She laughed. "It's all right if you can't remember any, there's a lot going on in that head of yours."

"Is there?"

"True, it's debatable, I suppose."

"I do have questions."

"I'm going to humor you this once—"

"How did she turn into a swan? Just at will? Was she a witch? Did she have some swan magic that—"

She covered his mouth with her hand again. "I've changed my mind. I'm not humoring you."

He suffered that for a few breaths before tugging away, kissing her knuckles, and standing. "Let me at least ward the clearing if we're going to stay here."

She watched as he did, feeling pathetic and useless and wondering if this was her second chance, her last chance. If she was supposed to do something, *say something,* that would pull him from disaster. He paused in the midst of casting a spell, pressing his fingers to his temples, his expression wrenching. After coughing into the crook of his elbow so hard she thought he was going to pass a lung, he spat out another mouthful of blood and kept going.

"Malachiasz?"

"Hmm?" He was flipping through his spell book and it took him a second to look over his shoulder at her.

She opened her mouth. She was going to tell him. She had to. She couldn't see this to the end, she wasn't as cruel as that, she couldn't be. Telling him now might be too late but at least then he would know, he could save himself, even if it meant she never saw him again.

"Can you actually keep anything out that wants to get in here?" Her words felt flat. They were the wrong words, and he shot her a bemused look.

"You doubt me?"

Anywhere else, no, but here? It was hard to fathom that he could keep anything out if it truly wanted to kill them.

She shrugged. He finished the spell and returned to where she was sitting, dropping down to rest on his heels in front of her. His fingers slid under her jaw as he cupped her face, tilting it up to his. He pressed his forehead to hers.

"*Towy dżimyka*, we will not die here."

That was too much. She fisted her hands in his coat, keeping her eyes closed to fight the threatening rush of tears. She failed spectacularly and he made a soft, distressed noise.

"Don't cry," he whispered. His thumb brushed a tear from her cheek. "You cry and you'll make me cry and where would that leave us?"

The laugh that bubbled out from her chest startled her and he grinned, pleased with himself and looking so much like the strange, silly boy she had met on the mountains that she almost burst into tears all over again.

She wondered how much of that boy was ever real. She hoped it had all been a part of his lies because the alternative was unbearable. The thought of killing that boy was impossible.

The thought of killing the boy before her, his body twisting with chaos, his smile cruel, was unbearable as well.

"*But necessary.*"

She flinched at Marzenya's voice and Malachiasz leaned back, his expression bewildered and a little hurt. She leaned forward, kissing him, a swift brush of her lips against his, but it loosened the tension in his eyes. And made her all the more miserable.

He kissed her forehead, and they prepared for the long night ahead of them.

Malachiasz was gone when Nadya woke.

## SEREFIN MELESKI

"So, should I be the one to point out that Nadya hasn't been behind us for the last ten minutes?"

Serefin whirled. Kacper looked sheepish.

"I only just noticed," he said.

Serefin swallowed back the urge to swear. Why were they being allowed to find each other only to be ripped away again? They hadn't seen Malachiasz at all—what had happened to him? Did Serefin really care? He wasn't sure. It had been hard to tell if Nadya cared, either, which was alarming.

He tightened his grip on Kacper's hand.

"Maybe we should stop? For the night?" Kacper said, gently, shifting his hand in a way that implied Serefin was maybe holding on a little too tightly. He couldn't help it; if he let go he was going to lose Kacper.

"What?"

"Sleep?"

"Here?"

Kacper nodded. His eye twitched. "You're going to fracture something in my hand."

Serefin relaxed his grip only marginally. "I don't think I'll be able to sleep here."

"That's fair," Kacper said. "But it's going to be dark soon and this is going to become all the more treacherous. It's better to stay in one place until we get a little bit of light again."

"If I let go of your hand, you're going to disappear," Serefin said, his voice cracking.

"I'm not. Has it quieted?"

It had. But Serefin didn't know when Velyos would start again, when the painful dragging at his chest would become insistent once more. He didn't want to be the one that disappeared in the darkness, leaving Kacper alone, but he had a terrible feeling that was exactly what was going to happen.

"We're going to see this through rationally," Kacper continued, then, wryly, "It's just Kalyazin. They're losing the war."

Serefin let out a breathless noise that was half laugh, half sob.

Kacper glanced over his shoulder. "We should go up that hill so we can see more clearly around us. And I have some spells I think can at least give us the illusion of safety, even if you don't sleep it will be better than stumbling through this place in the dark."

Serefin followed Kacper reluctantly, a strangled sound escaping him when Kacper carefully extricated his hand from Serefin's. But he didn't disappear.

This time.

What had happened to Nadya? Where did she go? And Ostyia? There had been a moment where they had been thrown back onto the same path as her, but it hadn't lasted for very long before they'd lost her again.

"This was such a bad idea," he muttered.

Kacper laughed. "I did try to tell you."

The top of the hill was, of course, more tightly packed trees and dense underbrush, but Kacper worked to clear the underbrush away while Serefin stood and listed until he was leaning against a tree. He was very suddenly exhausted.

*"You've stopped."*

Serefin flinched. *I'm only human. We get tired, you know.*

Velyos pulled, hard, and Serefin staggered a few steps. Kacper grabbed his arm, alarm passing over his features.

"You can't keep me here if he decides I need to go," Serefin said, his voice toneless in his ears.

"Yes, I can," Kacper murmured. "I'll chain you to a tree if I have to."

Serefin made a thoughtful sound. "You haven't been carrying chains with you all the way from Tranavia."

"I could be! I'm carrying a lot more than I probably needed."

"Including me."

Kacper rolled his eyes. "It's not like you'd ever ask for help. And I've had practice."

"Right, your thousand siblings."

"*Five.*"

"Unfathomable." He, apparently, only had the one.

"Yes, well, your sibling is a nightmare unto this world. The worst mine ever did was lock me in the barn overnight in the middle of winter."

"The worst?"

"No, that's a lie. Weira gave me the scar on my face. Hit me with a pillow—"

"What."

"That sent me crashing into a doorframe."

"A wonder you're still alive."

"I'm very resilient. Henryk once spun me an extremely convincing story about how easy it was to jump over a brushfire my father had set to clear a field because he had done it a thousand times."

"Kacper, no."

"I wasn't *completely* set on fire."

Serefin laughed softly. There was another shove, pressing him another step, but Kacper shifted so he was gripping Serefin's shoulders.

"Where did your hundred siblings end up?"

"Five."

"It's the same."

Kacper gently pushed Serefin until he was seated, his back against the trunk of a tree. "I *do* have rope if you want me to tie you up."

Serefin closed his eyes and shook his head. "I don't think it would make a difference."

Kacper folded himself down so he was sitting next to Serefin. He hooked one leg over Serefin's—so he would know if Serefin tried to get up and disappear, but the gesture also made Serefin warm.

Serefin leaned his head on Kacper's shoulder. "What are their names?"

"Borys is the eldest; he's going to keep the farm. Henryk is a merchant's apprentice. Weira married a shepherd, and Iwon has another year in the military."

Serefin frowned. That was only four.

"We lost Kaja to the war," he finally finished, softly.

Serefin let out a breath. "Ah."

"That so many of us survived is, frankly, a miracle. That I survived is . . ." He trailed off. "I remember when you promoted me, the letters I got from them were . . . weird."

"Weird?"

"It doesn't happen, Serefin. The *slavhki* don't notice anyone who isn't also nobility, let alone the High Prince. They were certain you were just using me as a human shield."

"Actually, I would have preferred it if you had been a bit less human-shield-like."

Kacper laughed.

"It was very disconcerting." Serefin cautiously took Kacper's hand again. "I was sent out to the front to die; it wasn't like I had anyone trying particularly hard to keep me alive until you came along, except for Ostyia. I hope your family doesn't think *too* ill of me."

"Just a bit of ill will is fine?"

"Well, that I'm used to."

Kacper kissed his temple. "I'm going to keep you with me. You're not going to do this alone."

Serefin hoped, desperately, that would be true.


## *TSAREVNA* YEKATERINA VODYANOVA

Katya was contemplating murder.

Rather normal for her, and she didn't generally act on those thoughts, but right now, oh, she wanted to very badly and she suspected that if she saw *anyone* in the wretched group she'd been dragged into, they were going to see the end of her blade.

What she was hoping for, however, was the Vulture.

Lightly disconcerted when literally everyone disappeared around her, but not too put out, she decided to set out deeper into the forest and hope for the best. If this ended in the Vulture's death, it would be worth it. If this accomplished what everyone seemed to think it would, it would be worth it. But, gods, if Katya wasn't exhausted and sick of jumping at every shadow. She thumbed the bracelet of icons around her wrist, wishing she had something more than magic that took time to prepare and use and wasn't even that powerful. It wasn't usually a thing she yearned for, magic like Nadya had, or even the damn Tranavians, but right now it would be some kind of assurance that if she came across something that lived in this forest, she would be able to survive it. Her blade wasn't quite so promising here.

She froze, voices from somewhere ahead of her, no, one voice. She frowned, the language passing by her until she realized it was Tranavian and it clicked. Katya slowly drew her sword.

Her steps weren't quite cautious enough as a breaking twig caused the figure to whirl around, blood dripping from a cut palm.

Ostyia. Well, Katya let her thoughts of murder drift slowly away. Not this one.

The Tranavian girl relaxed slightly. "You're not the *worst* thing this forest can spit out, I suppose," she said, in Tranavian.

"That's disappointing," Katya replied.

The Tranavian girl had blood on her that Katya suspected was not from her own magic. "What happened to you?"

Ostyia glanced at her jacket and shrugged. "Ran into . . . well I don't really know what it was. It was wolf-like? But it wasn't a wolf." She turned, peering into the forest with her hands on her hips.

Katya watched her carefully. She wore a patch over one eye, but Katya could see scars that the eye patch didn't quite cover. Did she lose her eye on the battlefield? Spear wounds were nasty things and Katya had seen a number of soldiers lose eyes to them and manage to pull through.

"What happened to your eye?"

"That's rude," Ostyia said without looking at her, kicking at some underbrush to see if it would uncover anything.

Katya shrugged, unconcerned. "This way."

"How do you know?"

"I don't, but staying in one place seems ill-advised while we still have light to move by, don't you think?"

Ostyia's lips twisted but she nodded and followed after Katya.

"I lost the eye as a child," she said after the silence between them had shifted into something less fraught. "Assassins. They were for Serefin, but I was caught in the attack."

"He got lucky."

"He had me." Ostyia shrugged. "Luck may have had something to do with it."

"And you don't resent him for it?"

Ostyia snorted. "No. Why are you talking to me?"

"Do you not like it?"

"I wouldn't go that far, I just figured it would be wiser to suffer in silence instead of potentially drawing this damn wood's attention."

"Wouldn't you?" Katya glanced over her shoulder at Ostyia, who immediately looked elsewhere.

She was extremely pretty, the harsh blood mage, with her sharp, angular features and wry mouth, and Katya caught herself wondering what it would feel like to take that still bleeding hand and kiss her. The thought struck her suddenly, unnervingly out of nowhere, and when Ostyia frowned because Katya had stopped walking and was *staring,* she cleared her throat and swiftly turned and—

Ostyia grabbed her wrist, wrenching her back a step before she walked face first into a tree.

"Blood and bone," she muttered. "Not when we're in the middle of a forest crawling with magic."

Ostyia had not let go of Katya's wrist and she swallowed. She wasn't usually this easily *flustered* but she couldn't exactly say she hadn't been watching the Tranavian girl ever since she'd shown up for Serefin and wanting to be noticed back.

Which was ridiculous of her. The girl wasn't only a Tranavian blood mage, she was close to the damn king. How many Kalyazi had she killed? Katya was being stupid, just because she was pretty.

But she was clever, too, and there was something about her loyalty to Serefin that Katya couldn't help but find compelling, which was weird, because she was the *literal enemy.*

"Are you always this obvious?" Ostyia asked. She started walking and had *not let go of Katya's wrist.*

"Sorry? Er, no. No? Not usually? It's all this magic, the forest—"

"Sure," Ostyia said.

Katya sighed.

"I just figured, well, you talk a big game, that this would go smoother, and not happen in one of your Kalyazi nightmare forests? But, ah, well, I can't be right about everything I suppose."

This wasn't fair, actually. Katya nearly tripped over a root and Ostyia laughed. She stopped walking, forcing Katya still as well.

"I am absolutely dying to know what would happen if I kissed you."

Katya swore softly. "Here?"

"Death is inevitable, your country is a hellscape, this seems to be a lull in the madness which only means it's preparing for something truly terrible, a calm before the storm, if you will, and I have been contemplating this for weeks now so why not?"

Katya took a second to consider that, before bending down and kissing Ostyia herself. The Tranavian girl laughed against her mouth before wrapping her arms around Katya's neck and deepening the kiss.

When they finally broke apart, breathless and flushed, Ostyia grinned brightly. "You are exceedingly good at this. Now, help me find my king and let's get the hell out of here. None of this is worth it."

Katya couldn't agree more.

EMILY A. DUNCAN is the *New York Times* bestselling author of *Wicked Saints* and *Ruthless Gods*. They work as a youth services librarian and received a master's degree in library science from Kent State University, which mostly taught them how to find obscure Slavic folklore texts through interlibrary loan systems. When not reading or writing, they enjoy playing copious amounts of video games and Dungeons and Dragons. They live in Ohio.